W9-ARS-537

MURDER AT THE GARDNER

MURDER AT
THE GARDNER

A NOVEL OF SUSPENSE BY

JANE LANGTON

ILLUSTRATIONS BY THE AUTHOR

ST. MARTIN'S PRESS · NEW YORK

F

Copyedited by Angelique Fralini
Design by Lance Hidy

Quotations from *I Trionfi* are reprinted from THE TRIUMPHS OF PETRARCH, translated by Ernest H. Wilkins, by permission of the University of Chicago Press. © 1962 by the University of Chicago. All rights reserved.

Library of Congress Cataloging-in-Publication Data

Langton, Jane.
  Murder at the Gardner / by Jane Langton.
    p. cm.
    ISBN 0-312-01479-1 : $17.95
    I. Title.
PS3562.A515M86 1988
813'.54—dc19

First Edition

10 9 8 7 6 5 4 3 2 1

FOR BETTY AND ALVIN

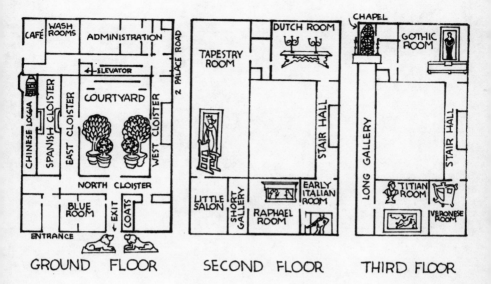

GROUND FLOOR

CAFÉ
WASH ROOMS
ADMINISTRATION
2 PALACE ROAD
CHINESE LOGGIA
SPANISH CLOISTER
EAST CLOISTER
ELEVATOR
COURTYARD
WEST CLOISTER
NORTH CLOISTER
BLUE ROOM
EXIT
COATS
ENTRANCE

SECOND FLOOR

TAPESTRY ROOM
DUTCH ROOM
STAIR HALL
LITTLE SALON
SHORT GALLERY
RAPHAEL ROOM
EARLY ITALIAN ROOM

THIRD FLOOR

CHAPEL
GOTHIC ROOM
LONG GALLERY
STAIR HALL
TITIAN ROOM
VERONESE ROOM

MURDER AT
THE GARDNER

THE PROCESSION

TITUS MOON met Catherine Rule on the back stairway of the Gardner Museum. They were both trying to do a little work before the meeting with Homer Kelly and the trustees at ten o'clock.

"Good morning, Titus," said Catherine. She looked at him brightly with one of her old yellow eyes, but as usual the other gazed past his head at things he could not see—islands in southern seas, landscapes of frozen tundra, monumental sandstone pharaohs towering out of the desert. "You're about to say your prayers?"

"That's right, Catherine. What do you suggest for this morning?"

Catherine started up the stairs to the room where she spent all her working hours repairing tapestries. "Pesellino," she said. "You'll never go wrong with Pesellino."

"Good," said Titus. "Pesellino it is." Nodding to the guard at the watch desk, he walked swiftly through the door into the west cloister.

Titus Moon was the new director of the Isabella Stewart Gardner Museum. As a public institution, his domain was much smaller than the Boston Museum of Fine Arts, its great neighbor along the Fenway to the northeast, and it was different in other ways as well.

At the Boston Museum there were hundreds of acquisitions every year; there were new galleries, whole new wings, and successions of new exhibitions—the prints of Degas, the art of Pompeii, the paintings of Renoir, of

Thomas Eakins, of Pissaro. All this growth and vitality were unknown at the Gardner Museum, where the collection never changed, where acquisitions were unheard of. From one decade to the next, Titian's *Rape of Europa* hung on the east wall of the Titian Room on the third floor, and the youthful Rembrandt in his feathered cap looked out from the north wall of the Dutch Room. Titus knew that if he were to come back in a hundred years, he would find Botticelli's *Chigi Madonna* still hanging over the same Florentine sideboard.

This everlasting sameness was no whim of Titus Moon's. Mrs. Gardner had insisted on it in her last will and testament. All was to be dismantled "**if the Trustees shall place for exhibition any pictures or works of art other than such as I own . . . or if they shall at any time change the general disposition or arrangement . . .** "

But Titus had invented a cure for the problem of excessive familiarity. He had taught himself to find freshness in the never-changing exhibitions by spending ten minutes every day with a single work of art—a carved wooden altar from Germany, a stained glass window from the Cathedral of Milan, a drawing by Raphael—gazing at it, sinking himself down into it, trying to absorb into himself the intent of its creator.

Today the very thought of Mrs. Gardner's will gave Titus a headache. Unfortunate things had been happening in the galleries, strange eruptions of whimsicality by a person or persons unknown, threatening the continued existence of the museum. The terms of the will were very clear. This sort of bizarre indignity must have been exactly what the founder of the museum had had in mind when she had directed the trustees, in such a case, to "**sell the said land, Museum, pictures, statuary, works of art and bric-a-brac, furniture, books and papers, and procure**

the dissolution of the said Isabella Stewart Gardner Museum . . ."

The trustees had been struggling with the problem for months, and so had the museum's security chief, Charlie Tibby, but so far without result. Therefore this morning they were trying a new tack. They were meeting with a former lieutenant-detective for Middlesex County, one Professor Homer Kelly.

3

Inviting Kelly to the trustees' meeting had been Titus Moon's idea. Titus had met Homer at a party for new members, and had pleaded with him to give the trustees the benefit of his advice. Homer had responded with a good-natured groan, but then he had agreed to come to the meeting and hear what was going on.

Titus looked at his watch. It was only quarter past nine. He would have plenty of time to devote himself to something in the collection. This morning in obedience to the suggestion of Catherine Rule, he walked upstairs to the Early Italian Room.

Of all the galleries in the museum, it was his favorite. Unlike many of the others, it was full of golden light. Four tall windows looked out on Palace Road and the Fenway, and another opened on the courtyard. But it was not only the windows that made the room bright. The Early Italian

4

Room glowed from within with the gold of altarpieces and panel paintings, with gold leaf beaten over gesso, polished until it shone on halos and wings and gilded skies. The Early Italian Room was hung with the dreams of the artists of the stony city-states of Italy. On the labels beside the pictures there were sonorous names ending in *a* and *i* and *o,* ringing Italian names that had resounded along the narrow streets of Siena and Florence, Ferrara and Venice and Mantua during the early Renaissance—Masaccio, Piero della Francesca, Ambrogio Lorenzetti, Gentile Bellini, Andrea Mantegna, Fra Angelico.

Pesellino's two panel paintings of *The Triumphs of Petrarch* hung on the east wall on either side of the door. They had been painted in the fifteenth century to adorn a pair of marriage chests. Rolling across them was a procession of triumphal chariots, each victorious over the one before, as

5

described in *terza rima* by the poet Petrarch.

Titus took up a position in front of the first panel and examined it with his usual care. At the far left was the chariot of Love, carrying a naked youth with bow and arrow, surrounded by pairs of lovers. The subject was mythological, but Pesellino had succumbed to the charms of daily life, and his lovers were young aristocrats of Florence, magnificently attired.

Next in the procession came the chariot of Chastity, who had subdued and taken prisoner the passionate youth. Chastity was a matron, modestly draped. Beside her the naked boy cowered in chains.

At the far right, squeezed into a narrow space (Pesellino had not planned ahead) was a skeletal hag whose chariot was a coffin. She was Death, cruel Death, who alone could conquer Chastity.

Moving to the other side of the doorway, Titus found

the chariot of death-conquering Fame, a splendid woman in royal robes. Around her were assembled the great men of the past.

But Fame was overwhelmed in her turn, unable to resist the slow depredations of Time. There he was, Father Time, a bearded old man carried swiftly forward by a pair of stags.

Last of all, Eternity superseded Time in final perfection and everlasting serenity, as God the Father lifted his hand to bless a new heaven and a new earth.

Titus walked up close to savor all the elegant little figures, then backed away, reflecting that Petrarch had merely been constructing another of those lists by which people had brought order to the chaos of the world. They had set up rosters of saints and levels of heaven and hell; they had enumerated the virtues and vices and sorted out the humors of the flesh; they had divided the human body into physical and spiritual halves. As long as something

could be itemized, it was under some kind of control, in an age when very little else was under control, when death was random and capricious, disease a series of ungovernable plagues.

Then Titus winced, aware that it wasn't just the men and women of the fifteenth century who had divided their lives into segments and subdivisions. Right here and now he, too, Titus Moon, had arranged his existence in separate parts, balancing them in the same spirit of order. Walking back downstairs, he amused himself by wondering just where he was on Petrarch's chart, at which of the six stages. Chastity had not grasped him, but neither had Love. He was triumphant nowhere. He certainly wasn't dead, nor was he exalted by Fame. In Pesellino's beautiful procession there was no place for him at all.

In the east cloister, an important reception for the benefactors of the museum was just getting under way. Well-dressed people smiled at one another with expressions of tortured good humor, as the light falling from the high windows over the courtyard made chalices of their glasses of cranberry juice. Flutelike tones fell upon the director's ear, and Boston umlauts whiffled at him, *hew-hah, hew-hew, hah-hah.* Titus stood among the benefactors and made a little speech, expressing his pleasure in meeting them here, outlining the entertainments of the morning.

Then he escaped to his office to look over the résumés of a couple of candidates for new assistantships, unaware that before the day was out he was to be struck down by a flaming shaft from the bow of the naked boy on the chariot of Love.

I
THE TRIUMPH
OF LOVE

Four steeds I saw, whiter than whitest snow,
And on a fiery car a cruel youth
With bow in hand and arrows at his side . . .
For this is he whom the world calleth Love:
Bitter, thou see'st . . .

—PETRARCH

CHAPTER ONE

THE BULRUSHES beside the water in the Back Bay Fens were like a jungle. Wandering among them looking for a lover, Edward Fallfold amused himself by envisioning tigers and elephants trampling the tall reeds, and livid green parrots flapping up into the gray Boston air.

But there were no tigers, no elephants, no parrots, and no lovers either, even though the weather on this day in late March was springlike and mild. The bulrushes were ten feet tall, with dry stalks that creaked and swayed as Fallfold parted them, trying this pathway and that. *Bulrushes here, bulrushes there.* The bulrushes reminded him of Titian's painting of *The Rape of Europa* in the museum, and he made a mental pun. *The bull rushes at Europa and carries her off.* But Edward Fallfold didn't want Europa, that portly wench with the heavy thighs. He wanted someone like the young man approaching him now.

"Hello," Fallfold said, giving the boy his charming smile, putting an arm around his broad shoulders. "What's your name? Look, why don't we go across the street to my room?"

Later he discovered that his young friend was looking for a job and a place to live. The boy was blond, strong, and tall, and Fallfold was immensely taken with him. "I think I can help you," he said, trying not to sound too eager. "Speak to Mrs. Garboyle. She's got an empty room. Another kid just moved out. And I'll bet I can get you a job as a guard in the museum."

"The museum? What museum?"

"The Isabella Stewart Gardner Museum. It's just down the road along the Fenway. I'm a trustee." Fallfold didn't bother to explain that he had very nearly been named director of the museum. Last year when the former director had been called to Yale, Fallfold had applied to become his successor, and he had come very close. There had been interview after interview. But at last, to his disgust, they had set him aside and chosen young Titus Moon instead. Fallfold had been offered the consolation prize of a place on the unpaid board of trustees.

"As a matter of fact," he said to his new young friend, whose name was Robbie Crowlie, "there's a meeting of the trustees this morning. Come on, I'm on my way there now. I'll introduce you to the security chief. He can always use a new guard."

"Well, okay," said Robbie Crowlie cautiously, "thanks a lot."

Fallfold beamed, and they went off together down the street, strolling along the Fenway past the dorms of Northeastern University, past the Forsyth School for Dental Hygienists and the Boston Museum of Fine Arts, in the direction of the Isabella Stewart Gardner Museum.

In the jungle of the bulrushes Edward Fallfold had found a new love.

CHAPTER TWO

HOMER KELLY was on his way to the meeting with the Gardner trustees. The truth was, Homer was in the dark about the history of painting and sculpture. But it was this very ignorance that was taking him there this morning.

It was all his wife's fault. If Mary Kelly had not thought her husband an ignoramus about art, she wouldn't have given him a membership in the Isabella Stewart Gardner Museum before she went off to New York City to take a course at Columbia.

If she hadn't given him a membership, he wouldn't have gone to the reception for new members. And if he hadn't attended the reception, Homer would never have met Titus Moon, the director of the Gardner Museum. And then he would never have been asked to go to the next meeting of the trustees, to discuss the museum's peculiar troubles and harassments.

But Mary Kelly *did* think her husband an ignoramus about art, and therefore she had set in motion the train of events that propelled him now, on this warm misty morning in March, in the direction of the Gardner to meet with the director and the seven trustees.

As Homer strode along the drive from a distant parking place, a fog hung over the Fenway, curling among the feathery fronds of the giant bulrushes on the shores of the sluggish little stream, draping itself over the dead stalks of the brussels sprouts and tomato vines in the public garden plots, wreathing over the curving road. Homer bowed his head against the blowing grit, and scattered the pigeons waddling across his path. The grit, he knew, was not important grit, not grit that counted for something. The pigeons were insignificant pigeons. In a way they were symbols of the neighborhood itself. Back at the turn of the century when Mrs. Jack Gardner had bought the land for her Venetian palace, Frederick Law Olmsted's emerald necklace of parkland was only beginning to emerge from hundreds of acres of heaped-up muck along Stony Brook and Muddy River. Mrs. Jack had expected fashionable Boston to follow her from Beacon Street with new ranks of lofty marble town houses. But fashionable Boston had gone elsewhere, and now the elaborate dwelling she called Fenway Court stood by itself.

Other public buildings had sprung up along the Fenway—the Boston Museum of Fine Arts, Simmons College and Wheelock and Emmanuel—and eventually the vacuum around them had been filled with blocks of houses. But they were not the sumptuous residences Mrs. Gardner had surely foreseen. Instead this whole sweep of road had a seedy and neglected air. Around the corner at the end of Avenue Louis Pasteur, the hospital complex was a choked mass of looming buildings, narrow streets, bumper-to-bumper traffic, and teeming pedestrians. And beyond the hospitals spread the ruined streets of Roxbury, thick with suffering life. But along the meandering artery called the Fenway, from one end, where you could hear the crack of a bat in Fenway Park, to the other, where the massive tower of Sears, Roebuck dominated a tormented intersection, the sidewalks were nearly empty. Homer was alone.

The Gardner Museum was a tall monument of pale brick with a tile roof like that of a villa on the Mediterranean.

Homer walked in the front door and introduced himself to the girl at the desk.

"Oh, yes, Mr. Kelly. The trustees are meeting in the Dutch Room. Go to the right around the courtyard, then up the stairs, and right again. They'll be expecting you."

CHAPTER THREE

THE PARTY for the benefactors was in progress in the east cloister as Homer made his way around the flowering courtyard. Hungrily he glanced at the plates of tidbits on the white tablecloths, the little cakes, the carafes of coffee, the pineapples impaled with morsels of fruit on toothpicks. But Homer had been invited to a meeting, not a party. Regretfully he climbed the stairs.

The reception in the east cloister was only the beginning of a festive day for the benefactors of the Isabella Stewart Gardner Museum. After their coffee and snacks, they would attend a lecture in the Tapestry Room and tour the greenhouses, then sit down to a grand luncheon in the Spanish Cloister.

All the benefactors were wealthy men and women, but in the Renaissance mind of Titus Moon, they fitted into categories. Some of them were cultivated lovers of art whose appetite could only be fed by looking at monuments of ageless splendor, by gazing at the green faces of fourteenth-century saints, or the marble folds of Greek and Roman draperies, or the painted skies of eighteenth-century landscapes. And of course there were scholars among the benefactors, learned men and women lost in their own specialties, with strong opinions about Flemish tapestries, or new theories about the cinerary urns of ancient Rome.

But many of the benefactors were rich women who favored the museum because it was a safe and attractive charity, worthwhile but not upsetting, unlike welfare associations or pressure groups for civil rights. In a casual way they admired the sculpture and the paintings, but best of all they loved dropping in with their friends to exclaim at the blossoming courtyard and eat lunch in the café.

Flower ladies, Titus called them in mild contempt, but he was well aware of their value to the museum. And he was grateful for the magnificent floral effects his head gardener had produced in the courtyard, where blue cinerarias were blazing now among trees of yellow jasmine, pots of arum lilies and pale narcissus, where throughout the year the garden burst into magnificent bloom with extravagant displays of lilies and orchids, cyclamen and azaleas.

"It's always so peaceful here," the flower ladies would say to one another, failing to notice the scenes of the Passion on the wall behind them, or the tragic marble head of Apollo beside the jar of Easter lilies, or the slave in the claws of a lion, above the container of sweet-smelling jasmine.

This morning the naked boy on Pesellino's panel painting, the cruel youth called Love, was sharpening his arrows for Titus Moon, and he was busy among the benefactors as

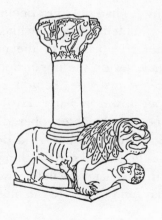

17

well, drawing his bow and taking careful aim.

His new victims were Beryl Bodkin, the wife of an impossible husband, and Fenton Hepplewhite, the husband of an impossible wife. Somehow these two unhappy people, crushed as they were in the grip of their wretched marriages, had stumbled upon one another in a nook between a Roman sarcophagus and a flowering jade tree. John Bodkin, the impossible husband, was absent at the moment because he was attending the trustees' meeting upstairs, and Madeline Hepplewhite, the impossible wife, had abandoned her husband in order to barge all over the galleries with one of the flower ladies. Thus Beryl Bodkin and Fenton Hepplewhite suddenly found themselves alone together.

Beryl and Fenton had never before exchanged a personal word. The noisy locomotives to which they were attached had always dominated their encounters with huge noises of *CHUFFA-CHUFFA-CHUFF* and furious whistle blasts. Towed along in the rear, they had never been shunted onto the same railway siding. Now, stunned, they greeted one another and began to talk, stuttering in their excitement, fearful of the return of Madeline or John.

For the moment they were safe from interruption. The meeting of the trustees had only just begun, upstairs in the Dutch Room, and Madeline Hepplewhite was at this moment dragging her friend, one of the new benefactors, through all the galleries on the upper floors.

In the absence of his wife, Fenton Hepplewhite expanded like a paper flower in water. His bowed shoulders straightened, his nervous laughter sobered, his sinews loosened their rigid grip on his bones. And Beryl's eager face was bright. She was finding all sorts of things to say; she was astonished at the things that were in her, waiting to be said.

It was a Monday, and therefore the museum was closed

to ordinary visitors. "I'm sorry," said the guard to Madeline Hepplewhite as she charged past him up the stairs. "The galleries aren't open today."

Madeline continued to sail upward. "I am one of the principal benefactors of this museum," she said, grasping the arm of her nervous friend, urging her along. "I think I have a right to go anywhere I please."

What could he do? He couldn't engage in physical combat with a benefactor. Swiftly the guard checked in at the watch desk, asking to be replaced at his post, then galloped up the stairs two at a time to follow Madeline Hepplewhite wherever she went.

Madeline was eager to play a proprietary role, to show off her treasures, her Velásquez, her Rubens, her Fra Angelico. "We'll just take a little whirlwind tour," she said to her friend, Viva Mae Biggy.

But the tour went on and on, exhausting the energy of the new benefactor, who wasn't really very much interested in art. By the time they reached the third floor, Viva Mae's eyes were glazed, she was glutted with masterpieces, she could absorb no more.

But in the Veronese Room she perked up. In the middle of the floor stood a solid object that was neither a painting nor a piece of sculpture.

"Oh, look at the sedan chair," she said, summoning a last spark of interest. "Imagine being carried around in that thing!"

"Muddy streets," explained Madeline Hepplewhite. "Filth everywhere. No standards of hygiene. Raw sewage running in the gutter."

"Oh, ugh," said Viva Mae, and then she gave a soft shriek. "Oh, Madeline, there's someone in it. Look, there's a man inside."

"Good heavens." Madeline moved forward and stared

19

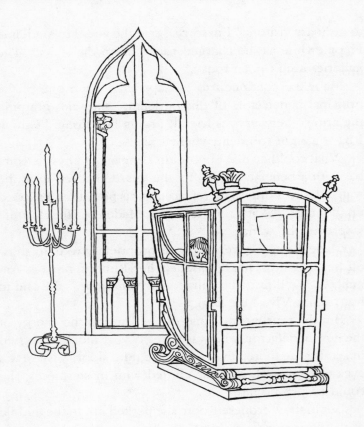

courageously into the sedan chair, mindful of her reputation as a fearless woman who had once climbed a tree at a garden party. "So there is."

The big man in the sedan chair was asleep. He lay cuddled on his side, his hands under his chin, his long knees drawn up.

Imperiously Madeline summoned the guard. "How, may I ask, did *he* get in here? What on earth has happened to the security of this institution?"

The guard too peered into the sedan chair. "Oh, no, not again," he said. "That's Tom Duck."

"What do you mean, again?" said Madeline Hepple-white. "Do you mean this sort of thing has happened be-fore? Who in the world is Tom Duck?"

"He's just this old bum. He's a friend of Titus Moon's. He keeps coming in off the street. He likes it here, that's the trouble. I don't know how he does it, but he gets in somehow. I'll call the watch desk. You ladies better get back to your reception."

"Well, all right," said Madeline. "But I'm really quite shocked. To think something like this could happen in an institution devoted to the protection of so many valuable things. I mean, Viva Mae was really quite frightened." Madeline frowned at the guard, regarding him as the visible representative of the establishment at the Isabella Stewart Gardner Museum. "I really am beginning to doubt whether this museum cares for what it has. Sometimes I wonder if I shouldn't change my will."

At last, to the guard's relief, Madeline and Viva Mae rejoined the rest of the benefactors, who were now touring the greenhouses. Thrusting her way along the narrow greenhouse aisle, Madeline looked for her husband Fenton. She couldn't find him anywhere. Where had he gone? At last she discovered him deep in conversation with Beryl Bodkin, the two of them sheltered by a gigantic rubber plant.

Shrewdly she guessed at the damage done in her ab-sence. Swiftly she swept him out of danger.

CHAPTER FOUR

I N THE DUTCH ROOM, the trustees sat on two sides
of the long Tuscan table, with director Titus Moon at
one end and Homer Kelly at the other. Around them
hung some of the most famous paintings in the museum—
three Rembrandts, a Vermeer, a Rubens, a pair of Holbeins, a Dürer. Even the illumination in the lofty chamber
was Dutch. It fell on the table as if it were slanting from
seventeenth-century windows, modeling in light and shade
a gathering of solid men and women of Amsterdam. Above
their sober clothing their faces glowed, and the air around
them was dark and shimmering. Their names might have

been Hoogstraten or Droochsloot or Schimmelpenninck.

But the seven trustees were not Dutch. Most of them were Bostonian. Their names were John Bodkin, Fulton Hillside, Preston Carver, Shackleton Bowditch, Peggy Foley, Edward Fallfold, and Catherine Rule. Edward Fallfold was a Virginian, and Peggy Foley had the pleasing blunt features of a middle-aged woman of Irish descent. But the rest were Anglo-Saxon Yankees with narrow faces that betrayed their inner convictions. Recognizing the tragic nature of earthly existence, they worked hard against the night that was coming, smiled with all their might, and saved leftover pieces of string. In repose, their features relaxed into melancholy. Their smiles, therefore, were triumphs of will. Their speech was a whiffle of *whee-whahs.*

Sitting together around the Tuscan table in their seven chairs, they were a study in the two ways Bostonians grow old—

1) they turn ever more pinched and shriveled, like plump fruit shrinking and withering;
2) they become ever more heroic and splendid like ancient trees.

Chairman John Bodkin was tending in the direction of the former, although he still had many years to go.

Carver and Hillside were too young to display either tendency. Their cheeks were round, their faces unformed and bland.

Catherine Rule was one of the latter. And Shackleton Bowditch, too, was a monument, grand and spreading like a white ash tree, even though his ancestry was not altogether pure. One of Shackleton's grandfathers had been an explorer, a seeker after rare Tibetan shrubs, and he had come home to Boston with a wife from a very different gene pool. Thus there was an unexpected streak of impish fancy

23

in Shackleton Bowditch, a breadth of outlook, an insistence on querying the very foundation stones upon which Bodkin, Hillside, and Carver so staunchly stood.

As trustees, all of them were new. In the last five years, the board had turned over completely. The seven competent men who had managed the affairs of the museum for so many years had vanished one by one, resigning or dying of old age. Their successors had been chosen a little hastily, although in the opinion of Titus Moon, the best among them were perhaps the most bizarre.

Catherine Rule and Peggy Foley were the first women to serve on the board of trustees. Some of the male members who had voted for them had lived to regret it. Oh, Catherine Rule was all right, although she was often stubborn about coming around to a sensible way of thinking. Catherine was the Conservator of Textiles, an international authority on the repair of tapestries. She was seventy years old. She knew everything there was to know about the collection.

Peggy Foley was something else again. A wealthy widow, Peggy had only a skimpy understanding of art history. She could pronounce the names of Botticelli and Rembrandt, but she muffed a lot of the others, like Teepolo, Goordi and Velsquaze. Fortunately Peggy was sharp as a tack about money. "Pick your people right the first time," her husband had told her before he died, "then give 'em a free hand. Hang in there, Peggy, back 'em up." "But how will I know the right ones from the wrong ones?" Peggy had wanted to know. "I trust you, Peg. You'll know what to do. You've got a good eye for a crook or a bimbo."

Six of the trustees often voted according to a pattern, with Bodkin, Hillside, and Carver on one side, cautious and statesmanlike, and Bowditch, Rule, and Foley on the other, impulsive and adventurous. The swing vote was usually Fallfold's.

24

Edward Fallfold was the only highly trained scholar among the trustees. His doctor's degree in art history had led to a life of learning. Fallfold had made a name for himself by writing scholarly articles and books, although this pursuit did little more than pay for his skimpy living quarters and keep him in well-tailored gray suits, immaculate shirts, and silken ties. In the past, he had held several teaching posts in local colleges, but he had lost them rapidly through flagrant attentions to one or another of the young men in his classes.

His failure to win the directorship of the Gardner Museum had been a bitter blow, but Fallfold had kept his disappointment to himself. His presence among the other trustees was genial and urbane, although somehow he failed to make intimate friends of any of the others. It was his own fault. Edward Fallfold knew only two ways of relating to his fellow men and women, either with indifference or with passion. The passion flared up suddenly and had a natural life span of four or five months. The indifference was constant, masked by an amusing manner and a glance that engaged the eyes of another human being for only an instant, then flitted away to rest on some inanimate object. Fallfold was given to puns and jocular remarks, and he had been known to flirt with Preston Carver. (Carver had recoiled.) Fallfold's views on controversial subjects were mildly sardonic. His vote was unpredictable.

Titus Moon himself, although he was the director of the museum, had no vote at all. But since Titus provided the agenda for the meetings, his proposals were usually the substance of the discussion.

In this setting, among these people, Homer Kelly felt out-of-place and seedy. This morning he had dressed with particular care, but with his wife away, he had overlooked a couple of small details. His shirt was badly rumpled and his tie was spotted with miscellaneous filth.

25

It didn't matter. Homer knew that his usefulness to the trustees lay not in some false air of respectability, nor in the fact that he taught a course in American literature at Harvard. What Titus Moon had cared about was Homer's reputation as a former lieutenant-detective with the district attorney of Middlesex County. This ancient connection was still getting Homer mixed up with crimes of a bourgeois and upper-middle-class nature. Here he was again, called in to hear some tale of woe in a scene of hushed intellectual pretension. While Fulton Hillside read the minutes of the last meeting, Homer gazed about him, longing for an honest felon, some low-down degenerate, some totally uneducated fink.

"Why me?" he had said to Titus Moon. "Why pick an aesthetic moron to help you out with your little problem, whatever it is? Surely there exists some mincing policeman who dotes on art?"

But Moon had said it didn't matter whether Homer knew one painter from another. The important thing was his nose for the identification of criminals. Homer was famous for his nose. "Our own security chief is a good man," Titus had said, "and he's done all he can, but without any result so far. We'll call in the police, of course, if we have to, but first we want to try to nip this thing in the bud without a lot of publicity."

The business meeting was over. It was time to explain to Homer Kelly the ticklish troubles afflicting the museum. Shackleton Bowditch began it. Shackleton was a Harvard Fellow, an acquaintance of Homer's from the old days of the bombing at Memorial Hall. "You see, Homer," said Shackleton, "it's these strange things that have been happening. That's why we've called you in."

"That's right," said Preston Carver, rubbing his hands nervously and raising his eyebrows. Carver's eyebrows

26

were arched and round like crescent moons, giving his face an expression of perpetual surprise, as if the world were a dangerous and shocking place. "There have been a number of peculiar incidents."

"It's that old tramp, for one thing," said Fulton Hillside.

"Oh, Tom Duck," said John Bodkin angrily. "Somebody's got to do something about Tom Duck." Bodkin looked meaningfully at Titus Moon. "It's disgraceful."

"Tom Duck?" said Homer.

"Oh, Tom Duck's not really part of the problem," said Shackleton Bowditch. "He's just an old guy who comes in here, turns up in the barn sleeping with the cats."

"He's a friend of mine, I'm afraid," explained Titus Moon to Homer. "An old alcoholic, ex-prizefighter. He's perfectly harmless, but somehow he keeps getting into the museum and alarming people. He's my responsibility. I'll work on him again."

"Well, if Tom Duck's not the problem," said Homer patiently, "what is?"

"The frogs," said Catherine Rule, looking at him slyly.

"Frogs?" Homer turned in astonishment to Miss Rule, who was sitting with her chair pulled away from the table, working on a piece of embroidery. At first glance, on being introduced to her at the beginning of the meeting, he had merely thought, *old woman,* but now he saw that she had fixed him with an extraordinary gaze. Her irises were yellow, her pupils black pinpoints. The right eye pierced him through, as if it knew his most terrible secrets and forgave them, while the left stared dreamily in another direction, contemplating wonders. Her dress was of crimson taffeta. It was a magnificent dress, a glorious dress. Even Homer in his oafish ignorance could recognize a great dress when he saw one, a dress that was surely at the height of contemporary fashion right now, and perhaps also at the dawn of time. Her face was lightly channeled with a thousand wrinkles, each seeming to express some distinctive attitude of mind, some cynical drollery. "The frogs in the courtyard pool," said Catherine, smiling at him. "Someone put pollywogs in the pool, and they turned into frogs, and pretty soon they were hopping all over the floor."

Homer scribbled *Frogs* on his agenda sheet. "What else?"

"The balloon," giggled Peggy Foley. "Somebody tied a balloon to Bindo Whatsisname. It's a bronze statue by Cellini, you know, the goldsmith." She waved her hands excitedly. "Oh, it's gorgeous, you've got to see it. But somebody tied a gas balloon to its ear. I mean, it was so funny!" Peggy cackled wildly, and her eyes rolled, and then her face fell. "Except that it was really just so terrible. I mean, we can't let it happen again, no, no."

"So far it doesn't sound very alarming," said Homer, writing *Balloon* under *Frogs*. "Anything else?"

Edward Fallfold cleared his throat and grinned at Titus. "There have been a good many much more damaging things."

"Much worse than frogs and balloons and Tom Duck," said Fulton Hillside, his brown eyes round with dismay.

"The pictures have been shifted," whispered Preston Carver, arching his eyebrows, leaning forward and speaking in a whisper.

"Shifted?" said Homer. "You mean, moved around from place to place?"

"They change places in the night," said Titus Moon. "The Crivelli and the portrait of Count Inghirami in the Raphael Room. The Botticelli and the School of Botticelli hanging across from it in the Long Gallery. The Rubens—" Titus gestured at the portrait of Thomas Howard on the

28

wall—"was hanging upside down. And someone pasted a mustache on van Dyck's *Lady with a Rose.*"

"Funny," said Homer grimly. "Ha, ha."

"I have to confess I found the blackboards rather amusing," said Catherine Rule, looking up from her embroidery. "The first one turned up in the middle of the Early Italian Room, a blackboard on an easel. Someone had drawn a picture on it with chalk, a crude picture of a cat—you know, the way children draw a cat, two circles with whiskers and a curly tail."

"The next one appeared in the Titian Room," said Peggy Foley eagerly, "right there in front of *The Rape of Europa,* with a lot of crazy scribbles on it, you know, like snarled-up yarn. And next day there was another one here in the Dutch Room with a *gallows* on it—you know, like when you play the game of hangman. I mean, it's really getting scary."

"Maybe it's just somebody with a warped sense of humor?" suggested Homer.

"Unfortunately," said John Bodkin, frowning at him, "these little jokes are endangering our continued existence as an ongoing institution. Do you know about the provision in Mrs. Gardner's will for the dismantling of the museum?"

Homer looked at him in surprise. "She wanted to dismantle her own museum?"

"Under certain conditions, yes."

Titus Moon explained. "It was something like calling the loss of a woman's virginity a fate worse than death. For Mrs. Jack Gardner, any change to her museum was so unthinkable that she preferred it to come to an end altogether, rather than allow her arrangements to be altered, or new works of art to be added."

"*New* works of art?" said Homer. "You don't mean those blackboards could be thought of as works of art?"

29

"Indeed they could," said Shackleton Bowditch grimly. "There's a sculptor in Germany who uses blackboards. He scribbles on them with chalk and calls it art. It's a pitiful mockery of craftsmanship and prowess, if you ask me, but some people take it seriously."

"Excuse me if I sound crass and irreverent," said Homer, "but what can Mrs. Gardner do about it, being dead and gone, even if things are being changed right and left? Who would insist on bringing an end to the museum?"

"We would," said John Bodkin. "As trustees, it is our duty to fulfill all the conditions of her last will and testament precisely."

"Now, John," murmured Catherine Rule, drawing an embroidery thread slowly out to arm's length, "so far it's mostly just a lot of foolishness."

"Right," said Titus Moon, "just a bunch of little dirty tricks. As soon as we find the culprit, the whole thing will go away."

"Don't forget," said Preston Carver, holding up a warning finger, "there's another last will and testament to be considered. One of our benefactors has promised to leave us a substantial legacy, but she keeps hinting she might change her mind if we don't take better care of the collection."

"Oh, Mrs. Hepplewhite," laughed Titus Moon. "She's a fruitcake anyway. She'll change her mind a thousand times before she dies, fifty years from now."

"Fruitcake or not, we need the money," said Carpenter solemnly. "As treasurer, I know whereof I speak."

"But I thought the museum had an endowment," protested Homer. "Didn't Mrs. Gardner leave plenty of funds for keeping the place going? Is a new gift so important?"

"Mrs. Gardner had no understanding," said Edward Fallfold, gazing seraphically at the painted Italian ceiling,

30

"of what it would take to run a museum sixty-five years after her death."

"Ah," said Homer, nodding his head, "I see. Look—tell me, does the perpetrator of all these jokes always manage to escape without being seen?"

"Yes," said Titus Moon. "The guards discover them when they come on duty at noon. Our security chief has doubled the night watch, but so far they haven't caught anybody in the act."

"Well, very good," said Homer, scraping back his chair. "Thank you, ladies and gentlemen. I'll talk to Mr. Tibby. I guess we've got our work cut out for us."

There was a general pushing back of chairs and gathering up of papers.

"I wonder," said Homer, "if someone could show me around? I mean, right now? I guess I ought to get better acquainted with the place. I'm afraid I don't know a single damn thing about art."

"I'll take you," said Edward Fallfold.

"Bring him to see me," urged Catherine Rule, nodding at Fallfold, smiling at Homer.

"Why don't you start with the rare books?" said John Bodkin. He turned to Homer. "Best things in the place, the early printed books."

"Books?" said Homer. "Mrs. Gardner collected books?"

"She collected everything," said Titus Moon. "So does John Bodkin. Especially books, rare books, right, John?"

Bodkin looked smug. "I do have a rather fine collection, if I do say so myself."

Fallfold led the way upstairs. "I think," he said, glancing back at Homer and uttering a dry laugh, "we should begin with Mrs. Gardner."

Homer had been reading a life of Mrs. Gardner, and he

31

looked up at Fallfold in surprise. "You mean Mrs. Jack Gardner herself, Isabella Stewart Gardner, who died, as I remember, in 1924?"

"The same."

CHAPTER FIVE

TITUS MOON ran back to his office, late for his appointment with the first applicant for a museum assistantship. Titus needed a couple of assistants right away, to help him prepare the new museum catalogue.

It was to be a complete catalogue of the entire collection, from Titian's *Rape of Europa* to the smallest scrap of bobbin-made lace. Everything was to be included—all the paintings, all the Greek and Roman sculpture, the Turkish bowls, the medieval wall reliefs, the rare books, the Parisian fans, the tapestries, the bishops' copes, the Japanese screens, the Venetian windows, the great French and Italian fireplaces, the furniture—there would be two or three thousand items in all. Of course there would be room for only the briefest of entries, but the listing was to be complete, and it was to include the very latest scholarship. The new catalogue was an enormous undertaking. Titus was going to need all the help he could get.

He was late, but so was Polly Swallow. Tearing past the courtyard, glancing breathlessly at the tall marble maidens poised over the flowers, Polly inquired the way to the director's office, then dodged along the corridor, threw open Titus Moon's door, slammed it back on its hinges, and presented herself front and center with a smile like fifteen exploding suns. Polly was a tall, strong girl with a big face and a torrent of brown hair. This morning she was dressed in layers of old coats, black sneakers, and striped stockings. "Here I am at last," cried Polly Swallow.

Titus shot out of his chair, which tipped over and fell to the floor with a crash.

"There was this accident on the T," explained Polly, grinning from ear to ear. "I'm sorry to be late."

She was overwhelming. She filled the room. She couldn't help it. Polly was an out-of-control enthusiast. She had always been crazy about everything, except for the things she violently detested. There she stood on the shining tiles in front of his desk, with 500,000 strands of healthy hair bursting out of her scalp and ten quarts of blood rushing bubbles of oxygen to all the chambers in her brain, where they were welcomed with glad cries and loud bangings of doors and joyous quaffings of effervescent goblets.

Titus was too stupefied to say anything. Silently he stood

34

gazing back at Polly, his girlish complexion flushed, his shirt collar unbuttoned, his tie wrenched open at the neck.

For Polly his silence was reproachful. "I mean," she said lamely, "I hope I'm not too late. I mean, I hope the job's still there." She was surprised that Titus Moon looked so young. He was almost like a tall baby, but he must be at least as old as she was, or how could he be the director of a museum? If only he would say something, and stop looking at her like God.

Then Titus found his voice. He gestured at a chair, and picked up her application, with its splashy handwriting, its exclamation points, its excited underlinings. "I looked over everything you sent in," he said. "It's very good indeed."

"Oh, I'm so glad," gasped Polly, flopping into the chair, arranging her several coats. "I mean I would just love to work here."

Titus tried to get a grip on the interview. "Tell me—" he began, but then Jim Boggs, one of the guards, stuck his head in the door.

"Hey, Titus," he said, "Tom Duck got in again. He was upstairs sleeping it off in the sedan chair. Guess who found him? Mrs. Hepplewhite! We've got him downstairs, but he's still zonked out."

"Oh, Lord," said Titus. He turned back to Polly. "Excuse me, it's an emergency. It'll take me an hour or so. Would you mind waiting till I get back? The café isn't open on Monday, but today they're serving a big lunch to the benefactors, so tell one of the waiters I said you could buy a sandwich. And there's the library. You might want to look at the books in the library. I'll show you where it is."

Polly beamed at him. "Oh, great. That's just great."

But instead of going to the café (Polly was broke), she wandered around the courtyard, and peered around the corner into the Spanish Cloister, where the luncheon for the

35

benefactors was at its noisiest, a polite roar ricocheting off the Mexican tiles on the wall. Then she drifted back around the courtyard, staring at the translucent petals of the cyclamen and the white blossoms of the orchids, thinking about Titus Moon.

Was he married? He didn't look old enough to be married, but he probably was. He seemed to Polly very different from the boys she had known at college in Ohio, athletic guys and social studies majors and M.B.A.'s. Oh, it had been fun going around with them, lots of fun, but after a while Polly had wearied of the way they laughed all the time, guffawing very loudly as if they didn't know who they were and were scared somebody might find out.

Titus Moon looked even younger than they did, with those white eyelashes and all those fountains of blood gushing up under his skin and surging back down, but at the same time he seemed a lot older. Polly liked the way his eyes had looked at her like dots, like nails in a board, like Judgment Day. Impulsively, enthusiastically, irrepressibly, Polly Swallow fell in love.

She had often been infatuated before, and she recognized the beginning signs. It was like throwing a ball in the air and watching it go up and up, flying higher and higher. Exhilarated, she looked around the courtyard and saw that the Gardner Museum itself was in on the secret. A smile was spreading over the face of Artemis the Huntress. The dancing maiden above the fountain rapturously tossed her veil. Before Polly's eyes, the potted lilies sprang up two stories tall, drenching the air with perfume.

Therefore when she saw Titus Moon beside the watch desk, supporting a tall, wasted man in blue jeans, Polly approached eagerly to see what was up.

"Can you manage him by yourself?" said the guard at the desk, looking at Titus doubtfully.

"Oh, sure," said Titus. But the man in his arms was slipping down, folding at the knees.

Instantly Polly sprang forward and helped Titus drag him to his feet.

"Oh, Gawd, I'm sorry," said Tom Duck. "My fault. Oh, my Gawd, I dunno what happened."

"It's okay, Tom," said Titus. "It's all right."

"Where are you taking him?" said Polly, holding Tom up on one side while the guard pressed the buzzer to open the inner door.

"To my car. It's just across the street." Titus pushed open the outer door and together they walked Tom Duck across Palace Road to the Simmons College parking lot. "I've got my own parking place behind the museum," explained Titus, "but sometimes I scoot in here when Simmons is on spring break. Here we are. Now if we can just get him into the back seat—"

"Why don't I come with you?" said Polly. "And help get him out again? He's a friend of yours, right?"

"Well, yes, that's right." Together Titus and Polly chivvied Tom Duck into the back of Titus's car, a small Honda that had seen better days, and then Polly crushed her large frame into the front seat.

Titus swooped the car out of the parking lot and told Polly about his hopes for the new catalogue. Then, while Tom Duck snored in the back seat, Titus explained Tom's history. "He was a middleweight boxer when he was a kid, only he got knocked on the head too often, and one day he sort of lost control and hit another fighter too hard and the guy died. So, poor Tom, they put him in a mental hospital and gave him shock treatments, and when they finally let him out seventeen years later, there wasn't much left of him. And then on the street, he turned into an alcoholic and that pretty well finished him off."

37

"That's terrible," said Polly. "How do you happen to know him? Are you a social worker or something in your spare time?"

"Oh, no. We just happen to live in the same house."

Polly glanced with alarm at the derelict neighborhood through which they were driving. There were boarded-up buildings, and empty lots filled with trash.

"It's not exactly a high-toned neck of the woods," said Titus. "Some parts of Dorchester are really nice, but not our part, I'm afraid."

"But I thought the director of the Gardner Museum had a beautiful apartment on the fourth floor of the building?" said Polly. "I mean,"—she smiled at him apologetically—"I read about it in a book."

"Oh, my apartment." Titus shook his head. "It's okay for ceremonial occasions. And sometimes visitors stay there—you know, museum curators and scholars. But wait till you see my house here in Dorchester; I mean, you've got to see the splendor of it all. It's just so—I mean, it's really so—" Words failed him, and he grinned at Polly. "Look," he said, gesturing at the flotsam slapping against the windshield, fluttering in the weeds in the trampled front yards, flattened against the sides of buildings, clotted in the gutter. "You see all that paper blowing around? You know what it is? It's letters, letters from the mayor and the city council and the legislature."

"Letters? You're kidding."

"Dear residents of Dorchester and Roxbury," said Titus loudly, "we beg to inform you that there are no funds this year for public housing in your communities. Therefore they will continue to rot from official neglect. God bless you all." Grimly he waved his hand at the gleaming towers of the city of Boston, rising far away, blue visions beyond the seedy storefronts along Massachusetts Avenue. "Plenty of money to build that kind of thing. Nothing to fix all this."

"Oh, right, I see what you mean." Polly looked around inquisitively as Titus turned onto Kansas Street. "Oh, hey, is this where you live?"

"This is it." Titus pulled up in front of a nondescript house. "Home, sweet home. It's such a nice contrast to the museum, don't you think? Something different to come back to at the end of a hard day."

Laughing, Polly got out of the car. "I must say, from the point of view of Kansas Street, the Gardner Museum looks kind of silly. You know, sort of effete."

Titus looked at her gratefully. "That's right. But on the other hand, when you look at this place from the point of view of the museum, it seems even worse than it is. I mean, where's the good taste, the refinement, the elegance? Come on, old Tom, easy does it."

"Oh, Gawd," moaned Tom Duck.

Together they got him out of the car and up the porch steps. A big piece of plywood had been screwed to the front door. Titus unlocked the door and pushed Tom in front of him into the narrow hall, then into a small room at the side, where he let him down gently on a deflated sofa. The room was full of mismatched furniture. Polly sat down on a plastic chair shaped to fit some semi-androidal form.

Titus joined Tom on the sofa and looked at him sternly. "Okay, Tom, how did you get into the museum this time?"

Tom Duck was perking up. He looked at Titus in a friendly way and nudged him with his elbow. "Took a bus. Guy inna greenhouse, frien' a mine, he lets me in. I carry stuff for him. You know, real heavy stuff. Then I wenta the men's room, took a bottle outa my pocket. You know." Tom made a swigging gesture and grinned angelically. "Oh, Gawd, I'm sorry. Really sorry. You know."

His guileless truthfulness was disarming. Polly couldn't

39

help smiling. She looked around the room, enjoying once again the incongruity between Titus Moon's two places of residence. The fourth floor of the museum was probably beautifully furnished with Oriental rugs and antiques. Here the dingy room was crowded with ungainly castoffs that had started life with wildly different aspirations of scruffy chic. Dirty blond Swedish modern from the 1950s was jammed against the tufted puffiness of Central Square rococo. Dime-store drapes hung slack at the window.

Then Polly stood up politely, as people came surging down the stairs. Titus introduced them—Mrs. Petty, a portly woman in her sixties, Joe Kelso, a young black man with feeble gestures and clumsy speech, and Bobby Dobbins, a tall, palsied boy with long hair. They were clustering around Titus, patting him, poking him, all talking at once, complaining, whining, laughing.

But Titus couldn't stay. Polly said goodbye and smiled hugely and shook hands all around, then followed him back to the car.

"Hey," she said shrewdly, "that's a special sort of place, right? And you're in charge, is that right?"

"They were living on the street," explained Titus. "So we bought this house from the city for a dollar and fixed it up. You should have seen it at first. The windows were broken, the ceilings were on the floor. We've still got a long way to go."

Polly looked at the trees growing along the sidewalk. They were stunted sugar maples, lopped and warped, but they were tossing gaily in the wind as if they were growing on the Champs Elysées rather than on Kansas Street in Dorchester, Massachusetts. She giggled, getting into the car. She couldn't help herself. "I mean, it's just so funny, the way you live in two such different places. The museum with all its—" Polly made an extravagant gesture and rolled

40

her eyes upward at a vision of infinite luxury and grandeur. "—and this, which is so—so humble, I mean it's just so—" Polly burst out laughing, as they drove through the ravaged streets of Dorchester, where a battle had apparently been fought the day before.

"Don't rub it in," said Titus. "It's a matter of perspective. I mean, I see Tom Duck at the museum leaning against some costly pillar of verde antique, and it throws the whole place into perspective, and I remember there's more to life than art and opulence. Some museum directors live in a beautiful prison and never escape." Then Titus laughed too and looked at Polly kindly. "Listen, you're hired. It's because of your muscles mainly. I mean, we've got all these great big heavy books."

Polly was overjoyed. "Oh, that's great," she said eagerly. "I don't care why you hire me, as long as you do." Polly's zest for the future boiled up. Her excitement about Titus, who was to be her new boss, made her heart beat loudly. Driving through Dorchester she was ready to change the world, to make everything new and fresh and good, beginning with the Gardner Museum's new catalogue. The task looked easy, delightful. She would make such a catalogue, such a wonderful catalogue!

But back at the museum her joy fell flat. Another girl was waiting for Titus. Only then did Polly remember that Titus Moon had two jobs to fill, not just one. This girl would be hired too. Polly could tell it as soon as she saw her.

And she was right. Titus had hired Polly Swallow because of her boisterous enthusiasm, because he recognized in her his own greediness for things well made, his own voracity for gnawing giants' bones. He hired Aurora O'Doyle because her qualifications were impeccable, be-

41

cause her uncle was Pertinax O'Doyle, the mayor of Boston, and because she charmed him right away.

The arrow of the cruel youth in Pesellino's painting impaled him with a passion for Aurora O'Doyle, not Polly Swallow.

In Titus Moon's neatly ordered life there had been only two items so far, both completely under control—aesthetics and ethics. In these two departments of human experience he was profoundly competent. In the relations between the sexes, he was a newborn babe.

CHAPTER SIX

"WAIT A MINUTE," said Homer Kelly. "Isn't that Adam and Eve?"

The painting hung on the wall of the Gothic Room. A flaccid Eve was languidly handing an apple to an indifferent Adam. Only the snake coiling around a branch over their heads seemed interested. It was watching the transaction intently.

Fallfold regarded the painting darkly. "Follower of Cranach. Too bad. The northern Protestants never did understand nudity."

"The snake is good though. They understood sin, all right."

"The snake is always good," said Fallfold, smiling broadly, showing yellow teeth.

Homer was still trying to get used to the overload of sublimity on his senses, the stimulus of painted legendary figures, gods and goddesses, apostles and popes, virgins and prophets. And it wasn't just the works of art. The rooms themselves were startling in the juxtaposition of their high dark spaces with the flood of gray light pouring down into the courtyard. He couldn't help marveling at the woman who had paid for it all, who had instructed the workmen, Fallfold said, by climbing on ladders and showing them how, who had bought enough works of art to fill the entire building.

Homer was reminded of the way he had felt at Versailles, where the multiplicity of golden rooms had made him physically sick. "Doesn't it seem greedy to you? I mean, the woman must have spent half her life buying things."

Fallfold's eyes lighted up. He glanced at Homer, then flicked his glance away. Homer had the feeling that for a second they had occupied the same volume of space and time, but only for a second. Fallfold kept himself at a Puckish distance, like a visitor from some fanciful place, some cloudland or island of Atlantis. "It's time you met her in person," he said. "Come on. She's right over here."

Crossing the room, they stood in front of John Singer Sargent's famous portrait of Isabella Stewart Gardner. "My God," whispered Homer, "she's alive, she's almost alive."

There she was, waiting for them, standing formally to receive them in her pearls and rubies. Her eyes were bold and merry, her lips were parted as if she were speaking, greeting them, as if she were saying, "Edward, what scandalous thing have you been telling Mr. Kelly? Don't believe a word of it, Mr. Kelly."

Homer whispered, as if she might overhear, "What do you think of her, honest to God? I mean, what was she really like?"

"Really like?" Fallfold stared insolently at Mrs. Gardner's clever, disarming face. "What are rich people like anyway? Are they different from other people? This one could point her parasol at anything on the continent of Europe—well, almost anything—and say, I'll take this, I'll take that."

"There was one thing she couldn't buy," murmured Homer, "eternal life."

Fallfold snorted. "Yes, alas, even the rich are mortal. It hardly seems fair."

"She didn't want to die," said Homer, staring at the portrait dreamily. "She didn't want to die and be forgotten.

44

I mean, even more than the rest of us, she didn't want to die. She wanted to be here still, through all time, right here in her own palace, with her own pictures exactly as she had arranged them, and her own name on the lips of everyone who came here, generation after generation. And here she still is, right here, where we can all meet her face to face. I mean, look at her; there she stands, almost breathing, almost alive."

"But the fact is, she's dead as a doornail," said Fallfold heartlessly, "in a mausoleum at Mt. Auburn Cemetery." He turned away, looking around vaguely. "There's a Giotto in here somewhere."

Homer admired the Giotto, and then they went downstairs and walked past the courtyard, where the tables in the east cloister were being cleared.

"Benefactors' day," explained Fallfold, staring at the boy who was collecting empty glasses on a tray. It was his new friend, Robbie Crowlie, in the green jacket of a museum employee. Robbie had worked fast. He had asked for a job, and he had been given one. Smiling to himself, Fallfold conducted Homer through a door to the foot of a stairway in the annex. "I promised Catherine I'd take you to see her. She's right at the top of these stairs. I'll be back for you in a minute or two."

The space allotted to Catherine Rule was brilliantly lit with fluorescent fixtures and banks of lights on metal stands. When Homer stuck his shaggy head in the door, she was bowed over a tapestry mounted on long wooden rollers.

She looked up and smiled at him in welcome, and once again Homer was enchanted by the way her right eye transfixed him, while her left surveyed the rest of the world, beholding its pitiful follies, judging it unworthy, casting it away. Her smile, too, was all her own. It was not like the obligatory cheery smiles of the bright suburban women who surrounded Homer and Mary Kelly in Concord— those good volunteers, those loyal moneyraisers and givers of dinner parties. Catherine Rule's smile was massive and forgiving at the same time. Her self-effacing amusement was that of an observer rather than a participant in human frivolity.

"Wow," said Homer, bending over the tapestry, "a thing like this must take forever to patch up."

46

"Twelve years," said Catherine, "as a matter of fact."

"Twelve years?" Homer was stunned.

"But I'm almost done." She leaned back, holding her narrow hands delicately in the air above the woven threads. "Only another two or three months. Then it will be hung back on the wall where it belongs. There'll be champagne." Her old yellow eyes sparkled. "A celebration."

Homer bent closer, trying to decipher the soft shadings, to see them as part of a picture. "How old is it anyway? What's it all about?"

"It was made in Flanders in the fifteenth century, or perhaps in France, in Picardy. It's the story of Jezebel." Catherine looked up playfully at Homer. "Jezebel thrown to the dogs."

"Jezebel thrown to the dogs! What a grim subject for a tapestry! I mean, imagine people working so hard and so long on something so horrifying! The dogs, as I remember, licked Jezebel's blood?"

"Oh, they loved bloodthirsty stories in those days. A nice gory tapestry was their version of a police show or a thriller. Look at this basket of severed heads."

Homer winced. "You're fixing moth holes, is that it?"

"Oh, yes, a few. But mostly I'm tearing out old repairs and redoing them. All these brown bits are eighteenth-century clumsiness."

Fallfold was standing in the doorway. Homer said goodbye to Catherine Rule, then turned impulsively to ask her a question, "Do you darn your own stockings?"

Miss Rule laughed gaily. It was a lovely abandoned warble. "Certainly not. I throw them all to hell."

47

CHAPTER SEVEN

HOMER'S NEXT STOP was the basement office of security chief Charles Tibby. Again Fallfold showed him the way, then left him, this time with a goodbye. "Good luck on your investigation," he said, with the wry chuckle that had drawn so many young men so easily out of the bulrushes, like a succession of little trout reeled in by a canny old fisherman.

"Thank you," said Homer. He shook Fallfold's hand in farewell, quelling the impulse to confess that he was flying under false colors, that he was totally inadequate to accomplish anything like a proper investigation. Glumly he recognized the signs of the self-abasement that always tormented him at the beginning of some stumbling new effort. Unhappily he knew that this preliminary self-abasement would lead only to more misery—self-flagellation, self-boiling-in-oil, and self-burning-at-the-stake.

But as he entered Charlie Tibby's office, he could see at once that Tibby was also tormented by doubt. Tibby was on the phone, but he flinched as Homer came in, obviously recognizing him at once as an invader of Tibby's personal territory. Tibby was a spare, distinguished-looking young man with a large black handlebar mustache and an expression of profound melancholy. The expression deepened as he waved Homer to a chair and groaned into the telephone, "Oh, no, Michelle, what's happened now? Oh, no, it's not Piggie again?" Clearly across Tibby's desk came the voice of an excited teenager and the bawling of a child. "Well, smack her one. No, no, don't do that. Did you try a pair of tweezers? Oh, God, call the doctor. Go ahead. If he can't see her right away, I'll come home. Okay? Okay." Charlie Tibby put the noisy phone down and closed his eyes. "My youngest kid. She put a jelly bean up her nose. That was the baby-sitter."

"Your wife is away?" said Homer. "So's mine. Things are tough all over."

Tibby looked at him glumly. "We've just been through the divorce court. Custody battle, the works. I won, but I'm beginning to wonder if it was worth it. Maybe I should have lost. My God, my kids are six and four. It's holy hell."

Homer was all sympathy. "I know what it's like. I've got this little nephew Bennie. He's—I mean, he's got all these older brothers and sisters, but he's worse than they ever were. The trouble is, his mother and father have had all they can stand, so they keep kicking up their heels and rushing off here and there, leaving him with guess who? Me. I'm lonely, they think, with Mary away. Bennie will be such good company. Holy horse collar, good company? The boy's a monster."

Charlie Tibby was charmed. Eagerly he leaned forward with his own tales of woe, and soon they were deep in the horrors of child care. When a beeper sounded at Tibby's belt, Homer was disappointed. He had more to say about Bennie, much more.

"Tibby here. What is it?"

"Trouble in the courtyard," said a voice from the wall.

"Right. I'll be there in half a sec." Charlie Tibby turned to Homer. "Want to come along?"

They galloped up the stairs, a couple of big men, both of them puffing a little. Hurrying past the watch desk at the Palace Road entrance, they came out into the west cloister.

Above the glass roof of the courtyard the clouds had

parted, and sunlight streamed down on the flowering jade trees, the cyclamen, the white azaleas. The party for the benefactors was breaking up. They were gathered in the north cloister in twos and threes with their coats over their arms, but they were not going home. Instead, they were staring at the little drama that was taking place before their eyes.

Madeline Hepplewhite, the impossible wife, stood stock-still in the middle of the garden, uttering cries of dismay and staring down at the front of her dress, while her husband Fenton hovered at one side. Beryl Bodkin, the wife of the impossible husband, knelt in front of Mrs. Hepplewhite, dabbing at her skirt. Around them lay the remains of a ripe pineapple, spread out in juicy pieces all over the old Roman mosaic that was the central ornament of the courtyard. Through oozing chunks of pulverized pineapple, the eyes of Medusa stared balefully upward.

Jim Boggs, the guard in the west cloister, told them what had happened. He was chuckling. "She deserved it. It was her own fault." He turned to Homer, explaining. "No-

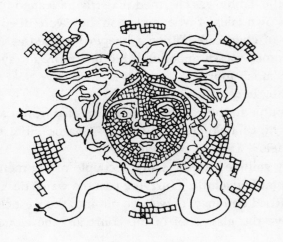

body's supposed to be out there in the courtyard. That's what those big pots are for, blocking up the entrances. But there she was, squeezing past that big jade tree to smell the flowers. And then this huge pineapple came sailing at her from across the way, *kersploosh*."

Homer and Charlie stared across the courtyard at the east cloister, but it was empty. "Oh, my God, that's terrible," said Charlie Tibby. "Madeline Hepplewhite, she's the same woman who found Tom Duck up there on the third floor this morning. She keeps threatening to cut the museum out of her will. And I understand the trustees are counting on getting the money. You know, a long time from now, some day in the far distant future." But Charlie Tibby was grinning as he stepped around the potted jade tree to come to the aid of Mrs. Hepplewhite.

The benefactors drifted away. They put on their coats and went out into the dazzling March afternoon, tittering softly over the affair of the pineapple, their party at an end. Homer Kelly waited for Charlie Tibby, but Charlie was still preoccupied with the outrage to the dignity of Mrs. Hepplewhite. Taking matters into his own hands, Homer ambled into the Spanish Cloister to see whether anyone was lurking there, some malevolent jokester with sticky pineapple juice on his fingers.

He found only a tall blond kid in a green museum jacket, soberly pushing a dolly of folding chairs. The kid had seen nothing, he said. Nobody had come dodging past him, running away from the east cloister.

Homer shrugged and let him go.

In the courtyard he found Charlie Tibby still assaulted by the loud exclamations of Madeline Hepplewhite, who was now demanding a personal apology from the director of the museum. Homer dawdled in the west cloister, pausing to admire an imposing Roman sarcophagus carved in

51

high relief. At once he was enchanted. It was a party, another party, a very different sort of party from the reception for the benefactors. On the front of the sarcophagus the sculptor had created a frolic of maenads and satyrs. They were dancing, swaying left and right, plucking the grapes that dangled from the vine over their heads. Some of the satyrs were slyly disrobing some of the maenads. Now that was a party, decided Homer, comparing it with the genteel celebration for the benefactors, deciding in its favor as a species of festive affair.

Edward Fallfold was in a hurry to get home. The morning had gone off very well, on the whole, and he felt rather pleased with himself. But he had to get back to the rooming house and buttonhole Mrs. Garboyle before she rented the empty room to someone else.

"His name's Robbie Crowlie," he told Mrs. Garboyle. "He'd be an ideal tenant, highly responsible. He's got a job at the Gardner Museum. Doesn't smoke or drink. No drugs. Clean as a whistle." Did Robbie smoke or drink or use cocaine? Who the hell cared?

"Well, you know me," said Mrs. Garboyle. "I just work

here. But I'll speak to the manager at the rental agency. He usually says okay."

"Good," said Fallfold. Exhilarated, he left Mrs. Garboyle vacuuming the stairs, strode past the open door of a messy room where four or five kids in various states of undress were listening to noisy music, entered his own room, slammed the door, and sat down at his desk to write another letter.

Fallfold had been writing letters for weeks. It was not an easy task. And it was always a delicate matter to choose the proper form of address for the director of a foreign museum. Should he say, *Mon cher Directeur, Musée du Louvre?* Or something less formal?

Deciding on a simple *Monsieur,* Fallfold wrote his letter and put it with the others in the box under his bed, to await its time.

Madeline Hepplewhite was shattered by her terrible day at the museum. But after dinner she summoned the strength to write in her diary as usual.

A frightful day! This morning—no, I can't go on! I am still too profoundly distressed! Tomorrow I will relate the appalling events of this dreadful day. Suffice it to say that my favorite two-piece Irish knit has been utterly destroyed, and that I am thinking seriously of removing from my will the bequest to the Gardner Museum. Goodbye for now, dear Diary! Weakened as I am by mortification and shock, it has taken all my courage even to say this much. (Gallantry under fire!)

As for Homer Kelly, he said goodbye to Charlie Tibby, picked up his car, parked it again near Copley Square, snatched a quick lunch at Ralph's Diner on Huntington Avenue, and spent the rest of the afternoon at the Boston

Public Library. By the time he found his car again and started for home, Storrow Drive was choked with traffic.

Wedged between commuters fore and aft, with impatient bastards in $20,000 sports cars dodging around his new Chevette, Homer glanced up, looking for comfort from the Citgo sign that rose over the low skyline of Kenmore Square. It was a beautiful sign, with geometrical triangles that continually waxed and waned, collapsing inward, then growing outward and shrinking in again. For years its Euclidian angles had given him pleasure, reminding him above the grinding of engines locked in first gear, above the choking fumes of a thousand exhausts, that a pure universe of truth and abstract perfection existed above and around and below it all, undergirding everything.

But today the sign wasn't there. Had he missed it? No, there it was, but, good God, they were tearing it down. A huge crane was attached to it; it was leaning sideways, drooping and falling. It was going, it was gone. What the hell? Homer swore and nearly ran into the guardrail.

The house on Fairhaven Bay in Concord was emptier than usual. Whenever he walked into it during Mary's absence, Homer found the small rooms pitifully hollow and silent. Now, leaning against the kitchen counter, he ate his usual supper, cutting himself slices of pepperoni, dragging crackers across a dish of butter, drinking consolatory glasses of ale. He had promised his wife he would fix himself proper meals, and he wasn't doing it; he knew he wasn't, but surely it would be her fault if he died of malnutrition, because she shouldn't have gone away and left him.

After a while the bleak condition of the kitchen wore him down—the soggy dish towel on the drainboard, the sticky dishes left over from yesterday, the greasy surface of the stove, the black bananas on the refrigerator, the nameless substance on the floor that stuck to his shoes. Picking up the phone, he dialed the number of the apartment Mary was subletting in the West Eighties in New York.

"Hello, darling. How are you doing? When are you coming home? How's school? How are all those gutsy women from the turn of the century?" As he spoke, Homer felt a pang of jealousy, still unreconciled to the awful fact that his wife would abandon him in order to study the women's labor movement, that she could stay away from her loving husband for the likes of Clara Lemlich, Rose Schneiderman, and Mrs. Oliver Belmont.

"Oh, Homer, they're great, they're just great. How are you, dear?"

"Well, as a matter of fact," said Homer boldly, "I hate to tell you this, but the truth is, I've fallen in love."

"Fallen in love? Oh, come on, Homer, you're kidding."

"No, no, it's true. Don't you think you'd better come home and nip this thing in the bud? I'm really a goner. This woman has got me hooked."

"What's her name?"

Detecting an anxious note in his wife's voice, Homer knew a moment of malicious pleasure. "Catherine Rule." He said it again, lingering on the syllables of the name of his beloved, "Cath-er-ine Rule. She must be seventy. She's wrinkled as a walnut. She repairs tapestries at the Gardner Museum, which is going through some kind of crisis. I mean, they've called me in, but so far I haven't the faintest idea what's going on."

Mary laughed. "Well, watch it, Homer. These seventy-year-old sirens are the worst."

"Oh, sure, I'll watch my step. What I mean is, Mary darling, maybe you should come home before I lose my head and go completely astray."

Next day was Tuesday. Once more the weather had turned cold. Homer spent the morning in Memorial Hall with a roomful of undergraduates, then picked up his car from the parking lot on Oxford Street, swooped across the Western Avenue bridge over the Charles River, and buzzed along Storrow Drive in an easy flow of midday traffic. As he approached the neighborhood of Kenmore Square, he remembered the Citgo sign and glanced up, hoping to see it re-erected. Good God, what was *that?*

The Citgo sign was no more. In its place, an enormous cartoon cat turned on its axis, grinning over the city of Boston, raising its top hat and putting it on again to salute the cars on Storrow Drive, the shivering rowers on the Charles River, the shallow dome of M.I.T., and the wintry midday sun.

II

THE TRIUMPH
OF CHASTITY

With her, and armed, was the glorious host
Of all the radiant virtues that were hers . . .
So moved she against Love.

—PETRARCH

CHAPTER EIGHT

CATHERINE RULE was an elderly virgin. This merely physical fact did not mean she was ignorant about sex and amorous craving. Perhaps the long hours of hovering over tapestries that told passionate stories of desire and barbarism had honed her sharp observation of the throbbing lives around her. She had time to be astonished, time to wonder and think, time for exactness of judgment.

It was true that the fiercely burning fires of her own youth had been banked long ago, because as she had grown older, her attention had been distracted by other things— by red birds and washing machines, by international disasters and shattered financial hopes, by yellow leaves and television repairmen, by nieces and nephews and works of art. But Catherine knew a good deal about lust just the same, and therefore when she invited Titus Moon and his two new assistants to lunch in the museum café, her veering gaze flickered from one to the other, and shrewdly she saw it all.

The tiny café was crowded with flower ladies, with suburban shoppers, with Friday-afternoon symphony-goers, with a scattering of true worshipers at the shrines of Titian and Rembrandt, Crivelli and Raphael, Veronese and Vermeer. The little tables were jammed together. Waiters threaded their way among them, bringing quiche and salad and pastry, bottles of white wine and imported German beer.

A little dizzy with the wine, Polly Swallow, Aurora O'Doyle, and Titus Moon were talking rather grandiosely about the new catalogue, about the museum, about the usefulness of public collections and the meaning to the individual gallery-goer of rooms full of great paintings.

"Oh, but they teach us something so important," said Aurora, throwing back one long panel of her hair. "Why can't we too become works of art? I mean, why can't our our whole lives be—" Aurora tossed back the other side of her hair—"harmonious and, you know, sort of like music? Everything we do? I mean, instead of walking, we could dance! Instead of talking, we could sing, or speak in verse! Why not?" Gracefully she lifted both sides of her hair and let them fall. The lilt of her voice was a melody. Her gestures were arabesques. Her dress and eyes and hair were all one color like a painting in monochrome. She was a butterscotch Botticelli.

Polly Swallow was struck dumb. Clumsily she dropped her fork.

Titus Moon was speechless too, but with infatuation. He wanted to get down on his knees.

"Didn't your name used to be Phoebe?" said Catherine Rule sharply to Aurora.

Aurora made a face. "Oh, I suppose so. I was named for my great aunt. When I was thirteen, my name was legally changed."

"But Phoebe is such a nice name," objected Catherine. One of her wild yellow eyes floated away from the other and fixed itself on Titus. "I remember your great-aunt Phoebe O'Doyle. She used to ride a big tricycle down Commonwealth Avenue."

Aurora glanced at Titus, as if to say, *These old crones.* But he was no longer looking at her like a panting dog. He had been chastened, mesmerized by Catherine. Under the glance of her singular left eye he was brought up short. Dizzily he shook his head, envisioning vessels far out at sea, their sails bellying in the wind, dolphins leaping in the waves. Soberly he cut a bun in half.

Polly Swallow sensed the difference and took heart. Picking up her dropped fork, she blew on it and then she too attacked her lunch.

Afterward she accompanied Catherine upstairs to examine the old textile catalogue, and choose brief entries for the new general listing of everything in the museum.

Already Polly was working hard at the task that had been assigned to her. She and Titus and Aurora had divided among themselves all the various collections as separate responsibilities. Titus had chosen the sculpture, Polly had begged to be allowed to do the painting, and Aurora had pounced on the furniture. Aurora had a feeling for the furniture, she said, having once thought of going into interior decoration. Words like *escritoire* and *chinoiserie* and *ormolu* were glib upon her tongue.

Polly was crazy about her job. It was too bad that she had fallen in love with Titus, too bad that Aurora O'Doyle with one toss of her long hair had shriveled the flowers in the courtyard; it was disappointing that the marble women no longer shared Polly's secret, that the recumbent knight in the Spanish Chapel no longer dreamed of a heart in flames. But after all, she was very lucky.

Writing exuberant letters home to her mother in Connecticut, Polly called her job *terrific*. Just moving around the building was a joyous privilege. Only a thin wall of brick separated her from the raw light of everything that was ordinary and everyday, of all that was Polly's former uninteresting life. Now she was enclosed in the dim radiance of glowing galleries, where saints' eyes looked at her, and dragons gaped at her, and gods and goddesses gazed calmly

61

past her shoulder. She was engulfed in mystery, in fantasy, in moral tales and stories of heroism, of Christian martyrdom and the defeat of gorgons. All the great cities of the past seemed alive in the Gardner Museum—Troy and Athens and Rome, Florence and Venice and Madrid, Paris and Tournai, even Kyoto and Baghdad. It was as though civilization had been wrung like a twisted cloth, and its juices had drenched the galleries.

Polly loved Titus Moon and she hated Aurora O'Doyle, but these strong emotions lived side by side in her healthy body without tearing her apart, because she had something else on which to lavish her affection—her job, the paintings, the enchanted air of the Gardner.

As an employee, Polly had proved herself a fast and accurate worker. She had calculated how many paintings must be catalogued in a week, and she was sticking to her schedule pretty well. Titus Moon was pleased, recognizing in Polly a special gift for seeing the entire forest as well as the small twigs and branches of the trees. In her appetite for detail, she never forgot the relation of small to large. He had chosen her for her voracious enthusiasm, and now he congratulated himself on the usefulness of that felicitous gluttony.

Today Polly was visiting Catherine's workshop for the first time. Leaning over the Jezebel tapestry, she asked excited questions. She wanted to see how Catherine made her repairs; she was delighted with the cabinet of embroidery skeins, the drawers of blues and greens and multiple shades of gold.

Catherine in her turn was interested in Polly's wardrobe, in her daily triumphs of delapidation, her layers of drooping hemlines and exaggerations of giddy socks. "My dear," she said playfully, "you have such a charming sense of style. Is that what people call punk?"

"Oh, no, not anymore," said Polly, looking down at herself ruefully. "Punk is out."

"Oh, I see. Well, whatever it is, I like it."

Catherine watched as Polly pored over the old textile catalogue, and smiled as it occurred to her that the girl resembled a clever machine for which the perfect use had not yet been found. She was like the little steam engine Catherine's brother had played with as a boy, a shining toy with cheery brass fittings. It had steamed and fizzed, and its powerful little piston had driven the flywheel around and around. But what was it good for? Polly was like that, a promising but untapped resource.

And then Catherine made up her mind. Whatever dangerous traps Phoebe O'Doyle was laying for that helpless young goose, Titus Moon, the boy must be saved at all costs, by the constant vigilance and interference of Catherine Rule.

Titus meanwhile was unaware of plots concerning his welfare. He was making his daily obeisance to a single work of art. Today he had chosen a fifteenth-century Italian painting in the Raphael Room, an *Annunciation* by Antoniazzo Romano.

It was a serene and lovely picture, with a kneeling angel Gabriel, a Virgin fair and bland, and the dove of the Holy Spirit descending in a shower of gold. The shower, thought Titus, was like the lecherous golden rain that had fallen from Zeus upon Danae. Here, of course, all lechery had been dismissed, leaving only innocence and purity. But more striking than the Immaculate Conception was the elaborate perspective of the painting, the two lines in the marble floor that rushed his eyes back to the majestic open doorway in the rear, to the hills and the ineffable blue sky. No matter how Titus tried to concentrate his attention on the figures, the perspective seized him and dragged him

63

away to the far door. There he longed to gaze out, and stroll into the landscape, to behold cypress trees and a river, perhaps, looping through a valley, and a miscellaneous cavalcade of saints—the Magdalen in a hairy skin, Catherine with her wheel, Sebastian naked and pricked with arrows.

"Hey, Mr. Moon," called one of the guards, "could you come here a sec?"

It was Robbie Crowlie, the new guard, a tall blond boy who looked very handsome in his loose museum coat. He was standing in the doorway between the Raphael Room and the Short Gallery.

Titus pulled himself away from the *Annunciation* and walked to the door, observing the prompt obedience of the surfaces around him to the laws of shifting perspective, the

drawing together of parallel lines to a vanishing point somewhere beyond the outer wall, beyond the little park, beyond the apartment buildings on the other side, beyond Huntington Avenue and the Green Line, beyond Roxbury, South Boston, and the harbor, on and on to the flat horizon where the sky eventually met the sea.

"What is it?" he said to Robbie, who was leading him across the Short Gallery into the Little Salon.

"It's in here," said Robbie. "I'm sorry, Mr. Moon, but I'm afraid something else has happened. Mr. Tibby told me what's been going on. I don't know if this is important or not, but it wasn't here yesterday."

Titus collected himself grimly. "Show me."

CHAPTER NINE

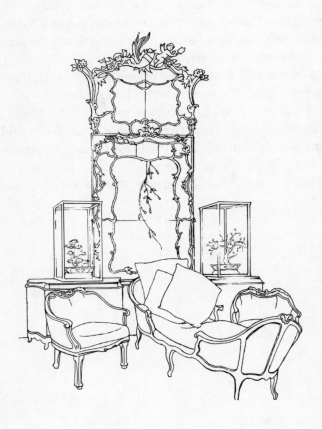

T HE LITTLE SALON was pale gray and gold, a
handsome chamber with French and Flemish tapestries adorning the eighteenth-century Venetian
paneling.

"What's the matter?" said Titus Moon. "I don't see anything wrong."

"The card game," said Robbie Crowlie. "There on the table. That wasn't here before."

Other guards were crowding in the door, staring at the cards laid out beside the Meissen clock. Before long the word got around, and soon four more staff members were gathered in the Little Salon—Polly Swallow and Catherine Rule, Aurora O'Doyle and Charlie Tibby.

"What the hell kind of game is it?" said Charlie. "It doesn't look like ordinary solitaire to me."

"I think I know," Polly volunteered. "It's solitaire, all right, a really fancy kind that's almost impossible to win. We used to call it Death."

"Death?" said Titus Moon.

"You see," said Polly, pointing at the cards, "they've been laid out in four rows face-up, and the aces have all been removed. You have to get the four rows in order by shifting the cards around so that they go in perfect suits from kings at the left. But the trouble is, you're stopped cold whenever the spaces turn up behind the twos. The first time, it's like a little stroke, and the second time, it's another heart attack, and the third time, it's a massive brain hemorrhage, and the fourth time, it's the end." Polly looked around apologetically. "Sorry to be so morbid, but that's the way we used to play it."

Aurora O'Doyle giggled. Today she was wearing a suit and blouse of butter pecan. Bored with the card game, she transferred her attention to the big mirror between the windows and murmured knowingly, "Venetian."

Catherine Rule looked up too at the delicate rococo fittings of the Little Salon. "Death," she said dreamily. "It seems an odd subject for this room, which was made for flirtation, for coquetry." She tossed her hand at the wall

67

over the table, where Boucher's *Car of Venus,* drawn through the air by swans, floated among billowing clouds and tumbling cupids. It had been painted for another room far, far away, for someone in the circle of Louis XV, perhaps even for Pompadour herself. For a moment the others stared at it too, falling under the spell of courtly dalliance.

For Titus, the contrast with the *Annunciation* was too great. The surrounding air of gentle licentiousness grated against the purity of Antoniazzo's unspotted Virgin. World views clashed in his head. He could feel the creak of passing centuries, the buffeting changes of time and tide. Reeling, he glanced at Polly, and took comfort in the innocence of her sneakers, the artlessness of the Band-Aid hiding a pimple on her cheek.

Charlie Tibby was questioning Robbie Crowlie. "Were you here yesterday? What time did you leave?"

"Sure, I was here, on duty between this room and the Short Gallery, just like usual. I left at five-fifteen."

"Are you sure the cards weren't here at that time?"

"Positive."

"So sometime between five-fifteen yesterday and noon today when you came in, somebody was here in this room, arranging the cards on the table. Christ. I'll speak to the night guards. Maybe they noticed something."

"But, Charlie," said Titus, "couldn't it have happened in the daytime while Robbie was on duty? After all, he's only human. He can't keep an eye on both rooms at once, not every moment of the day. Couldn't someone have been in here long enough to lay these cards down while Robbie was talking to someone in the Short Gallery next door?"

Charlie admitted it was possible. So did Robbie Crowlie. Charlie took a tiny camera out of his pocket, snapped a picture of the cards on the table, then swept them carefully into an envelope. "No fingerprints, I'll bet. No such luck.

I'll get in touch with Homer Kelly, but what can he do?"

They dispersed. But not before Catherine Rule, trailing after Aurora O'Doyle, observed the coquettish influence of the Little Salon.

Aurora was running after Titus Moon. "Are you going to the opening?" she said. "You know, the one at the Fogg Museum?"

"What opening?" mumbled Titus.

"They've got a new show, the drawings of Poussin. This afternoon at four."

"Well, I don't know."

"I'll take you. Meet me at my car at quarter to, okay? Oh, come on, Titus. Why not?"

Titus shrugged off the cramping effect of Antoniazzo's painting of the Immaculate Conception. "Well, okay. All right. I mean, I guess it's all right."

Polly Swallow strode ahead of them, whistling soundlessly, and Catherine Rule made a plan.

At twenty minutes to four, she went out to the staff parking area, knelt down with a cracking of old joints, and let all the air out of Aurora's left front tire, telling herself regretfully that Aurora's darling little red convertible would probably ride smoothly anyway, flat tire or no flat tire, powered as it was by swans and ringed about with cherubs.

But Aurora didn't think so. As Catherine unlocked the door of her own car, Aurora appeared with Titus, and discovered the flat tire. "Oh, shit," she said. "Damnitall, Titus, look at that."

"Oh, dear," said Catherine, "what a shame. Look, why don't you two come with me? I'm going to the opening." She beamed. "We can all go together. What a lark!"

And therefore Titus and Aurora were chaperoned all afternoon by an elderly maiden lady.

Aurora was shrewdly suspicious. She couldn't help noticing that the old woman had a curiously unsettling effect upon Titus. In the presence of Catherine Rule he seemed a completely different person. Wandering among the Poussins, he hardly looked at the reclining goddesses in red chalk, the temples reflected in sheets of water. He was awkward and thoughtful and had little to say.

And Aurora was right. Catherine Rule did indeed have a powerful jostling impact on Titus Moon. Once again it was the hypnotizing effect of her left eye. Catherine's right eye looked at him with a gaze that was at once transfixing and forgiving, but her roaming left eye seemed serenely unaware of him, as if it were beholding great pillars of universal justice and eternal value, somewhere above the roof of the Fogg Museum and the budding trees of Quincy Street.

In Catherine's company Aurora O'Doyle merely danced at the edge of his vision like a gnat in a cloud of other gnats.

CHAPTER TEN

ONCE AGAIN Madeline Hepplewhite was writing in her diary.

Michelangelo never took his socks off! This is a known fact! It makes one think seriously about the nature of genius. I am reminded of Professor Braithwaite's course in logic at Bryn Mawr. Can I recapitulate? Here goes!

Michelangelo was a genius.

Michelangelo was a dirty man.

Hippies are dirty men.

THEREFORE hippies are geniuses!

Query: are any hippies left these days? I never see them here in Chestnut Hill. Nowadays all the young people look so fresh and clean and nicely dressed. Which reminds me, whatever happened to Caroline Smithers, that girl at the end of the hall in my dorm, senior year? The one who never took a bath????!!!! I should have inquired of Peggy Honeywell, that time she asked me to remember Bryn Mawr in my will. (She was so thrilled when I told her I had already taken care of it, with a bequest more precious than gold!)

In mid-March there was a spell of severe cold. More than once Homer had to start his car with battery cables connected to his pickup truck. But spring was not to be denied forever. On the twenty-first of March, a thaw began to warm the frozen ground. Dank fresh smells floated up from the Sudbury River. Even inside the Gardner Museum, where it was spring all the time, there was a different quality in the light that streamed into the courtyard, a different feeling in the shadowy cloisters, in the great dark galleries—a sense of lightness, of freedom from the grip of giant frozen tongs.

Only in Charlie Tibby's windowless office in the basement was there no changing of the seasons. Homer and Charlie spent a lot of time down there in the bald light of the fluorescent fixtures, mulling over the schedules of the guards who had been on duty on the days and nights when unpleasant things had happened.

It was no easy task. There were thirty-eight people under Tibby's direction. Twenty-nine were guards who stood at strategic positions between the galleries and along the cloister walks and beside the staircases during the hours when the museum was open to the public. Nine were members of the watch, patrolling the museum at night. In addition there were ten people on the maintenance staff, seven gardeners, a number of docents and conservators, a curator and an assistant curator, the director and his two assistants, an archivist, a photographer, a café supervisor, a cook, three waiters and a sales clerk, as well as the seven trustees.

"Tell me about the trustees," said Homer, balancing his notebook on his knee and turning to a clean page.

"The trustees?" Charlie smiled, and moved the picture of Piggie and Dougie from the left side of his desk to the right. "Trustee number one, John Bodkin, president. Some kind of big tax lawyer, celebrated loudmouth. I feel sorry for his wife Beryl. Trustee number two, Preston Carver, vice-president and treasurer. Works for some big investment banking firm on State Street. Well, I suppose they have to have people like that on the board because of all the stocks and bonds they're supposed to be taking care of. Trustee number three, Fulton Hillside, secretary. Another highly respectable son of a bitch. Hillside's in real estate, big important properties, you know? No little rose-covered cottages or anything like that."

Charlie rearranged his pencils and went on to trustee number four. "Peggy Foley, great woman, terrific good sport. I wish they'd get rid of Carver and let Peggy do all the investments. That woman really knows her stuff. Who else? Shackleton Bowditch—"

"It's all right. I know Shackleton from the old days. Harvard Fellow, good man, soul of integrity. What about Edward Fallfold?"

Charlie laughed. "Charming guy, Fallfold. Doesn't like girls. I heard a rumor he was turned down for the director's job because Bodkin saw him coming out of the bulrushes with a young guy half his age."

"Bulrushes? What bulrushes?"

"Phragmites communis," said Charlie learnedly. "Those big reeds in the Back Bay Fens across the street. People use them for, you know, assignations. They're full of little paths, I guess, and forest glades and cozy nooks. Anyway, there he was, Fallfold, coming out of the jungle with some young kid. So his application was turned down and they chose Titus Moon instead. But just to show they were broad-minded, they asked him to be a trustee, because they were one short. And, after all, he's got all those degrees in fine arts. I mean he's a scholar, that's what they tell me."

"Which brings us," said Homer, leaning forward eagerly, "to the woman I love, Catherine Rule. Tell me more about Catherine."

"Oh, she's famous," said Charlie. "Catherine's an international expert on the repair of tapestries. She gets invited

73

to museums overseas to show them how to do it right. And her father was Henry Rule."

"Henry Rule?" Homer's jaw dropped. "Good God, the poor woman. Didn't he go bust in a really flabbergasting way during the Great Depression? Failed at copper mining, or something like that?"

"Oil wells, way up around Point Barrow in the Arctic Circle. They all came up dry. Hanged himself on one of the rigs. Too bad. So Catherine's a working woman, supports herself, always has. Lives on Beacon Hill."

"She can't be too badly off, if she lives on Beacon Hill?"

"Wrong side," said Charlie sorrowfully. "Down toward Cambridge Street with the cockroaches."

Homer shuddered in melancholy sympathy. "Okay, so much for the trustees. Do they all have keys to the museum?"

Charlie winced. "It's a sore point. The trustees voted themselves the right to have keys last year, before I came along. When they hired me as chief of security, I insisted it wouldn't do, so they agreed to give them up. But how do I know they didn't copy them first?"

"Surely that's a simple matter. Why don't you get all the locks changed?"

"Too expensive, they said. The trustees voted against it. So my hands are tied. The only other people with keys are me and Roger Wiseman, my foreman for the night patrol. And Titus Moon, of course. After all, the fourth floor is supposed to be his apartment. The gardener has a key to the greenhouses and the carriage house, naturally."

Then Charlie went on with his list of visitors to the museum, the crowds of people who came in during the day, the concert-goers on Tuesdays, Thursdays, and Sundays, the members and patrons and benefactors who came to lectures and luncheons and gallery talks. "And then there are the special visits. Good Lord, I almost forgot the special visits."

"Special visits?" said Homer, scribbling in his notebook.

"Special visits are special occasions when nonprofit organizations are allowed to use the museum. We charge them for security and catering."

"I see." Homer changed the subject. "Who was clearing up the tables after the reception for museum benefactors, when that pineapple was thrown at Mrs. Hepplewhite?"

"Only a couple of my people, as far as we could tell, Hilda Sorensen and Beanie Kenney. Oh, and the new kid, Robbie Crowlie. Hilda certainly didn't throw any pineapple. She's a big Swedish girl, heavy with Baltic gloom, absolutely reliable. I had a long talk with Beanie and the new kid. The three of them were together on the job, most of the time. Beanie has more sense than to do a thing like that. And why would the new kid want to embarrass Mrs. Hepplewhite? He doesn't know anything about her. The rest of us would be glad to embarrass her, no doubt. The woman's a menace."

Homer was hungry for lunch. He was starved for light and air. But it was still only eleven-thirty. Crossing one leg patiently over the other, he turned back the pages of his notebook to the scrawls he had made during his meeting with the trustees. "What about this old chap, Tom Duck? I gather he's part of the problem?"

"Oh, well, I guess so. But poor Tom's not clever enough to think up any of those dirty tricks. Oh, it's true, he killed somebody once, a long time ago in the prize ring. But all that behavior has been jolted out of him with shock treatments and all those years he spent in a mental hospital. Tom's just a big overgrown baby."

"But still—you say he killed somebody?"

Charlie Tibby slapped his knee and stood up. "Look,

you can talk to Titus Moon about Tom Duck. Come on, let's go up to his office and catch him before he goes to lunch."

Titus, as it turned out, was hungry too. "Look," he said, "why don't we go to my house in Dorchester? Mrs. Petty will make us some lunch. Tom's usually there at this hour. You can meet him in person."

So Charlie Tibby fitted himself into the back seat of Titus Moon's little Honda and Homer folded his six-feet-six-inch frame into the front seat, and Titus drove them to Kansas Street.

"Nice place," said Homer, at once divining the nature of the household. When Mrs. Petty produced a lunch of taco chips and canned ravioli, he smacked his lips. "Delicious," he said, spearing the last piece on his paper plate. "My favorite brand, I can tell. Chef Boyardee, right, Mrs. Petty?"

Charlie Tibby merely pushed the lumps of ravioli around with his fork, then confined himself to taco chips, as Tom Duck came in with a tray of Fig Newtons and cans of orange drink.

"Hey, there," said Tom, lowering his massive frame onto the sofa, taking Charlie by the arm and shaking him jovially. "Oh, whoops! Oh, hey, oh, wow, oh, Jesus Gawd, I'm sorry."

"It's all right," said Charlie, staring in horror at the ravioli in his lap.

"Tom, you don't know your own strength," laughed Titus. Vanishing into the kitchen, he came back with a wet dishrag and mopped at Charlie. "Look, Tom, these people want to know about you and the museum. They want to know why you go there and how you get in."

Tom crumpled a paper plate in his fist and grinned, showing gold teeth. "The museum? Oh, right. Lotsa flowers. Lotsa pitchers. Pretty kitties."

"Kitties?" said Homer.

"Inna garage. You know, the whatchamacallit. Gawd, I don't know. They got these nice little kitties. Friend of mine inna greenhouse, he lets me in. I help him, you know? Sweepa garage, feed the cats. I saw this other animal, Gawd, what's it called? Raccoon. You know. It comes around, name's Fred, awful cute."

"This friend of yours in the greenhouse," said Charlie, "what's his name?"

"Bart," said Tom, his ruined face lighting up. "Good ole Bart." He shook his head in awe at the museum and all its attractions. "All them flowers! All them pitchers! Gawd!"

"Well, thank you, Tom." Homer stood up. "We're grateful."

"And Tom's going to stay strictly away from the museum from now on," said Titus, looking at him soberly, "isn't that right, Tom? No more bus trips, no more greenhouse, no more Bart?"

Tom Duck beamed and nodded. "Oh, you bet. Thass' right. Jesus Gawd, you said it."

But Tom forgot. His wrecked memory completely lost Titus Moon's admonition. His friendly habit of dropping in at the Gardner Museum was stronger than the warning.

Next day he was back.

"Oh, hi, there, Tom," said Bart. "Hey, I'm not supposed to let you in. But, listen, I could sure use you today. The other guy's out sick, and the head gardener, he's in Dedham working on the nasturtiums. We've got all these Martha Washington geraniums, big heavy pots, there must be a dozen of them. My God, I can't even get 'em up on the dolly."

Together they wrestled with the first great terra rossa container, pushing the dolly at it, trying to scoop it up. Then Tom said, "Lookit, lemme have it." With no apparent

77

effort, he lifted the giant pot and held it against his chest. "Where you want it now?"

"Oh, hey," said Bart, flabbergasted, "you can't carry it like that."

But Tom was already striding easily down the greenhouse aisle. "Well, okay," said Bart, hurrying after him. "The geraniums are supposed to take the place of the cyclamens. I'll show you."

Under Bart's direction, Tom moved all the potted geraniums into the courtyard, and all the cyclamens back into the greenhouse. Then Catherine Rule had a problem with some of the textiles in storage—two of the heaviest tapestries were to be taken out for washing and relining. "Oh, Tom Duck," she said, smiling at him, "I'm delighted to see you. Could you and Bart help us out? We're desperate."

And after that Bart took his coffee break and Tom went to the men's room, and then Bart began potting dahlia bulbs, and forgot about Tom.

Therefore it was the Bryn Mawr 67's who found him. The Boston branch of the class of '67 was touring the museum on a special visit under the leadership of Madeline

Hepplewhite. They had just experienced a trying moment. One of Madeline's classmates had reached out to touch the Roman sarcophagus in the west cloister.

"Did you know, Phyllis," Madeline said sharply, "that no one on the staff of this museum, *no one,* not even the *director,* is permitted to touch anything?"

"Oh, goodness," said Phyllis, snatching back her hand. "I'm sorry."

Therefore when Phyllis saw Tom Duck sleeping in the Roman throne on the other side of the courtyard, she nudged a friend and began to laugh. No one was supposed to touch anything? Look at that crazy old guy lying there in the middle of everything! He wasn't just touching the sculpture, he was sprawling all over it! Soon the whole class was laughing, enjoying the sight of the strange-looking unshaven old man stretched out on the throne, dwarfing it, his head thrown back, sunlight pouring into his open mouth, his feet crossed on the marble footstool. Tom was wearing a miscellaneous outfit chosen from the box of secondhand clothing in the front hall of the house on Kansas Street. Today the box had been full of castoffs from a swanky church in Pride's Crossing. In his drunken stupor, Tom was natty in a pair of white polo pants that had seen service at the Myopia Hunt Club. His bare legs were thrust into a smart pair of golfing shoes.

Beryl Bodkin was also a member of the class of '67. This morning she lingered at the tail end of the procession in the company of Madeline Hepplewhite's husband Fenton. While the rest of the class was downstairs laughing at Tom Duck, Beryl and Fenton were still upstairs in the Raphael Room, straggling in the rear, staring vaguely at the velvet chasuble and the Canosan vase.

Then Beryl turned to the portrait by Pollaiuolo on the wall. "What a terrible face," she said dreamily. "She re-

minds me of someone I know, but I can't think who."

But then as Madeline Hepplewhite's voice rose imperiously through the window from the courtyard below, Beryl knew at once who it was she had been thinking of, and she glanced at Fenton in an agony of embarrassment.

Fenton looked at the picture and said nothing, but he blushed deep red. Instantly they turned their backs on the portrait and hurried after the others.

CHAPTER ELEVEN

"LISTEN," said Polly, "what's that?"

The cataloguing team was walking back from lunch. Titus stopped in the west cloister and looked up at the windows of the Dutch Room. "I didn't know there was a concert up there this afternoon."

"Concert?" said Aurora, frowning. "What concert?"

"Don't you hear it?" said Polly. "It's nice. Really nice."

"But it's Wednesday," said Aurora. "Concerts are Tuesdays, Thursdays, and Sundays."

"Maybe we'd better take a look," said Titus. With Polly at his heels, he hurried up the stairs.

"Don't be silly, Titus," Aurora called after them. "There isn't any music. I don't hear a thing."

But as Titus and Polly reached the top of the stairs, it was plainly audible to both of them, plangent notes from some sort of harpsichord, a threadlike soprano voice running softly down a scale to the plucked accompaniment of a guitar.

"It's probably for some special visit," said Titus, striding along the corridor. "I didn't know one was scheduled for today. I must have forgotten."

But there was no trio of musicians in the Dutch Room, no milling throng of polite guests. And the music had stopped.

The guard on duty was Hilda Sorensen. Hilda looked at them stolidly. "Music?" she said. "Vat music?"

"But we heard it," said Polly. "It was coming from this room, I swear it was."

Obeying the same instinct, Titus and Polly walked across the tiled floor to the little painting by Vermeer, and stood in front of it.

There they were, the right sort of music makers, the young woman in the yellow bodice thoughtfully playing the clavichord, the guitarist—or was he a lute player?—forever showing his back, the pensive singer keeping time with her lifted hand. As usual, Titus had the sensation that the tiled floor was reaching forward to slip under his feet, as though he too were standing in the same room, listening to an airy music that had only this moment ceased.

Then Polly's head went up. "There it is again," she said,

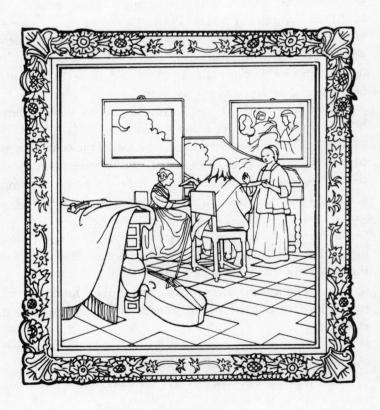

and at once they turned and ran down the hall in the direction of the Early Italian Room, drawn by an older music, an earlier simpler music, a stringy vibrating harmony of bows scraping across oddly strung instruments, of tinny-sounding horns.

But once again the ethereal music faded. "What's up?" said Jim Boggs, the guard on duty, looking at them in surprise.

"Did you hear any music just now?" said Titus.

"Music? Me? No, it's Wednesday. There's no concert on Wednesday."

But there were painted musicians here too, Fra Angelico's music-making angels, strumming on lutes and blowing horns and stroking a bow across a strange-looking viol, in honor of the assumption of the Virgin, who stood among them on a cloud, her hands raised in amiable wonder at finding herself transfigured.

"Quick!" said Polly. "Downstairs! There it goes again."

There was no mistaking it this time, the foot-stamping beat, the insane crashing of crazed guitars, the mad rattle of castanets. Down the stairs they plunged, racing around the courtyard into the Spanish cloister, to stand gasping in front of John Singer Sargent's enormous painting of a Spanish dancer, *El Jaleo.*

But this one too was silent. The women raised their castanets, the men crouched over their guitars, the singer howled at the ceiling, and the dancer stamped her heels on the floor, but the wild flamenco beat raged and resounded only within their own heads.

And then the bell rang, and this time they were close enough to turn at once. No hand had struck the great Japanese bronze bell that hung from the ceiling of the Chinese Loggia, but when they touched it, they could feel the deep shivering in the metal.

83

"It's very strange," said Polly.

"It certainly is odd," agreed Titus.

For a moment longer they waited, listening for some other harmony of instruments to strike up, but there was nothing more. Polly shrugged her shoulders and went back to work, and Titus wandered downstairs to talk to Charlie Tibby.

Charlie was fascinated. At once he wanted to look for hidden cassettes.

"Oh, right," said Titus. "It has to be something like that.

Except for the bell. The bell was real. It was still vibrating. We could feel it. That wasn't any cassette player."

"Sympathetic vibration," explained Charlie. "The bell was responding to some reverberation in the air, like the rumble of a truck on the street, or some resonance you couldn't even hear."

"Well, maybe," said Titus. "But I don't think a truck was going by. It's very peculiar."

Only later did Polly learn that Catherine Rule sometimes heard things too. Like Charlie Tibby, Catherine used the word *sympathetic*. In her case, she said, it was obviously just some sort of sympathetic displacement of noises in her own mind. "Actually, it isn't really music at all. It's horses' hooves and the clatter of arms and armor, the barking of hounds, sometimes a woman's cry. But you see it's probably all in my head."

"Armed men?" said Polly. "Why would you hear horses and armed men?"

"My tapestry," said Catherine softly. "Jehu's chariot assaulting Jezreel. Jezebel thrown to the dogs."

CHAPTER TWELVE

I N THE OPINION of Homer Kelly, March had little
to recommend it. March was a month of transition,
March was a mess.

On alternate afternoons, Homer took pleasure in walking into the Gardner Museum to surround himself with the
beauty and order of the Spanish Cloister, leaving behind
him the wild tangle of the natural world—the buckled bulrushes in the park across the street, the fluff-erupting cat-
tails, the polluted water, the trees tossing messy
miscellaneous branches against a background of random
cloud. In the world outside the museum, nature and mankind went right on tripping and stumbling all over themselves, while here, ah, here was harmony, here was
organized tranquillity. If the curving pattern of strigils on
one side of a Roman sarcophagus faced to the left, on the
other, they faced to the right. In the courtyard the dolphins
above the fountain wriggled their identical tails. In the
Gothic Room the painted hands of Mrs. Gardner were
clasped in the exact center of Sargent's canvas.

Homer stood in the hushed quiet of the Titian Room and told himself that somewhere in Boston at that very moment some wretched crime was happening in a squalid room among torn panties and dirty sheets, while here in the perpetual enchantment of this magical place, Zeus could carry off Europa in a pleasing swirl of chubby cherubs and floating veils.

The truth was, Homer had been won over. It was true that he still missed the plain living and high thinking of his beloved transcendentalists, back home in Concord. But there was something to be said, just the same, for the conspicuous consumption and aesthetic greediness of Isabella Stewart Gardner. She had indeed been an extravagant woman, lavish in personal expenditure, decking herself in rubies and pearls, with diamonds wobbling over her head on gold wires, but it didn't matter. She had loved good and beautiful things, she had brought them together here. Let everything else go to hell. In March, when nature was at its worst, let art reign supreme.

But art was unfortunately in trouble at the moment, and he, Homer Kelly, was supposed to be doing something about it. At the next meeting of the trustees, he was supposed to make a report on the progress of his investigation.

Progress had been slow. With the help of Charlie Tibby, Homer had made a calendar showing the dates of the various incidents that had occurred in the museum, and Charlie had added the names of the guards who had been on duty nearby. Only two had been present more than once, Hilda Sorensen and the new guard, Robbie Crowlie. Charlie had gone to Robbie's rooming house on the Fenway to interview him at home, but he had learned little of interest. And anyway Robbie was too new on the job to have been involved in any of the earlier incidents.

"Oh, he had some smoking materials of a doubtful kind

lying around," Charlie told Homer. "But I figured that was none of our business. And he put a letter in a drawer in a hurry when I came in. I caught a glimpse of the signature. Do you know anybody named Teddy? Nobody on my staff is a Teddy. How about Hilda? Did you talk to Hilda Sorensen?"

"I did," said Homer. "Hardworking serious girl, going to night school. Lives in a tiny room near Northeastern, wants to make something of herself. I can't see her hatching clever little criminal plots in the Gardner Museum."

Homer had gone away from the interview feeling sorry for Hilda Sorensen. The only glimmer of romance in her bleak and Spartan life had been the pictures from film magazines on her wall, Greto Garbo and Liv Ullman. They too were Swedish, Homer had reflected sadly, but otherwise their luminous beauty had little in common with Hilda's massive plainness.

At the trustees' meeting on the thirtieth of March, Homer reported briefly on these pursuits, and then he had the bad luck to arouse the ire of John Bodkin by saying that all the irregularities so far had been harmless. "Oh, some were irritating, like the shifting of the pictures, but some of the others were kind of funny, like the frogs and the balloon. And some were actually sort of charming, like the cards in the Little Salon. The latest episode, the mysterious music—did Titus tell you about the music?—the music was thoroughly poetic and delightful, don't you agree?"

"Delightful!" Bodkin was horrified. "Irritating! Do you call the manhandling of a precious Botticelli and a Raphael and a Rubens merely irritating?" And then for the first time, John Bodkin threatened to make a motion to dismantle the museum. "Our task as trustees is to fulfill the requirements of Mrs. Gardner's will. Those requirements have been flagrantly disregarded. The longer we carry on as if nothing were happening, the more we fail in our stewardship. Surely some of you must agree with me?" Bodkin looked around the table at the noncommittal faces of Shackleton Bowditch, Catherine Rule, Peggy Foley, Preston Carver, and Fulton Hillside. "Where's Fallfold?" he said sharply to Titus Moon.

"At home in bed," said Titus. "Just a cold, I think."

But Edward Fallfold was not at home in bed. He had called Titus with this excuse, but actually he was spending the afternoon in the Boston Public Library. Although by now the box under his bed was jammed with letters addressed to European art museums, Fallfold wasn't finished yet. Surely there were other museums he had never heard of—in Brussels and Oslo, in Prague and Monte Carlo, in Hamburg and Lisbon, in the ancient towns of Italy? In the catalogue room of the Boston Public Library, Fallfold plucked the Mo-My drawer out of the ranks of cabinets, and began running through the cards behind the tab for *Museums*.

CHAPTER THIRTEEN

I HATE *Aurora O'Doyle,* thought Polly Swallow, alone in her office next to Titus Moon's. *I loathe and detest Aurora O'Doyle.*

It felt good to say it to herself so positively. Her hatred was a wholesome thing, affording her a healthy amusement and an inward sense of revenge. Staring out the window into the Monk's Garden, Polly thought up new words for hating, like *abhor* and *disrelish.* "I disrelish Aurora O'Doyle," she said aloud, knowing at the same time that there was nothing she could do about it. She had to carry on as usual, and pretend to be a good sport. Aurora's power was too overwhelming. Even in the way she walked down the hall, Aurora displayed the imperial authority of all pretty women everywhere. Every day she ruled over Titus Moon with the soft tyranny of shoulder and breast and thigh.

When Polly's feelings ran too high, she left the office she shared with Aurora and went up to the workrooms on the second floor to see what the conservators were doing. On the day after the trustees' meeting, Polly found Catherine Rule bowed over the Jezebel tapestry as usual, sewing in the harsh light of the fluorescent fixtures. Pulling up a chair, Polly sat down across from Catherine, her hands in her lap. "I just wanted to say hello," she said, trying to sound cheerful. "I mean I've had lunch. You have too, right? Can I help? Hey, listen, I can sew. I really can. Little teeny stitches. Really!"

"All right," said Catherine, smiling, handing her a needle and thread. "Start right here. I'll show you. Do it like this."

They sat with heads bent, absorbed, like women sewing in ancient Greece, or medieval Italy, or China or Japan. Aurora O'Doyle found them like this when she came looking for Titus. "Where *is* he? I mean, I need to tell him something. He's coming for supper, and I forgot to explain where to park. Whoo, it's hot in here." Aurora pulled off her sweater and sat down.

"Oh, he's coming to supper, is he?" said Catherine, glancing at Polly, who didn't look up.

"Yes, and I've really got to rush off and pick up a few groceries." But instead Aurora leaned forward and stared at the work in progress. "I just don't see how you stand doing that, year after year. It must be so *boring.*"

"No," said Catherine, "I like it."

"I do too," said Polly, rethreading her needle. "I mean, it's restful. You can think about things."

"Well, it's not for me," said Aurora, tossing back one side of her long hair. "But then I've always been such a terribly *active* person." Tossing back the other side, she got up and rushed away, thinking about cheese and wine and a certain silver negligee in a shop window on Newbury Street.

"We, I suppose," said Catherine slyly to Polly, "are lazy and slothful."

"Oh, right." Polly laughed, then jumped up from her chair. "Oh, look, she left her sweater. I'll run and catch her."

"Wait." Catherine held up her hand. "Never mind. I'll be seeing her later. I'll take care of it."

"Well, okay. But maybe she's not coming back this afternoon."

"It's all right. Just leave it. Never mind." Reaching for the sweater, Catherine put it carefully beside her pocketbook.

Stupid old biddy, thought Aurora, racing away in the Car of Venus in the direction of the silver negligee. For once the old lady wouldn't be able to interfere. This time Aurora would have Titus all to herself. She spent the early hours of the afternoon rushing from store to store, then went home with her packages and bags of groceries.

At Mt. Vernon Street she found Mrs. Garboyle hard at work. It was the same Mrs. Garboyle who acted as caretaker in Edward Fallfold's rooming house, a hardpressed muscular woman who also spent several mornings a week cleaning gas-station restrooms here and there in the city of Boston.

"Oh, Mrs. Garboyle," said Aurora, giving a sharp glance around, "did you dust the Zagzig?"

"The what?" said Mrs. Garboyle.

"You know, the Zagzig. *The sculpture.*"

"Oh, the motorcycle," said Mrs. Garboyle, catching on, smiling cynically to herself. "Sure, I waxed it and polished it."

"Well, good. Now, would you run up and do my bedroom? Oh, and, Mrs. Garboyle, would you change the sheets?"

"I already did."

"Oh, but I want you to use the very best ones. You know, those really *gorgeous* ones with the eyelet edgings."

Refraining from sarcastic comment, Mrs. Garboyle went laboriously back upstairs.

Titus Moon was stunned by Aurora O'Doyle's duplex apartment.

"Of course I had to *gut* everything," said Aurora, as he stared up at her two-story living room with its bald white

92

walls and its display of contemporary art. At once he recognized a couple of early Lichtensteins and a hanging collage by a member of the Buffalo school, but he was flabbergasted by the Zagzig on the floor in the corner.

"Dead Indian," explained Aurora importantly. "Seymour Zagzig. He's been taken up by one of the really top New York galleries. Don't you just love it?"

Titus looked at the Zagzig. The parts were all there—the magneto, the two-cylinder engine, the chromium-plated exhausts—but they were scattered on a wooden platform as if in the wake of some ghastly accident. It seemed an awful shame. Somebody should reassemble the poor thing, or else put it out of its misery.

Aurora was proud of the Lichtensteins and the Zagzig, but her favorite possession was hanging over the mantel. It was an enormous purple Fatcat, balefully grinning at Titus. When Aurora threw a switch, it took off its hat, put it on, took it off and put it on again.

"I think of it as the interface between high art and popular culture," said Aurora. "Don't you agree? I mean, all those things at the Gardner, they're so aristocratic, so separated from the people, right? I mean, who paid for them, after all? Wealthy patrons, right? Or the church, isn't that right? Nowadays people go straight to the comics for artistic satisfaction. They live with it. They adore it. It's their *mise en scène,* their *milieu,* their *manière de vivre*—" Aurora stopped, her Sweet Briar French having given out.

It was comfortable in Aurora's apartment. Drinks in hand, they sat together on the puffy white sofa while Aurora gossiped about the highest levels of the art-collecting community. Titus sank deeper into the pillows, dazzled by the glittering pieces of the motorcycle. He could feel himself smiling. His smile was growing broader, and broader still. The silly chic of Aurora's works of art no longer bothered him. Even the Fatcat over the mantel began to seem comic rather than malevolent.

Aurora was full of praise. "Honestly, Titus, you're so gifted. You've got so much potential. I can see you going straight up the ladder. You won't always be stuck at such a poky little museum."

"Poky little museum?" said Titus, smiling indulgently. "You mean the Gardner?"

"The Gardner? Of course I mean the Gardner. Honestly, Titus, where's the *challenge?* You can't make new acquisitions; you've got the same stupid things on the walls all the time, you can't even arrange for traveling exhibitions. Listen—now that my uncle is the mayor of Boston, I can introduce you to some really fabulous people. I mean, it's been so exciting! I *know* people. I mean, listen, Titus, you could really go places. All I need is a go-ahead from you."

"But I like it at the Gardner."

Aurora wasn't listening. She was jumping up, running into the kitchen to tuck her little steaks under the broiler, thinking excitedly about the beautiful apartment on the fourth floor of the museum. Why didn't Titus live there? Why on earth did he choose to live in some squalid, ugly house in Dorchester? She would give a party for him on the fourth floor. She would invite all the right people. He would see how marvelous it was for a rising young museum director to entertain at home in genuine style. Aurora turned the steaks over and planned her campaign, lightly assuming that Titus's attachment to the house on Kansas Street was merely a quirk in his character, unaware that it was a deeply rutted track.

The steaks were done. Aurora whipped everything out of the kitchen and onto the table—the steaks rolled in freshly ground pepper, the new potatoes, the asparagus and the French bread, followed by strawberries, slices of old cheddar, and tiny glasses of liqueur.

When Aurora knelt in front of Titus and took off his shoes, it seemed to him the most natural thing in the world to stroke the long panels of her hair. Reaching up, Aurora undid his tie and slowly began to unbutton his shirt, while he kissed her throat and fumbled at the neck of her butter-nut-colored blouse.

"Wait, dear," murmured Aurora, slipping out of his grasp. "I'll be right back."

Thus, when the doorbell rang, it was Titus who answered it. His feet were bare. His shirt was hanging out, unbuttoned to the waist.

"Catherine!" he said, astonished.

"Oh, Titus," said Catherine Rule, beaming at him, handing him Aurora's sweater, "would you give this to Phoebe? She left it in my workroom by mistake."

Titus was suddenly conscious of his disarray. Holding the sweater under one arm, he tried to stuff his shirt into his pants. "Won't you—ah—come in?"

Catherine looked past him at the vision on the balcony, Aurora O'Doyle in a shining silver garment, her mouth open in dismay.

"Oh, no," said Catherine. Her right eye was looking at him with its usual benignity, but her wild yellow left eye wandered away from him, past elephants in Africa, temples in India, beggars in Shanghai, and then it raced across the Pacific Ocean and the continent of North America to come up behind him and pierce the tender flesh below his rib cage. "I'll just go along. Ta-ta, goodbye." Tossing her gnarled old fingers, Catherine vanished into a waiting cab.

Titus stood in the doorway, staring after the cab as it

drove away along Mt. Vernon Street. Aurora was moving up behind him, spreading her silken gown around him, pressing herself against him, fresh from the shower.

"No," said Titus, pulling away. "I can't, Phoebe. Not tonight." Snatching up his shoes, he shoved his bare feet into them and hurried back to the door, buttoning his shirt. "Forgive me." For a moment he stood on the top step with the light of dusk on his anguished face, and then he was gone.

Aurora was rigid. She stood frozen to the spot for a moment, then crossed the room and sank onto the sofa. The old woman was a witch! She was a Medusa, a gorgon! Whenever she showed her face, Titus was turned to stone.

But Titus, driving furiously away in the direction of Kansas Street, did not feel at all like stone. Instead he was torn by frustrated lust. It had been a rotten day from the beginning. All he wanted to do now was go home and go to bed.

But at the door of the house on Kansas Street, he was greeted by Mrs. Petty with the news that Tom Duck was missing.

"Oh, no, not again." Titus groaned aloud. Then he sat down at the telephone and began calling a list of Tom Duck's favorite saloons. On the sixth call, he found him. Tom was zonked out at the Red Rose Bar and Cocktail Lounge on Massachusetts Avenue.

"Oh, yeah, he's here," said Horry McDandy, the owner of the bar. "I was about to call you. I only served him a couple of beers, but he was already pretty well sloshed when he came in. He's sleeping it off in the office. Come and get him. He's all yours."

So Titus had to get back in his car and drive to the Red Rose and park double and carry Tom out of the bar with the help of McDandy and one of his regulars.

"Tom, you shouldn't have done it," he scolded on the way home.

"Oh, Jesus," moaned Tom. "I'm sorry. Jesus Gawd, I'm really sorry."

CHAPTER FOURTEEN

I T WAS the girl from the Gardner Museum coatroom who found the scrap of paper taped to one of the big front doors. Its message was alarming.

THIS BUILDING WILL BE BLOWN UP AT FOUR P.M.

Tearing it off the door, she ran to show it to Titus Moon. Titus at once summoned Charlie Tibby and Homer Kelly, who were hobnobbing once again in Tibby's basement office.

"My God," said Titus, "What are we going to do now?"

"It's just some crank," said Homer, looking at the note over Charlie's shoulder.

"But how can we tell?" said Titus. "Suppose it isn't? Suppose it's real? I can't take a chance."

"They've got a bomb squad at police headquarters on Berkeley Street," said Charlie Tibby. Turning abruptly, he hurried out of the room.

"Thank God, it's Monday," said Titus. "We don't have to worry about visitors." His face was ashen. "Look, Homer, I've got to make a decision. Do I start moving the most valuable things out of here as fast as I can? Or do I take a chance and leave them where they are? My God, Homer, the Titian, the Botticellis, the Vermeer, the Giotto! Good God, I can't just leave them to be blown up."

"Well, okay then," said Homer, "let's get going. Where do we start?"

In the beginning Titus had a system. All the off-duty

guards were called in, and the maintenance crew, and the galleries were divided among them. Soon the museum was swarming with rescuers. In the basement Charlie Tibby groped around among the ventilation pipes and the hot-air system with five men from the bomb squad, looking for plastic explosives or dynamite sticks or ticking clocks or anything out of the ordinary.

"What do you want me to do with this thing?" said Homer, standing at the foot of the stairs, holding the Giotto stiffly in front of him.

"Leave it here for now," said Titus, taking *The Presentation of the Infant Jesus in the Temple* and leaning it gently against one of the columns of the west cloister arcade.

"Oh, Titus, you poor dear," said Aurora O'Doyle. Handing him a Meissen shepherdess, she ran off to rescue a cup and saucer of which she was particularly fond.

"Why don't I stay here and take things as they come down?" said Polly Swallow, dumping on the floor the heavy file box from her office.

"Good," said Titus, looking around, distracted. "Oh, God, what about the Dutch Room? Is anybody working on the Dutch Room?"

"I'll find out," said Homer. Breathlessly he galloped up the stairs, followed by Titus, who had the three Rembrandts on his mind.

And so Titus Moon's system fell apart. Everybody began rushing everywhere. Nobody knew what had been saved and what hadn't. There were shouts from room to room. People leaned out of windows to yell across the courtyard, "Did you get the Vermeer?"

Downstairs in the west cloister, Polly tried to keep track, but she was too busy finding places to put million-dollar paintings. All the wall space around the courtyard was soon occupied. His Catholic Majesty, Philip the Fourth, King of

Spain and Portugal, stood on his head in the baby's tears, leaning against the Roman throne. A fourteenth-century altarpiece by Simone Martini glittered against a marble goddess.

"Where do they go from here?" Polly asked Titus, taking from him a drawing in a frame, the Michelangelo *Pietà*. She called after him as he puffed up the stairs again, "They can't just stay here."

Titus paused, then gasped his way back down. "We'll have to set up a safe place outdoors." Setting off at a swift pace, hurrying around the corner, he collided with a trio of

100

docents in the north cloister. They were carrying a big painting from the Tapestry Room, Bermejo's *Saint Engracia,* and one of the docents fell to her knees.

"Oh, I'm so sorry," said Titus. "Is she okay?"

"Oh, *she's* all right," said the wounded docent sarcastically, getting to her feet.

"Oh, forgive me," said Titus in confusion. Taking one corner of the painting, he sent the docent off to sit down.

The out-of-doors arrangement was not very satisfactory. Titus panted back and forth between his maintenance supervisor, Wally MacDonald, and a set of traffic cops who had suddenly appeared to divert the rush of cars. Wally and his crew were soon dragging a set of tarpaulins up from the basement, and spreading them on the grass across the street. Before long there were old masters reposing on them, or leaning against trees and highway signs, guarded by miscellaneous protectors—police officers, museum guards, Aurora O'Doyle in a gilded eighteenth-century armchair, and John Bodkin, who was sputtering with indignation. On the ground beside Bodkin, Benvenuto Cellini's portrait of Bindo Altoviti lay on his bronze back, gazing at the sky. Polly Swallow came running out of the museum with a Holbein under each arm, and deposited them carefully in the back seat of a police cruiser. After her came Homer Kelly with Sargent's portrait of Mrs. Gardner.

"Where shall I put her?" said Homer. "How about this nice maple tree here? Or would she prefer an oak?"

"I'll take her," said Aurora, looking at her watch. "But I can't stay long. I've got an appointment with the hairdresser at three o'clock."

Homer galloped back across the empty street and met Titus at the door. "Oh, Lord," said Titus, his chest heaving with exhaustion, "I can't find the Titian. It's not inside, it's not outside. Where the hell is it?"

There was a hue and cry, "Has anybody seen the Titian?" Two of the guards swore they had carried it out.

"Good God," said John Bodkin, "you don't mean you've lost the Titian?"

"It's all right, Titus," said Polly Swallow. "They sent over a truck from the Boston Museum. They've got it safe and sound. Don't worry."

"You're the director of this place?" said a stranger in a purple coat. "I'm from the *Globe*. Can you tell me why anybody would want to blow up the Gardner Museum?"

"Oh, for Christ's sake," said Titus, "not now," and he rushed back inside for the Dürer, the Crivelli, the Pesellinos. Good Lord, had anybody rescued Botticelli's *Chigi Madonna*?

Homer saw him a moment later leaning over the courtyard from a second-story window with a small object in his hand.

It was one of the little Han bears, a two-thousand-year-old statuette of gilt bronze. "No, no," cried Homer, "don't do it, Titus. I can't catch. I'm all thumbs." But then Polly Swallow snatched up a bishop's cope that had been draped over a headless marble figure in the corner of the courtyard. "Here, Homer," she said quickly, "take this end," and between them they deftly caught the little Chinese bear.

It was getting very late. An officer from the bomb squad stood in the middle of the courtyard bawling, "Everybody out." He raised his voice to a bellow and yelled up to the

upper story windows, "This building is now being evacuated of all personnel."

"Oh, God, not yet." Titus Moon's head disappeared from the window of the Early Italian Room. Homer raced upstairs to find him, but only after ten minutes of shouting through empty galleries and fighting off the men who were trying to clear the building did Homer come upon him at last, downstairs in the north cloister, trying to lug to safety the monumental head of Apollo.

"Christ, Titus, let me help you."

"Mother of God," shouted a burly officer, looming up behind them. "I said everybody OUT."

It was ten minutes to four. Outdoors the street had been cordoned off. The entire block had been cleared of students, including all the occupants of Roxbury Community College, the Massachusetts College of Art, Simmons College, and the Boston Latin School. At the other end of the Simmons parking lot, crowds of people stared in the direction of the museum, obviously anticipating a large and satisfying explosion.

Titus was nearly fainting with despair, mumbling to himself all the things he had left behind. "The Dante editions," he said frantically, shaking Charlie Tibby by the shoulders, "where are they? Oh, Lord, did anybody save the Dante editions?"

"Of course I saved the Dante editions," said John Bodkin. Opening his briefcase, he displayed them safe and sound, three leather-bound early printed books of enormous value. "I'm surprised you didn't think of them before. I must say, it's a good thing I just happened to drop by."

And then they missed Catherine Rule. Polly couldn't find Catherine anywhere. "It's her tapestry," she said desperately, appealing to Homer. "I'll bet she's in there trying to save her Jezebel tapestry."

They ran back in together, pushing past the protesting bomb-squad man at the door. And there indeed was Catherine, dragging her tapestry down the stairs like a rolled-up rug. "Twelve years," she said faintly, as they took it from her. "I couldn't let anything happen to it."

Carrying the tapestry between them, Polly and Homer picked their way among the rescued paintings, the Venetian chairs tipped at odd angles on the grass, the marble busts wrapped in velvet brocade, and laid it gently down on one of the tarpaulins. Then Polly urged Catherine into the police cruiser. Shifting the Holbeins delicately to one side, Polly crawled in beside her and sat down on the back seat.

Titus Moon refused to give up. He was still fuming, running over in his head all the things that had not yet been saved. "It's too late, Titus," warned Homer. "Relax. You've done all you can. Don't worry."

But Titus would not be comforted. "Hey, stop him, somebody," shouted Homer, as Titus charged back across the street.

There was no one to stop him. The bomb squad had left the building. Homer had no choice but to run after Titus by himself. Stumbling into the middle of the courtyard, he shrieked, "Come out of here, you fool. Titus, for God's sake!"

Titus was upstairs somewhere, shouting back.

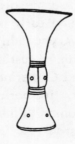

"What, what?" croaked Homer. "Titus, come down!"

"The ku, the Chinese ku." Titus appeared at one of the windows of the Dutch room, brandishing a bronze vessel. His breath came in gasps. "It's—three thousand—years old. I couldn't—leave it behind."

"Come on down, you idiot! It's five minutes to four!"

But once outdoors with the Chinese ku, Titus remembered something else. "Oh, Lord, the Egyptian hawk," he said, choking. "I'll just go back for the hawk. It's right there in the courtyard. I'll be right back."

They had to take him by the arms and restrain him, while he babbled about the hawk, and the *al-Jazari Automata,* and the Mantegna *Sacra Conversazione,* and the oldest tapestry in the museum, the *Amazons Preparing for a Joust.*

"It's four o'clock," said Charlie Tibby, his voice sepulchral. Pushing Titus down on the curb beside the road, he got down beside him and together they waited for the blast.

Dog-tired, shivering with tension and physical strain, Titus put his head in his hands. Somebody handed him a cup of lukewarm coffee. The crowd had increased. There were clusters of Charlie's museum guards, docents and curators, gardeners and conservators, and the supervisor of the café. A television crew from Channel 7 had talked its way past the roadblock. Half the administration of the Boston Museum was on hand. Even Aurora O'Doyle's uncle, the mayor of Boston, was strolling around, making his presence felt, although Aurora had long since vanished to have her hair done. On the other side of Evans Way Park, the big ladder trucks of the Boston Fire Department were lined up, their hoses already connected to a couple of hydrants. Beyond the cordons and roadblocks, crowds of students from the Northeastern dormitories along the Fenway gawked and waited, along with legions of people from apartments on the park. They were all waiting expectantly for the Isabella Stewart Gardner Museum to fall down.

Homer could guess how the explosion would begin. The structure would rock slightly on its foundation, and then a crack would rush up the facade, and slowly one side would collapse, and then the other, in a tremendous thundering catastrophe of falling brick and stone and a blinding cloud of dust, smashing the fragile ceramics, shredding the tapestries, shattering the Greek and Roman sculpture, crushing the lovely pointed windows from Venetian palaces.

At five minutes after four, Homer said to Titus, "I'll bet it was just a hoax."

"I hope to God you're right."

At quarter past four they were still in doubt.

At half past four some of the off-duty museum guards went home, the television crew went away to record the arrival at Logan airport of a Japanese industrialist.

At quarter to five, Homer suddenly cried out in a loud voice, "April first, it's the first day of April, April Fool's Day. We should have known."

There was a general groan, and embarrassed laughter. In spite of the magnitude of the possible disaster, in spite of the value of all the things that would have been destroyed, most of the onlookers felt oddly gypped, as though they had deserved a splendid spectacle after waiting around all day.

But Titus was enormously relieved. "Thank God," he said. Heaving himself to his feet, he at once began directing the return of everything to its proper place.

Homer stayed to help. He fetched and carried with everyone else until all the works of art were back where they belonged, until Cellini's bronze likeness of Bindo Altoviti was returned to its golden column, until Botticelli's *Madonna of the Eucharist* was hung reverently once again over the Florentine sideboard, until the little bronze bear was restored to its shelf in the Early Italian Room, and the Ku to the Dutch Room on the table beneath Zurburán's *Doctor of Law,* and the Michelangelo drawing mounted once again on its folding panel in the Short Gallery, and Sargent's portrait of Mrs. Gardner re-installed in the Gothic Room above the fifteenth-century Spanish chest.

And therefore Homer was on hand when Titian's *Rape of Europa* came back from the Boston Museum of Fine Arts. The Boston Museum's new curator of European painting was in the truck as it pulled in, and he hopped out to say hello to Titus Moon. "I just wanted to be sure it got here safely," he said, looking on enviously as the Titian was lowered to the ground. "God, it's a great painting. I hate to part with it. I wish it were ours."

"Well, it's not," said Titus gruffly. "Listen, I'm really grateful to you people for taking it under your wing."

"It was a pleasure, believe me." The curator climbed back in the truck, and watched covetously as Titus and Homer carried the huge picture back inside.

They were too tired to carry it all the way to the third floor without stopping on the way. Hanging on to the railing halfway to the second floor, Titus again tried to calm his own doubts.

"I had no choice, did I, Homer? I was forced to take the thing seriously. Suppose the building had blown up after all? How could I have faced the trustees if I had made no move to save the collection?"

"You did the right thing," agreed Homer, as they heaved the painting up off the steps again and carried it back to the Titian Room. "You certainly did. Yes, sir, Titus, you were a hero. If that place had blown up, they would have given you a medal for trying to save everything. I mean, the way you kept going back in there, endangering your own life for the sake of some paltry work of art, it was truly incredible. It was selfless devotion of the most courageous kind."

But when Homer said good night at last and went looking for his car, it occurred to him that Titus Moon's mad dashes into the museum at the last possible moment could have been due to something other than personal courage and loyalty to the museum's priceless collection. Suppose Titus had known from the beginning that the threat wasn't real, that no dangerous explosive was hidden away somewhere in the Gardner Museum? In that case he would have been free to run in and out as much as he pleased in a conspicuous show of bravado, knowing all the time he wasn't about to be blown to kingdom come.

CHAPTER FIFTEEN

THERE WAS no all-day parking anywhere in this part of Boston, no seven-tiered parking garages, no public parking lots. On the morning of the bomb scare Homer had wedged his Chevette into an odd little space between a couple of driveways on Forsyth Street and hoped for the best.

Instead, of course, the worst had happened. Sourly Homer pulled the parking ticket from under his windshield wiper and stuffed it in his pocket. He would think about it later. Right now he was starved. He made up his mind to park double on Huntington Avenue in front of Ralph's Diner, eat one or two of Ralph's special cheeseburgers, talk to Ralph in a friendly way, and then go home, his health and spirits restored.

But Ralph's Diner was gone. In its place Homer was appalled to see a glass and plastic storefront under a huge sign projecting way out over the sidewalk, FATCAT FAST FOODS. The sign was animated with a big purple cat in a top hat. The cat was rubbing its stomach around and around with its paw.

Homer recognized the creature. It was the same monstrous animal that had taken the place of the beautiful triangles on the Citgo sign in Kenmore Square. Fatcat—the name had a threatening sound, ominous and intimidating. This Fatcat was staring down at him now with a bullying leer. Homer was repelled, but at the same time he was hungry. He pushed open the door and went inside.

To his relief he found Ralph himself behind the counter. "Hey, Ralph," cried Homer, "how about one of your good old cheeseburgers? Hey, listen, what's up? What's all this? What's happened to those nice spin-around stools and all those lovely flyspecked mimeographed menus and the lemon-meringue pie in the little display case and the Orange Crush sloshing around in the machine? It was all here last month, and it was precious to me, Ralph, dear to my youth, close to my heart. What have you done with it? Where, I ask you, have truth and beauty gone? What's the story?"

Ralph folded his arms grimly. "Don't look at me. It's not my fault. It's Fatcat."

"Fatcat? Oh, you mean that big cat over the door?"

Ralph was amazed. "You haven't heard of Fatcat?" Turning swiftly, he picked up a packaged cheeseburger from the steam table, slapped it on a paper dish, and slid it across the counter. "Well, watch out. Fatcat's taking over the world. I had this long lease on my diner, but then one day this smooth-talking character came in and offered me a job with Fatcat Fast Foods at one-tenth of what I used to make, and I said no way, but before I knew what was happening the whole place was bought out from under me, and next day they came along with a bulldozer and tore the place down. I hardly had a chance to unscrew the coffee-maker and drag out the refrigerator."

Homer was horrified. "But that's terrible. Couldn't you do anything? Couldn't you fight back?"

"Against Fatcat? They must have a thousand lawyers."

Saddened, Homer unwrapped his cheeseburger and took it to one of the tiny plastic tables. The day had been long and hard, what with the bomb threat and the evacuation of everything from the museum and then the task of returning all of it to safety once again. And now there was

110

this dismaying news about one of his favorite places to eat. The world was going to the dogs. Or rather, apparently, to the cats.

Edward Fallfold was curious to find out how Titus Moon had reacted to the note on the front door. Judging by the distant blatting of police loudspeakers, he guessed that the museum staff must have taken the note seriously. When the first fire truck thundered past his window, bells ringing, sirens screaming, Fallfold grinned. Such a small effort on his part, with such an enormous result!

Ten minutes later Mrs. Garboyle thumped at his door and told him excitedly that everybody was running down the street to see a building blow up. Didn't he want to come? Fallfold demurred, and explained that he had to go to the library. So while everyone else rushed to the left along the sidewalk, Fallfold turned right and headed for Huntington Avenue and the Green Line, intending to go on with his important correspondence.

Today he would start on the great collectors. Once again his principal problem was the form of address. How did one begin a letter to the Duke of Northumberland? The duke was one of the few really wealthy men left in the British Isles. By right of inheritance (and shrewd connections with a popular brand of ketchup), the duke still owned six great country houses, among them the magnificent Fishbeck Hall, the splendid Boxgrove House, the charming Spoke-shave Manor. Perhaps, wondered Fallfold, you merely said, *Dear Duke?*

There was always a reference work to answer any question. Under the great coffered vault of the reading room in the Boston Public Library, Fallfold sat at a table and studied a book called *Protocol,* flipping the pages from the forms of address for senators and congressmen to the correct ways to approach archbishops and ambassadors, and finally to the things you could say to a king.

His attention wandered. Fallfold glanced around at the tall windows of the reading room, and up at the gilded bosses of the lofty vault. His sense of dispossession was afflicting him. An event that had happened when he was only three years old had wounded him so profoundly that the scar still puckered and chafed whenever it was rasped by external events. Now the thought of the Duke of Northumberland's various pieces of real estate had set it tingling once again.

It didn't matter that Fallfold had forgotten nearly everything. It was enough that his mother remembered, that together they had preferred a dreamlike European past of imagined splendor to the living American present, vulgar as it was, and coarse. Fallfold did not, for example, have any recollection of his father, who had died in the Second World War. He had forgotten, too, the house from which, through certain unfortunate paragraphs in various documents of inheritance, they had been turned away. Of course Fallfold knew what had happened to the house since then, and it enraged him, but he had taken care never to return to it, never to see it again in its present fallen state. Therefore the house itself and all the rest of his early childhood lived on in his mind only as a glowing and amorphous cloud.

Except for one thing—Fallfold remembered one part of the house in vivid detail—the great stone platform in front, where the huge close-fitting marble paving made a pattern of lozenges alternating with squares of red and white. Fallfold's pulse quickened now as he thought of those red and white squares. The white ones had been jolly and safe. Young three-year-old Teddy had played with his blocks and his trucks for hours in the white squares, while someone had dozed nearby—his mother, perhaps, or a servant.

But the dark red squares, with their squirming darker veining, had been dangerous and terrible. They were like the inside of a snake little Teddy had seen one day on the road. The snake had been run over by a car, and its slimy contents had gushed out all over the gravel. The snake had been still alive, still twisting and flopping, still heaving itself up and falling down again in bloody coils.

Like the snake, the dark red squares in the stone courtyard in front of the lost house had been thrilling and horrible, and so exciting they had made the blood rush to his head. Whenever he had stood in the middle of the dark red squares, young Teddy had soon begun to scream and scream, and then the woman had risen from her chair and had taken him away.

Teddy had known perfectly well that he should always stay on the happy white squares, but sometimes he couldn't stop himself from toddling across the intersection of white with red, because there was only the most delicate infinitesimal point between them, so small it was like nothing at all, and he could leap across it with the smallest jump and find himself in a savage land.

The twisting patterns of the dark red squares in the courtyard had cast their livid shadows over the rest of Fallfold's life. Leaving the house with his mother had been like stepping forever out of the white and into the red. Alone together they had crossed the sea and settled in a new country, where his mother had lived in pathos like a queen in exile.

Luckily, after growing up under the overcast sky of her loss, her sense of a world's despoliation, the youthful Fallfold had stumbled upon the white squares once again in the paintings of the High Renaissance and the baroque. He remembered the delight with which he had first gazed at a color photograph of gods and goddesses by Tiepolo, his rapture at beholding great bundles of flesh lightly borne up on archipelagoes of cloud, his excitement at the queenly madonnas of Tintoretto, the wanton boys of Pontormo, the dalliance of Poussin's lightly clad divinities. Their overlife-size images had given back to Fallfold a semblance of the unknown world he had lost, its dignity and grandeur, its spread and scope, its sense of blessing. These painted fantasies had charmed and distracted him, freeing him from all that was paltry in his diminished life.

But sometimes the red squares still called to him, untamed, barbarous and wild, dark with possibility. He had only to step across the infinitely small point between white and red. Whenever he liked, Fallfold could stroll across the Fenway and prowl among the bulrushes. There they lay, ready-to-hand, the tumultuous red squares.

CHAPTER SIXTEEN

HOW COULD a woman like Madeline Hepple-white exist? How can impossible people ever be explained? There are such persons in every circle, men and women who rub everyone the wrong way. Madeline had been an only child—perhaps that was the explanation in her case. If only she had experienced the abrasive encounters supplied by brothers and sisters, she might have been knocked into some better shape, she might have been less domineering. As it was, she had grown up to become a rich and friendless adult. Her husband Fenton had long since learned how to protect himself by self-effacement, by losing himself in the woodwork, by devotion to his job. Others who encountered Madeline Hepplewhite soon learned how to flatter and exploit her, but no one loved her.

The strange thing about people like Madeline is their failure to understand their own condition. Madeline would have said that she had hundreds of friends. Yet in her unconscious hunger for real companionship she had found it necessary to manufacture a friend, one who could not get away. She had created one from whole cloth. Her friend was her diary.

Madeline was deeply attached to her diary. It was like a replica of herself, another Madeline, a twin in whom she could confide. Daily she sought it out. Every evening she sat down in privacy to describe the triumphs and failures of the day. Over the years she had developed an easy conversational style of journal keeping, one she was rather proud of, and therefore as each year's entries were completed, she had them bound in leather. Now the twelve volumes stretched across an entire shelf of the bookcase in her bedroom.

On the day of the bomb scare at the Gardner Museum, there were important things to be set down. Madeline was furious that no one had called to tell her what was happening. She had learned about the embarrassing affair from the evening news. Angrily she sat down at her desk and took out her pen.

> A bomb scare at the Gardner! What a disaster! All those glorious old masters rushed pell-mell outside and dumped in heaps on the sidewalk! All for nothing! Tom Brokaw was just a little bit sarcastic. Who can blame him? The Crivelli leaning against a fire-hydrant! The Titian in a pickup truck! At least it has helped me make up my mind at last. Tomorrow, first thing, I'll call for an appointment with the director of the Boston Museum of Fine Arts. Subject for discussion? The transfer of my bequest to that institution. I will feel so much easier in my mind, knowing it will some day be in the hands of a responsible and ongoing museum whose stewardship is not in doubt.

Mrs. Hepplewhite's decision to transfer her legacy from the Gardner Museum to the Boston Museum of Fine Arts was the first consequence of the bomb scare. The second was the temporary loss of the three editions of Dante's *Divina Commedia*.

Titus Moon's first act on Tuesday morning was an inspection of every work of art that had been carried out onto the street the day before. There were grass stains on one of the chasubles, dust on the outer guard of Catherine Rule's *Jezebel* tapestry, and small particles of dirt in the crevices of some of the great gold frames. Otherwise no damage had been done.

But the Dante editions were missing, those priceless examples of the work of the early printing press.

"Why, of course I took them," said John Bodkin, when Titus anxiously called him to inquire. "In all that confusion of going in and out, I thought they'd be safer with me. I must say, I've enjoyed looking them over. What a gem that 1481 edition is! Do you realize it has two engravings actually printed with the text, as well as seventeen tipped in? What a treasure! All of them, of course, after designs by Botticelli."

"Well, bring them back," said Titus faintly. "If anything should happen to them while they're in your care, our insurance wouldn't cover it."

"Well, of course I'll bring them back."

"Today?"

"Good heavens, not today."

"Tomorrow?"

"Well, I'll see."

But Bodkin took his time. It wasn't until a month later that his wife Beryl returned the three volumes to the museum, apologizing for her husband's delay. "He's just been so busy," she explained to Titus Moon.

"Thank you, Beryl," said Titus, greatly relieved, suspecting she would get hell when Bodkin discovered that his pilfered books were gone.

The most important consequence of the bomb scare was the emergency meeting of the trustees, called on Tuesday evening by John Bodkin at his own house on Marlborough Street. Titus Moon was not invited. Neither was Homer Kelly. Only the seven trustees climbed the elaborate staircase to the reception room of quartered oak on the second floor. Beryl was there to welcome them. Hastily she served seven cups of coffee and some rather clumsy cookies, then hurried away.

"I've called this meeting," said John Bodkin, "to consider whether some ultimate step should not now be taken."

"Ultimate step?" repeated Shackleton Bowditch dryly. "What do you mean, ultimate step?"

"I mean the dismantling of the museum. The sale at auction of all the works of art."

Catherine Rule jabbed herself painfully with her needle, and Shackleton Bowditch said simply, "Never."

"But, John," said Peggy Foley, giggling nervously, "it isn't as bad as that. After all, there wasn't really any bomb. The museum is safe and sound. It's still right there, all in one piece."

Edward Fallfold smiled gaily, and spread his hands palm outward. "Surely all this foolishness will pass, sooner or later."

Preston Carver and Fulton Hillside nodded in agreement, and made harrumphing noises. "Dismantle the museum? That's ridiculous," said Carver. "Totally uncalled for," said Hillside. "I mean, it's just a lot of practical jokes, that's all it is. Not robbery and murder."

Then Shackleton Bowditch, the Harvard Fellow, talked about the student strike at the university during the Vietnam War, when it had looked as if the place would never function normally again. Everything had gradually quieted down, Shackleton reminded them, and now the school was altogether too quiet for its own good. The students were apathetic, dormant, quiescent. "But I suppose that's what the museum needs right now, that sort of peace and quiet. The quiet of the grave. After all, that's what we are really, an elaborate mausoleum dedicated to the memory of a self-willed wealthy woman."

And then Shackleton went home to sort his stamp collection, a task he kept for those occasions when the latest idiotic decisions by the president of the United States were upsetting him, or when, as now, he lost all faith in the human race.

III
THE TRIUMPH
OF DEATH

. . . I beheld a banner dark and sad,
And a woman shrouded in a dress of black . . .
I am that one whom all ye mortals call
Fierce and relentless; ye are deaf and blind,
Night falls upon you ere 'tis eventide.

—PETRARCH

CHAPTER SEVENTEEN

LIKE HOMER KELLY and Titus Moon, Charlie Tibby had not been invited to the last meeting of the trustees. But he said the same thing as Fulton Hillside. "It's not as though anybody has stolen anything, or committed a murder."

"No," said Homer, "but the bomb scare was an escalation of the war. Until this thing is stopped, the museum will be in a state of siege." And then Homer brought up his reluctant suspicions about Titus Moon. "What do you think? I'll bet you've never even asked him where he was during any of these episodes, isn't that a fact? Doesn't he have keys to the entire building and an apartment on the fourth floor, whenever he chooses to use it? Who else could wander around in the middle of the night so easily, keeping his distance from the guards patrolling the building, doing anything he pleases? Moving the pictures around, for example?"

"Titus?" Charlie was taken aback. His response was entirely unprofessional. He didn't want anything to do with such a suspicion. "Titus wouldn't do anything like that, not Titus Moon. He wouldn't endanger the collection. He wouldn't get the museum in that kind of trouble. Anyway, don't ask *me* about the moving of the pictures. I was on vacation when all that kind of thing was going on. The trail was pretty cold when I got back."

"Vacation? You were on vacation?"

"It was Christmastime. I took the kids to the Virgin Islands."

Homer narrowed his eyes craftily. "How do I know you were in the Virgin Islands?"

"How do you know?" Charlie looked at Homer solemnly. "I'll get Dougie and Piggie to testify in court. I'll put Piggie on the stand." Raising his right hand, Charlie assumed an expression of childish innocence and said in a falsetto treble, "Daddy thpanked me when I thtole Dougie'th thea-thellth. And, gueth what, I wet the mattreth in the hotel, and Daddy had to pay them sixthty dollarth."

"Oh, all right. Just kidding." Homer laughed and brought up once again his own troubles with his nephew Bennie. "This Friday, good Lord, you know what I'm in for? Bennie's got a day off from school, so naturally his mother called me up. I've got to take the little monster to that new amusement park way out on Route 128—what's it called? Fatcat Park. Can you imagine a worse fate? And that's not all. His mother gave my name to Bennie's teacher, Miss Brisket, and next week I've got to accompany his class on the school bus for a field trip. They're coming *here* for a field trip. Miss Brisket thinks her little urchins should be exposed to the artistic heritage of the ages, that's what she told me."

Charlie Tibby had stopped listening. "Friday? Did you say you're going to Fatcat Park on Friday?"

Homer could feel it coming. Wincing, he put up one hand to ward off the blow. But it came anyway.

"Listen, Homer," said Charlie, "next Friday is Good Friday. Piggie's day-care center will be closed, and Dougie goes to a Catholic kindergarten, so that's going to be closed too. But the museum will be open, so I have to be here. I've been on the phone all morning, trying to get a sitter. I don't suppose you'd take them along? The two of them? Dougie and Piggie? I mean, you know, I'd bring them over early and pay their way?"

124

Homer was trapped. "Well, okay," he said feebly. "Why not?"

Charlie was exuberant. "Oh, great, Homer, that's just great. They'll be good, I promise. They're really cute little kids, Homer, honest they are."

It was true, Homer had to admit it—Dougie and Piggie Tibby were certainly cute little kids. But they were even younger than Bennie, and Homer couldn't help noticing a dangerous light in Piggie's eye. The two of them sat in the back of the car in shy silence, staring suspiciously at Bennie in the front seat, while Homer drove south on 128, wondering how a man of his distinction, a scholar of his international renown, a man who had lived in dignified communion with other rational human beings all his life, had sunk as low as this. By what wrenching of the natural order of things had this cup been brought to his lips?

At the entrance to Fatcat Park a colossal purple Fatcat grinned at them from a giant billboard, lifting his top hat on and off just like the Fatcat looming over Kenmore Square. The three children began to perk up. When Homer bought their tickets and led them into the main street of the miniature village, all self-restraint left them. Breaking away, they ran screaming down the street in an abandon of joy.

Homer had forgotten how violent children were. He ran after them, shouting, but in an instant they came tearing back, demanding ice cream cones and Fatcat balloons. The balloons were free, but the cones were a dollar-and-a-half apiece.

Homer shelled out. A moment later he shelled out again for the scary ride through Fatcat's Mousehole Madhouse, which was full of giant rats plunging at the little cars as they hurtled through the dark. Homer emerged from the mousehole unnerved and shaking, but Bennie and Dougie and Piggie were emotionally unscathed. The ride had merely sharpened their appetites. They surrounded him, demanding lunch, pointing at the Fatcat Fast Foods Boutique next door. Obediently Homer led the way, but it was a full half hour before they worked their way to the other side of the boutique and came out into the sunshine, appetites glutted, the children's faces smudged with ketchup.

The new street was the main drag of Fatcat Park, Kittycat Promenade. It was lined with architectural monuments, a child-sized lighthouse, a miniature Statue of Liberty, a windmill of concrete and plastic, a tiny Empire State Building, a Styrofoam igloo and a fiberglass wigwam.

It was a long afternoon. Not until three o'clock were they finished climbing the Statue of Liberty and the Empire State Building and crawling into the igloo and the wigwam and buying pinwheels and comic books in the windmill. And they weren't done yet. Bennie was demanding to go up in the lighthouse.

"Oh, Bennie," groaned Homer, and then he stopped in his tracks. Beyond the lighthouse and the igloo was a house, a beautiful house, an Elizabethan manor house of tawny lichen-covered stone. Its bays and recesses were filled with tall windows, and the flat leaded surfaces of the windows were warped, so that the small pieces of glass reflected the light in angled facets like sparkling gems. There were niches with stone canopies, there were playful sphinxes and obelisks along the roof balustrade. It was as if a swan had settled among the starlings. What was this splendor doing here?

"Come on, you kids," said Homer, tugging at Dougie and Piggie. "We're going in there."

"But Uncle Homer," whined Bennie, who was tired of being the oldest child instead of the youngest, bored with holding Dougie's hand, sick of doing whatever the little kids wanted. "You said we could go up in the lighthouse. I want to see the optical system. I want to see how it works."

"Later, Bennie, later." Homer picked up Piggie, who was dragging sleepily behind. "This is going to be really interesting, Piggie, Dougie, Bennie. Wait till you see."

Before the doorway of the Elizabethan house lay a broad courtyard of stone flags. Inside they found themselves in a lofty light-filled hall, its high windows looking out over the Styrofoam igloo and the fiberglass wigwam. The house was cool and still. Above them the plaster ceiling was intertwined with circles and polygons, around them the walls were covered with linenfold paneling.

Fatcat Park fell away. Even the children were silent, awed by the perfection of this accidental culmination of usefulness and majesty, this grandeur magnified by the passage of time.

With Piggie on his shoulders, Homer inspected the painting enclosed in paneling above the flat Tudor arch of the fireplace. It was a portrait of a small child, a modern portrait, pleasing in its ancient setting. "Hey, look at this little guy, Bennie, Dougie, Piggie."

"He's not as big as me," said Piggie, taking pride in being four years old.

"He must be grown-up by now," said Homer. *Or old,* he thought, *or dead.* Feeling more tender toward all children in honor of this painted child, Homer set Piggie down on the floor and they all joined hands and walked out of the beautiful house.

At the entrance he stopped to examine the battered device above the door. It was a coat of arms, a heraldic stone shield divided in two parts. A carved worm made an S-curve on one side, and a carved gate a sort of lattice on the other. It was a pious reminder, decided Homer, that we should lock up all earthly desire, and remember that *though worms destroy this body, yet in my flesh shall I see God.*

As they drove away from Fatcat Park, he was overcome by the melancholy of the thing, by the sadness of some ancient family's decline. It seemed so depressing that this house of golden Cotswold stone, this piece of poetry and joy, should have been taken apart and reassembled in an obscene playground three thousand miles from its own greensward in Surrey or Yorkshire or Kent, an ocean away from its own ancestral hills and valleys, stables and barns, its own massive cedars of Lebanon.

Charlie Tibby was waiting for them in his car at the end of the driveway on Fairhaven Road. "Hello, everybody," he said cheerfully, with the enthusiasm of a father who has been away from his children all day. "How was it, Homer? Not too bad?"

"Oh, no," said Homer, aware of the hollow echo in his voice. "We had a good time, right, Dougie? Right, Piggie? And there was this house—"

"House?" said Charlie. "What house?"

"Oh, they've got this house there. Tudor, or Elizabethan, or whatever you call it."

"Oh, right," said Charlie, picking up a whimpering Piggie, who had been sleeping on the back seat. "I guess I read about it in the paper a few years ago, before I started working at the museum. They took it all apart and shipped it over here and put it back together in Fatcat Park. You saw it, did you, the house? What was it like?"

"Oh, never mind," said Homer. "It doesn't matter. It was nice, that's all. Really nice."

CHAPTER EIGHTEEN

THE DIRECTOR of the Boston Museum of Fine Arts was delighted to grant an interview to a wealthy woman like Madeline Hepplewhite. But when they met in his handsome office on the third floor of the museum, he dealt her a severe blow. He flatly refused to accept her bequest.

Madeline rushed straight to the sanctuary of her diary.

My feelings are terribly hurt! I am at sixes and sevens, wondering what to do. Shall I try to restore my childlike faith in the Isabella Stewart Gardner Museum? Shall I attempt to rebuild my trust in Titus Moon? Tomorrow I'll go straight to the Gardner on a quiet little tour of inspection, just me, all by myself. I'll see if my affection for those beautiful galleries is still strong enough, still true-blue enough, in spite of the carelessness and incompetence of Titus Moon, to restore my old sense of commitment. Oh, if only Fenton were more interested in my great undertaking! If only there were someone to share my confusion and bewilderment, some wise counsellor to guide me! But I am so alone! I have no one in whom to confide! (Only you, diary dear!)

Is Titus Moon worthy of my gift, my darling treasure?

Homer Kelly's trials with his nephew Bennie were not yet over. On the day after Madeline Hepplewhite's disastrous meeting with the director of the Boston Museum of

Fine Arts, Homer found himself in the company of twenty-three eight-year-old children on the way to the Gardner Museum in a school bus.

It was an appalling situation in which to find himself, but certainly it was in no way menacing. It was not the kind of episode you would expect to end in tragedy—unless of course Homer himself should give way to temptation and strangle a couple of the little girls, the ones with the shrillest voices. The metal walls and ceiling of the school bus had no sound-absorptive capacity. Screeches and shouts rebounded and ricocheted from one end of the bus to the other, and rattled from side to side. The seats had no springs. For Homer the ride into Boston from the Alcott School with Bennie's class was torture. The children screamed at each other and sang at the tops of their lungs. Their voices crackled around him in a rending, deafening roar. The bus driver and Miss Brisket had endured it many times before, and they seemed resigned to the pandemonium, but for Homer it was a frightful virgin experience.

In the Gardner Museum, Miss Brisket took charge at once. "Now remember, children, we're all going to be very quiet, isn't that right? Do all of you remember what we are *not* going to do, ever, ever, ever, not even once?"

"TOUCH ANYTHING," shouted the class in unison. In the Spanish Cloister they crowded around her, chastened in spite of themselves by the strangeness, by the battered Roman sarcophagi, by the twelfth-century portal with its staring limestone heads, by the look of things that were very, very old.

Bennie had been in the museum before with his Uncle Homer. He was anxious to show off. "Look," he said, "this is the Spanish Chapel. See the dead knight? See the stained glass?"

Miss Brisket handed out pieces of paper. "A game," she announced brightly. "We're all going to play this wonder-

130

ful game. As we walk through the museum, we'll check off
the things on the list. The first one to find everything wins
the game.''

Homer glanced at the list, and winced. Miss Brisket was
pandering to childish bloodthirst. "Find the blunt instrument," the list began. "Find the man-eating lion. Find the
man whose skin is being torn off. Find the monster with
eyes in its stomach. Find the dead lady.''

Madeline Hepplewhite had been a naughty girl at
boarding school, always in trouble for one thing or another.
Now that she was a grown woman, her naughtiness had
become quixotic and self-indulgent. Rules did not apply to
her, only to other people. Therefore on the day when Miss
Brisket's third-grade class was to visit the museum, Made-

line talked her way into the building before the noon opening hour. At her insistence the guard on duty at the Palace Road entrance called Titus Moon.

"Someone wants to get in early?" said Titus.

"It's Mrs. *Hepplewhite*," said the guard, with heavy significance.

"Mrs. Hepplewhite!" Titus was startled. He had heard a rumor that Madeline had been seen entering the office of the director of the Boston Museum of Fine Arts, and he had guessed why—she was arranging the transfer of her much-talked-of bequest. "Why," he asked warily, "can't she wait until twelve o'clock?"

The guard consulted Mrs. Hepplewhite. "Let me speak to him," she said, taking the phone. "Titus? I simply must come in at once. I have a terribly important decision to make. I just want to walk around freely for an hour or two while I make up my mind."

Titus grimaced. The woman was comparing one museum with the other, deciding which one she liked best. He was sick to death of Mrs. Hepplewhite and her legacy. The woman was impossible. But what could he do? "Well, all right," said Titus. "Just be sure you stay on the first floor until the guards take their places. The museum is officially closed today, but a lot of children are coming in at noon."

"Of course," said Mrs. Hepplewhite. "Certainly."

But Madeline Hepplewhite was still the naughty girl she had been at boarding school. Finding no guard had yet been stationed in the west cloister, she nipped softly upstairs to the second floor. Below her she could hear children's treble voices on the other side of the courtyard. Should she begin with the Dutch masters or the Italians? Choosing the Early Italian Room, she tiptoed down the hall. But then she was surprised to find that someone had come into the room before her.

132

"Good heavens," said Madeline Hepplewhite, "what are you doing with the Fra Angelico?"

Without taking any thought at all, he knew what to do. Swiftly he put the little painted panel back where it belonged with his gloved hands, and then he stepped quickly out of the light square onto the dark one, leaping across the infinitesimal point where the two squares met, as easily as if he were once again a child.

"There'll be a short delay," said Robbie Crowlie, coming on duty at the foot of the staircase. "One of the guards is out sick. We're shifting the security staff around. It'll just be a minute or two."

Miss Brisket clapped her hands. "Who wants to go to the boys' and girl's rooms?" With Homer Kelly's help, she shepherded the children to the rest rooms behind the courtyard. Here Homer was cast in a new role, one that took all his attention. Therefore he didn't miss Bennie right away. In fact he didn't miss him at all until they were gathered once more at the foot of the stairs, waiting for the signal to begin their tour of the second floor.

Suddenly there was Bennie, catapulting *down* the stairs instead of up.

"How did *he* get there?" said Robbie Crowlie angrily.

Bennie was clutching his game sheet. His face was white. Shoving his way through the other children, he threw himself against Homer and began to cry.

"Bennie, for heaven's sake," said Homer, heaving him off the floor and holding him in his arms, "what is it?"

"The dead lady," sobbed Bennie.

"The Botticelli," explained Miss Brisket dramatically. *"The Tragedy of Lucretia.* There she lies with a knife in her breast. Bennie, you shouldn't have gone upstairs by yourself. That was really a dreadful thing to do."

133

But Bennie was hysterical. While the other children looked on, astounded by this lapse of dignity, Bennie wept and clung to his Uncle Homer. When Jim Boggs, the extra guard, came hurrying around the courtyard to conduct them upstairs, Homer tried to put Bennie down, but Bennie merely hung on with a stranglehold around his uncle's neck. Homer had to carry him up the stairs, pausing halfway to catch his breath.

It was Miss Brisket and Jim Boggs, therefore, who came upon the body of Madeline Hepplewhite on the floor of the Early Italian Room. Jim at once turned and blocked the doorway against the surging invasion of third graders, while Miss Brisket gasped and backed away. Jim shouted over the heads of the children to Robbie Crowlie at the foot of the stairs, "Get Charlie."

Homer was still on the stairs, surrounded by a throng of eight-year-olds. "Okay, now, Bennie," he said, guessing the truth about Bennie's dead lady, "you go downstairs with Miss Brisket. I've got to see what's going on." He set Bennie down and watched him hurry along with the others as a frantic Miss Brisket, gulping and dabbing at her face, drove them before her. Then, parting the tide as it fled around him, Homer climbed slowly to the second floor and entered the Early Italian Room.

"Christ almighty," said Jim Boggs, staring in horror at the floor, where a woman lay on her back, her skirt awry, her pink jacket flapped up under her, one side of her head crushed and bloody. "It's Mrs. Hepplewhite."

Homer recognized the woman who had been the target of a ripe pineapple at the reception for museum benefactors. Since then he had heard other things about her, all spoken in sly disparagement. She had not been a likable woman, he knew that. But it didn't matter whether she had been likable or not. Homer looked down at her and

thought of other dead people he had seen in his time, men and women whose lives had been cut short by acts of violence. Once again he was overcome with the thought of all the trouble nature had gone to in the first place, in order to create this complex bundle of protoplasm. He couldn't help thinking of its silent secret beginnings inside its mother, its slow growth in the dark as the microscopic fingers took shape, and the bones formed cavities and prominences, and the miniature organs expanded and began to function, until at last the perfect infant creature was ready to be born. All that work and preparation, all that miraculous growth and diversity, here gone utterly to waste.

Looking away, Homer glanced up at the wall above the

135

body of Mrs. Hepplewhite, and made a painful joke. "Maybe Hercules did it," he murmured to Jim Boggs. Jim too looked up at Piero della Francesca's Hercules. The great muscles of the monumental figure were slack and soft, but Hercules was gazing solemnly at the world and brandishing his club, as if to say, *Who's next?*

The painted club was obviously Miss Brisket's "blunt instrument," but it had not inflicted the blow that had killed Madeline Hepplewhite. As Charlie Tibby came running into the room, Homer found the murder weapon. It was sharp rather than blunt. It was one of the four tall Spanish candlesticks standing in a row along the east wall. They were large and heavy and dangerously pronged, and one of them was out of line. The plug that electrified it had been pulled from its socket. Homer did not doubt that a drop or two of Mrs. Hepplewhite's blood would be found in its wrought-iron crevices. *Killed with a candlestick in the billiard room,* he thought to himself callously, watching as Charlie Tibby knelt beside Mrs. Hepplewhite, his face convulsed with anguish.

When the police came, Homer was glad to see his old friend Campbell from the Department of Public Safety. Campbell cocked an eyebrow at him, took one look around the Early Italian Room, and swiftly commandeered the four Spanish candlesticks. Moving across the room into a thicket of golden altarpieces, he introduced Homer to Lieutenant-Detective Bleach.

Bleach was a tall, pale, plump young man. He looked pitiable to Homer, but his job in Suffolk County was the same one that Homer had once held in the office of the district attorney for the county of Middlesex. Homer told Bleach and Campbell what had happened, and then he said goodbye and left them with Charlie Tibby, because he had to go home with Bennie and Miss Brisket and the rest of the third grade, back to the Alcott School.

In the school bus Homer jammed Bennie next to a window, and sat beside him to keep the little bastard safe and sound. It had been a close call. The guard on duty at the Palace Road entrance to the museum had made it clear that Mrs. Hepplewhite had entered the building only moments before Bennie had encountered her body in the Early Italian Room. Bennie must have arrived on the scene right after the deed was done. A moment earlier, and he might have been lying beside Mrs. Hepplewhite, one perfectly good and rather lovable nephew, dead and gone.

Fenton Hepplewhite was informed of his wife's death by a distracted Titus Moon. Titus called him at the factory in Jamaica Plain, where Fenton was president of a baling wire company. Titus had to speak up loudly above the clatter of machinery, as billets of steel were drawn through successively smaller dies and wound around giant spools.

"Dead?" Fenton couldn't believe it. He cupped his hand over his left ear. "Is that what you said? Madeline's *dead?*"

When he put the phone down, Fenton felt nothing. But a few minutes later, as he hurried back to his office, it hit him with full force, and he burst into sobs. Weeping, he opened the door and astonished his old secretary. He told her what had happened, and said he was going home. "Of course you are, of course you are," said the secretary.

But on the way home something else invaded Fenton's grief, a sense of dizzy expansion. Madeline dead? His impossible wife was dead?

Across the city of Boston on Marlborough Street in the Back Bay, Beryl Bodkin heard the news in a roundabout way from her husband. John Bodkin had merely dropped

137

in at home to use the phone. Titus Moon had called him, and now he felt it his duty at this time of crisis to inform all the other trustees about the murder *in the museum* of one of their chief benefactors. After delivering this bombshell, he summoned each of them to another emergency meeting.

"We can't go on like this," he said to Fulton Hillside. "The thing has escalated out of control."

"But what about the money, the bequest in her will?" faltered Fulton. "Won't the Gardner be getting a lot of money from Mrs. Hepplewhite's estate?" Then it occurred to Fulton that he must be sounding rather heartless. "Believe me, I'm terribly sorry. It's a terrible tragedy, oh, yes, indeed."

Bodkin returned to the important facts of the case. "We certainly should be getting a lot of money, unless she changed her mind at the last minute, the way she kept threatening to do. But it's not Mrs. Hepplewhite's will I'm worried about, it's Mrs. Gardner's. You know, Fulton, she foresaw a situation like this, the possibility of disrespect and disaster, and she made provisions for it. We've got to pay more attention to her legally expressed desire. Right, Fulton?"

"Well, I don't know," said Fulton. "Maybe. Maybe not."

As John Bodkin hung up and paused to look for Preston Carver's number, his wife Beryl turned away and went down to the cellar to look at her old bicycle. She found it in a corner behind an empty fish tank. It had a flat tire. Thoughtfully Beryl wiped the dusty handlebars with the hem of her sweater. The bicycle was all that remained of her early life before she had married John Bodkin. Everything else in the house had been bought for her with money from the comfortable income of her husband, but the bicycle was hers alone. She had earned the money for it by working after school in the public library in Rutland, Vermont.

Beryl was stunned to learn of the death of Madeline Hepplewhite. And like Madeline's husband Fenton, she was aware of an odd division in her response. On the one hand, she felt pity for the poor dead woman, and on the other, a guilty sense of shock at her own irrepressible glee.

The meeting of the trustees was held in Bodkin's book room, where the air was fragrant with the pleasant smell of expensive leather bindings. It was the second emergency meeting of the trustees in as many weeks. This time, with the tragedy of Mrs. Hepplewhite's death still quivering in their nerve endings, they listened patiently as Bodkin brought up once more the question of the dismantling of the Gardner Museum and the sale of its contents at auction, in accordance with the stipulations of Mrs. Gardner's will.

"The thing is getting out of hand," he said. "This wasn't a joke, it was murder. I'd like to see Homer Kelly laugh it off. I think it's time that we did our duty as trustees." Bodkin stood up and leaned against the fireplace with its dainty carved swags and curlicues. "I wonder if you people are aware of the prices now being paid on the auction market for really valuable works of art? Eleven million for a Mantegna? Nearly forty million for a van Gogh? Think what the masterpieces in the Gardner must be worth all together!"

"But what difference does it make," said Catherine Rule, "how much they're worth, if we don't intend to sell them?" Glancing down at her sewing bag, Catherine could just see the tip of a bulky envelope above the canvas of her half-finished chair cover. The letter had appeared in her mailbox only that morning. Should she say something about it now? No, it was too soon. And she didn't believe it anyway. It was altogether too absurd.

The other trustees shared Catherine's opinion about the dismantling of the museum. Bodkin's motion was highly unpopular. It was voted down, six to one.

IV
THE TRIUMPH
OF FAME

Then, as I gazed across the grassy vale
I saw appearing on the other side
Her who saves man from the tomb, and gives him
life.

—PETRARCH

CHAPTER NINETEEN

FAME SUCH as the Isabella Stewart Gardner Museum
had never known came to it now. In the nearly ninety
years since Mrs. Gardner had first opened her Venetian palace on the Fenway, the museum had been famous
among lovers of art, artists and scholars, students and flower
ladies. But now, as news of its troubles spread, its name was
familiar to every schoolchild in the city, every furnace re-
pairman, every endodontist and software engineer.

On the morning after the murder of Madeline Hepplewhite, the *Boston Globe* published the dramatic circum-
stances, relating them to the bomb scare of the week before.
And somehow the story about the other dirty tricks came
to the ear of Chip Geyser, anchorman on the six o'clock
news at Boston's Channel 4. Chip recited the entire list of
episodes, making it clear that the funny business was no
longer funny.

Once the story was out, there was no containing it. Next
day the *Boston Improviser* picked up on Chip Geyser's revelation with the headline, TRICKSTER TURNS TERRORIST.

That did it. The word *terrorist* ruined everything. Once
uttered in the open air, it oozed like a drop of acid into the
national consciousness with the help of Tom Brokaw and
the NBC evening news. And Brokaw improved on the
story—"One of the most famous small art museums in the
country, the Isabella Stewart Gardner Museum in Boston,
is suffering from a rash of dirty tricks, culminating in acts
of terrorism and murder. Because Mrs. Gardner's will re-

143

quires the termination of the museum in the event of the improper preservation of the works of art, it is rumored that the entire collection may be sold at auction."

Homer Kelly was listening to the "NBC Nightly News" at home in his bleak empty kitchen, as he tried to find a clean frying pan for his potatoes. Instantly he called up Titus Moon. "Did you hear that?"

Titus was furious. "I sure did. Who the hell told Brokaw about the will?"

"Oh, anybody can look up a will. In Boston they're on file in the probate court of Suffolk County. The question is, *why* did somebody look it up? Those people at NBC must have been tipped off. Somebody must have told them, somebody who knew about it."

"Well, my God, it just provides more fuel for Bodkin and his nutty idea. He keeps talking about the duty of the trustees to carry out the provisions of Mrs. Gardner's last will and testament. He thinks we should dismantle the whole place. You know, sell out. Fortunately none of the other trustees agrees with him."

"I suspect," said Homer gloomily, "the word *terrorism* isn't going to do the museum any good. People will think the place is like Beirut or Belfast. They'll stay away in droves."

"My God, I never thought of that."

And as it turned out, to Titus Moon's chagrin, Homer was right. The day after Brokaw's announcement, attendance at the Gardner fell off sharply. The audience for the afternoon concert by the Atlantic Brass Quintet was very small. Special visits were affected too. The American Society of Microbiology canceled the party for two hundred guests that was to have been held on the first of May in the Tapestry Room. Governor Dummer Academy called off an alumni celebration for May twenty-fourth. The American

144

Society for Adolescent Psychiatry followed suit. So did the staff of the *Boston University Law Review.*

In the empty galleries, guards had no one to keep an eye on. They brought books and magazines on the job to pass the time. At noon the usual crowd of hungry people no longer pressed up against the door of the café. Even the flower ladies had stopped coming to the museum. Now they met for lunch in the cafeteria on the ground floor of the Boston Museum, carrying their salads outdoors on sunny days. Betty Gore, the supervisor of the Gardner's tiny restaurant, cut down her order for fresh scallops and began freezing her excess supply of Viennese pastries.

Shackleton Bowditch tried to comfort Titus Moon. "Oh, it will be a nine days' wonder. You'll see."

But a week after Madeline Hepplewhite's death, the Gardner Museum continued to be a private place, as though it belonged only to the director and his staff. Doggedly they went on with their usual tasks. In the textile-repair workshop Catherine Rule bowed serenely over the *Jezebel* tapestry, and in the catalogue office on the first floor Polly Swallow never paused in her huge mission of assembling the great inventory. Aurora O'Doyle, unfortunately, was thrown completely off course by the latest events, and her analysis of the Venetian mirrors in the Little Salon and the eighteenth-century console tables in the Titian Room began to be neglected. Instead she ran off to New York to study comparison examples in the great auction galleries of Sotheby, Parke Bernet.

CHAPTER TWENTY

THE SUCCESS of some enterprises can be traced to ingenuity, business experience, hard work, competent colleagues, and a rational understanding of the requirements of the job.

The success of others comes from something quite different, something rather like the sensitivity of an artist, or the delicate perceptions of a spider poised on the trembling threads of its web.

There was just such a gifted man at the controls of the great Parisian auction gallery of Fouchelle et Fils on the Boulevard Saint Germain. When Gerard Fouchelle read in the Paris edition of the *International Herald Tribune* an article about the mounting difficulties of the Isabella Stewart Gardner Museum in Boston, Massachusetts, and the odd provisions in the will of Mrs. Jack Gardner for the dissolution of the museum, the filaments of his attention were suddenly pulled taut. At once he felt the presence of prey. He could smell the blood of Rembrandts and Botticellis and Holbeins.

The Galeries Fouchelle were at that moment going through a slack period. Oh, they were doing very well with bisque figure groups and Fabergé boxes, but Gerard Fouchelle had customers waiting for really important items, extremely valuable works of art of exactly the kind that hung on the walls of Boston's Gardner Museum. A toilet-paper king in Taiwan was yearning for a Botticelli; a generalissimo in Chile was hungry for Italian madonnas; a consortium of South Korean businessmen wanted genuine old masters for investment purposes; and a Third World dictator with a plump bejewelled wife was on the lookout for a Boucher or a Fragonard.

Within the hour Gerard Fouchelle was on the transatlantic phone, consulting his American representative in the Galeries Fouchelle on Dartmouth Street in Boston's Back Bay. The conversation was so promising, Fouchelle immediately packed a large bag and took the next plane. In Boston he settled in at the Ritz and called Frederique Paquette of the Dartmouth Street gallery to his suite. Together they went over the situation in more detail. In the next few days, there were countless phone calls and many swift expeditions of inquiry.

The result was rapid progress. Frederique had heard rumors about the trustees. From a reliable source he learned that one of them was actually calling for the dismantling of the museum, here and now, in accordance with the terms of Mrs. Gardner's will. What was more, the man was himself a collector of early printed books.

Fouchelle was delighted. He smiled radiantly at Frederique. "And what is the name of this trustee?"

"Bodkin. John Bodkin."

"Let us begin with Bodkin."

They got to work at once. The very next day a flattered John Bodkin was happy to conduct an important visitor from Paris around the Isabella Stewart Gardner Museum. Not only was the visitor distinguished as a gentleman and scholar, he was also the proprietor of one of the most famous auction houses in the world. What was even more significant, the central offices of the auction house were in Paris. Bodkin remembered at once the stipulation in Mrs. Gardner's will that any auction of her collection should be conducted in Paris, France. Fouchelle's appearance in Boston was like a windfall from the fates.

Bodkin found it hard to stop grinning as he escorted Fouchelle around the museum. His guest was a handsome young man with wavy brown hair and the strong facial creases Bodkin attributed to the muscular contortions required in speaking French.

But his English was impeccable. "How very fine," he said, admiring the Terborch. "Exquisite," he murmured, standing before Uccello's portrait of a young lady. But when he held in his hands the Landino edition of Dante's *Divina Commedia* and turned the pages to see the engravings after Botticelli, the word that came to his lips was "Glorious." John Bodkin beamed.

Over lunch in the Monk's Garden, with the warm sun of a lovely May day dappling the little tables and chairs, Fouchelle talked easily about a first edition of the *Canterbury Tales* he had once handled, knocking it down for $49,000, and a *St. Albans Chronicle* of 1497 that had gone for $75,000. Bodkin bragged eagerly about the prices he had paid for the books in his own collection.

Only then did Fouchelle raise the question of the possible liquidation of the museum. What a terrible thing it would be, how very unfortunate! Raising his hands, he gazed upward in supplication. But if—heaven forfend!—such an awful thing should happen, if an auction house like Fouchelle et Fils were to be chosen to manage the sale, there was no reason why a private transaction should not be conducted simultaneously on certain items—the Dante volumes, for instance. As a matter of fact, in gratitude for the choice of Fouchelle as exclusive agent and auctioneer, there might be a free transfer of one or two things to the trustee who arranged the matter. These private exchanges were altogether traditional and customary, well-known in the world of the fine arts whenever large quantities of very valuable paintings, tapestries, furniture, etcetera, were to be put on the market.

"Is that so?" said Bodkin greedily, feeling once again within his hands the crushed levant morocco of the Landino edition of Dante's *Divina Commedia*.

CHAPTER TWENTY-ONE

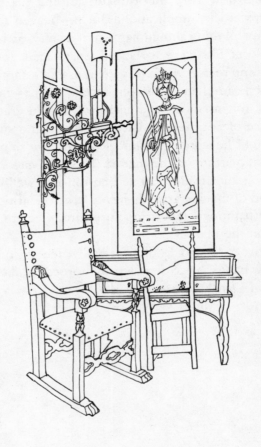

T HE LITTLE FIRE was burning merrily. It took
Polly Swallow a moment to realize that there wasn't
usually a blaze in the middle of the Tapestry Room,

the fire looked so warm and cheerful. Two or three of the hundreds of matching wooden chairs had been broken up and set alight. A wisp of smoke wafted sideways toward the windows opening on the courtyard.

Where was the guard? Hilda Sorensen was usually here on Tuesday mornings. Hilda was always so reliable. Where could she be?

There was a fire extinguisher around the corner in the Short Gallery, but Polly had never noticed it. Instead she beat at the flames with one of the undamaged chairs. Then she used it as a poker, shoving pieces of burning wood left and right on the tiled floor and stamping on them with her heavy boots.

Soon there was more smoke than fire. Polly's eyes stung, but she went on stamping. At last, coughing and choking, she stepped back. There were no more licks of flame, no bright sparks, no red embers. The smoke too was thinning.

Polly went looking for Charlie Tibby. On the way she found Hilda Sorensen giggling with Becky Stover, the guard on duty in the Raphael Room. Hilda looked at Polly guiltily, and started back at once to her post, explaining, "I yust went to the ladies'."

But when Polly told her what had happened in the Tapestry Room while she had been gone, Hilda burst into tears and changed her story. "Yeesus! I vas tired of being all alone. I yust vanted to talk to somebody."

When the phone rang in Homer Kelly's house in Concord, Homer had just come in. The cheerful ringing pleased him, because the empty house always felt especially forlorn at the moment of walking in. Whenever his wife was away, Homer felt oddly inconsequential, as though his days were index cards filed under *Miscellaneous.* Eagerly now he picked up the phone and said hello. And when he heard about the fire in the museum from Charlie Tibby, he was glad to run down to his car and drive back into the city.

But Homer was feeling rebellious. The murder of Madeline Hepplewhite had indeed been a tragedy, and he was working on the matter zealously with the help of Tibby, Campbell, and Bleach—but the fire didn't affect him one way or the other. After all, what did it matter if the whole place burned down? Life would go on. People would still get up in the morning and pour cement and move crates and feed chickens and drive taxis, whether or not the brocaded walls of the Gardner Museum were hung with Rembrandts and Titians. All those flossy masterpieces weren't useful in any way. They didn't serve any visible function. If you looked at the museum from a purely practical standpoint, what good was it? The miscellaneous statuary didn't stalk around a lumberyard sorting planks, it didn't check out groceries in a supermarket. It just stood there, not moving a muscle.

Whizzing along Route Two, Homer looked across the highway at the steeple of a church in Belmont, and it occurred to him that the practice of religion didn't accomplish anything useful either. It wasn't getting on with the world's work. For that matter, what good were poetry and literature, what good was all that stuff he had been telling his students that very morning? You couldn't slam the door of a poem and drive it to work, you couldn't saw through a two-by-four with a novel. Smugly Homer chucked all the delicate impalpable values of the human spirit out the window and drove into Boston, wrapped in the mantle of utilitarian self-righteousness.

"I can't believe it was serious," he said to Charlie Tibby, as they stood with Titus Moon and Polly Swallow, looking down at the charred wood and scattered ashes of the fire.

"I mean, I doubt somebody was really trying to burn the place down. If they'd wanted to do that, they would have set fire to one of the tapestries."

"But, good lord, Homer," said Titus, "look at the ceiling. If Polly hadn't come along when she did, those dry old beams could have caught fire. The whole building could have burned down. It was an incendiary act, it was arson. Just look at this room." Titus turned on his heel and swept his arm in a gesture that included the *Abraham* and *Cyrus* tapestries, the fifteenth-century Spanish painting of *Saint Engracia,* the Persian manuscripts. "You don't start a fire for a joke in a room like this."

"Where were you when this was going on?" said Homer, glowering at him, remembering his suspicions about Titus Moon's apparent heroism during the bombing episode.

"Just around the corner in the Dutch Room," said Titus, "doing my exercises."

"Exercises?" said Homer.

Charlie Tibby laughed. "Titus exercises his understanding of the collection. He studies a different thing every day. You know, he just picks something and stares at it for a while, taking it all in."

"Portrait of Mary Tudor this morning," mumbled Titus.

"There was a guard on duty while you were there in the Dutch Room?" said Homer.

"No, I dismissed the guard. I like to be by myself."

"Ah," said Homer, "so you were admiring Mary Tudor. Bloody Mary, right? She was an arsonist herself, burned people at the stake, isn't that right?"

Polly objected warmly, "Poor Mary Tudor, she really had a bad press. It wasn't really her fault."

"Well, it was Hilda Sorensen's fault this morning," said Charlie angrily, pushing bits of blackened wood around

153

with his foot. "I could wring the girl's neck. By all rights she should be fired, but she's been so reliable so far, I guess I have to give her another chance."

"Hey," said Polly, "is there a broom closet around here someplace? I'll start sweeping up all this stuff."

"Better leave it," cautioned Homer. "Public Safety will want to take a look."

Homer and Charlie Tibby went back to the security chief's office in the basement, and together they talked to Bleach on the phone, and Bleach promised to come right over with Campbell. Then Homer drove back to Concord to pursue an idea of his own.

The truth about Mrs. Gardner's will had become a public revelation when Tom Brokaw mentioned it on the NBC evening news. Who had told Brokaw?

On the same counter with the telephone in Homer's grubby kitchen were several heaps of dirty dishes. Homer put his elbow on a sticky plate and settled down patiently to work his way through layers of secretaries and receptionists and assistants to the right person among the news gatherers at NBC. There were maddening delays, as he was shunted from here to there, and once he was cut off by mistake. Growling to himself, he began again, and at last he was connected to a reasonable woman in the background-research division of the news department.

"Oh, yes, that was me," she said. "One of the Gardner trustees told me that. I got a list of the trustees, and began calling them one by one. I remember it took me four tries. It was some man, I forget his name. Needles and pins, something like that. I remember thinking of needles and pins."

"Well, there are only seven of them. How about Bowditch, Foley, Rule, Carver, Bodkin, Fallfold, Hillside?"

"Bodkin! That's the one. Isn't a bodkin a kind of needle? Or a sharp pin or something like that?"

"So it is. Well, so it was Bodkin. Well, actually, that figures. Bodkin has been pushing for the exact execution of the terms of Mrs. Gardner's will." Homer pushed a plate of petrified peas out of his way and leaned on his elbow and turned confidential. "Listen, you haven't run into my wife anywhere, have you? Tall woman with dark hair, sort of really calm? I mean, she's got this stupendous sort of lovely calm. Name of Mary Kelly?"

"Your wife? She's here at NBC?"

"Oh, no. But she's in New York. I just thought you might have met her on the street."

"She's run out on you, has she? Gee, I'm sorry, Mr. Kelly. Matter of fact, I did the same thing. My husband worked at home all day, but he always left things in a mess. Whenever I came home from my job, there were all these dirty dishes all over the place. I got so I couldn't stand it anymore. Well, so long, Mr. Kelly."

"No, no, it's not like that. I didn't mean—"

But the woman was gone. Homer put down the telephone, scraped back his chair with a powerful shove, snatched the dishpan from under the sink, washed the dirty dishes, made his bed, plumped the pillows on the sofa, and picked up some dust kitties that had blown into a corner. Then he called his wife Mary.

"Oh, hello, darling," cried Mary, sounding glad to hear his voice.

"Just finished cleaning house," said Homer pompously. "Why don't you come home for the weekend? You won't have to lift a finger."

"Honestly, Homer? Well, maybe I will. I do miss you, dear. Tell me, are you eating properly? Are you washing the dishes?"

CHAPTER TWENTY-TWO

AS HOMER KELLY entered the museum, Titus Moon tore past him, pulling on his suit jacket.

"Hey, where you going?" said Homer.

"Oh, it's Tom Duck again. He keeps going to this bar on Massachusetts Avenue and passing out. They just called me."

"I'll take you," said Homer. "My car's right across the street."

"Well, thanks."

The Red Rose was a sports lover's bar. Autographed memorabilia of the Red Sox and the Bruins and the Celtics hung all over the high walls and behind the bar above the tiers of bottles. This afternoon the television was noisy with the excitement of the crowd in the tenth inning of a tie game with the Cleveland Indians. Horry McDandy helped Titus and Homer lug Tom Duck out of the office, but Horry kept glancing over his shoulder at the screen, watching the top of the Indians' batting order strike out. As Homer pushed the street door open and Titus shoved Tom outside, there was a vast roar of exultation from ten thousand Cleveland fans as the Red Sox left-fielder crashed into the fence with the winning run sailing over his head. "Oh, shit," shouted Horry, and then the door swung shut and the sound of the television faded, and Tom Duck slumped to the sidewalk.

"Oh, migawd," he said, "I'm sorry. Oh, Jesus, I dunno

how I got here. Honest to Gawd, I'll never come here again, right, Titus? Honest to Gawd."

Homer pushed on one side of Tom and Titus went around and pulled from the other, and together they got him into the back seat of Homer's car. "Did you see the *Globe* this morning?" said Titus, getting into the front seat beside Homer. "That fire was a disaster. The thing is escalating. You know, everybody out there is enjoying it, in a grisly kind of way. It's a story, a continuing story. They want more, still more. What's going to happen next, that's what they want to know. It's like chapters in a thriller, with the suspense building up all the time. It's got its own momentum, its own—"

"Manifest destiny," growled Homer, pulling away from the curb.

In the back seat Tom Duck leaned drunkenly out the window. "Hey, guys," he cried, waving both arms at the sky, "lookit the kittycat. Isn't that cute?"

"What kittycat?" said Titus.

"Up there," said Homer, leaning forward, staring up at the enormous image of Fatcat poised over Kenmore Square. "Talk about manifest destiny, talk about the onward march of destruction! Talk about disaster!" Then he got down to brass tacks, and asked Titus about John Bodkin. Was Bodkin a likely candidate for the role of trickster, murderer, arsonist? Bodkin, after all, was the only trustee who was pushing for the logical result of all the terrible things that had been happening, the closing down forever of the Gardner Museum. If the end of the museum was what he wanted, then a combination of murder and mayhem was certainly the way to get it.

"Oh, I doubt it," said Titus. "He's just stuffy, that's all. He's a guardian and protector of Mrs. Gardner's will, and the will says certain things, and therefore, come hell or high water, Bodkin's going to obey the letter of every paragraph, every sentence, every punctuation mark, every—"

"Jot and tittle," supplied Homer, who was himself fond of long parades of parallel phrases.

"I don't think he has the imagination to dream up the kinds of things that have been going on. And murder is surely out of his ken. I mean, murder just isn't respectable."

"Certainly not," said Homer.

But Bodkin was on Homer's mind. Therefore on the following Saturday afternoon, he found himself on the front steps of the Bodkin's house on Marlborough Street, ringing the doorbell and admiring the opening buds on the magnolia tree in the little front garden.

It was Beryl who came to the door. Her face was flushed, her hair was dripping wet, her pleasing plumpness was wrapped in a bathrobe. Radiantly she smiled at Homer. "Oh, come in," she said. "Do come in."

But her husband loomed behind her. "Beryl," he said disapprovingly, "is that any way to go to the door?"

"Oh, gosh, I guess not," said Beryl, cowed, and she scuttled away down the hall.

Homer in his turn found it difficult to maintain his self-esteem in the overpowering presence of John Bodkin. The man was physically impressive, his voice was loud, he subjugated everything around him. The umbrella stand huddled in the corner, the rug flattened itself against the floor, and Homer wanted to pull his forelock. Resisting the impulse, he followed Bodkin to his book room, and asked him to explain his whereabouts during the murder of Madeline Hepplewhite.

Bodkin grinned, showing six rows of enormous teeth. "I was at work, naturally, in my office on Milk Street, discussing taxes with the president and vice-president of the A-1

158

Pest Control Company of Providence, Rhode Island. Afterward we went to lunch at Lockober's, and I had steak and kidney pie. The exterminators had roast beef. I left the waiter a very large tip, so I think he'll remember me. Titus called me when I got back to the office, to tell me Madeline had been killed, and I promptly went home and notified the other trustees."

"Well, thank you anyway," said Homer, getting up, looking around forlornly at the shelves of splendid leather bindings, intimidated in spite of himself.

CHAPTER TWENTY-THREE

GERARD FOUCHELLE and John Bodkin quickly became fast friends, at least on the surface. In the week between Fouchelle's arrival in Boston and the burial of Madeline Hepplewhite, he was a dinner guest at Marlborough Street. There he was charmed by Bodkin's wife Beryl, but Bodkin himself struck Fouchelle as a classic example of the loud and vulgar American, a stereotype he had seldom actually encountered. With careful courtesy, he masked his repugnance and behaved like an intimate friend.

About the future of the Gardner Museum, at any rate, they were in complete agreement. Polite shilly-shallying had given way to candid frankness. Both Fouchelle and Bodkin had the same desire, to see the trustees vote at last for the dissolution of the museum. Their personal interests did not need to be mentioned again. The tempter had been understood by the temptee. Bodkin would get his pick of the rare books, Fouchelle the vast commission on the sale of immensely valuable works of art.

"You can hold the auction right here in Boston, of course," Bodkin said, "in the museum. It's true that Mrs. Gardner's will specifies Paris, but you're a Parisian firm, after all, and it would be absurd to crate up all those paintings and pieces of sculpture and pay the insurance to transport them across the Atlantic. I'll talk to the board. It's no problem."

But their first enormous obstacle was the current refusal by the other trustees to vote for the dismantling of the museum. On the morning of Madeline Hepplewhite's memorial service, Bodkin and Fouchelle sat together in Bodkin's famous book room, studying the list of trustees, looking for a soft spot, trying to guess who might be vulnerable to an approach of this kind or that.

"Forget Catherine Rule," said John Bodkin. "She's hopeless. So's Bowditch. Now what about Peggy Foley? I doubt she would do us any good. Edward Fallfold? Hmmmm. Hold him in abeyance for now. He's an odd duck. I haven't the faintest idea what makes Fallfold tick. That leaves—" Bodkin's pencil stopped at Preston Carver's name. He tapped it several times. "Possible," he said. "Quite possible."

"Ah, Preston Carver," said Gerard Fouchelle eagerly, reading the name aloud. "What does Carver do?"

"He works for an investment firm," said Bodkin. "Cuthbert, Bigelow, and Cuthbert. They do institutional investments—Harvard, Wellesley College, the Museum of Science." Bodkin's eyes lit up. "Harvard? Say, you know, we might be able to work out something there. If the museum were to be dismantled, the assets would all go to Harvard. I mean, Harvard University is the ultimate beneficiary, did you know that? Assets! Surely the assets would include not only the building and its contents but the entire portfolio of investments?" Bodkin looked at Fouchelle significantly. "You know," he said, crouching closer, "I could suggest certain things to Carver. If his firm were to handle the transfer of the Gardner portfolio to Harvard, it would certainly be a feather in his cap. Suppose I just take Carver aside and talk the matter over?"

The memorial service for Madeline Hepplewhite took place in the chapel on the third floor of the Gardner Museum. Fortunately Madeline had been an Episcopalian, like

161

Mrs. Gardner herself, and therefore the service in this con-
secrated place of worship was appropriate.

The chapel was very small, little more than a wide corridor at the end of the Long Gallery. There were stained glass windows and sixteenth-century choir stalls, and very few places to sit. Titus Moon hoped that some of the friends and relatives of Mrs. Hepplewhite would be put off by murder and bomb threats and arson, and stay home.

But they didn't. Scores of Madeline Hepplewhite's acquaintances came anyway. Loyally they climbed the stairs to the chapel to attend the service. Beanie Kenney and Jim Boggs and Becky Stover began bringing up extra chairs from the Tapestry Room.

The officiating clergyman was the rector of the Church of the Advent. *I am the resurrection and the life,* he began, and everyone rose.

All the trustees were present, along with most of the staff. Standing with her husband behind Fenton Hepplewhite, Beryl Bodkin studied the back of Fenton's neck. Although the month of April was only half advanced, his neck was already freckled and sunburned. Beryl found herself wondering whether the manufacture of baling wire made it necessary to spend a great deal of time out-of-doors. Then she chastised herself. She mustn't think about Fenton. Casting down her eyes, she looked at her shoes, but she couldn't bring Madeline into her mind. Instead she thought about her old bicycle, with its flat tire. The bicycle had become for Beryl a heroic symbol. How did you fix a flat tire?

The clergyman called for prayer. In the last row of chairs, Catherine Rule bowed her head, ran her finger over the carving on the Roman grave altar against which her knees were wedged, and tried to think kindly about Madeline Hepplewhite.

O God, intoned the clergyman, *whose mercies cannot be numbered; Accept our prayers on behalf of the soul of thy servant Madeline, and grant her an entrance into the land of light and*

163

joy . . . In his homily the priest praised Mrs. Hepplewhite's energy, her generosity and good works, and then once again it was time for prayer.

Titus Moon prayed obediently, trying to arouse in his mind some sort of tepid affection, struggling to forget the fact that he had detested the living woman. It was difficult, if not impossible. Titus could think of nothing but her legacy, the one she had so often held over his head, her possible bequest to the Gardner Museum. *Oh, Lord,* he prayed, *may she not have changed her mind. May she have left us a generous gift in stock certificates, or cash, or certificates of deposit, or mutual funds, or anything else that is negotiable in a Boston bank. Oh, God bless Madeline Hepplewhite, God bless her benevolent heart.*

In the solemn murmured greetings after the service, Titus shook the hand of Fenton Hepplewhite and expressed his sympathy, hoping in spite of himself that the bereaved husband would let slip some morsel of information about his wife's intentions. But Fenton merely looked at him sorrowfully and hurried away.

However, to Titus Moon's relief, Madeline Hepplewhite's last will and testament shot through probate court with astonishing speed. It was only the end of April when her attorney called to say that Mrs. Hepplewhite's benefaction to the museum would be delivered that afternoon in a large van.

"A van?" said Titus, flabbergasted. His heart sank. He made a feeble joke. "What is it, gold bullion?"

"You'll find out," said the attorney grimly.

Titus hung up, trying to guess what valuable object belonging to Mrs. Hepplewhite would require delivery in a van. There had been something ominous in the tone of the lawyer's voice. For the rest of the morning Titus devoted himself to an examination of Polly Swallow's teeming notebook, and then he had lunch with Aurora O'Doyle. Back in his office he kept jumping up and peering out the window, thinking he had heard the sound of a truck. When the van arrived at last and began unloading boxes on the cement floor of the carriage house, he rushed out to take a look.

Kneeling on the pavement, he opened his jackknife with trembling fingers and began to rip open one of the hundreds of identical cardboard containers. Then he leaned back in dismay. It was full of new books, large books bound in red leather. Titus riffled the pages of one of them, then closed his eyes and tried to collect himself. Standing up mournfully, he spoke to the men who were tussling more boxes out of the van. "Wait, stop, hold it a minute. We don't want them here."

Sadly he called a meeting of the trustees and informed them that Mrs. Hepplewhite had not, after all, left the museum out of her will. From a box on the floor, he took several of the red-leather volumes and began handing them around the table. Homer Kelly was present at the meeting, and he took his copy cautiously, as if it might nip his fingers.

Titus Moon's voice was hollow. "Mrs. Hepplewhite has bequeathed to the Gardner Museum five thousand twelve-volume sets of her diary, with permission to sell them at a price not less than a thousand dollars a set."

"Good God," gasped John Bodkin. "Holy horse collar," said Homer Kelly. Around the table there were exclamations of revulsion and disgust. Then Edward Fallfold tittered, and Catherine Rule threw back her head and laughed.

Shackleton Bowditch glared at an open page of the book in his hand and read it aloud.

Shopping! How I detest it! Spent the entire week looking for summer togs, matching shoes, bags, sporty casual clothes in navy and beige. This is a MUST. KEEP TRY-

ING. Today Friday, to Symphony in the pm. Exquisite performance of the Unfinished, then some awful modern thing. Must speak to Ozawa about sticking to the classics.

Shackleton slammed the book shut, then looked up gravely. "This, I gather, is her entire gift to the museum?"

"I'm afraid so," said Titus Moon.

Catherine Rule put down her embroidery, dragged her chair closer to the table, and cleared her throat. If John Bodkin had not begun talking tirelessly at that moment, she might have said something important. Oh, well, thought Catherine, better to wait.

"It's the last straw," Bodkin was saying. "And I'm afraid I must now inform you of still more bad news. Our insurance premium has doubled. It was the bomb scare, I think. The Paul Revere Insurance Company was rather distressed at that particular incident. Of course I did my best to change their minds. You will remember that the president is a close friend of mine, Putnam Farhang, an old classmate. I invited the Farhangs to supper, really put on the dog. My wife worked for two days, cooking up a fancy meal. But it was no go. Putnam told me it wasn't just the crazy things that have been happening around here lately, endangering the collection. He said the works of art themselves have quadrupled in value in the last ten years. As a matter of fact, I have myself been talking with an expert in the field"— Bodkin cleared his throat self-consciously—"who informs me that our paintings alone are worth millions upon millions of dollars. Therefore, Putnam said, we were lucky to get off with only twice our usual rate."

"Oh, dear," said Fulton Hillside, putting pale fingers to his lips.

"Golly, that's just terrible," said Peggy Foley.

Catherine Rule picked up her needlework. Edward Fall-fold looked slyly around at the others. Shackleton Bowditch lost himself in gloomy examination of an ancient wormhole in the table. Preston Carver cast down his eyes and said nothing.

"What's more," Bodkin went on, "I'm sorry to report that our investments have declined sharply in value at the same time."

"It's part of the general decline," said Carver, piping up at last. "The Dow-Jones is way down, inflation is taking off."

"With the natural consequence that our income has suffered, right, Preston?" said Bodkin.

Then Bodkin and Carver began talking learnedly about the museum's portfolio, of which they were the particular guardians. Their faces were long, their pronouncements melancholy.

When they paused at last, Catherine Rule leaned forward eagerly. "Why don't you buy gold instead?" Her expression was angelic. Her right eye looked mildly at Bodkin, her left gazed vaguely in the direction of Wall Street and found it wanting.

"Gold!" Bodkin snorted contemptuously.

"Well," said Titus Moon, heaving a deep sigh, "I have to get back to work. Is there anything else to come before the meeting, Mr. Chairman?"

"Indeed there is." John Bodkin shuffled his papers and exchanged a sidelong glance with Preston Carver. Then, pulling a slip of paper from his pocket, he reworded the motion he had made at the last meeting of the trustees. "In view of the disintegrating financial position of the museum and the continuing violation of the terms of Mrs. Gardner's will, I move that the Isabella Stewart Gardner Museum be terminated and its contents sold at auction."

167

"Second the motion," mumbled Preston Carver, when no one else spoke up.

This time, to the amazement of five of the trustees and the astonishment of Homer Kelly and Titus Moon, there were two affirmative votes. One was Bodkin's; the other was Carver's.

After the meeting, Homer walked along the Fenway with Edward Fallfold. "You live down this way, do you?" said Homer.

"Oh, along here somewhere," said Fallfold, seeming anxious to dismiss the subject. He was dapper in a light tweed jacket. "Excuse me, I usually walk in the park at this hour."

"Well, it's a great day for it," said Homer kindly, and then after Fallfold dodged across the street and plunged into a stand of bulrushes, Homer decided to take advantage of the afternoon himself. He would enjoy the warm day while it lasted. The first week in May was chancy. Tomorrow there might be rain and sleet.

At once he came upon a new discovery, the rose garden. Charmed, he wandered along the path, watching as the bushes were pruned. Piles of thorny dead twigs lay on the ground. Homer's mind felt thorny too. He felt snagged and rasped and pricked with resentment against Bodkin and Carver and all the other money men in the city of Boston. Oh, they were necessary all right, of course they were, or the world wouldn't function, the capitalist system would come to an end; the great cities of the world would fall into ruin and decay. But Homer hated them.

Angrily he wandered across the grass to the public garden plots and watched a couple of old men turning over the soil. Now *there* was honest work. Those old guys would soon be planting seeds, and after a while the peas and beans and squash would come up and be eaten, and that was nice. Direct action upon the earth followed by direct result upon the stomach. It wasn't like the abstract transactions of the money market, those billions of electronic negotiations on video screens around the world, resulting in turbulent indirect consequences to millions of innocent bystanders.

Homer ambled slowly in the direction of the baseball diamond, sauntering past another mighty stand of the tall reeds that grew in such jungle profusion along the edge of the water. Half the young men of Boston seemed to be going into the jungle or coming out, and for an instant Homer thought he caught a glimpse of Fallfold. Turning away, he followed a path thick with young couples and families with strollers. From beyond the trees came the shouts of boys playing baseball.

Then Homer shook his head, correcting himself. He was wrong, dead wrong. The financial people were just as honest as the men who were digging the soil over there in the vegetable garden. They were honest about greed. Excited by this discovery, Homer walked to the crest of a little bridge and gazed down at the polluted water, where spongy brown masses clouded the sluggish stream as it crawled slowly in the direction of the Charles River.

Bodkin and Carver were honestly interested in money, that was the point, and they didn't pretend otherwise. They didn't claim to be doing good, or serving mankind, or saving life, or creating beauty, or increasing human knowledge. By contrast, the rest of the population of Boston preened itself on its ethical standards. They were all teachers or poets or nurses or archbishops or whatever. But what did they really think about in the small hours of the night— their IRA's and income taxes and whether or not they should shift their tiny nest egg from this little venture to that? Greed was a universal condition, a consequence of the

169

fall of man, of Adam and Eve and the apple of original sin. Bodkin and Carver made no bones about it. By being honest they were able to go after luxury and affluence whole hog. With singleminded integrity they could dissociate business and morals. Capital punishment was on the rise? Good! Invest in hangman's nooses. The Gardner Museum was going down the drain? Too bad, but what could they do about it?

And then it occurred to Homer that the museum itself had been founded on the successful investments of Mrs. Gardner's father, and the shipping and railroad interests of her husband Jack. Art for the public was not spun out of nothing. It did not float on the air, nor hang on diaphanous walls of spiderweb.

CHAPTER TWENTY-FOUR

AFTER CLOSING hours on the day of the trustees'
meeting, the night watchman in the museum was
Beanie Kenney. Beanie had been told not to carry
his portable cassette-player on duty, but the warning didn't
make sense to Beanie. Therefore tonight, just as usual, he
was wearing his earphones as he walked from gallery to
gallery, gyrating to the beat of last year's Newport concert
by the Soft White Underbelly. Three electric guitars
whomped and crashed in Beanie's ears and the mournful
caterwauling of the lead singer split his skull.

What did it matter that he couldn't hear anything else?
He could see perfectly well.

Thus when Beanie's flashlight swept over the east wall
of the Titian Room, he didn't need to look twice to see that
the Titian was missing. Instead of the painting there was
only a large dark-crimson rectangle where the brocaded
wall had been protected from the light for the better part
of a century. The great mythological canvas illustrating a
scene from Ovid's *Metamorphoses,* painted for King Philip
the Second of Spain and later possessed by Philip the Fifth,
the Ducs de Gramont and d'Orleans, the Marquis of Staf-
ford, the Earls of Berwick and Darnley, and at last by Mrs.
Gardner, for whom Berenson had snatched it from under
the nose of the Kaiser Friedrich Museum—*The Rape of
Europa,* the most famous painting in Mrs. Gardner's collection, was gone.

In a panic Beanie called Becky Stover at the watch desk

on his intercom, and Becky called Titus Moon and Charlie
Tibby, and Charlie called Homer Kelly.

Homer had spent the evening with Titus Moon, patrolling the back streets of Dorchester, looking in various bars
for Tom Duck. They had found him at last in a low-down
hole on Genoa Street, and taken him home. Now, driving
into town again in the middle of the night, Homer cursed
the Isabella Stewart Gardner Museum, which looked inward upon its own fantasies, turning blank blind walls of
brick to the actual world outside. What difference did it
make if one painting or another disappeared forever? Let
the museum come to an end and be dismantled, let the rest
of its fabulous collection be sold; let the money transform
the city of Boston into a metropolis of alabaster, with houses
of ivory and ebony for all the Tom Ducks of Dorchester.
Let there be schools of silver and gold for the unemployed
teenagers of Dorchester. What good were painting and
sculpture when people were living in misery? What possible
use were pictures hanging on a wall?

At three o'clock in the morning, Route Two was empty
of traffic. Homer sped past the Alewife parking garage,
rounded the two sets of rotaries, and plunged across the
bridge to Storrow Drive, snarling to himself. The trouble
was, the money wouldn't go to the welfare institutions of
the city of Boston, it would go to Harvard University.
Instead of rearing alabaster dwellings for the poor, it would
merely reprivilege the already privileged, and swell the
coffers of the institutions to which Harvard's millions were
entrusted—enormous corporations like Dow Chemical,
Exxon, General Motors.

Storrow Drive was empty too. Homer whizzed along
the Fenway, chiding himself for his sociological irritation.
It was merely a cover for his own inadequacy. He was
making no headway at all in finding the prestidigitator who

had performed all those dirty tricks and murdered Madeline Hepplewhite. Charlie Tibby wasn't getting anywhere, either, and neither, apparently, were Lieutenant-Detective Bleach and old man Campbell. The nastiness was going on and on. When would it stop?

The Titian Room looked vacant and shocking without its principal work of art. Homer stood with Titus Moon and Charlie Tibby and young Beanie Kenney staring up at the empty wall. He remembered now what the painting looked like. It had been rather good, as a matter of fact, he couldn't deny it, a genuine smashing crashing masterpiece, one of the great daubs of the western world—the woman on the back of the bull, Zeus in the shape of a beast kidnapping Europa so that she could give birth to Minos, and populate the continent that would be called by her name. "Well, for Christ's sake," Homer said, "where can the damned thing be?"

Then Titus Moon, who had been calm in the face of arson and mysterious music, who had behaved with heroism on the day of the bomb scare and functioned effectively even after the murder of Madeline Hepplewhite, poor Titus went completely to pieces. He couldn't stand up. Lowering himself carefully into one of the gilded Italian armchairs, he put his head in his hands. "My God," he kept saying. "Oh, my God."

"Listen, Beanie," said Charlie, "you've sworn you didn't see anybody. Did you by any chance *hear* anything?"

"Hear anything?" Guiltily Beanie wished he had removed his earphones, which were still dangling around his neck. What he had heard, of course, was the raving of three insane electric guitarists hollering *GOTCHA, GOTCHA, GOTCHA* at the tops of their lungs, while the demented drummer thumped and banged and the guy on the synthesizer made funny bleating noises like blowing on a bottle, and immense tremendous crashes like colliding locomotives. Any soft scrapings or creeping footsteps or quiet murmurings among thieves would have been utterly overwhelmed. "No, not that I remember."

Then Titus Moon brightened, and he stood up. "Maybe somebody moved it to some other part of the building. Hey, has anyone looked around? I'll bet it's someplace else right here in the building."

Charlie shook his head. "We looked, Beanie and I. We've been all over. You can't hide something as big as that. The thing must be six feet by eight, counting that heavy gold frame. You can't shove a thing like that behind a potted plant."

"But how," said Homer, completely baffled, "would anybody get something that size out of the place? It must have taken some doing."

Titus suggested they notify Lieutenant-Detective Bleach, then go home and think about it some more tomorrow. He, for one, couldn't keep his eyes open at this hour of the night.

Next morning, bright and early, he welcomed Homer into his office, while Charlie Tibby showed the empty wall in the Titian Room to Bleach and a couple of investigative officers whose specialty was stolen property. Both Titus and Homer were suffused with gloom.

"There was a party in the museum last night," said Titus, "while you and I were prowling around looking for Tom Duck. I suppose we'd better think about that."

"One of those special visits?"

"That's right. Fatcat Enterprises was holding a big shindig. Normally we don't permit profit-making groups to use the museum, but in the case of potential big givers we sometimes make exceptions. And since most of the other

174

special visits have been cancelled, we were glad to liven the place up a little, as though things were back to normal."

Homer couldn't believe it. "You mean that comic-strip character has filtered into the museum too? What kind of enterprises has *he* got, besides that third-rate amusement park and a couple of fast-food places here and there?"

"Oh, you know," said Titus, "it's like any big corporation. They're into all sorts of things. From the funnies they went on to comic books, then to stuffed toys and boxed cereal and junk food and soapflakes and heavy industry and microchips, and I don't know whatall. Fatcat's a big deal right now. As a result they need tax relief, so they've got this big foundation for giving money away. We're hoping for some of it ourselves, so naturally we allowed them to put on a party here last night. We were darn glad they didn't call it off in spite of the rotten publicity we've been getting lately."

Homer yawned, and looked around Moon's office, admiring the hangings on the wall. They came from Turkestan or Afghanistan or Tashkent, or some place else unimaginable to Homer. He thought of men on little ponies dashing across the steppe. Moon's office had an air of Mongol daring. "I didn't see anything about the missing painting on the news this morning, did you?"

"No, but I think we've got to release it to the press right away. After all, the more people who know what the painting looks like, the less chance the thief will have of selling it. Not that I think profit was the motive."

"It wasn't just one thief," said Homer. "That painting weighs a ton, remember? And it's way too big for the elevator. It must have taken at least two strong guys to carry it out." Unless, thought Homer, the thief was some muscle man like Tom Duck. Again he imagined Titus Moon in the

175

role of crafty betrayer, coming back to the museum in the middle of the night with his friend Tom.

But if he was guilty, Titus was putting on a good imitation of a museum director in mourning. "I admit I feel personally humiliated. What kind of a stupid fumbling caretaker allows women to be murdered on his premises and then loses the gem of his collection? What kind of careless, negligent, slipshod—"

"Shut up," said Homer kindly. Then the phone rang, and he listened with half an ear while Titus talked to Campbell on the phone. The conversation went on and on. Homer picked up a huge notebook that lay on Titus Moon's desk, and flipped the pages. "Say, this is nice about Rubens," he murmured to himself. "*Swashbuckling application of paint,* that's really good. Who wrote this stuff? It's great."

"Oh, that's Polly Swallow," said Titus, putting down the phone. "It's her part of the new catalogue."

"Polly Swallow? That big girl with the sneakers?" Homer put the notebook down and went back to the problem at hand. "What sort of security arrangements did you have last night during the party for the Fatcats?"

"Oh, we had guards all over the place. The Fatcat people wanted to see the museum, and a bunch of the trustees were on hand, so some of them gave little guided tours. Bodkin wasn't there. Neither was Catherine Rule. Peggy Foley says she took a lot of people around before the festivities. Fallfold took some more of them afterward. We had guards in all the rooms, so it must have cost Fatcat Enterprises at least six-hundred dollars for security alone. Naturally at a party they only stop to look at a few things. The Titian was one of them. Robbie Crowlie was the guard in the Titian Room. Nobody walked off with it while he was on duty. Charlie Tibby has already put Robbie through the mill."

"Did they have refreshments at this affair? You know, tables with a lot of food?"

"Oh, sure. Betty Gore usually has four folding tables set up for this kind of party, there in the east cloister. One for the fruit punch, one for the wine, two with various sorts of cold food. We do the catering ourselves, out of the kitchen in the café."

"Four tables," said Homer. "How big were they? Not as big as a Venetian masterpiece, I take it?"

"Well, there's one big one, maybe five by nine. The others are smaller."

"Suppose a couple of people carried the Titian down the back stairs—you know, the stairway beside the chapel—then removed it from the building covered with a white cloth, as though it were one of the tables?"

Titus nodded his head slowly. "I think," he said, "we should have another go at Robbie Crowlie."

But Robbie was a watermelon seed. He squirted right out of their fingers. "I went downstairs with the last of the visitors. Ask Mr. Fallfold. He was with me, along with a whole lot of other people. I don't know their names, those Fatcats, but you could probably find out."

"I will," promised Homer grimly.

And then he did his best to discover whether Robbie was telling the truth. He called Edward Fallfold.

"Yes," said Fallfold, "Robbie was with us. We went downstairs together. I asked him about his future plans. Did he want to be a museum guard all his life, that sort of thing. And, as I remember, he said security was a good field. He's studying for some kind of exam so he can get a job as a licensed bodyguard."

Then Homer talked to Robbie Crowlie once again, buttonholing him in the guards' room in the basement. "Tell

177

me, Robbie, what did you and Mr. Fallfold talk about last night?"

"Oh, he asked me about my future," said Robbie smoothly. "I told him about getting a job as a bodyguard. You know, as a personal bodyguard for some rich guy. Or, you know, maybe a rock star."

There was no disagreement there. Nevertheless Homer made up his mind to devote the rest of the day to the corroboration of Robbie's story. Maybe Charlie Tibby's entire security staff was getting off easy. All of them had been questioned and requestioned, but not a single one had actually been fired. Maybe if Charlie Tibby were to get rid of all eighty-seven guards, the malevolence would stop. Had Robbie Crowlie left the Titian Room last night with the others as he claimed, or had he remained behind and lifted a famous painting from the wall, with the help of an accomplice?

Maybe some of the Fatcats could tell him whether Robbie had been telling the truth. Maybe they would remember whether he had gone downstairs with them. Somebody might even have seen him leave the building. Where were they now? Where in the city of Boston were the central offices of Fatcat? Homer left the museum with a mission, to search out and pin down in their lairs those true lovers of art and culture, those worshipers of beauty, the top executives of Fatcat Enterprises.

CHAPTER TWENTY-FIVE

DRIVING THROUGH Kenmore Square, Homer was once again confronted with the colossal Fatcat towering over the rooftops, taking off its neon top hat, putting it on and taking it off again. Once more he regretted the loss of the old Citgo sign, with its charming triangles that swelled and shrank, and swelled and shrank. There was something ominous about the exchange of the one for the other, the substitution of a funny-paper feline for an equilateral triangle drawn in the sky by the calipers of God.

Once again Homer flipflopped in his posture toward the Gardner Museum. Thank God for it, he thought, as he made a U-turn in the middle of Kenmore Square. A cop yelled at him and blew his whistle, but Homer drove serenely away, picturing the Gardner Museum poised on a giant seesaw with Fatcat, all its works of art judged in a competition with Fatcat's comic-strip fables.

On the one hand, the galleries of the museum were alive with the myths and legends by which people had understood their existence in time and eternity for thousands of years—from the hawk of the sun god Horus to the Crucifixion of Christ, from the domination of popes and kings to the rise of the middle class. The Gardner Museum was a distilled essence of the history of the world, its works of art were crystallized cross sections of the life of the imagination.

Fatcat, on the other hand, was merely a leering image of

the unimpassioned mind at its feeblest. Where the hell was it anyway? Homer leaned out the window and hollered at a passerby, then found himself suddenly in Copley Square. Here he was mollified by the vision of the mirrored surface of the John Hancock building. As usual the gleaming tower seemed lightly poised on its foundations, as if it were made of azure air instead of thousands of tons of concrete, steel, and glass. At least some of the contemporary works of man were not altogether loathsome.

But Fatcat Enterprises was not in Copley Square. Homer found it at last, another tall glittering building next to the Prudential Center and Copley Place—glassy, glossy, and flossy. Parking his car under the building, Homer grumpily paid a large sum on account.

Striding out of the parking grotto, he glared around at the new Boston, remembering when this part of the city had been a tacky wilderness of empty lots and seedy shopfronts. On the whole he had liked it better. Copley Place and the Prudential Center and the expensive shops on the ground floor of the Fatcat building were milling with a race foreign to him now. On this warm day in early May it was clear that they were an excessively clean people, these pink strangers, with spotless white shoes, gleaming hair, and round healthy arms. They looked terribly young to Homer, who by contrast felt sour and disheveled and old. But he told himself that his eyes were shining with a shrewd hard light that was absent from theirs. It was the light of civilization and culture, he reflected smugly, the light of art and beauty, the light of shrinking and expanding triangles. These people weren't civilized. They were some new race of ignorant savages who had been plunged into bubbly bathtubs, yanked out and shaken and dried off and dressed in bright new clothes. Homer stalked through the ground-floor arcade of the Fatcat building, glowering at everyone he saw, hating their jolly smiles and brilliant teeth.

One of the stores in the arcade was a purveyor of Fatcat gifts and greeting cards. As Homer walked past the window on his way to the elevator, two girls were cooing at the display. "Don't you just adore Fatcat?" said the one in the

181

baby-blue T-shirt. "I've got this Fatcat notepaper, and like I use it whenever I write to my boyfriend. Oh, Fatcat's so *cute.*"

"No, no," said Homer eagerly, stopping to admonish her. "You don't mean *cute. Cute,* you see, is a corruption of the word *acute,* meaning sharp or clever. What you mean, I suppose, is *adorable.* Fatcat's adorable, right?"

The girl gaped at him. As Homer walked away in the direction of the elevator, he could hear her tittering with her friend. Actually, he decided, correcting himself, she had probably been using the word with perfect accuracy. Fatcat was certainly sharp and clever, if anybody was. Look at the way he was taking over the world.

Homer glanced at the list of names and offices beside the elevator. It was apparent at once that the entire building was occupied by Fatcat Enterprises. How was he going to find the executives who had gathered at the Gardner Museum last night? Entering the elevator, Homer chose a floor at random and pushed the button.

Facing him as he got out on the sixteenth floor was the desk of a Fatcat receptionist. She looked just like the people downstairs, clean as a whistle and fresh from the tub. A man with an attaché case stood in front of her. "I have an appointment with Mr. Chalk," the man said.

"Whom shall I say wishes to see him?" said the receptionist in accents of chilling refinement, picking up the phone.

Homer was shocked. Once again he interfered. Leaning over the desk he said benevolently, "No, no, not *whom. Who. Who* shall I say wishes to see him? It's the subject of the verb *wishes,* you see, not the object of the verb *say.* I mean, I can see how you'd go wrong, it's so easy to take the nearest verb and fit the pronoun to that, but in this case—"

The girl behind the desk pierced Homer with an icy

glance, and hissed at him. The man with the attaché case fell back. Saddened by the grammatical unreceptiveness of the receptionist, Homer walked away down the hall, looking for an open door.

Where was he anyway? At what level of this vast enterprise? How could he find the central pulsing heart of this great establishment, the throbbing core, the soul and spirit, the nub, the marrow, the pith, the running sap? Finding a door marked GRAPHIC ARTS SERVICES, Homer pushed it open.

He had entered an enormous room full of small compartments. The separating walls were only chest-high. From his altitude of six-feet-six, Homer could see bent heads and crouching backs in all of them. Everyone was hard at work.

Homer was pleased. Here, surely, he would find the visionary genius who had invented Fatcat in some moment of inspiration, some flash of creative fire. Here, if anywhere, was Fatcat's sacred birthplace.

"Excuse me," said Homer, speaking to a young woman walking toward him along the corridor, "could you direct me to the creator of Fatcat?"

She was a handsome girl with short blond hair and enormous glasses. "Sure, this is it. You've come to the right place." Grinning at Homer, she scooted past him and dodged into a compartment.

Mystified, Homer followed her in. "You mean, *you* did? *You* invented Fatcat?" In one glance, he saw that he was right. Laid out on her drawing table were renderings of Fatcat on acetate.

"Me? Oh, no, not me. All of us." The girl waved her hand around the enormous room. "It's everybody. We all make Fatcat."

Homer gasped. "But who started it? I mean, who had the idea in the first place?"

183

"Oh, Lord, I don't know. It was a committee. They took the big heavy-lidded eyes from Garfield"—the girl made a clever face, and suddenly became a cartoon cat—"and the teeth from Heathcliff, and the grin from the Cheshire Cat, and the wisecracks from Morris, and the white gloves from Donald Duck, and then they colored it purple to look different from the others, and behold!" With uprolled eyes and tossing hand, she brought Fatcat into being. "Now, excuse me, I've got to finish this by lunchtime."

The next floor of the building was peopled by balding young men with raffish mustachios, sharp suits, and deep tans. They all looked alike to Homer. Sadly he imagined their great-grandfathers, back home in the old country—muzhiks in felt boots, Cossacks in furry hats, Armenians in baggy trousers, coalminers from Lancashire, Irish potato farmers—how different from one another they would all have been! This look-alike conformity seemed a comedown, a falling away of natural dignity.

Homer approached a young man carrying a roll of maps. "I wonder if you could help me? I'm trying to find some of the people who attended a Fatcat party last night at the Isabella Stewart Gardner Museum."

"Oh, hey, no kidding? Sure, I was there. Great party. Great place!" The young man with the deep tan introduced himself to Homer as Larry W. Oversole. "It was our big night, the annual bash for Fatcat Investment Properties. That's our department."

"Investment properties? You mean Fatcat's in real estate too?"

"Oh, sure. Fatcat owns half the city of Boston. Well, maybe not half." Oversole smirked modestly, and invited Homer into his office, a jazzy little compartment paneled in plasticized oak, with huge paintings on the walls, giant swirls in livid colors. Beneath the paintings there were framed photographs of Fatcat properties. Oversole pointed them out to Homer. "New high rises, we build them, rent them. Old estates, we buy them, turn them into useful deluxe spaces, sell them. That kind of thing."

Homer was dismayed. On the seventeenth floor of the Fatcat building he could feel the ground disappearing beneath his feet, forests and fields, daisies and buttercups, vanishing under concrete. All the daisies and buttercups in the world, all the fresh green grass . . .

". . . So that's what I told this guy last night. I told him, wow, what we could do with a place like this!"

Homer had not been listening. He had missed something. "A place like this?"

"The Gardner Museum." Oversole was excited. Spiral rays shot from his eyes. His mustachios quivered. "See, that's my specialty. I redesign. I look at some old place, say a bunch of town houses on Commonwealth Avenue, and like right away I know what to do, rip out a wall here, a floor there, stick in a couple of lavs for every suite, bring in new lighting, carpeting, louver drapes, corporate art."

"Corporate art?" said Homer.

Oversole pointed at the paintings on his wall. "Stuff like mine. You know, important art. So pretty soon you've got a lot of new luxury office space. I mean, that's what I do, right?" Oversole gestured at the tiny pin in his buttonhole. "Got this last night," he said proudly, "for doing it the mostest and the bestest."

Homer blanched. "You mean, you'd like to do that sort of thing to the Gardner Museum?"

Oversole turned confidential. "Well, like I heard this rumor, I mean it was in the paper. You guys are in some kind of trouble, right? I mean, you've got your problems. So I says to this guy, listen, if worst comes to worst, I'm right here, ready and waiting, here's my card." Oversole illustrated his story by whipping out a card and handing it to Homer.

It was a little piece of gold pasteboard—ah, there was no bottom to the vulgar good taste, the barbarous refinement of this young man.

> ## LARRY W. OVERSOLE
>
> REAL ESTATE MANAGEMENT CONSULTANT
>
> FATCAT ENTERPRISES   975-9750

Homer pocketed the gold card, his head spinning. "So who was this guy," he said, "the one you were talking to last night?"

"Oh, some character who was showing us around. You know, tall distinguished sort of guy, classy dresser. You know."

"Fallfold," said Homer, pouncing. "Edward Fallfold. What did he say in reply, when you suggested that the Gardner Museum would make a desirable investment property for Fatcat Enterprises?"

"Well, I could tell he was interested. But he shook his head and said no way. The place wasn't for sale. So I said, I just thought I'd mention it. I mean, you never can tell, right? Like you keep on planting seeds all over the place, right?"

"Did you see Mr. Fallfold leave the museum? Did the guard go downstairs with you? I mean, did everybody leave the galleries at the same time?"

"How should I know?" Oversole winked at Homer. "To be honest with you, I was sort of heavily involved in a new relationship with this cute girl from Data processing."

Homer left the office, but not before complimenting Oversole on his tan. "Say, you must have been in the Caribbean or someplace like that."

"Tanning parlor," explained Oversole. "Lunchtime, right down the street. You work out in the gym with all this state-of-the-art equipment, and then you relax on these couches under ultraviolet light and take a snooze. Hey, guy, you ought to try it. You look kind of like a fish's belly yourself. Or like, you know, something under a rock."

Homer went away defeated, after spending another hour on the seventeenth floor of the Fatcat Building, failing to find anyone who could remember whether Fallfold and Robbie Crowlie had been left by themselves in the Titian Room at the end of the gallery tour. His afternoon had been wasted.

Except that it had given him a new and rapturous understanding of the virtues of the Gardner Museum. Here was Fatcat Enterprises, a mindless, faceless institution, sleekly anonymous, undertaking enormous ventures, shifting the globe on its axis, with no one in charge but corporate nerds, amoral middlemen, and executive hooligans. Mrs. Gardner, on the other hand, had been a vital and intelligent and slightly eccentric wealthy woman, totally responsible for the building she had created, a woman of strong personal taste who had left her signature on one small part of the world, to be enjoyed by everyone ever after.

As Homer got off the elevator he was feeling so lonesome and depressed, he decided impulsively to call his wife in New York City. Around the corner he found a bank of telephones.

"Fish's belly, that's what he said," he complained to Mary indignantly. "Like something under a rock, he said."

"Why, Homer, of course you don't look like that," said

Mary stoutly. "You're not pale like a fish's belly. It's more like—let's see now—"

Another blow was coming. Homer braced himself.

"A parsnip. It's the way a parsnip looks after you cook it. That's it. A boiled parsnip."

"Thanks a heap," said Homer bitterly. But on the way back to the car park, he stuck his face up into the sunshine to banish a little of his vegetable paleness.

"Hey, guy, what you looking at?" said a passerby curiously, looking up too.

"Perfect beauty," snarled Homer. "The ideal of human perfection, unattainable, alas, in this evil world."

CHAPTER TWENTY-SIX

THE DECISION to publicize the theft of Titian's *Rape of Europa* was unanimous. Charlie Tibby and Homer Kelly and Titus Moon and Lieutenant-Detective Bleach and all the trustees agreed that it had to be done.

Charlie spent an entire day calling trucking companies and bus depots, customs house brokers, air freight offices, the freight department at Conrail, and the central offices of Amtrak. Then he began on marine shipping, ransacking the Yellow Pages, picking out the Hermann Ludwig Company (International Freight), the Commerce Handling Company (Air and Sea Shipping, Steel Strapping & Container Stuffing), the ABC Transportation Company (Door to Port Economy Service), then running down the list of all the rest. It was absorbing work. Along with the bluff voices on the phone came a vision of the oily harbor, with crates descending into cavernous holds, knocking against the gunwales of huge seagoing vessels.

Titus Moon's part of the job was the alerting of the TV networks. He was successful at once. Within the hour, camera crews from two of the local stations were setting up lights in the Titian Room, while Titus stood in front of the empty wall displaying a large color reproduction of *The Rape of Europa*.

It was Homer's task to inform the managing editor of the *Boston Globe*. Homer, too, had no difficulty. The managing editor caught fire right away. Next morning the theft of the Titian was proclaimed on the front page, with a reproduction of the missing masterpiece in livid color, as if it were a winning Red Sox pitcher or a Hallowe'en jack-o'-lantern or a newly elected president. For the *Globe,* the theft of the Titian was pure gold. The troubles of the Gardner Museum had become an ongoing story, with new chapters appearing all the time like episodes in an exciting serial adventure.

But Horry McDandy didn't follow the news. Whenever the *Boston Globe* arrived on the doorstep of the Red Rose Bar and Cocktail Lounge, Horry extracted the sports section and threw the rest away. The television set over the bar was tuned to sporting events, game shows, and police-action dramas. You could sit on a stool at the Red Rose Bar and watch wisecracking young homicide squad guys, one black, the other white, hurl themselves into cruisers and slam the doors with a *punkshing* sound and take off with a squeal of tires and a roll from side to side and a high accelerating whine, and never know there was a real world of trouble and sorrow just outside the door.

So when Horry's friend Scotty Greep in the secondhand store down the street, just beyond the H. & R. Block income tax office and Victor's Unisex Hair Salon, told him about the painting he had for sale, Horry had no suspicion there was anything wrong.

"Hey, Horry," said Scotty on the phone, "how'd you like a big picture over the bar? You know that high ceiling you got? Plenty of room for a picture. I got this huge naked woman. Well, you know, half undressed. Real work of art. High-class stuff."

"Hey, no fooling?" Horry was interested at once. He had often thought of lowering the ceiling, because it was far too high for the long narrow space of the Red Rose, but maybe a painting was what the room had always been waiting for. Horry remembered a tavern in Rome, New York, where two luscious painted nudes reclined on pillows over the long fumed-oak bar, their succulent breasts and stomachs and thighs pearly white with blue veins, reminding him of fresh-caught fish in a bucket, or pork bellies in a barrel. "Sure I'd like to see it. How much will it go for?"

Scotty was coy. "Just wait till you see it, Horry. I mean this is genuine world-class stuff, I kid you not. Come on over. It's right here. I mean, she's huge, this big woman, just a veil, that's all she's got on, sitting on the back of this great big cow."

"A cow?" gasped Horry. "A woman on a cow?"

CHAPTER TWENTY-SEVEN

POLLY SWALLOW was running away from Titus Moon's office, where she had come upon Titus and Aurora O'Doyle locked in each other's arms. Their fixation had become oppressive. It wasn't just that Polly was jealous—although she was, she certainly was—it was also embarrassing. Titus was like a panting dog, and Aurora a bitch in heat (a purebred bitch, a best-in-show, well-cared-for bitch).

Polly retreated to the tapestry workshop and spent an hour with Catherine Rule, plying needle and thread. It was consoling to be with Catherine. Polly said nothing aloud about Titus and Aurora, but Catherine looked at her cleverly as though nothing escaped her.

Catherine had not yet given up her fight against the machinations of Aurora O'Doyle, but she knew it was a losing battle. She had thrown herself in Aurora's way as often as possible, and these forays had usually been successful. On each occasion Aurora's power over Titus had wilted and shriveled away. But Catherine could not match Aurora's trump card, which was infinite opportunity. A hundred times a day she could be alone with Titus, and the silver negligee would always be waiting for him every night. Were they sleeping together? Catherine didn't know.

Neither did Polly, although she thought about it often enough at two o'clock in the morning. She wondered about it now, as she sat with her head bowed over the tapestry, stitching away at the dog lapping Jezebel's blood.

Abruptly Polly put down her needle, said goodbye to Catherine, and hurried across the hall. In the sculpture repair studio she found Harry Blackman cleaning the stone head of Aphrodite, giving it a good scrub.

"Oh, isn't she lovely!" exclaimed Polly. Remembering her reading, she said learnedly, "Influenced by Praxiteles."

"Well, I wish we had the rest of her," said Harry, giving Polly a wink. "Hey, listen, does she remind you of anybody?"

"No," said Polly, but she knew at once who he had in mind. Excusing herself quickly, she went away, going nowhere in particular.

Therefore it was Polly who discovered the absence of another important painting. Trailing disconsolately through the galleries, she walked into the Gothic Room and missed it at once.

"Where's Mrs. Gardner?" she asked Hilda Sorensen, the guard on duty.

"What?" said Hilda, who didn't know much about the collection.

"The Sargent portrait of Mrs. Gardner, it's not there." Polly pointed at the empty space above the Spanish chest in the corner. The life-size portrait of Isabella Stewart Gardner, the founder of the museum, its guardian angel and pervading spirit, was gone.

193

"Yeesus," said Hilda, "dot's right. Oh, my God, Charlie vill fire me now."

And Charlie did. Poor Hilda was not given another chance to make a mistake. Weeping, she turned in her green jacket and went away for good.

The disappearance of a second celebrated painting was crushing news to Titus Moon. He groaned aloud, and called for Charlie Tibby. Later he had lunch in the Simmons College cafeteria with Homer Kelly.

"It's so damned humiliating," he said to Homer. "How can I notify the trustees? Bodkin will say, *I told you so, we've got to close down the museum and sell everything, because Mrs. Gardner is turning in her grave.*" Miserably Titus thought of the ridiculous figure he would cut among all the local museum curators and directors if the news got around that the portrait of Mrs. Gardner was gone from her own museum. "Do we have to spread the story? What if we just shut up about it, and didn't let on? We could put up one of those little notices—THIS PICTURE REMOVED FOR CLEANING. Why not?"

Homer pondered. "You mean, you and I and Charlie agree to shut up about it, and we tell Hilda Sorensen and Polly Swallow not to say anything either? That won't get your picture back, Titus. Look, I'll ask Bleach if he can be discreet, but we really ought to be doing the same things for this picture that we're doing for the Titian. We ought to let the whole world know what it looks like."

"The Titian, oh, God, the Titian. Where in hell is the Titian?"

Homer leaned forward and looked at Titus keenly. "You know what I'm beginning to think? Some fanatic in our midst is an enemy of Mrs. Gardner. Or an enemy of all she stood for. Who do you know who despises her for her

194

wealth, or her artistic taste, or her self-indulgence, or her ability to satisfy almost any whim that came into her head? Or perhaps there are still old grudges against her, here in Boston? Any suggestions? How about some young servant in Mrs. Gardner's Beacon Street house, living in the attic, broiling in summer, freezing in winter, earning three or four dollars a week, with Thursday afternoons off for good behavior? Well, I guess that's unfair to Mrs. Gardner—to suggest she was anything out-of-the-way as a cruel employer. It was the same for all those young Irish girls working in Boston. My own forebears were in service around here, the whole lot of them, and their resentment has come down in the family. My own grandmother could have nicked that portrait, if she were still alive." Homer put down his coffee cup and took pity on Titus Moon. "Look, I'll speak to Bleach. Maybe he'll shut up for a week or two."

But when Bleach was approached with the news and the request to keep it dark, he wasn't sure he could oblige. "I just don't know if we can keep it a secret from the press. I mean, after all, we're not the CIA." And Campbell in Public Safety responded in the same way, only he said they weren't the KGB.

But surprisingly enough, the theft of the Sargent painting remained a secret for more than a week. The trustees were informed, of course. And John Bodkin passed the news along to his friend Gerard Fouchelle.

The two of them gloated over the double disaster, the embarrassing loss of two great works of art from the museum they were trying to destroy. "Wait till the next meeting of the trustees," said Bodkin, grinning. "I'll pick up another vote. All it takes is two more. It's only a matter of time."

"The two paintings must of course be found," warned Fouchelle, clicking his tongue, thinking prudently, as he always did, of the ultimate value on the auction block of the collection as a whole.

CHAPTER TWENTY-EIGHT

HOMER WAS AWAKENED next morning by the croaking cries of a flock of geese. They were barking like dogs over the house. He cursed the geese because he didn't want to wake up from a very interesting dream about—about—what was it about? As it slipped away from him he made a lunge after it, but it scrambled away on its runty legs and disappeared forever.

Sighing heavily, Homer got out of bed and went to the window to watch the squadron of geese flap low over Fair Haven Bay. The wind blowing the curtains was fresh with the rank smell of the river, where sixty million different things were bursting into disorderly life, jostling each other aside. The geese, too, were disorderly as they struggled to get into some kind of formation. Noisily they shifted and changed direction, squawking hoarsely, shouting at each other to shape up. Homer enjoyed the sense of mix-up and confusion. Geese were supposed to fly in orderly arrow-shaped wedges, but they hardly ever did. Their echelons were always ragged and lopsided, as jumbled and chaotic as everything else in the life of the wild.

It was the second week of May. Driving in from Concord, Homer chose Trapelo Road and Concord Avenue, attracted by the flowering front yards and the pale green bushy tangles along the pavement, where miscellaneous saplings surged out of the ditches, fighting for light and air, urgently blossoming. It was chaos again, like the thick competition of the pickerel weed and buttonbushes and alders along the bottom of his own front yard. But it was a fresh and sunlit and sweet-smelling chaos. Homer thought again of the systematic tidiness of the Gardner Museum. This morning the place was going to seem dried up and shrunken, dark and old, the paintings merely cracked old boards smeared with crumbling necromantic mixtures.

But then he forgot about the museum, about order and disorder, as chaos erupted in the convoluted pipes and electrical connections of the Chevy's internal combustion engine. There was something seriously the matter with the car. The stupid machine had been giving Homer trouble lately. Now he was aware of an ominous failure of power. As he droned down the hill in second gear, Homer hungered once again for the faultless perfection of the Gardner Museum, where everything obeyed some Athenian law of harmony and proportion, blissfully removed from the weedy rambunctiousness of nature, the oily insolence of man-made machinery, and the cussed unruliness of the real world.

Oh, God, he was stalled in Belmont center. Commuters were honking furiously behind him, beeping *what the hell, what the hell.* At last Homer got his car on the move again, very slowly, and as it turned cautiously under the railroad bridge, it occurred to him that his pretty little image of the museum as a place of harmonious perfection was wrong. The scramble and confusion of the real world, its cockeyed dishevelment and incoherent turbulence, had moved right into the sacred precincts. They had invaded the holy of holies. The Isabella Stewart Gardner Museum was no longer sacrosanct. It was just like everything else, a doomed and hopeless muddle.

The Chevy crept along Concord Avenue. The trouble must be in the carburetor. Maybe it was dirty, maybe the fuel-air mix was wrong. If only he could get to McKinnan's

Garage on Huntington Avenue, all would be well. Mr. McKinnan would know what to do. Mr. McKinnan with his greasy duckbilled cap and blackened fingernails would fix it. He could fix anything. His garage was an automechanical Valhalla, a place of grimy poetry and joy. Homer smiled broadly, remembering the grubby walls, the smell of new rubber tires, the wrenches clanging on the floor, the men shouting above the noise of the compressor.

It was a long way for a sick car to go. Homer drifted slowly along Storrow Drive while angry motorists whizzed past him, turning their heads to shout. At last the car made it all the way to Huntington Avenue, but then Homer couldn't find McKinnan's Garage. He drove right past the corner where it had once been, then turned around and came back, unable to believe his eyes.

McKinnan's Garage was gone. Its place had been taken by a shiny new gasoline station, a clean little island of gas pumps under a floating plastic roof. Above the roof rose a big mean-looking Fatcat. This time it was lashing its tail and showing its teeth. PUT A FATCAT IN YOUR TANK, said the puffy cloud over its head.

Homer was aghast. The faceless empire of Fatcat was seeping farther and farther into the body of the republic like a malignant growth, metastasizing in the extremities, invading lymph nodes in the armpits, corrupting vital organs—Fatcats lifting their top hats, Fatcats rubbing their stomachs, Fatcats lashing their tails. Homer pulled up beside one of the pumps, hoping against hope that the kid who pumped gas would be able to do something about the carburetor.

But there was no kid pumping gas. All the pumps were self-service. Nobody was in attendance at all, except for a small child in a tiny building that housed only a pair of rest rooms and a little cubicle with a cash register.

Homer strode into the cubicle and slammed the door behind him. "Where the hell," he said, speaking between his teeth, "is Mr. McKinnan?"

The small child had her back to him. No, it wasn't her back; it was her front, obscured by a torrent of hair and a copy of the *National Enquirer.* Her eyes were invisible behind the mop, like a Yorkshire terrier's. "I only been here since Tuesday," she said sulkily.

Homer stared at the headline on the front of the *Enquirer*: BABY BORN PREGNANT. He opened his mouth to say something, then thought better of it. Storming out of the cubicle, he got back into his troubled car and drove away, seeking help from a careless city, thinking about cats—Fatcats, thin cats, all kinds of cats. Mrs. Gardner, for instance, had liked cats, big cats, wild cats, lion cubs. She had taken a pair of cubs for rides in her carriage; she had romped with a full-grown lion in the zoo. She had bought stone lions and set them up outside the door of her palace. Now *there* were a couple of cats that were cats, thought Homer, remembering the way Mrs. Gardner's Italian lions lay on their haunches, dignified, snarling, splendid. They didn't lift their hats or rub their tummies or otherwise behave themselves unseemly. Once again Homer thought kindly of the wealthy Mrs. Jack. Seen against the background of Fatcat's enormous anonymous holdings, her museum was a tiny bastion of civilization in a barbarous world.

Mrs. Garboyle saw Homer drive away, as she came out of the ladies' rest room with her can of cleanser. Mrs. Garboyle wasn't interested in the filling station's customers. She had something else on her mind. Hurrying into the cash register cubicle, she addressed the mop of hair behind the counter. "Hey, honey, what's that lady doing in the ladies' room?"

"Lady?" said the mop. "What lady?"

"I mean the picture of a lady. Gave me a scare. I mean, she looks right at you. There's this big picture in there, a lady standing like this, life-size." Mrs. Garboyle pulled up her neck and stood proudly erect with her hands clasped. Then she relaxed, and giggled. "I almost said, *'Excuse ME.'* I mean, what's a big picture like that doing here?"

The mop of hair shrugged. "How should I know?"

"Okay if I use the phone?" And then Mrs. Garboyle called her boss at the cleaning company and told him about the picture. But he, too, hardly listened to the woman he had hired to scrub all the Fatcat filling stations on Huntington Avenue. *These old cleaning ladies, they were half-cracked to begin with, or they wouldn't be cleaning toilets.*

"But what am I supposed to do with it?" said Mrs. Garboyle.

"It's not my problem. Why don't you call—uh—the lost and found?"

"What lost and found?"

But her boss had hung up.

Mrs. Garboyle was a tough and intelligent woman whose hard life had not been her fault. She put down the phone, understanding that she would have to decide for herself what to do with the painting in the ladies' room, and went back to wash the floor. Then she put away her cleaning materials and washed her hands. Reaching across the wet tiles, she wriggled the picture away from the pipe behind which it had been wedged, dragged it outdoors, and propped it against the wall while she unlocked her car. Then she took it home to her basement apartment in the rooming house on the Fenway where she was caretaker, and hung it among her other pictures—the kittens in a basket, the calendar with views of Prince Edward Island (her birth-

201

place), and the photograph of her son, who had been killed in the Tet Offensive.

Later that day she ran upstairs to speak to Edward Fallfold as he came in the door. Mr. Fallfold, she knew, was an expert on art, because he was something important at the museum down the street, not the Boston Museum but the other one. "Oh, say, Mr. Fallfold," said Mrs. Garboyle, "you ought to see the picture I found. Want to come down? I've got it right in my front room on the wall."

But Edward Fallfold was not interested in Mrs. Garboyle's collection of miscellaneous frights. He had seen her basement living room once, with its baskets of kittens and its Alpine landscapes painted on velvet. "No, thank you," he said with an absent smile, and then he hurried up to his room, his footsteps fading on the carpeted stairs.

Therefore it was a week before Mrs. Garboyle learned the true nature of the painting in her possession—while she was cleaning Aurora O'Doyle's apartment.

During the morning she had the place to herself. She dusted the Dead Indian and stood on a chair to wipe down the Fatcat over the mantelpiece. It gave Mrs. Garboyle a cynical pleasure to perform these tasks scrupulously. Her attitude toward these two pieces of high contemporary art was ironic. She felt only contempt for her employer, knowing her own superiority in the eyes of a just God, if there were such a thing, which there wasn't.

When Aurora burst in to use the phone, Mrs. Garboyle gamely turned off the vacuum cleaner and started cleaning a smear of guacamole from one of the cushions on the puffy white sofa.

"Oh, didn't you know?" breathed Aurora into the phone. "Well, of course it's a big secret, and you mustn't tell a soul, because darling Titus is beside himself with

202

embarrassment. It's not only the Titian that's missing from the Gardner Museum, my dear, it's Mrs. Gardner herself. Somebody stole the Sargent portrait, you know the one, of course you do. She's standing there in her black dress with the plunging neckline and the pearls around her waist, remember? Staring at you in this *uncanny* way, *life-size?* Well, naturally, poor Titus, it was just too much. So they're trying to find it by talking to dealers sort of on the sly, because, honestly, just between you and me, dear, the museum is on the skids. No, I mean it, honestly. I'm trying to get Titus to desert the sinking ship, but the foolish boy feels so loyal."

Mrs. Garboyle recognized her painting at once, and she was astounded, but craftily she didn't say anything. She went on dabbing at the spot on the cushion while Aurora finished her phone call.

"I just called to tell you I can't come to dinner tonight after all. Oh, I know, you've probably gone to all *kinds* of trouble." Aurora looked at her hand, as though it held a fan of cards, then plucked one shrewdly. "I've got to stay home and work on that *pesky* catalogue. *So* sorry."

The Gardner Museum was only a few blocks away from Mrs. Garboyle's dark apartment in the basement of the rooming house. When she got home, she went to work immediately. Putting the painting down carefully on the floor, she wrapped it in brown paper and tied it up with string. Then she summoned young Rick from the front steps, where he was sweeping up cigarette butts, and together they carried the big package down the street. At the door of the museum, Mrs. Garboyle sent Rick home, and then she dragged her awkward bundle inside.

"You'll have to check that package," said Jim Boggs, who was sitting at the desk in the museum entry.

"Oh, I think they'll let it in," said Mrs. Garboyle triumphantly, unwrapping the brown paper.

"Oh, my God," cried Jim. "Wait a sec, I'll call the director."

And of course Titus came running. He gave the picture one glance of joyful recognition, then grasped Mrs. Garboyle's hand and shook it violently. "Thank God," he said. "Oh, thank the Lord."

"Well, I knew it was something," Mrs. Garboyle said. "I mean, I said to myself, this has got to be somebody." And she told him how she had found it in the ladies' room of the Fatcat filling station.

Titus laughed and beamed, and took her back to his office for the reward he suddenly decided she should have, writing out a check for a thousand dollars in a rush of good feeling without asking the trustees first. "This is a happy day for us," he said gratefully. "We're so glad to have her back." When Mrs. Garboyle left with her check, Titus ran downstairs to tell Charlie, and then he called Homer Kelly and Lieutenant-Detective Bleach and John Bodkin, chairman of the trustees.

But next morning he was less pleased when he saw the *Boston Globe.* The secret was out. Somebody had leaked the news of the theft of the picture and its reappearance in the ladies' room of one of the Fatcat filling stations on Huntington Avenue. Was it Mrs. Garboyle? If so, Titus regretted his thousand-dollar check. But she hadn't seemed like that kind of woman.

And that evening the television newscasters had a field day with the latest episode in the ongoing story of the misadventures of the Isabella Stewart Gardner Museum. Their jokes about Mrs. Jack Gardner and the ladies' room were merciless. Titus could feel the dignity and reputation of the museum sliding still farther in public regard. Not

204

only was it a dangerous place to visit, it was also faintly ridiculous. He switched off the set in the disreputable parlor of the house on Kansas Street and felt his cheeks flush hot and red. All over the country, right now, people were snickering. They were laughing at the Gardner Museum, and more specifically at its director, Titus Moon.

But for Gerard Fouchelle and John Bodkin, this new proof of the decline of the museum in public opinion was a piece of good news. It was grist for their mill. "This won't do us any harm," said Bodkin. "Don't forget, we're only two votes short. Who's next?"

CHAPTER TWENTY-NINE

A S IT TURNED OUT, the next vote in favor of ending the life of the Gardner Museum was already falling into place without the interference of Bodkin and Fouchelle. Foster Hillside, the secretary of the board of trustees, was succumbing to a different sort of pressure.

Foster was the junior partner in a fashionable real estate firm with central offices on Dartmouth Street. The firm also managed branch offices in the suburbs, as far west as the town of Nashoba and as far south as Cape Cod. Its employees were much more discreet and well-bred than the bold buckoes on the seventeenth floor of Fatcat Enterprises. But the ambitions of its chief were similarly large and wide-ranging. In fact, the senior partner had recently been talking about the possibility of opening more offices in the wealthy communities along the North Shore, where the sale of large estates would surely yield high profits.

But this morning the senior partner had something else on his mind. He had been studying the morning paper. Calling Foster into his office, he tapped the front page and handed it across his desk. "Your museum," he said, "its difficulties seem to be multiplying."

Foster took the paper. He had not yet heard about the humiliating resurrection of the Sargent portrait of Mrs. Gardner. "Good Lord," he said.

"Interesting paragraph there," said the senior partner softly, "about Mrs. Gardner's will."

Foster looked suspiciously at the column of print that had interested his boss. It minced no words.

The continuing disarray at the Isabella Stewart Gardner Museum has increased speculation that the museum will be dissolved and its valuable collection sold at auction, in accordance with the terms of Mrs. Gardner's will.

"But that's ridiculous," said Foster. "It can't happen. The trustees would have to vote for it. We're not about to do anything like that. Oh, it's true there's been some agitation in that direction." Foster thought of John Bodkin's crazy motions at the last two meetings, and Preston Carver's sudden decision to vote on Bodkin's side. "But the rest of us won't stand for it. You'll see."

"It would certainly be a tragedy," agreed the senior partner, "an awful shame, if something like that were to happen." He looked at Foster sympathetically, then gazed dreamily out the window at the feathery trees along Commonwealth Avenue. "A nice piece of property, that building."

Foster looked out the window too. "Building? What building?"

"Her palace. Mrs. Jack Gardner's palace on the Fenway."

"Oh, you mean the museum?" Foster was startled. "You mean, as a piece of real estate? Well, I suppose it is."

"If it should ever go on the market, with you on the board of trustees and all, our firm might have an inside track. What do you suppose the place is worth? I mean simply as a property, without its contents? Considered merely as a splendid shell to be turned into condominiums, perhaps, or luxury apartments?" The senior partner's voice was almost inaudible. His ethereal notions floated on the air, insubstantial, almost nonexistent.

"Well! I don't know." Foster tried to concentrate. What indeed would be the value of a Venetian palace, one of a kind, unique, complete with four stories of glorious rooms, a lofty glass-roofed courtyard, extensive greenhouses and a beautiful garden? He made a rapid calculation. "Twenty million, perhaps? Maybe more?"

"And our percentage of twenty million, Foster?" murmured the senior partner. "What would that be?"

"Well, I suppose it might be a million-eight? I mean," said Foster, badly flustered, "if we took our usual nine percent."

"One million, eight-hundred thousand? Good gracious, we could open a whole flock of offices on the North Shore

with one million, eight-hundred-thousand dollars, couldn't we, Foster?"

"Well, yes, I suppose we could."

"That is, of course, in the unlikely event the building should ever come on the market."

"Yes, yes, of course, but I doubt very much it could ever really happen."

"But if it did, Foster, if it did?"

The senior partner's words hung in the air, delicately suspended. When Foster left the room, they wafted out with him through the door and wreathed around his head as he sat at his desk—*But if it did? If it did?*

CHAPTER THIRTY

"TOM, YOU promised me. You said you'd never go back to the Red Rose."

"Oh, Jeez, that's right. Gawd, I dunno how it happened. I'm sorry, honest to Gawd."

"You can pull up right here," said Titus to the taxi driver. Manhandling Tom Duck out of the back seat, he held him upright while he fumbled in his pocket. "How much?"

"That'll be eighteen bucks, mister."

"Eighteen—but that's highway robbery."

"Listen, kid, my job don't normally include lifting no drunks off the sidewalk. I got bursitis, you know? Eighty dollars it cost me last time, not counting the cortisone. You want to make a formal complaint?"

"Oh, no, what the hell." Titus counted out eighteen dollars and handed it over.

"Gee, thanks for the big tip." The taxi pulled away with a squeal of tires, barely giving Titus time to drag Tom's big feet up on the sidewalk.

"Hey, Titus, honest to Gawd, you ought to see the pretty pitcher in Horry's bar. I mean it, Jesus, swear on a stacka bibles."

"Now, come on, Tom, pick up your feet."

"Honest, I'm telling you, I swear, there's this pretty pitcher. Huge, really stoo-pen-dous. Gawd."

"Can you manage the stairs? Come on, Tom, don't lean on me so hard."

"Listen, why dontcha go and see? Horry's Bar. Red Rose somep'n or other. I mean, my Gawd, you should see this pretty pitcher."

"Oh, sure, sure."

But Titus Moon would never have gone back to Horry McDandy's bar to see the pretty picture, if Tom hadn't let him down again the very next week.

"I thought I'd call you first thing," said Horry on the phone. "He just came in, but he looks bad, and you know as well as I do what will happen. He'll pass out."

"Oh, Lord, hang on. I'll be right there."

And there it was, on Horry McDandy's wall. A pretty picture, just as Tom had said. A really pretty picture. It looked so natural over the bar in the Red Rose that Titus didn't react at once. He saw it out of the corner of his eye as he looked around for Tom, and then he swung around and stared at it, transfixed.

Horry had mounted a light over the picture so that Europa's pink flesh glowed, and the rolling eye of the bull flashed lewdly, and the sea was opalescent like the inside of a shell. There it hung, the missing masterpiece, next to the suspended television set, on which a lackadaisical game with the Orioles was grinding on. The Red Sox had started the year in good form, but during the month of May they had lost almost every game. Today in Baltimore the pitcher was losing his grip, there had been three bases on balls, and the coach was strolling out to have a little talk on the mound. Horry McDandy's regular customers were reaching for their fourth refills, yelling jocularly above the gigantic noise of Stevie Wonder on the jukebox, and some of the younger guys were throwing darts and punching in their scores on the monitor screen.

Titus had to shout to make himself heard. "Hey, Horry, just a minute." Grabbing Tom Duck around the waist with one arm, he gestured with the other at the picture over the bar. "Listen, that's a new picture, right?"

"Oh, right." Horry beamed at it. "Brand new."

"Brand new? Where'd you get it?"

"Where'd I get it?" Horry was distracted by the baseball game. The pitcher had just thrown his fourth base on balls, bringing in the winning run for the Orioles. Everybody at the bar groaned and booed. "Guy I know," hollered Horry. "Antique dealer couple of doors down. Paid plenty

212

for it. I mean, you can tell, right? It's a really high-class piece of work."

"How much did you pay for it?" shouted Titus, still trying to collect his wits.

"Well, I don't mind telling you, it was plenty. Picture like that, they don't show up every day of the week. Twelve hundred dollars I forked over, matter of fact," said Horry proudly. It was clear that Horace J. McDandy was the kind of guy who was willing to pay for quality merchandise, for a genuine oil painting like this or a mink coat for his wife or a Caddie Eldorado.

It brimmed to Titus Moon's lips to tell Horry the truth about the painting, that it was worth hundreds of thousands of dollars. But that could wait. Horry would get his money back, and then some.

Hundreds of thousands of dollars? No, no, that was chicken feed. Titus corrected himself savagely. Titian's *Rape of Europa* was worth millions. Millions upon millions.

Titus lugged Tom Duck outside and deposited him in his double-parked car, then went back into the bar and took Horry McDandy aside. "Listen," he said with solemn emphasis, gripping Horry by the arms and shaking him. "I'll be back in a little while. In the meantime, whatever you do, don't leave the bar unattended, even for a minute or two. Stay here, understand? Don't move, do you hear me?"

"Well, okay," said Horry McDandy, mystified. "Right you are."

CHAPTER THIRTY-ONE

T HE RETURN of the Titian was accompanied by the same mixed reviews that had greeted the recovery of the Sargent portrait of Mrs. Gardner. A Titian in a saloon was almost as funny as a portrait in a ladies' rest room. There were more sneers than cheers. Titus soon found himself caricatured on the editorial page of the *Globe*. There he was in the cartoon, swilling beer in a sozzled condition under a picture of a girl on a bull, mumbling "Picture? What picture?"

But the cartoon didn't trouble him nearly as much as a letter in the paper the next day. It was signed by the curator of European painting at the Boston Museum of Fine Arts.

It has become evident that the Isabella Stewart Gardner Museum is a seriously troubled institution. Its difficulties would not call for public comment if national treasures were not involved. When all the principal works of art of a famous museum are rushed out-of-doors, helter-skelter, as they were a few weeks ago, when a painting precious to the city of Boston turns up in a filling station, and another of immense value to the world at large is discovered in a bar-room, one must surely begin to question the competence of the Gardner staff and its security department as guardians of the priceless works of art in their care.

Perhaps it is time to obey the wise provisions of Mrs. Gardner's will, to dismantle the museum entirely and entrust this glorious heritage to the care of other institutions better able to safeguard it for ages yet to come, for the wondering eyes of our children, for the reverence and awe of generations yet unborn.

Titus felt this attack keenly. Of course he knew that the author of the letter had an ax to grind. He remembered the way the man had looked longingly at the Titian on the day of the bomb scare. It was the curator's first year at the Boston Museum, and he was obviously trying to make a splash. He must be picturing how easily the entire contents of the Isabella Stewart Gardner Museum could be trundled down the Fenway into his own splendid galleries.

"What a snake in the grass," cried Polly Swallow, running into Titus's office with the newspaper in her hand.

"No," said Titus, trying to be fair, "he's probably persuaded himself that our collection just isn't safe. He really cares about pictures, I know he does."

But the insult rankled. Titus went downstairs and talked to Charlie Tibby. But Charlie was doing all he could. He had been working with Bleach on the Fatcat filling station problem, and Bleach was going up and down Huntington Avenue, talking to the people who occupied the buildings within sight of the filling station, looking for someone who might have seen a passerby carrying a package, a long flat package of the right size and shape to have been the portrait of Mrs. Gardner. So far, nobody remembered seeing such a person or such a package.

"And Homer's out there right now," said Charlie, "talking to the guy in the antique shop on Mass Ave. You know, the one where McDandy says he bought the Titian."

"Well, that should get us somewhere," said Titus hopefully.

*   *   *

But the owner of the antique shop was only another innocent bystander.

His name was Scotty Greep. Scotty stood in a narrow aisle between tippy stacks of dressers with swollen drawers and chairs with worn-out caning and framed photographs of deceased club women, and told Homer about the phone call.

"I don't know who the hell it was. Queer voice, like somebody was pretending to be a woman, you know? Only maybe it was a woman, I don't know, who knows? Do I want this picture, he says, or maybe she says. He don't want no money for it, he says, or she says, because it's cluttering up his attic, he says, he's moving and he don't have no room for it, so is it okay if he brings it around some day, so I says okay, and he hangs up, or maybe she hangs up, and next day when I come in, here's this big package leaning against the door, wrapped in newspaper. So I think, hey, you know, it's like a whatchamacallit, a windfall, and then I remember Horry's bar and his high ceiling, and I figure the picture will just fit, so I call Horry and he comes around and likes it fine, so I got a sale right away." The owner of the antique shop looked anxiously at Homer. "Hey, you won't say anything to Horry about me getting the picture for nothing? Like sometimes I sell stuff for less than I pay for it, just to get it out of the way. I mean, that picture was worth every penny of twelve hundred, right? I wasn't cheating him, right?"

"No, indeed," said Homer, gazing disconsolately around at the dark crowded interior of the antique shop, wondering what to ask Scotty next. When he couldn't think of anything, he went away dissatisfied, after refusing a terrific bargain on a secondhand Panasonic color television set in perfect working order, a Mediterranean-style console model.

In this last week of May, rain had fallen every day, tearing all the blossoms from the flowering trees in the Monk's Garden, bowing the thick stalks of the bulrushes in the Fens, making new gullies in Homer's steep driveway, dampening the spirits of city dwellers and suburbanites alike.

Homer despaired.

CHAPTER THIRTY-TWO

JOHN BODKIN'S spirits, however, continued to rise. The comic quality of the morning news did not depress him as it did Titus Moon. In fact he found the very damaging letter from the Boston Museum curator positively exhilarating. Surely, he told Gerard Fouchelle, it was time to call another meeting of the trustees and try his motion once again.

The two of them had been putting their heads together, running down the list of trustees, looking for another soft spot. After eliminating this one and that one, they had homed in on Fulton Hillside. And then Bodkin spent an evening talking to Hillside, explaining, cajoling, soliciting his vote. But Hillside merely looked at him with boiled eyes and promised nothing.

Therefore when Bodkin called a meeting of the trustees for the thirty-first of May, it was fifty-fifty in his mind whether or not he would pick up another supporter.

Trustees' meetings were easy for Catherine Rule. She merely had to rise from the chair in her tapestry repair studio and find her way to the gallery where the meeting was to be held on that particular day. But this time Catherine was late, because just as she put down her needle, someone burst into her workroom.

"Registered letter for Catherine Rule," said Aurora O'Doyle brightly, appearing at her side, a vision in creamy beige.

"Why, thank you, Phoebe," said Catherine, looking at the letter in surprise.

"My name is Aurora," said Aurora severely. "Sign here. The mailman's waiting downstairs."

Catherine signed, then put the letter aside and smiled at Aurora and picked up her needle and threaded it carefully with flesh-colored thread and began filling in the hand of the eunuch who was grasping the arm of Jezebel, and Aurora left, disappointed.

As soon as she was alone, Catherine opened the envelope and began to read. It was a long letter, accompanied by thick wads of reports and affidavits. She spent a full twenty minutes looking at it, reading it over three times very carefully. At last she stuffed it into her workbag and hurried downstairs to the trustees' meeting in the library.

"I'm *so* sorry to be late," she said, smiling at the rest of the trustees gathered around the table.

The meeting was already underway. Homer Kelly had finished his report on Bleach's failure to find a witness in the neighborhood of the filling station where the portrait of Mrs. Gardner had been deposited. Homer had also confessed his own lack of success in discovering who had delivered the Titian to the antique shop on Massachusetts Avenue.

As Catherine sat down, Titus Moon began to comment dreamily that perhaps the works of art themselves were conspiring against them. "I still hear music," he said. "It was the Terborch the other day, and this morning I'll swear I heard a toot from Cupid's horn, and Polly hears strumming from the harp in the Little Salon whenever she walks through the Short Gallery." Titus looked gravely at John Bodkin. "And, it's funny, I've often thought the building talks to itself. Have you ever noticed? I mean, think of the windows in the courtyard, the way they stare at each other across that big empty space. You'd think they'd have things to say to each other, after all those centuries of looking down on doges and ambassadors, princes and contessas, and, who knows? Stranglers and poisoners—all sorts of people must have floated past in gondolas, down there on the Grand Canal, including all those great north Italian painters—Giovanni Bellini, Giorgione, Carpaccio, Titian himself, not to mention Mrs. Jack Gardner on her way to the Palazzo Barbaro."

Catherine was enchanted. She clapped her hands. "Tintoretto, Tiepolo!"

"The Brownings," cried Edward Fallfold, getting into the spirit of the thing.

"Byron, Shelley," boomed Homer joyfully, "Anthony Trollope!"

"My grandfather visited Venice during his wanderjahr in 1877," said Shackleton Bowditch, overcome with sentimental nostalgia. Turning to Homer, he explained that it was this very same grandfather who had brought home a new kind of lily from Tibet.

"Well, you know what?" began Peggy Foley. "*My* grandfather—," but John Bodkin thundered at her, "STOP."

There was a sudden silence. Everyone looked at Bodkin. Slowly and methodically, he then began a recitation of everything that had gone wrong in the museum, from frogs to stolen paintings, from arson to murder. The list would have been tedious, if in its accumulated malevolence it had not sounded so deadly.

At the end he paused, and Catherine Rule wondered whether she should speak up and tell her news. She cleared her throat and pulled her chair forward, ready to begin. But John Bodkin in his domineering way ignored her, and repeated his earlier motion.

It was now somewhat expanded with eloquent coercive phrases.

Whereas the will of Mrs. Isabella Stewart Gardner calls for the dissolution of the museum in the event of a change in the general disposition of the works of art, and whereas the orderly conduct of the museum has been violently disturbed, and whereas the disturbance continues without check or abeyance in spite of all efforts to return the institution to stability, IT IS MOVED THAT THE MUSEUM BE DISMANTLED AND THE COLLECTION SOLD AT AUCTION.

"Second the motion," murmured Preston Carver.

John Bodkin glared around the table at Edward Fallfold, Catherine Rule, Peggy Foley, Preston Carver, Fulton Hillside, and Shackleton Bowditch. "All in favor?"

Homer winced. This time the vote was three in favor and four against. Fulton Hillside had joined the enemy. Homer watched as Bodkin, grinning with pleasure, reached across the table to clap Fulton on the shoulder.

Homer had a naturally suspicious nature. What, he wondered, was Hillside going to get out of all this? And Bodkin and Carver? He strongly suspected there were reasons greater than compliance with the terms of Mrs. Gardner's will and the safety of the works of art. Studying their strong-jawed Yankee faces, he told himself that bribery was inconceivable. Bribery, at least, of the ordinary low-down kind. What other sort of bribery was there? Could there possibly be corruption of a highly respectable nature, skulduggery of the most exquisite tastefulness, graft of a truly cathedral-like dignity?

The meeting was over. Catherine Rule rose from her chair hesitantly, wondering once again whether she should have spoken up. Perhaps it was just as well she hadn't. Her letter was too new, its contents too astonishing. She needed time to absorb it. She needed time to talk to the lawyers.

Then she would call a meeting of the trustees herself, and announce her decision.

Catherine went back upstairs and took up her needle and bowed gratefully over her familiar task. She was almost done. Her twelve years of work on the Jezebel tapestry were coming to an end.

Titus Moon was badly shaken by the dangerous closeness of the vote. Taking Homer Kelly by the arm, he pulled him around the corner into his office. "Good God, Homer," he said, his voice trembling, "one more vote on their side and the museum will be finished. The whole thing." Titus lifted his hands, including in his gesture all the sunlit spaces, the great galleries, the relics of Greece and Rome, the silent paintings hanging on the wall.

"Somebody's getting at those people," said Homer indignantly. "Somehow or other. I don't know how. What would they get out of the death of the museum? That's what I want to know."

"Oh, I suppose they're only performing their duty as they see it," said Titus Moon, leaning over backward as usual, trying to be fair. "There's no denying that Mrs. Gardner's will is very clear about what should be done in the event of a serious threat to the collection as it stands. But, you know, Homer, I'll bet that paragraph in her will was just her way of making a strong case for leaving things the way she had arranged them. *This is my palace,* she was saying. *And you'll damn well keep it exactly the way I left it.* She couldn't have wanted it to be dismantled and all her collection dispersed around the world. She couldn't really have meant it."

"No," agreed Homer, "I'm sure you're right. Where does her immortality go if everything is broken up? She wouldn't want the trustees to vote for the end of the Isabella Stewart Gardner Museum. Never." And then Homer groaned as he understood what Mrs. Gardner really wanted. He could feel her looking at him with that direct gaze of hers, telling him, ordering him, making her wishes known. *Find the troublemaker, Homer Kelly,* she was saying, speaking up clearly from the grave. *Shake up Tibby, prod Bleach, encourage Campbell. Do something. Do it NOW.*

Edward Fallfold never lingered to chat after a board meeting. None of the other trustees interested him in the least. It was true that Preston Carver had once attracted his attention, but when his mild advances had been rejected, Fallfold had given up on the whole company. Today he walked out-of-doors into the glory of a perfect May afternoon, congratulating himself on his restraint. So far he had been a follower, an inconspicuous follower. He would continue to be a follower, merely switching his allegiance to the other side. When would it be the right moment to tip the scales? All the letters he had written were ready to go; in fact in his eagerness, he had already mailed a few of them. The moment for changing sides was nearly at hand. Soon, very soon, he would vote with Bodkin.

Restraint was all very well, but Fallfold had endured enough of it for one day. And he was beginning to tire of young Robbie Crowlie. Plunging across the street, Fallfold thrust his way into the drenched tangle of tall reeds. Warm drops of water fell on his head, on his shoulders, releasing him from the lofty exaltation of purity and whiteness, bathing him in the moist blood heat of the dark red squares.

CHAPTER THIRTY-THREE

EVEN WITH his museum endangered by forces of destruction from within and without, Titus Moon kept to his routine of studying a single work of art every day. This afternoon he walked uncertainly through the Raphael Room into the Short Gallery and looked around. Then he remembered Michelangelo's drawing of the *Pietà*. Under the eye of guard Robbie Crowlie, Titus turned the folding panels carefully until he found the Michelangelo, then stood in front of it, gazing at it, his hand on the edge of the panel.

At once he was lost in the drawing, wandering in it as though the musculature of Christ's rib cage were the geography of some imaginary country. Absorbed, he drifted along the dead arms and traveled among the massive folds of the draperies, and climbed to the bowed head of Christ and the tragic upraised arms of the mother. Her eyes were lifted to heaven. Behind her rose part of the cross—the drawing had been cropped—inscribed with words from Dante's *Paradiso: nonuisipensa.quanto.sangu* . . . —*ye little think how great the cost in blood . . .*

Turning away, Titus gave Robbie Crowlie a melancholy smile, and then he walked upstairs to the third-floor corridor where the *Jezebel* tapestry was being rehung. Catherine had at last completed her twelve years of repair.

Perhaps, thought Titus sadly, she had finished the tapestry only just in time to see it hammered down on the auction block. But whatever its future destiny, there was to be a celebration tomorrow in Catherine's honor, auction or no auction. Already the catering crew was arranging tables in the Gothic Room, jingling the champagne glasses. Downstairs Polly Swallow was writing a poem. Somewhere Shackleton Bowditch was composing a speech.

"Oh, dear," said Catherine, glancing at Titus, "we've got it wrong somehow. See that long wrinkle? We'll have to take the whole thing down and try again."

"Right," said Titus. "Bring it down again, Buddy."

Patiently two men on ladders pulled the tapestry free

225

from the long lath on which it was mounted with hooked tape, then lifted it and attached it again with greater care. "There," said Titus, "that should do it."

"Oh, I'm so glad to see the whole thing at once," said Catherine, looking at it greedily as the ladders were removed. "I haven't seen all of it in a very long time."

"I wish we could hang it somewhere else," said Titus. "The glare from the windows on either side really kills it. I'm going to put a spotlight on it, Catherine, damned if I'm not."

"Oh, isn't it beautiful," cried Polly Swallow, running up the stairs. "Oh, aren't the colors bright! Poor Jezebel, she looks so frightened up there in the tower! Oh, how red the blood drops are!"

Catherine was worn-out. She sat down on the top step of the marble stairs. She had been up all night, doing over a tiny section of the tapestry at the place where she had begun to repair it twelve years before. The tension in the new threads hadn't been right—in those early days she didn't yet have a feeling for it. And last night it had troubled her, that little bunched place in the corner, so she had stayed up and worked until dawn.

It was five o'clock. The working day at the museum was over. The maintenance crew went away with its ladders and rubber hammers. Titus invited Polly and Catherine to his office for a drink, in honor of a job well done. "And I want to hear what's next on your docket, Catherine," he said, rummaging in his closet for the sherry.

"Well, a seventy-year-old woman ought to be forced to retire, I suppose. But the truth is, Titus, I've got my eye on *Esther and Ahasuerus.* It's full of little holes and clumsy patching. I'm itching to get my hands on it."

"Oh, Catherine," said Polly, "not another twelve years of work?"

226

"Twelve years? Well, I guess so." Catherine laughed merrily. "In twelve years I'll only be eighty-two."

When their drinks were finished, Titus offered to drive Catherine home. But of course she had her own car. She would get home by herself, she said.

She was utterly exhausted. But after saying good night to Polly and Titus, Catherine changed her mind about going home. She was overcome by a desire to see her finished tapestry again, to admire it alone, all by herself, to bask in it without anyone watching.

The guard on duty at the bottom of the stairs had left, but surely no one would mind if she spent a few minutes by herself on the third floor? Quickly Catherine began to climb the first of the two long stone staircases. Then she slowed down. Oh, she was tired. Her shoes hurt her feet. Six steps up, she sat down and took them off. There, that was better. But she was still worn-out. She had to hang on to the banister and haul herself up from step to step. Oh, but she was old, so old. Slowly and painstakingly, Catherine dragged herself up the first flight and walked soundlessly along the second-floor hallway.

But halfway up the second flight she could hear small sounds from the floor above. Someone was still there.

Catherine was disappointed. She had wanted to be alone with her tapestry. But she climbed on slowly in her stocking feet, then stopped cautiously and looked up through the marble balusters to see who it was.

Then she gasped and cried out. Someone was cutting the tapestry to ribbons.

Hearing her cry, he turned at once, his foot poised for an instant on the infinitesimal point where the light square met the dark, and then he reached down like one of Jehu's henchmen, grasped her like a helpless Jezebel, and threw her out the window into the courtyard three floors below.

V

THE TRIUMPH
OF TIME

Your grandeur passes, and your pageantry,
Your lordships pass, your kingdoms pass; and Time
Disposes wilfully of mortal things . . .
And fleeing thus, it turns the world around.

—PETRARCH

CHAPTER THIRTY-FOUR

"TIME," SAID the surgeon in the trauma unit of Brigham and Women's Hospital to Titus Moon, "it will take time. We'll have to wait and see. She's survived her first night. All we can think about now is keeping her alive. After that, it's a matter of slow recovery. The brain hemorrhage has paralyzed her right side. Her left arm is broken, but otherwise it's just a matter of scratches and severe bruises. Whether she'll recover her mental activity again or not, it's too soon to tell." He shook his head doubtfully. "When a woman seventy years old has a catastrophic accident—well, normally one doesn't hope for much."

It was Titus who had found her lying in the courtyard. After saying goodnight to Catherine and Polly he had worked in his office for a while, trying to catch up on his own additions to the new catalogue. But the sherry had made him thickheaded. He soon gave up and walked down the hall to tell the guard at the watch desk he was going home. And then he heard the mournful music from the courtyard.

"Good God," he said to Roger Wiseman, the night patrol foreman, "what's that?"

"What's what?" said Roger.

Titus ran into the west cloister and stopped to listen. There it was again, that wild half-savage keening, that agonized lament from the time of the creation of the world. It was streaming across the courtyard from the north side, rising and falling, half barbaric, half attuned to the profoundest human feeling. Swiftly Titus ran around the corner to the north cloister, as the voice of the singer rose again to a single eerie note, then slid down in anguished inquiry and faded away in bewildered torment, as though appalled at some inalterable and universal terror in the nature of things. *Ye little think how great the cost in blood.*

The singing faded away. There was only the monumental head of Apollo lying on the stone railing, just as always. But its lips were slightly parted, and its eyes stared upward toward the windows on the west side of the courtyard, as though witnessing some awful disaster.

And then Titus saw Catherine lying in the ground cover of baby's tears beside the potted geraniums.

At first he had only one thought, was she still alive? Bowing over her, horrorstricken, Titus detected a faint fibrillating pulse. He shouted for Roger, and Roger quickly called an ambulance. Then Polly Swallow emerged from somewhere, uttered a cry of distress, tore off her coat and

threw it over Catherine. When the ambulance came, she begged permission to go along.

The museum was soon swarming with policemen. Charlie Tibby came rushing back. It was Charlie who discovered the vandalized tapestry. With Campbell and Bleach, he groped around on the floor of the third-floor corridor, picking up fragments of cut thread. Homer Kelly drove in from Concord in a rage. All the guards who had been on duty in the late afternoon were called in and questioned. So were Roger Wiseman and Titus Moon. When Bleach and Campbell left at last, Titus sat down at his desk, reluctantly deciding he had to call John Bodkin. As president of the trustees, once again Bodkin had to be kept informed.

When the call came, John Bodkin was eating a light supper with his wife Beryl in the kitchen of the house on Marlborough Street. Titus Moon's message was a shock, and Bodkin gasped in dismay, as people do at such times. But as he put down the phone, other reactions sprang to the surface. Instantly he thought of the votes that might now tumble into his lap. He turned to his wife, his eyes shining with excitement, and told her the melancholy news.

At once Beryl burst into tears and rushed from the room. She was overreacting as usual, decided her husband, mildly irritated. But with Beryl out of earshot, he lost no time in calling Gerard Fouchelle.

"Three to three it will be now," he chortled into the phone, "at the very least, with Catherine in the hospital. And after such a disaster, who knows? We might even pick up all the rest of the trustees. Six to nothing, how would you like that?"

Then Bodkin called Bowditch, Carver, Hillside, Foley, and Fallfold, conveyed his terrible information, and interrupted their various expressions of grief, both real and

233

feigned, to announce another emergency meeting for the next morning.

Only then did he go looking for his wife. To his annoyance, Beryl was missing. She wasn't anywhere on the three floors of the tall house. At last he ventured into the basement, and there he found her. She was polishing her old bicycle in the dim light of a fifteen-watt bulb, her face streaked with tears.

"What on earth, Beryl Bodkin, are you doing down here in the dark?" he said testily, exasperated as always by another exhibition of unconventional behavior.

"Oh, I don't know," murmured Beryl. "I just thought I might take up bicycling again. Do you know if we have a bicycle pump anywhere? I mean, I've got this flat tire." And then Beryl drooped her head over the handlebars of the bicycle and sobbed aloud.

Next morning the trustees met once more in the Dutch Room. Soberly they sat around the Tuscan table under the eyes of Mary Tudor and Thomas Howard and Sir William Butts and Lady Butts and the young Rembrandt, and listened to Titus Moon's report on Catherine Rule's condition.

"It isn't good," he said. "I'm afraid that if she survives at all, she'll be—" He couldn't go on.

Around the table there were shocked sounds of distress. Peggy Foley wrenched her pocketbook this way and that, looking for a handkerchief. Shackleton Bowditch found his, and blew his nose. "My dear old friend," he said.

It wasn't until John Bodkin brought up yet once again his motion for the termination of the museum that Titus realized with a pang the additional significance of Catherine's absence. The vote for dismantling would now be brutally altered. "You can't vote on it today," he said angrily. "Surely you can wait until she comes back?"

234

"You just said," pointed out Edward Fallfold heartlessly, "that she's *not* coming back."

Titus sucked in his breath. Which side was Fallfold on? So far he had voted with Catherine and Bowditch and Foley. Was he now going to join the opposition?

John Bodkin picked up the sheet on which he had typed his carefully worded motion, read it aloud, then took another vote—and Titus breathed a sigh of relief. It was three to three. Fallfold had not yet deserted them. But Titus suspected that Fallfold's vote was a shaky thing. It was crucial but unpredictable, unsupported by eloquence or argument, as though he merely tossed a coin, careless which way it came down.

After the meeting, Titus went looking for Charlie Tibby. He found him in his basement office with Bleach and Homer Kelly. Charlie was glum, Bleach was pale and frustrated, Homer was enraged at his own stupidity and furious at Bleach and Tibby for not being cleverer than he was. "Catherine Rule was too precious to lose," he said, pacing back and forth in the crowded little office, waving his arms, "a pearl among women, a benefit to the human race. She's indispensable. Why didn't they push John Bodkin out the window instead? Or Fulton Hillside? Or Preston Carver? Or me, for that matter? You and me, Bleach! You too, Charlie! They could have pushed the three of us out the window, and who would ever grieve? We're washouts, the lot of us. We'd never be missed."

Charlie Tibby ignored Homer's raving, and explained to Titus what they had discovered so far. "Two big slits in the *Jezebel* tapestry. The notion is, somebody was beginning to cut it to pieces, and Catherine caught the person in the act, so she was tossed to her death, only please God it won't be her death. If she can only be restored to consciousness, she can tell us who did it. Right now, I gather, it's touch and go."

"What about the knife that was used on the tapestry?" said Titus. "I don't suppose it turned up anywhere?"

"Probably a pair of scissors," said Bleach dolefully. "A knife wouldn't have made such clean cuts. No, all we found were a couple of little heaps of thread on the floor, bits of the wool and silk the tapestry is made of."

"And her shoes," said Charlie. "Catherine's shoes were halfway up the stairs to the second floor. Nice and neat and side by side, as if she took them off and put them there herself on the way up."

Then Bleach went back to headquarters on Berkeley Street, and Homer galloped off to teach a class, and Titus took Charlie upstairs into the north cloister to look at the head of Apollo. "I didn't tell Bleach about this," Titus said, "because I knew it would sound sort of dumb. But, listen, Charlie, Apollo was singing, I swear he was. That's when I found Catherine. If it hadn't been for the singing, I wouldn't have come out here to listen. I would have gone out to my car and then she wouldn't have been discovered until the night guard went by. And the guard might have missed her. He might not have seen her at all."

"No kidding," said Charlie, obviously doubtful. Nevertheless he made a thorough search of the garden below the head of Apollo, and poked into the nooks and crannies in the capitals of the neighboring columns, and examined the deep recesses of the carved stone altar hanging on the north wall. He even peered into the yawning mouth of the stone gargoyle beside the altar. Then Charlie and Titus went back to the basement to explore the heating ducts under the floor, looking for an electronic device that might have released into the air the haunting strains of music Titus had heard with such passionate attention.

236

They found nothing, nothing at all. "But I heard it," insisted Titus.

"Well, if you say you did, you did," said Charlie.

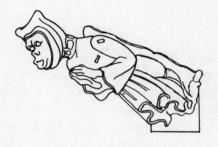

CHAPTER THIRTY-FIVE

BRIGHAM AND WOMEN'S Hospital was only a
few blocks from the Gardner Museum, in the great
complex of hospitals crowded together between
Brookline Avenue and Huntington. Homer Kelly quickly
got into the habit of dropping in on Catherine Rule whenever he went to the museum.

At first he merely sat beside her bed while she lay insen-
sible, recovering from the operation that had removed the
clot from the left side of her head. Her face was puffy and
swollen and suffused with blackened blood. There were
huge black patches on her limp right arm. The left arm was
enclosed in plaster. Even the fingers of her left hand had
individual casts. She had fallen on that arm, the doctor said,
and shattered all the brittle bones. Sitting beside the window, Homer read books and wrote letters to his wife.
Sometimes he found Titus Moon in Catherine's room, or
Peggy Foley, or Polly Swallow.

Polly had been hit especially hard by what had happened
to Catherine. Her cheerful optimism was sorely tried. Like
most middle-class American children she had been brought
up to believe that all was well around her, that nothing bad
could happen, nothing really bad, at least not to anyone she
knew. But now she feared she had not been told the truth.
This then was the truth, and not the other.

Catherine improved very slowly. Two weeks after she
was taken to the trauma unit, her swelling subsided, but not
until a month later did she become fully conscious, making

grating sounds in her throat, moving the toes of her left foot, opening her mouth to be fed. Her eyes had lost their piercing magic, but they saw Homer and Titus and Polly; they saw Shackleton Bowditch and Peggy Foley, and her visitors knew that the person inside the scarified outer flesh was something like the Catherine they had known before. When they spoke to her, she responded with the ghost of a smile on the left side of her face, and seemed to be listening with all her might.

"She'll be having speech therapy soon," said the head nurse to Polly and Homer. The head nurse's name was Judy Pringle. She was a large sensible young woman, the nurse manager in cardiac rehabilitation. "Physical therapy has already begun," she said, standing beside Catherine's bed, looking down comfortably at her charge.

"Will she be able to talk again?" said Polly. Then she glanced at Catherine, embarrassed, seeing Catherine's eyes swivel to the nurse, waiting for her answer. Perhaps she shouldn't have asked such a crucial question in front of Catherine.

"That's what they'll be working on," said the nurse calmly. "It may take a while. But she looks pretty eager, if you ask me."

"May we ask her questions?" said Homer. "Could we ask her to nod once for yes and twice for no? Would that be all right?"

"Well, you can try it," said the nurse. "Did you hear that, Miss Rule?"

Catherine's head wobbled. Was she nodding?

"Catherine, do you know who attacked you?" said Homer softly.

Catherine closed her eyes. They could see her struggling. Her head fell back, then dropped to the side.

"I think it's too soon," said Judy Pringle. "Miss Rule,

239

could you blink your eyes for yes and no? Once for yes, twice for no?"

Homer repeated his question, but blinking didn't work either. Nor could Catherine command her eyes to look left and right to answer yes-or-no questions. No part of her body was under her control. Homer despaired, picturing the tangle of severed neurons in her head, flailing around in the dark. "It's all right," he said. "Don't worry. You'll be better soon."

"Better leave now," said Judy Pringle. "I think she's had enough for one day."

Next morning Catherine had another visitor. As he came within the sphere of her vision she recognized him at once with a jump of her heart. Almost without thinking, she knew what to do. When he moved to the foot of the bed she gazed vacantly past him at the far wall, dropping her lower jaw, letting her tongue loll.

He was staring at her, frowning with concentration. "Catherine?" he said.

She made no sign that she had heard. Her heart beat painfully. She was relieved when a junior nurse came in with a tray of pills in little paper cups. "Miss Rule?" said the nurse.

Catherine continued to stare blankly at the wall.

The nurse turned to Catherine's visitor. "This *is* Catherine Rule, isn't it? I'm new. This is my first time on this floor."

"Oh, yes, it's Catherine Rule."

"Miss Rule," said the little nurse loudly, "time to take your pill." She put down the tray on the table beside the bed, tugged Catherine up against her pillows, then picked up a glass of water and a pill from one of the paper cups.

Catherine's tongue still drooped. She gazed dreamily through the nurse, as the pill was put on her tongue and the glass of water lifted to her lips. "Swallow, Miss Rule," said the nurse.

But Catherine stupidly let the pill roll off onto the blanket.

"Oh, dear," said the nurse.

"Well, I'll be going now," said the visitor cheerfully, and he made a swift exit, congratulating himself on Catherine's total mental degeneration. The woman was a vegetable, she was utterly senile.

But as soon as the sound of his footsteps faded, Catherine looked merrily at the nurse and opened her mouth in a way that meant *try again.*

"Well, now, that's better," said the nurse, as Catherine swallowed the pill. "What was that all about anyway?"

And Catherine smiled a lopsided conspiratorial smile.

That afternoon Homer Kelly came upon Edward Fallfold in the Veronese Room. Fallfold was gazing at a painting by Tiepolo, an oil sketch of *The Wedding of Barbarossa.*

He hardly seemed aware that Homer was coming up behind him, but he began talking right away. "Look at it," he said, still gazing, "look at the shimmer of the white satin, the big patch of red, the massing of those huge lumps of clothing, the focusing of the light."

"Oh, right," said Homer, peering at the picture. "I see what you mean. Huge lumps of color, right, right." For the first time in his life it dawned on Homer that there might be more to a picture than its subject matter. "Say, that's really nice."

"Nice?" Fallfold turned and looked at him sharply.

"What you said." Homer gave Fallfold a wide delighted grin. Fallfold promptly misinterpreted it, and Homer had to back away in confusion. "Oh, sorry," he said, "I've got to rush off now. Student conference in Cambridge. Sorry, sorry."

But on the way downstairs, Homer had to resist a temptation to run around the galleries and look at all the pictures in this fresh new way. It was thrilling. What a teacher Fallfold would have made!

This chance encounter was the beginning of a new interest in Fallfold on Homer's part. After all, the man was a fascinating and promising enigma—Fallfold, the oddity among the trustees. Was it not possible that he possessed a key that would let him into the museum any time at all? Charlie Tibby had deprived all the trustees of their keys, but he had not changed the locks. Fallfold could easily have had his key copied before turning it in. And might he not harbor a grudge against the institution whose trustees had failed to hire him as director? And, with the exception of Catherine Rule herself, was he not the only trustee with the scholarly understanding to perpetrate witty practical jokes among the masterpieces?

To all of these questions the answer was yes. And there was something else—Fallfold's peculiar way of looking at people, or rather his way of *not* looking at people.

Homer was interested in the study of criminal physiognomy. In his opinion it was a sadly neglected science. He himself had classified a few archetypes. The popular imagination was, as usual, wrong. No common felon ever exhibited the lip-curling snarl of the fictional villain, or uttered his hideous laughter. Most murderers merely looked at you blankly, like bank clerks or notary publics. There was also the insolent stare of the juvenile delinquent, the glassy-eyed dreamy expression of the drug addict, the gaunt ravaged look of the alcoholic.

Fallfold wasn't like any of these. It was his singular manner of allowing his gaze to drift away that interested

242

Homer, or rather—Homer looked for the right word—to *float* away as though buoyed on a sea of egocentrism. Perhaps Fallfold indulged in that psychotic concentration upon himself that was a genuinely criminal tendency, a kind of solipsism, a disbelief in the existence of other people.

And then there was the fact that Larry W. Oversole of Fatcat Enterprises had handed Fallfold his gold card, explaining that the Gardner Museum was a promising site for real estate speculation, and Fallfold had not repulsed him altogether. *I could tell he was interested,* Oversole had said.

It was a tiny fact, a microscopic fact, but it added up nicely with all the rest.

Thus Homer began to draw nearer to Edward Fallfold. Like mathematical asymptotes, the two approached closer and closer. In obedience to this new gravitational principle, Homer went back again to the thick file of recorded interviews Tibby had collected with all the guards, with the night patrol, with every member of the staff, with the director and the seven trustees.

And at once, examining Fallfold's responses to Tibby's questions, Homer made a promising discovery—how could they have missed it? Fallfold's alibi for the time during which Catherine Rule had been attacked relied on the supporting testimony of the young guard called Robbie Crowlie. Fallfold had walked with Robbie in the park across the street, he said, from four-thirty that afternoon until suppertime.

Homer flipped the pages and looked at Crowlie's record. It was the same as Fallfold's. Yes, Robbie said, he had been with Fallfold from the time that he, Robbie, left work at four-fifteen until the two parted company around six o'clock.

"Right," said Charlie Tibby. "I remember now. It was those damned bulrushes again. You know Fallfold, he answers the call of the jungle." And then Charlie made a Tarzan-like whinnying noise, and laughed. "It's no crime, after all."

"But they backed each other up once before, remember? The night the Titian was stolen."

Charlie sobered. "That's right. So they did. Well, for Christ's sake, we'd better look into it."

But before they could probe deeper into the coincidence of interlocking alibis, they were thrown seriously offcourse. Like asymptotes, Fallfold and Homer Kelly had been approaching one another more and more closely. But now, like asymptotes, they seemed destined never to meet.

It was Homer's own fault. He thought of a new way of getting information from Catherine Rule. Surely this time she would reveal the name of her attacker. It was perfectly simple. Since Catherine could open her mouth to be fed, she could open it to mean "yes," she could close it to mean "no."

In the company of Charlie Tibby, Homer went back to the hospital and explained the system to Catherine. Then Charlie sat down on Catherine's bed and leaned toward her intently. "Was it a stranger who attacked you, or was it someone you knew? Just open your mouth, Catherine, if it was someone you knew."

Catherine was stunned. Her moment had come, and it was so important. What was she to do? She must open her mouth! But she couldn't. Catherine's jaw was clamped shut. "Mmmmmm, mmmmm," she said through clenched teeth.

At last her mouth flew open, but Charlie had already asked another question. "Then it was a stranger?"

Catherine's eyes filled with tears. She wanted to shake her head, to close her mouth, to say no. "Uuuuuhhhh," she moaned.

But they misunderstood. They got it wrong. "A stranger then," said Homer Kelly sadly. "Too bad."

And then they went away, leaving Catherine frustrated and furious. "Here now," said the nurse who came in to take her pulse and temperature, "your pulse is way up. What got you so excited?"

But Catherine could only murmur, "Mmmmmmm, mmmmmm," while angry tears rolled down her cheeks.

CHAPTER THIRTY-SIX

J OHN BODKIN was planning a dinner party. It was going to be a rather heavy-handed party. The guests, he told his wife, would be Shackleton Bowditch, Peggy Foley, and Edward Fallfold.

"Really, John," said Beryl timidly, "don't you think they'll know perfectly well why they've been invited to dinner?"

"Purely social occasion, purely social," insisted Bodkin. "Tell you what, I'll ask Homer Kelly too."

"Oh, John," said Beryl, greatly daring, "I know you want to persuade them to vote to bring an end to the museum, but I hope—I hope they persuade you to change your mind instead."

Her husband turned huffy. John Bodkin reminded his wife that it was he, not she, who was a member of the board of trustees of the Isabella Stewart Gardner Museum. He, not she, was burdened with the responsibility of determining what would be the desire of Mrs. Gardner in appalling times like these. So if Beryl would kindly keep her nose out of his affairs, he would be grateful.

Beryl tightened her lips and remained silent. Dutifully she went to the kitchen and took down her file of recipes for company. But she couldn't keep her mind on the job. From the kitchen window she watched a young girl ride past the house on a ten-speed bicycle. The girl had a pack on her back, she had long streaming hair, she was wearing a pair of ragged jeans. Oh, where was she going? She looked so wild and free!

All the guests accepted John Bodkin's invitation, and all of them arrived promptly on the evening of the dinner party. Bodkin greeted them at the door, heartily the welcoming host, while Beryl was still in her apron, flustered, her hair awry. Peggy Foley promptly followed Beryl back into the kitchen to help out, while Bodkin handed out the drinks and led the men into the book room to admire his collection of early printed editions.

"I don't like to brag," he bragged, "but it's a fact that I'm making something of a name for myself as a collector of early editions of Dante's *Divine Comedy*. Of course none of mine is as fine as Mrs. Gardner's, but I think I can truthfully say this one is rather splendid. My father swept it right out from under the nose of the monks at Monte Cassino during the war. After the destruction of the abbey there was a period of confusion, and he got it for almost nothing."

"Is that so?" murmured Homer Kelly, looking at the book over Bodkin's shoulder, interested as always in other people's criminal obsessions.

"Early product of the printing press, I gather?" said Shackleton Bowditch. Shackleton was a voracious reader, but he was content with secondhand paperbacks in a condition of near-disintegration.

But Edward Fallfold was a different sort of book lover. Taking the Monte Cassino Dante carefully from Bodkin, he turned to the first page of the *Inferno,* and translated reverently, *"I woke to find myself in a dark wood."*

"Very pretty, Fallfold," said Bodkin. "I don't read Latin myself. Never tried. Damned dead language."

Homer blushed for Bodkin, who didn't know that his splendid edition of the *Divina Commedia* had been written in Italian, not Latin. He glanced at Fallfold, who was closing his eyes as if in physical pain. *"They see as they are worthy,"* Fallfold said peevishly, quoting Dante again, and Homer snickered.

"What's that?" said Bodkin, guessing he had been insulted, but Beryl and Peggy came in to announce dinner, and the moment passed.

The roast beef was delicious. Beryl smiled with relief as it was praised, and pushed back strands of damp hair. They all ate their portions gratefully, with the exception of Bodkin, who kept up a running fire of argument on the subject of Isabella Stewart Gardner's last will and testament. Beryl's shy attempts to change the subject were promptly squashed. Even the jocular interruptions of the irrepressible Homer Kelly were ignored. Homer gave up, and passed his plate for seconds.

After dinner, Beryl made one more try at asserting herself, urging her husband to serve coffee in the living room rather than in his private den. When she failed, she ran into the kitchen for the coffeepot and lingered as long as she could, because she hated the den with all her heart.

As always, the guests were taken by surprise. "Oh," squealed Peggy Foley, gazing at the object in the middle of the room, "what's that?"

"Good God," said Shackleton Bowditch.

Homer Kelly laughed out loud, then stopped abruptly as he saw the wince of torment on the face of Fallfold.

In the center of the room rose a towering monument of galvanized iron trash cans, reaching to the ceiling.

Bodkin laughed with satisfaction. "Budgie's latest. You know Budgie? All the rage in New York. Trash cans are his thing."

"Hey," said Homer, "watch it. It's about to go over."

"Ha, ha, that's the game, you see. Actually they're full of cement. But it gives the illusion, you see, of insecurity. Metaphor, right? For our throw-away culture. Trash, all trash, ready to go over any second. Budgie has this sort of really marvelous contempt. Cosmic disdain, that's what they call it in New York."

"But how does he get it to teeter like that?" said Homer warily. "I mean, every time you get near, it seems about to fall on you."

"Oh, that's his genius. Don't ask me how he does it. It's supposed to make you feel uneasy, right?"

"Well, it succeeds very well," said Shackleton Bowditch solemnly.

"If that's art," said Peggy Foley firmly, "I don't want anything to do with it."

Beryl Bodkin set down the coffee tray on the table in front of the sofa, and told herself to go out first thing in the morning and buy a bicycle pump.

CHAPTER THIRTY-SEVEN

I T WAS a fine day in late June when the trustees met once again in the Dutch Room and voted to close down the museum forever. After the vote had been taken, Titus Moon left the Dutch Room and went back to his office and sat down at his desk. Beside him the south window dropped sunlight on the floor, where it flickered in yellow nickels and dimes among the moving shadows of the leaves of the magnolia tree outside. Titus stared at the fluttering images and knew that before long he would never see them again. The magnolia trees and the garden and the galleries in all their splendor would be lost—to him, at any rate, and to everyone else in the city of Boston.

The vote had been four to dismantle, two to preserve. Bodkin had won. Somehow he had persuaded Edward Fallfold to vote on his side. Why had Fallfold changed his mind? Once again the man had offered no arguments, no explanations. It was as though he merely tossed his mental coin, and watched it come down tails instead of heads.

Homer Kelly had also been present at the meeting. He had watched in stunned silence as Edward Fallfold joined Bodkin, Hillside, and Carver to vote for the dissolution of the museum, against the losing votes of Foley and Bowditch. And then, almost at once, the same majority prevailed for Bodkin's hasty motion that the auction should take place in the museum on the twenty-first of September under the auspices of Gerard Fouchelle, president of Fouchelle et Fils of Paris, London, New York, and Boston.

Afterward Homer sat immobile in his chair as Titus Moon hurried away without a word, while the other trustees stood up solemnly, shuffling their papers, preparing to depart.

And therefore Homer saw something Titus missed.

He saw Edward Fallfold move away from the long Tuscan table in the company of Fulton Hillside. He saw him lean over Hillside and hand him something.

Homer stood up and craned his neck. Hillside was staring at the thing in his hand, a little piece of glittering cardboard. He was nodding his head.

Homer made the connection at once. It was the gold business card of that investment-properties creep, that health-club degenerate, that luxury-office-suites bullyboy, Larry W. Oversole of Fatcat Enterprises. On the day when Homer had spent a few minutes in his office, Oversole had told Homer he had given one of his cards to Fallfold. And now Fallfold was passing the same card along to Hillside.

Wasn't Hillside himself some kind of real estate and investment-properties ratfink? Then what did it mean, this newly forged little link? Something sinister, Homer had no doubt. Something of a catastrophic nature. He could hear the clap of final doom, the raucous blare of the last trump. An eschatological pall fell over Homer, a sense of final things. The world was in convulsion, it was the end of time. With a colossal reverberating shiver and thunder, the dead were throwing back the lids of their tombs and rising for the judgment. No, no—Homer corrected himself—in the case of the Gardner Museum, the judgment had already occurred. In the monumental scales of justice the museum had been teetering and wobbling, and now it had plummeted with the rest of the damned into the abyss of hell, where grinning little Fatcat devils would prod it and poke it with their sharp little forks for the rest of eternity.

251

Homer walked across the floor, treading on hot coals. At the top of the stairs he caught up with Shackleton Bowditch.

"This is indeed a sad day," said Shackleton, looking at Homer from under his great gloomy eyebrows.

Homer glanced down the stairs and saw Peggy Foley hurry toward the door, dabbing at her eyes. Edward Fallfold and Fulton Hillside were going their separate ways, but Homer could see a glint of gold as Hillside thrust Oversole's card carefully into his pocket.

Homer looked back at Shackleton. "What do you think made Fallfold change his mind?"

"Maybe," said Shackleton Bowditch, "it has something to do with his sexual preferences."

Homer was astonished, the phrase sounded so odd on the lips of an elderly man like Shackleton Bowditch. "His sexual preferences? You mean people who prefer the company of their own sex are less dependable than the rest of us? Surely you don't mean that?"

"No, I don't mean that at all. I mean we're more used to finding ourselves in exposed positions, more accustomed to taking the blame."

"We? You mean, you too—?"

"I happen," said Bowditch, with enormous dignity, "to be of the same persuasion."

"But I think Fallfold's vote today was absolutely craven," said Homer.

"On the contrary. It may have been an act of courage." Shackleton nodded gravely at Homer, walked out of the museum, and stalked south to Huntington Avenue and the Green Line, intending to spend the rest of the afternoon with his stamp collection.

Homer went looking for Titus Moon. He found him in his office, looking out the window.

Titus turned his pale face to Homer, and spoke as if he

252

couldn't believe it. "It's all going on the auction block, Homer, all of this, the whole blessed thing. It's the end, the end of everything."

Homer felt sickeningly responsible. After all, if he had done his job, the end might never have come. "It means the murdering bastard has won, whoever it is. We haven't been able to track him down, and now he's driven the museum right over the brink. Why the hell? Why in the name of *Christ* would anybody want to do that?"

"I don't know, Homer. It doesn't matter now. It's all over. Oh, by the way, you should be congratulating me. September twenty-first is my wedding day. Aurora and I are going to be married on September twenty-first. She's just sent out the invitations." Titus Moon's voice was hollow. "Big coincidence. We'll have to share the building with the auction, because Aurora's arranging a big ceremony in the courtyard, by special permission of the trustees."

Homer was staggered. He had met Aurora O'Doyle, flouncing around the museum in her sharp little heels, *crash, crash, crash,* and he had stepped aside and given her free passage. Homer was dumb about a lot of things, but not about women—unlike poor Titus Moon. "Well, ha ha," said Homer with forced enthusiasm, "how nice. At least something will be starting while the rest of the world is ending. Good for you. What are you going to do for a living after the museum closes down?"

"Oh, I'll be okay. Aurora can probably get me a job in some little art firm in New York. She knows a lot of people there. Pretty soon I'll be selling contemporary artists like Budgie. You ought to see Budgie's work, Homer. He's a specialist in trash cans, big international superstar."

"I know," said Homer gravely. "I saw."

"And who's that guy who drops clothing on the floor in piles? Another genius. And then there's that other guy

253

who stacks rolled-up rugs around a gallery. He's my favorite."

Titus's sarcasm was terrible to hear, worse than groans, worse than tears. Homer said goodbye, then called his wife. "For God's sake, Mary, come home."

"But what made Fallfold change his mind?" said Gerard Fouchelle, shouting into the transatlantic line, grinning at his secretary on the other side of the Louis Quinze table in the central offices of Fouchelle et Fils in Paris. Fouchelle had come home to the Boulevard Saint Germain to carry on the affairs of his business until such time as John Bodkin should call him back to Boston. That moment had apparently come. The connection was poor, but across three thousand miles of windswept ocean, Fouchelle got the gist of Bodkin's good news. "How did you persuade him?"

"It wasn't my doing," said Bodkin. His voice was thin and faint, but unmistakably triumphant. "I told you, the man's inscrutable. I couldn't move him an inch. I gave up trying. Then this morning he suggested we vote again, and to my flabbergasted amazement, he came down on the right side. Moon didn't like it. Neither did Bowditch and Foley, naturally. But the die is cast. Of course I moved right in with my suggestion about your firm, and they were too stunned to argue, so that's all right, and I suggested a date, and they bought that too, September twenty-first. Will that give you people time to—"

Fouchelle uttered an exclamation in French, then collected himself. "Oh, but of course. But the catalogue, how will we get out the catalogue in time? We've got to list all those thousands of separate items, *mon Dieu.*"

But Bodkin made consoling noises. "The catalogue? Ah, I see, of course, you'll need a catalogue. Well, don't worry, I think I can help you out on the little problem of the catalogue. When are you coming over?"

"*Immediatement. Ce soir.* Tonight."

CHAPTER THIRTY-EIGHT

FOR POLLY SWALLOW as for Homer Kelly it was a double blow, the fatal vote of the trustees and Titus Moon's approaching marriage to Aurora O'Doyle.

When Peggy Foley told her the awful truth about the museum, Polly couldn't realize it for a minute. Numbly she watched Mrs. Foley hurry tearfully away, and then she looked back at the paragraph in her notebook where she had been stopped in mid-sentence. Polly had been writing about one of Guardi's views of Venice—*the antic sweep of cloak and flapping tent.* Picking up her pencil, she stared at the sentence, wondering how she had meant to finish it. Then with an awful wrench, she thought, *It doesn't matter. There isn't going to be a catalogue anyway.* Dismayed, she pushed back her chair and ran into Titus Moon's office.

"There won't be a catalogue," said Polly, choking. "It's all over. The Gardner Museum, it's all finished. And so is the catalogue. No one needs it!" She banged her fist on the huge file box on Titus Moon's desk, so chockful of her typed cards of descriptions, of new information, of the results of her eager researches. "All wasted. It's no use to anyone."

Titus looked up at her, his face paler than usual, his hair more violently red. Then he stood up and wrapped his arms around her. "I'm awfully sorry," he said, holding her tighter, murmuring meaningless syllables into her ear.

His embrace was lovely, it was warm and enchanting. Polly wanted to kiss him and be kissed, but when he let go, she backed away, not knowing where to look. Her eyes were glittering. They felt enormous, like the eyes of lions.

"I'm going to get married," said Titus desperately, shuffling the papers on his desk.

"You are?" said Polly, trying to conceal her dismay, utterly crushed. "Well! Listen," she went on, babbling too fast, "you don't need me here anymore. I mean, you hired me to do the catalogue, and there isn't going to be any catalogue, so—"

"You've got to stay," said Titus, looking at her in anguished appeal. "You can't leave. The people who believe in this place have got to keep going until the end. Please, Polly, we've got to keep the bloodsuckers at bay, at least until it's all over."

"I know what I'll do," said Polly, brightening. "I'll work on Catherine's tapestry. I've been repairing it during my lunch hour. Now maybe I can finish it by the time she's out of the hospital."

"Good, that's wonderful," said Titus humbly.

Then Aurora O'Doyle came in with samples of monogrammed wedding napkins and pictures of wedding cakes. Aurora obviously hadn't heard the news about the vote of the trustees. But if Titus told her about it after Polly left, Aurora was not laid low by the news. Polly saw her later, showing the cake pictures to Betty Gore, the supervisor of the café. "I can see this one in the Chinese Loggia, can't you? You know, we'll set up a table there and the cake will be silhouetted against the windows. It's going to be the most beautiful wedding in the world. Don't you just love the Della Robbia wreath on top? It's all sugar. No, honestly, it's true, they do all those little peaches and pears in pure sugar."

Before Polly went home to her Cambridgeport apartment, she stopped in once again at the hospital. This time

257

she must be very careful, she knew that. She mustn't say anything to Catherine about the meeting of the trustees. She mustn't let anything slip about their terrible vote to dismantle the museum. The truth might be too painful for Catherine to endure, now that she was so ill.

Polly thought sadly of the future auctioning of Catherine's tapestries, all those elaborate woven patterns she had worked on with such care and patience over the years. No, Catherine mustn't hear about the auction.

So instead Polly talked about her own work on the vandalized *Jezebel* tapestry. "It's easy," she said to Catherine. "It's just straight cuts. It's like mending a stocking."

But Catherine didn't seem interested in the tapestry. With her keen intuition she apparently sensed that something else was wrong. "Mmmmmm?" she said, trying to lift her head from the pillow. "Mmmmmm? Mmmmmm?"

Homer Kelly came in then, tearing off his jacket. "Hot," he said. It had been a week since his last visit. Immediately he sensed a difference in Catherine, a new alertness. She was looking at him sharply. Her eyes were wide open. She was staring at him with that old skewering glance that struck to the bone. Homer felt the universe teetering, resting uneasily on its fulcrum, while she examined it in the light of history and the chief end of man. Since this extraordinary emanation was normal for Catherine Rule, he was delighted to witness it again.

"I've been telling her about the *Jezebel* tapestry," said Polly. "I've started to repair it. It's going to be good as new." Polly looked meaningfully at Homer, conveying some message she couldn't say aloud. Homer understood at once. *Don't tell her,* that was what she meant. *Don't tell her about the vote. Don't tell her the museum is going under. Don't tell her the vultures are gathering.*

"Mmmmmm? Mmmmmm?" said Catherine again. It

258

was a question, an urgent question, and this time they both knew what she was trying to say. Had the trustees met again? Had they voted? Without her presence on the side of the angels, had the vote gone the wrong way?

Both of them professed not to understand. Homer talked heartily about a nutty thing he'd seen on the Milldam the other day, and then he ranted and railed about the abominable behavior of the administration in Washington, and Polly talked breezily about Aurora's approaching marriage to Titus, taking a melancholy pleasure in the spasm of distress that convulsed Catherine's face.

Then once again Catherine raised her crucial question, straining her throat to say hoarsely, "Mmmmmm? Mmmmmm?" She looked at each of them in turn with her piercing gaze, then lifted her eyes to the ceiling in despair.

She wanted to know what was happening. She was desperate to know.

When the therapist came in, Polly kissed Catherine and went away. Homer stayed to watch Catherine's impassioned determination turn eagerly in a new direction. Lying motionless and speechless on her back, yet she pulsed with ardent interest. At the therapist's direction she worked the fingers of her paralyzed right hand, and moved her fragile feet in little arcs, and tried to say consonants, attempting a *B* and a *D*, failing, closing her eyes in anger at herself, trying again.

Homer had to leave too. His wife was coming home at last, and before she arrived, he had to do something about the disorder in the kitchen, where muck and grime had crept outward from the walls and something putrid was spoiling in the refrigerator. Patting the slight promontory that was Catherine's left knee, he winked at her and said goodbye.

The therapist was encouraging. "Don't you worry," she

259

said to Catherine. "You're doing fine. I'm going to get your speech back, if it's the last thing I do. Now, you know what happens next? You're going for a ride to the patient lounge."

The therapist disappeared, but pretty soon a husky young orderly came in and transferred Catherine expertly from the bed to a wheelchair, then rolled her down the hall and around the curving corridor to a big open room.

The patient lounge was furnished with brightly upholstered sofas and chairs. A row of wheelchairs was stored against the wall. "Okay now?" he said, bending over her. Then he introduced Catherine to another patient, Betty Fawcett, and left them alone together.

Betty Fawcett was a spastic woman whose head and arms were in constant motion. She was sitting on a sofa, wearing a flowered smock and slippers. "Hello, there, Cath' Rule," she said, looking in a friendly way at Catherine, hurling her right arm over her head in greeting.

"Mmmmmm," said Catherine cordially.

"How're you?" said Betty, rolling her head, throwing up her feet and rocking backward.

"Mmmmmm," said Catherine, nodding her head slightly, smiling at Betty, pleased to find that the two of them were enjoying an exchange of a sort, a genuine human exchange.

She watched, fascinated, as the other woman began a new series of mad flailings. Betty was trying to take things out of the pocket of her smock. One by one she extracted a package of cigarettes, a folder of matches, and a tin ashtray. "Not s'posed to," said Betty, giggling and hiccuping, throwing up one arm at the NO SMOKING sign on the wall. Next there was a long struggle with the matches, as Betty tried to light the cigarette clenched in her teeth. Before she accomplished it, she had singed her nose, burned a hole in her smock, blackened her glasses, and set her hair on fire.

"Mmmmmmuh!" warned Catherine, as the smoke curled up from Betty's frowzy head.

But Betty only laughed and pawed at her scalp until the smoke stopped. Then she enjoyed her cigarette, getting the wrong end in her mouth half the time, sprinkling ashes on the floor, grinning at Catherine in raffish satisfaction, choking and laughing and coughing. When a nurse came in and scolded her and took her cigarette away and confiscated the rest of the pack, Betty only laughed some more. It was obviously the joy of her life to defy the rules, to be outrageous rather than docile. After all, thought Catherine, what good did it do to be docile? No fun in that.

When the nurse went away, Betty was restless. Her face fell. She was obviously looking for new worlds to conquer. Catherine thought of something. She fixed her eyes on a newspaper lying on the low table between them, then glanced up at Betty, looked back at the newspaper meaningfully, and made her questioning noise, "Mmmmmm?"

Betty Fawcett was used to inarticulate signals. She caught Catherine's wish right away. "Jussa minute," she said, beginning a deliberate attack on the project. First she flung out her right arm, but it missed the table. Then she tried the left, but it went astray. At last she stood up and wobbled around the table and reached down and picked up the newspaper between finger and thumb, waved it spasmodically in the air, and tossed it high. By some miracle it landed in Catherine's lap.

Catherine was delighted. She smiled lopsidedly at her companion, who was whooping with rapture, said thank you with another "Mmmmmm," then dropped her eyes greedily to the newspaper, which lay folded on her lap, upside down.

There was a big headline at the bottom of the page—

SIKHS RIOT
IN PUNJAB

It took Catherine a little while to decide that there was some sort of trouble in India. Then she turned her attention to an upside-down headline in another column—

GARDNER AUCTION
SEPTEMBER 21

The paper slipped from Catherine's lap, and her eyes filled with tears.

"Ooh, whassa matter?" said her new friend, throwing herself forward in her chair.

"Nnaaah-hah," said Catherine, sobbing.

"Oh, too bad. I'm sorry. Don't cry."

CHAPTER THIRTY-NINE

G ERARD FOUCHELLE was no longer a lurking
presence behind the scenes at the Gardner Museum. He was front and center. His minions from

the Paris office of Fouchelle et Fils were everywhere. There were experts in the art of the Italian Renaissance, in classical sculpture, in the Gothic painting and sculpture of northern Europe, in European painting of the sixteenth and seventeenth centuries, in furniture and decorative art, in rare books, in the art of Islam and the Orient. They were soon buzzing around the museum in twos and threes, whispering among themselves.

The news of the coming auction spread like wildfire from Boston to New York to Texas, from Paris to London to Berlin. Curators from museums all over the world came flying to Boston to examine for themselves the treasure trove that was about to appear all at once on the market, as though a pirate ship had risen from the bottom of the sea overflowing with emeralds and pearls. Slowly they wandered through the galleries of the Gardner Museum, standing for hours in front of single works of art, stroking their chins, walking up close with magnifying glasses, consulting the old museum catalogues, pointing out to each other places where the paint had been abraded or wormholes filled in, taking note of losses of original pigment or overpainting by later hands or discolored layers of varnish.

But the masterpieces were masterpieces still, and the museum directors and experts and representatives of wealthy collectors grew thicker on the floor. They spoke in English and French, in German and Italian and Spanish, in Korean and Chinese and Japanese, in unrecognizable tongues from remote exotic cities.

All the great museums of the world were sending deputations. There were delegates from the Metropolitan in New York and the Kimball Museum in Fort Worth. For the director of the fabulously wealthy Getty Museum in Malibu, California, it was a golden opportunity for the enrichment of his collection of Renaissance painting. There were emissaries from the National Galleries of Washington and London, ambassadors from the Rijksmuseum in Amsterdam, the Pinakothek in Munich, the Louvre in Paris, and from other museums scattered across the continent of Europe.

The curator of European painting at the Boston Museum dropped in nearly every day to commune with Titian's *Rape of Europa*. The sacred names of Mellon and Simon and Annenburg were a murmuration in the air. The Third World dictator who wanted Bouchers and Fragonards was visiting the United States on a buying spree, and he made a side trip to Boston with his wife. A manufacturer of cement in Argentina came back again and again to look at Antoniazzo's sacred *Annunciation*. And from various mysterious corners of the world Gerard Fouchelle had grubbed up other bidders who represented only themselves and the fortunes they had made in Bolivian tin mining, or telecommunications in Tokyo, or soft drinks in Naples, or paper diapers in Cincinnati.

"Where did they all come from?" said Titus Moon to Homer Kelly. "Some of those people were here before the vote was taken. That guy from the Louvre, I know I saw him in the Dutch Room the day before that last meeting of the trustees. Fallfold brought him in. They were in there together, staring at the Vermeer."

"Vultures," said Homer dismally. "They see the poor dying creature fall to its knees and then they start circling around, even before it utters its final death rattle and keels over."

There were to be seven days of sales in the Tapestry Room—Fouchelle had figured it out. The auction of the paintings would occupy three days, sculpture was allotted one, and everything else was to be packed into the remaining three—tapestries, furniture, Japanese screens, ceramics,

265

fans, lace, books and autograph letters, prints and drawings. Even the great French and Italian fireplaces were to be sold and wrenched from the walls.

During this long tormented summer of degeneration and ferment, Titus Moon was uncooperative. Instead of acting as gracious host to museum directors from all over the world, he crouched in his office, trying to finish his part of the doomed comprehensive catalogue.

He wasn't the only dissenter. The entire staff was split down the middle. Some of the conservators were willing to cooperate with Gerard Fouchelle and his colleagues, some resisted their approaches altogether. When Fouchelle discovered that he could make no headway with Titus Moon, he went one step down to Polly Swallow. Polly smiled at him courteously, but she seemed curiously ignorant, even though Fouchelle had been told she knew almost as much about the collection as Moon himself.

So he had to make do with Aurora O'Doyle. Aurora didn't seem to know very much either, but she was delighted to be of service. In company with Fouchelle, whom she called Zherard, she clashed around the galleries on her noisy little heels, chattering in her pretty Sweet Briar French (Aurora had spent her junior year in Paris), *Mais oui! C'est magnifique, n'est pas, Zherard? Voyez vous! C'est tres, tres fantastique, n'est pas?* and gesturing extravagantly, while Fouchelle kept his own hands quietly at his sides.

The trustees were divided too. Shackleton Bowditch and Peggy Foley never showed their faces, preferring to grieve in privacy, but John Bodkin was everywhere, ingratiating himself with all the distinguished visitors. Edward Fallfold, for his part, was a strange mixture of graciousness and pugnacity. He had fallen all over himself to welcome the delegation from the Louvre, but to the man from the Getty Museum in California he was positively hostile. "Listen, Edward," said Bodkin, after observing a rancid encounter between the Getty man and Fallfold, "you could at least be polite. The Getty is absolutely rolling in money for acquisitions. They're *required* to spend a hundred million a year. They've *got to.* And they might as well spend it here." But Fallfold merely snarled at him and begged to be let alone.

As for Preston Carver, he too was very much on hand, making himself useful to Gerard Fouchelle as a financial advisor. Carver's little notebook was soon filling up with Fouchelle's estimates on the bids to be expected for individual works of art, along with his own figures on the daily shift in the value of the museum's investments on the Dow-Jones. The market was rising in optimistic surges and Fouchelle's staggering guesses at the prices to be expected for Mrs. Gardner's treasures were mounting astronomically.

"Six hundred million, that's what he predicts," Carver chortled to his wife, and then in giddy excitement, they began talking about finding a little holiday place on the Costa del Sol.

Trustee Fulton Hillside had his hands full with the real estate transaction, because the building itself was now on view as a merchandisable product. Fulton had an important buyer lined up, ready to take over the main edifice. There were to be exclusive shops in all the galleries and an elegant restaurant in the courtyard. For a while there had been a snag, the problem of zoning. The neighborhood was zoned for apartments, not commercial development. But the firm's senior partner was an old hand at dealing with the board of appeals. "No problem," he told Fulton. "We'll fill up the garden with housing for the elderly, then plead hardship because the old folks will need shopping close at hand. The board will fall for it. See if they don't."

One day Titus Moon cornered Fulton Hillside in the

Little Salon. "Okay, Fulton," he said, "who's going to buy the building?"

"Oh, it's just this big syndicate. I mean, naturally it would have to be something substantial, the transaction is going to be so costly."

"What big syndicate?" said Titus suspiciously.

"Oh, you know. You must have seen their new building next to Copley Place, Fatcat Enterprises." Fulton hastened to explain. "Upmarket! It's their first upmarket venture. They want to turn the building into fashionable shops, with a four-star restaurant in the courtyard. Oh, don't worry, they're not going to use that cartoon cat, good heavens, no. They've created a whole new logo, Titus, a designer Fatcat to go with the general class of the architecture. They intend to make it a showplace. And listen, they're signing up the chef from the *Q. E. II.*"

Titus Moon's heart sank. "What about the greenhouses and all the flowers, the potted plants, the palm trees? Are they part of the deal, Fulton?"

"Oh, no, we've got that all squared away." Fulton glanced up nervously at the tapestry on the wall, a sixteenth-century Flemish masterpiece burgeoning with ripe peaches and bunches of grapes, blossoming with flowers, luxuriant with arbors and hedges and all the lush growth of a fruitful earth. Swiftly he turned away and fastened his gaze safely on the Meissen clock. "The greenhouses go to a tomato grower in Waltham, as soon as he makes sure his poisonous sprays won't pit the plexiglass surfaces." Fulton had hit another land mine, and he cleared his throat and pawed the air. "The potted plants are going to a corporate interior landscaping firm in Hartford. You know, for lobbies and executive offices." Fulton giggled tensely. "We've got everything worked out."

"I can see you have," said Titus, and then he laughed

too, a sepulchral guffaw from the depth of his hollow bowels. From the spinet in the corner came an answering note of discord.

Trustee Catherine Rule was the only one who was uninformed about the daily plunge of events. Everyone continued to keep her in a state of frustrated doubt. Whenever Titus visited Catherine at Brigham and Women's, he found the deception increasingly difficult. He would make his usual ghastly effort at cheery monologue, trying to avoid talking about the museum altogether. But Catherine merely looked at him with those mad eyes of hers and made noises in her throat as though she wanted to tell him something, or ask him something, as though she wanted him to try harder to listen and understand. But Titus couldn't understand, and therefore he gabbled on, and went away with the terrible news still locked in his head, knowing how bitterly it would affect her if she were told, unaware that she knew the worst already.

As for Gerard Fouchelle, he was thoroughly satisfied with his preparations for the auction on September twenty-first, except for one essential thing, the preparation of a set of catalogues. For a collection like this no expense must be spared. For the paintings alone, there should be two glossy volumes in a slipcase. They must be ready no less than three weeks before the sale. Fouchelle had the old museum catalogues to work with, but his fingers itched for the new entries Titus Moon had been preparing for his grand comprehensive compendium of everything in the museum.

John Bodkin had a suggestion. "Try Aurora O'Doyle. She's been working on the catalogue, and she's engaged to Titus Moon."

And Aurora had agreed at once. "Of course," she said. *"Enchanté!"* But when she approached Titus, he proved to be stubborn.

"No," he said, "they can't have it."

Aurora couldn't budge him. *"C'est tres ridicule,"* she complained to Fouchelle and John Bodkin. *"C'est too absurde!"*

But Bodkin wasn't through yet. "Where does Titus keeps his notes?"

"Oh, they've got this huge file," said Aurora. "Polly's got it now. It's right there on her desk." Aurora's beige eyes widened. "You mean you'd like me to—well, I could, of course I could!"

"Good girl," said Bodkin. Gerard Fouchelle merely smiled.

CHAPTER FORTY

HOMER KELLY saw the loose sheets of the splendid new auction catalogues later that summer on a visit with his wife to Beryl Bodkin. Homer and Mary had been seeing a good deal of Beryl lately, ever since Homer had noticed at the dinner party in June an interesting bifurcation in the Bodkin family. The wife, he guessed, was not in total sympathy with the husband. In Beryl's nature there were dignified corners into which she retreated whenever her husband's arrogant forcefulness became too overwhelming. And yet she must know a great deal about his wheelings and dealings. Why could she not be a partisan in the enemy camp?

Homer persuaded Mary to join him in striking up a friendship. Together they called on Beryl, together they took her to lunch, together they attended some of the last concerts at the Gardner Museum.

Today in the Bodkins' living room, the proof sheets for the auction catalogues were spread out along the table behind the sectional sofa, where John Bodkin had been going over them with Gerard Fouchelle the day before.

"It seems so sad," said Beryl, picking up the dazzling reproduction of Bermejo's *Saint Engracia* that was to be the cover illustration on the slipcase. "I wish all this weren't happening."

"What a delectable picture!" said Mary Kelly, admiring Saint Engracia's plucked eyebrows, her jeweled crown, her blond pigtails, her transparent veil, her sweet self-conscious piety. "Who'll get it now? Some wealthy scoundrel, I'll bet, some worthless member of the jet set." In her months away from Homer in New York, Mary had been studying the troubles of the women's labor movement in Manhattan, and she had lost all patience with shop bosses, hard masters, top brass, wealthy owners, the establishment in general. The idea that works of art should become the exclusive property of the rich and powerful seemed to her a manifest injustice.

When the telephone rang, Beryl ran to answer it. Glumly Homer picked up a sheaf of loose pages and sat down to read them over, but he couldn't help hearing from the next room Beryl's gasp of pleasure. "Oh, Fenton!" she said, her voice trembling, "Oh, Fenton, dear, how are you?" Then Homer stopped listening, his attention grasped by a phrase in the description of the Rubens portrait of Thomas Howard. *Swashbuckling application of paint,* said the text beside the picture. Where had he seen it before? *Swashbuckling application*—why, yes, of course, it was Polly Swallow's pretty phrase about the Rubens portrait of Thomas Howard. Homer remembered reading it in Titus Moon's office.

He grimaced. It was too bad. Polly Swallow had cravenly handed over her notes to Bodkin and Fouchelle. She had given up. She had gone over to the enemy.

Beryl was back, her face suffused with color. Impulsively she hugged Homer and kissed Mary. She hardly seemed to understand when Homer asked whether he could borrow a set of proofs. "Proofs? Oh, proofs! Oh, certainly! Of course!" Then Beryl changed the subject, and said what was next to her heart. "Oh, Homer, would you help me with my bicycle? I've got this pump, this new bicycle pump, but I don't know how it works. Oh, please, Homer, Mary, would you show me? You would? Oh, thank you, thank you a thousand times! How kind, how wonderfully kind!"

Homer ran into Polly Swallow that afternoon at the museum, catching her on the wing as she raced around the corner of the Spanish Cloister and came out into the sunlit glow of the court. He couldn't resist a nasty impulse to accuse her. "I see you've been writing up things for that man Fouchelle."

"What?" said Polly, rushing on by, turning to keep him in sight, walking backward in long strides.

"His catalogue," said Homer, bringing it out from under his arm. Then as Polly still looked blank, he said, "You wrote all the descriptions in this thing, right? I recognize your fine Italian hand."

"I what?" Polly stopped cold. "I didn't, I didn't. What are you talking about?"

He handed her the pages of the Fouchelle catalogue, and she gazed at them in disbelief, stopping to read and exclaim. "Yes, I wrote that, I mean, they're my words all right, but I never said anybody could use them." She was stupefied. "So that's where my notes went. My file box! It was missing for two or three days. Somebody stole it and copied all the cards. But that's terrible. It's just terrible."

"Any idea who could have taken it?" said Homer, relieved to find his instinctive character analysis of miscellaneous specimens of the human race still justified.

"No, no, I don't. Well, maybe I do. But it's so rotten, so really rotten. So *two-faced.*"

Charlie Tibby came up to look at the file box, a huge accordion-pleated cardboard container bursting with too many pieces of paper. "I suppose we could take fingerprints, but if it's Aurora O'Doyle you're thinking of, she had access to the file anyway, didn't she? I mean her prints would be all over it anyway, wouldn't they?"

"Oh, never mind," said Polly, who had had enough of hating. "It doesn't matter now."

But Homer spoke to Aurora O'Doyle just the same. And Aurora was highly amused. *"C'est extraordinaire!* Why would I do a thing like that? And why would anybody care? Titus's catalogue is no good to anybody. There isn't going to be any catalogue. You know," she said confidentially to Homer, "I'll bet Polly took it home and forgot it was there." Aurora tapped her head significantly. "The truth is, Polly's been terribly forgetful lately. Oh, I can't blame her. We all have so much on our minds."

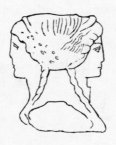

CHAPTER FORTY-ONE

T HE SUMMER was over. Catherine had been in the hospital for more than three months. Her paralyzed side was recovering its functions slowly. Daily she worked in the rehabilitation department with the physical therapists, the speech therapists, the occupational therapists. There were exercises for her left arm, even though it was still covered in plaster. Catherine had to lift the cast straight up and rotate the heavy plaster from the shoulder. She had to work the tips of her fingers. The paralysis in her right arm was somewhat improved. Now she could inch the fingers of her right hand across a table and pick up pegs, although she still dropped most of them.

Speech continued to be a struggle. Catherine was in too much of a hurry. There were questions she wanted to ask, things she was desperate to say, but she still couldn't form the words, she still couldn't discipline her lips, her tongue, the flow of air from her lungs. She was too eager, too impatient. When would she learn to slow down?

"Take it easy, Catherine," said the therapist. "You're coming along nicely. Just relax. Now, let's start again with the easy ones. Say *Ah.*"

"Ahhhhh," said Catherine, slumping back in her wheelchair, closing her eyes, starting all over again from the beginning.

"Say *E.*"

"Eeeeeee."

"*Ma.*"

"Mmmmmaaaaa."

"*Mama.*"

"Mmmmmaaaammmmaaaa."

"Very *good.* Now don't worry. You're doing great, just great. Bonnie will take over now, and work on those fingers."

"Aw ri'," said Catherine sorrowfully, frustrated that she couldn't try the next exercise, that she couldn't master the more difficult syllables. She looked up as the physical therapist sat down at the low table beside her. "Essel?" said Catherine eagerly.

"Essel? Say it again, dear. Tell me what you want."

Catherine forced her tongue to articulate the *N* before the *C,* but this time it came out *Ennel.*

"It's all right. Take your time. I'm not going away."

"Pppp," puffed Catherine, then "essel."

"Oh, pencil. You want to try to hold the pencil? Well, okay, let's see if you can do it this time."

Once again the therapist produced the pencil-holding device, a strap that wound around the curved fingers of Catherine's right hand. "There, now here's a piece of paper. Let's see you write your John Hancock."

Anxiously Catherine bent to the task. She couldn't get her forefinger and thumb tightly around the shaft of the pencil, but she could shove it straight up toward the top of the paper to make a straight line.

"That's not a *C,*" said the therapist. "Do you want to start over?"

But Catherine was hurrying on, pushing the pencil across the paper, making two shaky horizontals to the right of her straight line. *Now, once again, shove the pencil from the bottom to the top, but on the diagonal this time. Good! Now make another diagonal slanting the other way, meeting the first one at the top. Now another horizontal across the middle.* There! She could do it! She could write!

"What are you writing, dear? I don't understand."

Catherine looked at the therapist triumphantly. Then in her elation she was struck with fear. Her face puckered in worried lines. She forced her lips into the right posture to deliver a *W*, and said, "Wha' daaay?"

"What day? It's Friday. Pay day," said the therapist, smiling. "Let me see, it must be the twentieth of September. No, the twenty-first. Why, what's the matter? Miss Rule, are you all right?"

"Twe'irss'? Oh, no." Catherine raised the feeble fingers of her right hand a few inches off the table. Her face crumpled with dismay, and she threw herself back in the wheelchair.

"Miss Rule, I think you need to go back to your room and lie down. Wait till I get someone to take you. I'll be right back."

But when Catherine was returned to her own floor, she had no interest in lying down. She spoke up over her shoulder to the young woman who was pushing her wheelchair. "Lowjh," she said. "I wan' lowjh."

"The patient lounge? Why, sure." Expertly the nurse's aide whirled the chair and pushed it down the curving corridor to the lounge, where Catherine found herself alone, as usual, with Betty Fawcett.

"Hello, there!" cried Betty, happy to see her, grinning and flinging herself left and right. Her cigarette flew across the room and burnt a hole in the cushion of an empty chair. The nurse's aide spoke to Betty crossly, put the fire out, confiscated her cigarettes, and left swiftly.

"Lizzen, Beh-ee," said Catherine. "Lizzen."

"Oh, right," said Betty, nodding her head violently up and down.

277

"I wan'—I wan'—." Catherine stopped to take a deep breath.

"You want what?" Betty threw her right leg up and tossed out her arms to Catherine to show her goodwill.

Suddenly Catherine felt better. Her tongue was under more control. The words she needed came to her. "I wan'—other—whee'—chai'."

Betty's head swiveled, looking around. "You want other whee' chair?"

"Mo-er," said Catherine, struggling. She had never tried to say so many things at once. "Mo-der. Mo-der-ize whee'-chai'."

Understanding Catherine at last, Betty tossed her entire body off the sofa. Flinging herself across the room to the row of wheelchairs stored in the corner of the lounge, she grasped one and jerked it in and out. There was a tremendous rattling and entangling of metal arms and footrests, but at last Betty pulled one wheelchair free and dragged it across the floor. "Motorized whee'chair, right here, at your service."

"Oh, Beh-ee, 'ank you. Oh, 'ank you." Catherine's eyes filled with tears.

"You wanta get in?"

"Yeh, yeh, oh, yeh, I do." Catherine looked up at Betty in timid appeal, and held her arms up as high as they would go. Her half-paralyzed right arm rose only a few inches, but her broken left arm in its plaster cast went almost straight up in the air.

"Jussa minute." Betty tugged at the motorized wheelchair, clattering it against the wall and dragging it back, until at last she had it lined up beside Catherine's. "Now, less go, okay? Whoop, whoop! *UPSADAISY!*"

For a moment there was a wild melee of loose arms and legs, a mad wobbling of feeble limbs in the air. Then Betty

278

plopped Catherine into the motorized wheelchair more or less right-side up, and backed away, roaring with laughter. Plunging forward again, she made swabbing motions at Catherine until she had her sitting upright. Then she stumbled backward and flopped down on the sofa. "Mish' accomplish'," she said, grinning hugely, reaching into the pocket of her bathrobe for another pack of cigarettes.

"Oh, 'ank you, Beh-ee. Now, show meeeee. Show meee—how do it."

"Pusha bar. See? Juss pushabar the way you wanta go. Right? Thass right! Good for you!"

"Goo'-bye, 'ank 'oo!"

"Goodbye! Have a happy day!"

CHAPTER FORTY-TWO

T HE DAY of the auction and the wedding had dawned clear and fine, with a thin mist giving way to a warm smoky haze. Trees here and there put out tentative branches of color, as though the proprietor of a dry goods store had unrolled huge bolts of orange silk and might shortly roll them up again.

The complexity of the day's arrangements had been worked out by Aurora O'Doyle, who had organized everything with an iron hand. Only the wedding guests were to enter by the Fenway door. Everyone with a reservation for the auction was to come in by the Palace Road entrance, to be routed by way of the rear corridor and the back stairway up to the Tapestry Room. Large printed directions were mounted on the iron fence at the front of the building and beside the door on Palace Road. The wedding was to begin promptly at noon, the bidding for the auction at one o'clock. There was to be no intermingling of the two functions. Aurora had been firm.

Homer Kelly came in early, dodging past the guard at the Palace Road entrance with a nod and a smile. Mary had chosen to stay home. "It will be a big enough crowd already," she said, pulling on her blue jeans. "And I don't know any of those people. I'll take the canoe out on the river."

At the museum Homer peered inquisitively into the courtyard, where the bride was supervising the hanging of garlands. Aurora's winsome charm had temporarily vanished. It was apparent that Aurora O'Doyle had been born to command, to control vast armies on the field of battle, to turn the enemy's flank with a charge of cavalry, to send ten thousand men to death or glory. "Up, up," she cried. "A half inch up. No, no, that's much too far. Haven't you got eyes? Can't you see?"

Titus Moon was not in his office. Homer turned away, disappointed, and headed downstairs, seeking the windowless serenity of Charlie Tibby's basement hideaway, where it was always midnight, where the overhead fluorescent fixtures cast down forever the same harsh light.

"How long will you be keeping all your security people?" said Homer, looking at the chart on the wall with its long list of guards and night watchmen.

"This is the last day," said Charlie grimly. "Tomorrow they bring in a security management service. From now on the whole thing will be somebody else's responsibility. Maybe they'll hire some of my kids. I hope so."

"What about you, Charlie? What are you going to do from now on?"

"Oh, I don't know. Maybe I can get a patrolling job. You know, as a night guard with a dog in some technical plant out Route 95 or someplace. Nobody's going to hire me to be in charge again. Not after this mess." Charlie changed the subject. "How's your little nephew?"

"Who, Bennie? Don't ask me. I haven't seen Bennie lately. His parents have taken over. How about Piggie and Dougie?"

"They've been with their mother all summer. I'm about to get them back. You know, it's funny, I sort of miss them."

"Yes," mused Homer, remembering his wild day at Fatcat Park. "There's certainly something cunning about Piggie."

"And Dougie, right? He's cute too, right?"

"Oh, of course! Dougie too. Delightful child."

"How's it going upstairs?"

"I don't know," said Homer. "I felt sort of in the way."

Charlie pushed back his chair. "Come on. I'll show you what we're doing. We've got all the guards here at once. Nobody's going to get away with anything, not today, no way."

It was true. Charlie's people were everywhere. But on the second floor they were hardly noticeable in the crush and commotion of auction preparations by Gerard Fouchelle and his organization. A closed-circuit television screen was being wired up in the Raphael Room, where a specialist would transmit the bids of the less important ticket holders to the auctioneer in the Tapestry Room by way of an intercom. A bank of telephones for long-distance bids had been installed in front of the auctioneer's platform. Next to the platform, a couple of men were arranging the disposition of the bid desk, where bids sent in by mail could be called out at the appropriate moment. The rest of the big room was jammed with chairs. Fifteen-hundred tickets had been distributed to would-be bidders from all over the world, and somehow every one of those people had to be accommodated.

Homer and Charlie left the auction gallery and walked through the little adjoining hall to the Dutch Room. Here the guards were in overwhelming evidence, because the room had become the depository for everything that was about to be auctioned. Famous paintings stood on their edges in big cardboard boxes mounted on dollies—Raphaels, Tintorettos, Guardis, Rembrandts, a Veronese, a Coello, a Dürer. Titian's *Rape of Europa* had an extra-big carton to itself. Homer watched as paintings from the Gothic Room were carried in from the elevator. Giotto's *Presenta-*

tion of the Infant Jesus was clutched to the breast of the director of Fouchelle's Boston gallery, Frederique Paquette. Two elegant young men in pink shirts carried the Sargent portrait of Mrs. Gardner.

"Que dois-je faire de Madame Gardner?" said one of the young men, looking around for an empty box.

Frederique Paquette deposited the Giotto tenderly in a container with two Holbeins and a Mabuse. *"Là-bas,"* he said, pointing imperiously at a window. Obediently the two young men set the Sargent portrait down gently on the floor, leaning it against the frame of the window as though Isabella Stewart Gardner were looking down for the last time into the courtyard of her Venetian palace, and then they strolled off to get something else.

"Charlie?" said Becky Stover, crooking a finger at him. Charlie Tibby disappeared with Becky to attend to a staffing problem—one of the kids responsible for the Fenway entrance had broken out in chicken pox—and Homer was left to himself. He stood at one side and indulged in his favorite habit of staring. It was always a good way to pass the time, because when people acted in character it was reassuring, and when they didn't, it was electrifying.

Fulton Hillside was there too, conducting someone through the Dutch Room. Homer watched inquisitively as Fulton gestured at the ceiling, the windows, the damask-covered walls. Then Homer recognized Fulton's companion, and he winced. It was the amiable goon from the investment-properties department of Fatcat Enterprises, Larry W. Oversole, the guy who spent his lunch hours in a tanning parlor, the one whose gold card had been passed along from Fallfold to Hillside. Obviously Fallfold's little hint about a connection between Fatcat's investment-properties department and Hillside's real estate firm had taken hold. Oversole had indeed planted a seed in fertile ground.

The seed had grown and blossomed. Now Oversole could put to use on a grand scale his talent for repulsive redesign.

Homer looked around at Mrs. Gardner's majestic Dutch Room, trying to see it with the eyes of Larry Oversole as a set of lavish commercial suites embellished with fancy decor, its walls sporting important corporate art instead of Rembrandts and Holbeins. It was too painful, and he gave up right away.

At once his attention was caught by a group of newcomers in the Dutch Room. Preston Carver was there with a little band of companions. The others were strangers to Homer, but he was struck by their family resemblance to Carver. Their faces were similarly pink and shining, their heads were balding to the same degree, their suits were dark with the same distinguished gravity. Homer moved up behind them, pretending to gaze at works of art to left and right.

" . . . entire proceeds to be invested," Carver was saying, "with the exception of course of the auctioneer's commission of ten percent. Fouchelle informs me we can expect upwards of five hundred million, less his commission, naturally. My firm will at once put the proceeds into short-term treasury bills."

"Only seven-percent return on treasury bills right now," said one of Carver's companions, sounding a little sour.

"Right," said Carver, "and therefore we'll lose no time in moving everything into the university's customary investment portfolio. Of course we'll have to be careful not to put a wobble in the market, with totals as substantial as these. But that," he said with a modest smirk, "is the sort of thing we're good at."

They were Harvard investment types, Homer decided. Carver's important friends were about to become the recipients of all this booty. Now they were moving away, stepping carefully among the cardboard boxes, paying no attention to the masterworks that were about to be taken to Fouchelle's Last Judgment. Homer could barely hear their final protestations.

"Oh, we trust your firm completely," said one.

"Implicitly," said the other.

For Homer, it was a morning of melancholy revelation. Before his eyes the springs of action were bubbling, that gushing fountain called conflict of interest. He knew now why Preston Carver had voted for the end of everything. Carver had been transformed from a trustee with a sense of stewardship into an interested party. His own firm was handling the transfer of the Gardner portfolio to Harvard University. What percentage would be taken on such a transfer by a highly respectable brokerage house? Eight percent? Carver wouldn't get it, naturally, but surely there would be a handsome bonus, even perhaps a partnership, as a reward for this faithful gathering in of the sheaves.

And Fulton Hillside's reasons were also as transparent as glass. Fulton was in real estate. Thanks to the sly interference of Fallfold, Fulton and Fatcat were in cahoots. It was as simple as that. What was the going rate for real estate commissions these days? Something like nine percent, wasn't it? Eight percent in the one case, nine in the other. That explained two of the four votes to finish the museum. But what about Bodkin's? What about Fallfold's?

Homer got out of the way as *The Rape of Europa* was wheeled past him on its way to the Tapestry Room. When Gerard Fouchelle himself came into the Dutch Room in the company of John Bodkin, Homer managed to saunter near and plant himself in front of the portrait of Philip the Fourth, as though he were fascinated by Philip's malformed Hapsburg jaw.

But Homer's eyes were skewed sideways, and his ears

were cocked like a dog's. His eyesight had always been keen, and his hearing had been sharpened by a lifelong nosy curiosity about other people's affairs. Now he witnessed a passing of objects from Fouchelle to Bodkin, and he heard the murmur of Bodkin's excited acknowledgment. Bodkin was smoothing the leather covers of books, he was examining the title pages, then slipping the books into a large case and buckling the buckles and strapping the straps. Only a fragment of what Fouchelle was saying reached Homer's ears, but it was enough. ". . . deserve it," said Fouchelle. ". . . all your kindness."

Kindness? What kindness had John Bodkin performed for Gerard Fouchelle? Well, it was obvious. He had persuaded the trustees to hire Fouchelle's firm, and now he was being rewarded with the three editions of Dante's *Divine Comedy*. The precious books would not appear in the auction catalogue. They would not be pounded down under the hammer. They were Bodkin's compensation for services rendered.

Three of the betraying votes were now explained. There remained only one more, Edward Fallfold's.

What was Fallfold's interest in all this? Was he being paid by Fatcat Enterprises for making the connection with Hillside? Homer doubted it. Oversole had handed a gold card to Fallfold in the same way he had given one to Homer, like a faithful husbandman sowing his grain on fertile and infertile ground alike, in the hope that one seed in a thousand would one day bear fruit.

Therefore—Homer struggled with the riddle—what *was* Fallfold's true interest in this formidable collapse?

CHAPTER FORTY-THREE

WANDERING BACK through the Tapestry Room, Homer went looking for Fallfold. The Tapestry Room was full of people making last-minute preparations for the auction. At one side of the platform, a television crew was busily setting up high-intensity lamps and attaching microphones to the rafters.

"Whoops, excuse me," said Homer, tripping over a cable, saving himself by clutching a $40,000 camera.

"Watch it there, man," said the grip, and then the camerman seized Homer's arm. "Hey, fella, is it true a billion dollars is going to change hands here today?"

"Oh, I doubt that," growled Homer. Stepping carefully over another swarm of snaking cables, he made his way through the Raphael Room into the Early Italian Room, still looking for Fallfold. Here he paused to watch another pair of Fouchelle's employees remove paintings from the south wall and carry them down the corridor to be ticketed and stored for their turn on the auction block.

Everything was coming down. In gallery after gallery, the walls were bare. The museum was denuded. Soon it would no longer be a museum at all, merely a piece of negotiable real estate for Hillside and his friends from Fatcat Enterprises.

Homer watched gloomily as another Fouchelle minion came in with a big painting and put it down against the wall. *"C'est okay?"* he said, glancing at Homer.

Homer shrugged, and the minion vanished. The paint-

ing was one Homer recognized, *Adam and Eve* from the
Gothic Room upstairs. He remembered looking at it with
Fallfold months ago. The snake, he noticed, was still steal-
ing the show, still coiling down from above to witness
humanity's first colossal blunder—so emblematic, thought
Homer, of the way the human race had gone right on

falling over its own feet and missing opportunities for advancement and destroying everything it could get its hands on, like today, like now, like right here and now.

Turning away from Adam and Eve, Homer huddled at the other end of the room among the altarpieces, embedding himself in beaten gold, the gold of icons, the gold backgrounds surrounding the Virgin, the gold halos of saints. Gold, gold, it was all gold, it was a nest of gold. Like fish that survive only under water, saints and angels breathed only in gold air. The flood of gold washed over Homer, the gold of Florence and Siena and Venice. In a gilded trance, he wandered from one altarpiece to the next, remembering the images of saints in the Catholic parish church of his childhood. The saints were old friends, politely displaying the symbols of their martyrdoms. The place was a thicket of moral tales.

Homer allowed himself to be instructed. Drenched in gold, he moved from one Christian lesson to another, from St. Catherine with her wheel, to Elizabeth of Hungary with her bouquet of miraculous roses, to John the Baptist in his furry suit, to St. Francis with his tonsure and brown robe, to the central mystery of the Crucifixion. And here was a bishop saint, who was he? The bishop carried only a staff in the shape of a crozier, a shepherd's crook, to snatch runaway souls back into the church, to gather all his lost sheep safely again within the sacred fold.

Perhaps it was the crisis in which Homer found himself, or perhaps it was the gold effulgence around him that went to his head. His mind cleared, and seized on the word *fold*, and then it jumped back to Bennie and Piggie and Dougie and the visit to Fatcat Park, and the beautiful house with the stone crest over the door. The crest had been carved with a worm and a gate. But it wasn't a gate, it was a fold, a sheepfold. And the worm was not a worm, not a worm that

eats a dead body, it was a snake. It was like the snake in the picture leaning against the wall, the painted snake that looked down on Adam and Eve with such comic interest. It was the original fall from grace, the fall out of all that was beautiful and innocent and good into the harsh world of death and corruption, poverty and terror and general nastiness.

The symbols on the battered shield over the door of the beautiful house in Fatcat Park were a visual pun on the name Fallfold. And the boy in the picture inside the house was the child who had grown up to become a man named Fallfold, the very same Edward Fallfold for whom Homer was looking right now.

Then the gold lapped back away from him, the air thinned and turned colorless once again, and Homer was released from his gilded spell. Through the window over the courtyard he could hear someone with a French accent testing the microphone in the Tapestry Room across the way. "Item number one, *The Rape of Europa* by Titian. Item number two—eh? *Qu'est-ce que c'est? Ah, pardonnez-vous moi,* Booch, Butch? Turn it down."

Once again Homer went looking for Fallfold. Coming upon John Bodkin at the head of the stairs, his case of treasures clutched under his arm, Homer asked where Fallfold might be found.

"Haven't seen him," said Bodkin, smiling like a cat with a canary inside. "But he lives just down the street at number 45 on the Fenway. You might find him there."

"Thanks," murmured Homer. Running past Bodkin, he hurried down the stairs, made his way outdoors, and sprinted along the curving drive, leaving behind him the newly decorated courtyard, which Aurora O'Doyle had transformed into a vision of paradise. Garlands were twisted around the columns, and hung between them in charming swags. The union of Aurora O'Doyle and Titus Moon was to take place in front of the Roman throne, which was filled with a great spray of summery flowers. Red carpets had been laid over the gravel paths. In the cloisters the bridesmaids were gathered in chattering bevies, looking like the angels in Fra Angelico's *Assumption of the Virgin.* The colors of their velvet gowns were pink and purple and apple-green and cobalt-blue, like those of the little figures in the *Très Riches Heures* of the Duc de Berry. Aurora's wedding gown was white velvet with gold bands around neckline and hem. Her uncle, Pertinax O'Doyle, the mayor of Boston, was hanging around, ready to perform the ceremony, and a Renaissance quartet was tuning up on the landing of the staircase outside the Dutch Room. It promised to be the most beautiful wedding in the world.

With half an hour to go, Aurora swept her attendants into the Blue Room, which she had fitted up as a dressing room. There she examined them like a drill sergeant in-

291

specting recruits. Sweat had unkinked the spit curls on her forehead, so that they fell around her face like little snakes. Aurora pinned them up again, then snatched a dried flower from the basket carried by the flower girl, her little cousin, the mayor's youngest daughter. "Good God, what's that doing there? Brown! I can't have a single speck of brown! Thank God, I saw it." Aurora raised her voice. "Bridesmaids, check your flowers!"

The flower girl started to cry. "Oh, Cecily," hissed Aurora, "don't be silly. Can't you understand, weddings have to be perfect? Absolutely perfect?" To herself she prayed that Titus had actually gone out and bought a new suit. He had refused her design for a costume, but had promised to get something decent in dark blue, say, or a soft olive-green.

CHAPTER FORTY-FOUR

T HE RUSTED GEARS in Homer's brain were grating together, trying to free themselves from the corrosion in which they had been locked like seized pistons in the cylinders of an unlubricated engine. So far only a few cogs were moving freely.

1. Edward Fallfold as a trustee of the Isabella Stewart Gardner Museum had voted for the dismantling of the museum.
2. By passing along Oversole's gold card to Hillside, Fallfold had betrayed an interest in seeing the museum become the property of Fatcat Enterprises.
3. Fallfold had once lived in the beautiful house that had been taken apart and reassembled in Fatcat Park.
4. Perhaps Homer and Charlie Tibby had placed too much reliance on Catherine Rule's feeble attempt to tell them whether her attacker had been someone known to her or a perfect stranger. *What if, after all, she had been thrown into the courtyard by someone she knew very well?*

The cogs whirled separately, failing to mesh. If only Homer could take Fallfold aside and talk to him, maybe the rest of the jammed machinery would loosen up.

Number 45, the Fenway, was a four-story brick town house, a little seedy around the edges. It was obviously a student rooming house. On this pleasant day in late September the lodgers were milling around the front steps.

Homer addressed them all at once, raising his voice. "Does a Mr. Edward Fallfold live here?"

There was an undercurrent of sardonic laughter, and then a thin girl in a baggy sweater spoke up. "He lives here, but he's not here now. I saw him go out a couple of hours ago. He does a lot of stuff at the Gardner Museum."

"And he's not been back? Are you sure?"

"Positive."

"You see, I'm trying to get hold of him right away. He's not at the museum, so I thought—"

"Maybe Mrs. Garboyle knows where he is. She's the super." The girl pointed to a basement door three steps below the sidewalk. "You could ask her."

Homer descended the steps, wondering how to seize this opportunity. If only he could see Fallfold's room in Fallfold's absence! How could he ingratiate himself with the building superintendent? Then Homer remembered a ruse he had been cherishing, a little stratagem he had been holding in storage until its time should be ripe. The time was now.

He knocked smartly on the door. Instantly it was opened by a wiry little woman with dyed black hair. "What can I do for you?" said Mrs. Garboyle.

She was a stranger to Homer. He was unaware of her intimate connection with the portrait of Mrs. Gardner; he didn't know she worked for Aurora O'Doyle. "Oh, excuse me," he said unctuously. "I'm sorry to bother you, but I've just come back to Boston for the first time in thirty years. I used to live in this house as a boy."

Mrs. Garboyle was enchanted. "Hey, no kidding! Golly, I bet it wasn't a rooming house thirty years ago, right?"

"Oh, no, indeed. It was just me and my family living

294

here, that was all." Homer gazed upward with sentimental longing at the high brick facade. "Oh, the bliss of a happy childhood! Ah, how much water has gone over the dam since then! How many dear dead faces shall I see no more!"

"Well, say, why don't you come in?" said Mrs. Garboyle hospitably. "You want to look around?" She gestured at her dark little kitchen. "I suppose it was just the servants down here in the old days?"

"Oh, yes, the butler, right," said Homer. "And ah—" He racked his brain for fragments of "Upstairs, Downstairs," the gossip of Mr. Hudson and Mrs. Bridges. "The cook! The parlor maid! They did all the food preparation down here, of course, and the—ah—laundry." Homer put his hand on the newel post of the stairway and gazed yearningly upward. "I wonder if my old bedroom is still the same?"

"Well, say, how would you like to see the rest of the house?" Mrs. Garboyle was captivated by this fantasy of the return of the son of the house to his boyhood home. In her harsh and luckless life it was a moment of mystery and romance. On the first floor, she threw open doors and exhibited the two parlors, the kitchen, and the dining room. They were battered chambers full of nondescript furniture. Two girls were making coffee in the kitchen. They glanced up resentfully at Mrs. Garboyle.

Homer followed her eagerly, reciting fibs about his childhood. "Oh, here it is, the dear old front hall. Gussie and I used to slide down this very banister. We rolled our hoops down these very stairs." Hoops? Wasn't he going back a little too far?

But Mrs. Garboyle didn't notice the anachronism. She led him upstairs, then stood in the hall swinging a bunch of keys. "Which room was yours?"

"Oh, gosh." Homer rubbed his chin thoughtfully. "I

295

think it was on this side. No, it may have been on the other side. Yes, I think Gussie and I switched bedrooms once. But perhaps it was on the third floor?"

Obligingly Mrs. Garboyle opened all the rooms, after giving each door a good thump. One of the doors opened on a surprise. Robbie Crowlie was standing in front of a mirror, pulling on his green museum jacket. He looked inquiringly at Homer. "Hey," he said, "what's the big idea?"

Homer promptly shut the door. "No, no, that's not it. Now, where could it have been? I'll know it right away."

And of course Homer did know Edward Fallfold's room, as soon as Mrs. Garboyle turned the key in the lock and threw back the door. Unlike the other rented rooms in the house, this one was not littered with clothing. The bed was not a tumble of grubby sheets. Over the dresser in delicate gold frames were drawings in red chalk. Even Homer could make a stab at their provenance. Eighteenth-century France, he guessed, sketches by Watteau. They had hung on the walls of the beautiful house before it was lost to Fallfold's family forever.

"This is it!" he cried. "We found it!" Walking in, he closed his eyes in nostalgic ecstasy. "Oh, how many times after the hurly-burly of a day at school did I come here to confide in my boyish diary!" Homer crossed to the bay window and looked out at the tall waving fronds of the bulrushes across the street. "There was this girl I loved, Gloria—ah—LaStella. I used to look out the window and dream about Gloria LaStella."

"Gloria LaStella!" Mrs. Garboyle was stunned. "But I knew Gloria LaStella! She lived right around the corner! Married now, naturally, to a big highway contractor. Really doing well for herself. She had this pretty brown hair, right?"

"That's it!" cried Homer, in a transport of delight and

terror. "The color of dark molasses, I always said Gloria's hair was."

"Or was it blonder then?" worried Mrs. Garboyle, frowning. "Yes, yes, I think it was. She was a real platinum blonde when she was a kid."

"Oh, that's right! Now I remember! I used to dream of stroking her flaxen hair!" Homer was way out on a shaky limb. He inched a little farther toward disaster. "Oh, Mrs.—"

"Garboyle."

"Oh, my dear Mrs. Garboyle, might I stay here alone for just a moment, and reflect on the past? Just for a minute or two, so that I can close my eyes and feel my boyhood around me once again?"

"Well, I don't see why not," said Mrs. Garboyle stoutly, completely caught up in Homer's farfetched saga. "I'm sure Mr. Fallfold wouldn't mind. Just shut the door when you go out. I'll be downstairs in my apartment."

Homer felt a little ashamed of himself as Mrs. Garboyle went out and shut the door. But he didn't let his shame prevent him from pouncing at once on Fallfold's desk.

There were no papers in sight. The top of the desk was excruciatingly neat. Homer pulled open the drawers. They too were tidy. Fallfold kept his tax records in the left-hand drawers, and clean paper and pencils in the drawers on the right.

Homer shut the drawers and looked around the room vaguely, thinking about his own work space at home, his own technique for storing documents. There were any number of good systems for controlling the supply of paper that washed in and out of any normal scholarly household. One way was to simply pile everything in separate heaps. Homer subscribed to this school of paper storage, although he knew it left something to be desired—on his own desk the piles were always drifting toward one another and mingling.

Homer also prided himself on his file drawers, where everything was carefully put away except for the great stack of things that lay on *top* of the file drawers waiting to be filed. There was also a basket for stuff he hadn't sorted yet, and several shelves for projects begun but not yet finished, and notebooks of miscellaneous scribbles, and heaps of drafts for work-in-progress, and piles of fresh paper and folders of Xeroxes, and works in manuscript by colleagues, and a tin container for letters he had forgotten to answer. There was also a sofa in Homer's study with a splendid long virgin surface on which to pile things, and one mustn't forget the piano in the living room and the top of the refrigerator in the kitchen. The floor was a last desperate resource, providing space for orderly sortings in geometric rows. You merely had to step around the rows cautiously, or if that was impossible, walk across them delicately on tiptoe.

But Fallfold seemed to have a different system altogether. There were no papers anywhere in sight. There were no piles, no files, no sofas inundated with paper, no rows of documents on the floor. The room was stark, furnished only with the exquisite pictures on the wall, a bed, a dresser, the desk with its electric typewriter, a bookcase, a table with a lamp beside the window, and a couple of upholstered chairs.

Homer examined the books, and found several by Fallfold himself—*North Italian Painting of the Renaissance, Roman Painting of the Counter-Reformation.* Homer glanced through them. As an art historian, Fallfold seemed perfectly presentable. Homer put the books back, then had a new thought, and got down on his knees. Ah, there they were, under the bed, four or five boxes of Fallfold's papers.

Eagerly Homer pulled out one of the boxes and spread the top layer of papers on the bed.

He had hit pay dirt at once. The uppermost sheet bore the heading, *The Rape of Europa.* But the typed list below the heading was not about Titian's painting. It was a list of other works of art in Mrs. Gardner's collection. Homer ran his eyes down the list and found a sameness in it.

Giovanni Bellini/Giorgione, *Christ Carrying the Cross:* Willed by the Loschi family to the town of Vicenza. The will was broken in spite of riots in the streets when Mrs. Gardner bought it through Berenson. Berenson to Mrs. Gardner—*It would be much easier for you in your vast trunks to get the picture out of Italy without risk of discovery than for me.*

Velásquez, *Portrait of Philip IV:* Mrs. Gardner to Bernard Berenson—*Yes, on the Velásquez . . . only do be a dear and get it cheaper if you can. I am so poor . . .*

Raphael, *Pietà:* Mrs. Gardner to Berenson—*Can it be sent to me smuggled . . . so that I may get it as soon as possible without any duties?*

Berenson to Mrs. Gardner—as for *getting hold of the great things,* the only way it could happen was by *smoothing the way by a copious expenditure of money.*

Botticelli, *Madonna of the Eucharist* (the *Chigi Madonna*): Sold to Mrs. Gardner over the protest of the Italian government against the loss of the Italian patrimony of art. It was rumored that the dealer Colnaghi had the picture painted over, in order to smuggle it out of the country as a modern painting.

Piero della Francesca, *Hercules;* the *Cyrus* series of tapestries; and other valuable furnishings and works of art, brought into the United States as articles belonging to a Mrs. Emily Chadbourne, in an attempt to avoid duties.

From the garden of Sallust, headless statue of a woman: The Copenhagen and Berlin Museums were eager to buy it, but Mrs. Gardner got it.

Corneille de Lyon, *The Dauphin François:* Berenson to Mrs. Gardner—*The price I could get it for—eight thousand lire—is absurdly cheap.*

Bermejo, *Saint Engracia:* Mrs. Gardner won it by outbidding the museums of Brussels and Budapest.

The list went on and on. It was a list of grudges against Mrs. Gardner, against her riches, against the triumph of her avid acquisitiveness, her habit of carrying away to America the national treasures of Italy, France, and Spain, her conspiracies with Berenson to pack away all her precious plunder in the holds of transatlantic steamships without paying duty.

Homer wanted to stick up for the woman. She wasn't any worse, after all, than most of her wealthy contemporaries, J. P. Morgan, for instance, or Mrs. Potter Palmer. It wasn't as though she had snatched altarpieces from churches in the middle of the night. Almost everything had been legitimately for sale. And she wasn't the only one who had tried to avoid import duties.

Homer glanced guiltily at the watch he had bought in Switzerland, remembering that he had gone through customs wearing it on his wrist—and yet he considered himself an honest man. Clucking his tongue in self-disapproval, Homer flipped through the rest of Fallfold's list, and put it back in the box. Then he picked it up to look again at the last page.

Something had been scrawled across it in a wild hand, as though scribbled in a fit of temper. It was *R*-something. *RIB CAGE?* No, not rib cage. Try again. *BILLAGE?* 'Twas *billage, and the slithy toves?* No, not billage. Homer gave up, and dipped into another cardboard box for another set of Fallfold's papers.

The next sheaf was an interesting bundle of letters from abroad. The first was from a certain Signora Beatrice Chigi Ferracini.

> Caro Signore Fallfold,
>
> I am not a rich, and therefore I cannot buy the picture of Botticelli which one time belong to the great-grandfather, il principe Chigi. To me send that picture, please, because it is in my family so many year. I expect that picture subito. Signore, me lo mandi immediatamente, per favore!

The letter was obviously from some descendant of the previous owner of the *Chigi Madonna,* the painting that had been part of the Italian national patrimony. Signora Beatrice Chigi Ferracini wanted it back, all right, as Fallfold must have hoped she would, but she wasn't about to pay for it.

The next letter bore the splendid crest of the Musée du Louvre, and it requested the date of the possible sale of the paintings mentioned in Monsieur Fallfold's letter. Another was a delicately worded inquiry from the museum in the Vatican, and there were letters from the Prado in Madrid, the Dresden Gallery, the Rijksmuseum in Amsterdam, and museums and galleries in a lot of other European cities. What had Fallfold been up to?

Well, obviously he had written to all of them to tell them about the auction. Then Homer riffled through the letters again, glancing at the dates. They didn't make sense. Bewildered, he looked at them again. The letter from the Louvre was dated March 16. The others had been written in April and May.

Homer raised his head and gazed absently out the window at the bulrushes in the park across the street. What did it mean? Fallfold hadn't voted to dismantle the museum until after the attack on Catherine in June. Yet all the time he had been voting no, Fallfold had been alerting European museum directors about the coming auction.

Homer pawed through the box. Yes, it was true. All the letters had come from across the Atlantic. There were no envelopes with American stamps from museums in California or New York City or Chicago.

Then he stiffened. Someone was running noisily up the stairs. Alarmed, he dropped all the letters back in the box, shoved the two boxes under the bed, and draped himself against the bedpost in an attitude of rapture. Across the hall a youthful voice shouted, "Hey, stupid," and a door slammed.

With a sigh of relief, Homer let go of the bedpost. *Stupid is right,* he said to himself, as revelation like a stream of lubricating oil seeped among the jammed machinery in his head. The word that had been scrawled across the last page of Fallfold's list of grudges was *PILLAGE.* And the heading at the top of the list was *THE RAPE OF EUROPA.*

Mrs. Gardner had raped the continent of Europe. The most famous work of art in her collection was a metaphor for her own act of rapacity in grasping at all that was most precious in the older culture across the sea. Oh, she had paid for it, of course, with money wrought by her father in his iron mill, with dollar bills blown into her husband's lap by the wind that drove his sailing ships around the world. She had reached up her arms and caught the fluttering showers of greenbacks as his locomotives shrieked and thundered across the nation on transcontinental rails. Yes, she had paid for them, but perhaps there had been rapine in her heart just the same.

302

Homer remembered what Fallfold had said, standing before Sargent's portrait of Isabella Stewart Gardner. "This one could point her parasol at anything on the continent of Europe—well, almost anything—and say, I'll take this, I'll take that." *Can it be sent to me smuggled?*

What did she care, after all, for the European patrimony of art? She had wanted things, she had wanted the best of things, she had wanted the very pinnacle of the most precious things in the world, and she had got them. They had been packed in enormous crates and shipped from Paris, they had descended into the holds of gigantic vessels, parted forever from the places of their origin—altarpieces sacred to generations of men and women in the little hill towns of Tuscany, portraits of women who had given birth to princes, of men who had sought glory among popes and kings in Rome and Paris, Madrid and Sicily, portrayals in paint and stone of the classic legends and Christian stories that had excited European imaginations for two thousand years. Away they had gone to the new world, to the rude muddy banks of a little creek in the city of Boston, at the whim of a wealthy woman with a will of iron.

To Fallfold, it had indeed been the rape of Europe. No wonder, then, that it was Titian's painting he had stolen from the museum, and then the portrait of Mrs. Gardner herself. Her crime had been like the tearing up from the British countryside of his own ancestral house, in order that it might be set down in Fatcat Park. Her life of acquisition had been a life of pillage. Fallfold couldn't fight back against Fatcat, but he could destroy the Gardner Museum. Mrs. Gardner's palace was about to suffer the same degradation as his own childhood home—Fatcat was going to get it. Whimsically but thoroughly Fallfold was carrying out its destruction. And murderously. Homer remembered the bludgeoning death of Madeline Hepplewhite and the desperate condition of Catherine Rule, and hardened his heart against Fallfold. The man was a brutal killer, after all.

Letting himself out of Fallfold's room, Homer said an affectionate goodbye to Mrs. Garboyle, picked his way around the kids on the front steps, and ran all the way back to the museum.

It was almost noon. The wedding guests would be gathering in the cloisters around the courtyard. At the front entrance Becky Stover waved Homer in, but he had no interest in watching Titus Moon make the biggest mistake of his life. Brushing past the knots and clusters of well-dressed wedding guests, Homer ran up the stairs to the second floor, while Aurora O'Doyle's musicians played ancient melodies on the balcony over the courtyard.

The Tapestry Room was nearly empty, except for two or three police officers and a couple of the regular museum guards. Everybody else must have gone off to lunch, or else they were downstairs waiting to witness the sacrifice of Titus Moon on the altar of matrimony.

One of the guards was Robbie Crowlie. "Excuse me for busting into your room just now," said Homer. "I didn't know you lived in the same house with Fallfold."

"Anything wrong with that?" said Robbie pugnaciously. Too pugnaciously, decided Homer. The connection between Fallfold and Robbie Crowlie was stronger than ever. Robbie was living in the same house as Fallfold, ready to lend a hand any time at all, the faithful boyfriend and loyal junior partner.

"Do you know where Mr. Fallfold is?" insisted Homer. "I'm trying to find him."

"How should I know?" retorted Robbie.

The other guard was Beanie Kenney. He looked at Robbie in surprise. "He was here just now, with Polly

Swallow, and they were talking about Miss Rule. You know, the old lady in the hospital. And Polly said she was a lot better, so Mr. Fallfold decided to go see her. He had just enough time, he said, to go to the hospital and get back for the auction."

"Oh, God," cried Homer. Leaping over cables, knocking down chairs, he charged around the corner to the back stairs, plunged down them three at a time, surged out the door onto Palace Road, and raced in the direction of Brigham and Women's Hospital.

Fallfold had tried to kill Catherine once. It would be easy enough to do it again, and finish the job this time. There she lay, utterly helpless, her life hanging by a hair. How easy it would be to snap that fragile thread!

CHAPTER FORTY-FIVE

THE PROBLEM was one of control. She was compensating too much in each direction. In the motorized wheelchair Catherine Rule rolled down the corridor of the hospital, veering left and right. Pausing, she waited a moment, then started again, pushing her wrist against the control bar more gently. There, that was better.

The nurses' station was just around the corner. To Catherine it was like a fortification overlooking a narrow place in the river, and she was an enemy vessel. She must slip by without attracting attention. She paused again and listened. All was silent at the fort. Catherine waited until she heard the nurse on duty speak up. She recognized the voice of her friend Judy Pringle, the nurse manager on this floor. The lunch cart had arrived, and the transportation aide was checking in at the nurses' station, running down the list of patients, matching the trays with the rooms for which they were destined.

"Room 30, Speranza and Digby, two blands, right? Room 32, O'Rourke, liquid diet, Benecetto, regular. Room 34—"

Catherine took a deep breath and sailed forward, curving around the corner slowly and gracefully, keeping eyes front.

Judy glanced up just long enough to recognize her favorite patient and say, "Go for it, Catherine," before looking back at the list. "Room 40, that's Mrs. Greenberg. She shouldn't be bland. She's regular now."

Catherine slowed down at the end of the corridor and reached out with her left foot to push open one of the double doors, expecting to hear Judy call her back. The door swung open, the wheelchair glided through, Judy was still preoccupied. The door flapped shut. On the other side Catherine waited a moment, expecting Judy to come to her senses. But there was still no outcry, no thud of running feet.

Catherine smiled and rolled away, feeling free as air, hearing the call of the open road. Which way now? Where was the elevator? She had often been taken up to the rehabilitation floor on the elevator, but she had never found the way by herself.

The hospital corridors were like curving lanes, opening out into windowless waiting rooms, branching and branching again like forking paths in a labyrinth. Catherine found herself thinking of a Flemish painting in the Gardner Museum, the story of *David and Bathsheba.* Beyond the lascivious King David, ogling the naked Bathsheba from a window, lay a maze of green hedges—surely an astonishing horticultural achievement for the landscape of Jerusalem in biblical times. Perhaps the maze represented the tortured complexity of human relations. More probably, it was just an adornment in an amusing picture full of mannerist detail.

Here in the hospital there was a reason for all the curving paths branching left and right. All of these doors opened on useful spaces. Oh, which path was the right one? Would this door open on the elevator corridor? Gently Catherine putt-putted through it.

Whoops, wrong turn. Before her rose another armed fortress, another nurses' station. And this nurse seemed more alert than Judy. She looked up sharply and stared at Catherine and said, "May I help you?"

Whisking her wheelchair around in a circle, Catherine

smiled at the nurse, then bumped briskly through the door in the other direction. *She went thataway,* she told herself triumphantly, as a sign materialized on the wall in front of her, with an arrow pointing to the right: ELEVATORS.

At last she had found the familiar corridor, the wide hall with its lofty windows. Catherine put on speed and whizzed down the hall, feeling jaunty and mettlesome, and brought herself to a gallant curving stop in front of the elevator.

What to do now? How was she to push the down button? it was no mean trick. Fingers wouldn't do it. Catherine maneuvered the chair closer and tried her right elbow. Ah, that did it.

Now she must back around until her wheelchair was facing away from the elevator, and wait for the doors to open. How long would it be before Judy discovered she was missing, and set up a hue and cry? Altogether too soon. Then Catherine winced, as a familiar doctor strode down the corridor and stood beside her to wait for the elevator.

It was Dr. Balk, the neural surgeon. Even though he had saved her life, Catherine cordially disliked Dr. Balk, and she knew he would guess at once that she had no business gallivanting around the building in a motorized wheelchair. In fact he was looking down at her now with a frown. "Miss Rule, what are you doing here? Where do you think you're going in that thing?"

"Phys' 'erapy," lied Catherine hopefully, knowing she couldn't get away with it. Physical therapy was upstairs. He was sure to notice she had punched the DOWN button.

Dr. Balk opened his mouth to protest, but at that moment the elevator doors slid back and his attention was instantly grasped by the shapely operating room nurse within. The nurse's eyes were rimmed with black, and her green wrapper was pulled tightly around her.

"Debbie," cooed Dr. Balk, staring at her lecherously as

308

he held the elevator door open for Catherine, "that was a tricky little lumbar laminectomy we did together yesterday. I love the way you swab cavities. Nobody else swabs cavities the way you swab cavities, Debbie." Adroitly Catherine moved her wheelchair into the elevator, while Dr. Balk and Debbie edged together beside her.

"Oh, thank you, Dr. Balk," breathed Debbie. Her name wasn't Debbie really, decided Catherine, it was Bathsheba. She was rising pink and dripping from the pool in King David's garden. As the elevator stopped on the ground floor, Bathsheba strolled out, putting a cigarette to her lips. King David hurried after her, whipping out a match, bending all his attention to the task of lighting the cigarette, while Bathsheba touched her left hand to his fingers.

It was a tender episode. Catherine removed herself from the elevator entirely unnoticed. While Dr. Balk and Debbie moved off in one direction, Catherine turned her wheelchair and rolled away in another, aiming herself at the lobby.

The lobby was the main entrance to the hospital, with a set of large glass doors that opened and shut automatically as people entered and departed. It was crowded with every kind of miscellaneous human being. Elderly men and women in wheelchairs sat waiting, staring at the doors, waiting for transportation, attended by younger relatives. Doctors in white coats walked around them, heading for the cafeteria. There were outpatients on the way to appointments, tall nurses and short nurses, fat nurses and thin nurses, all going somewhere on important errands. Black men with easy swaying walks pushed cleaning equipment through the clotted lobby, past rows of men and women and restless children all waiting for something, for good news or bad news, for taxis or nursing home vans or the automobiles of sons-in-law to pull up on the street outside.

Catherine paused and studied the situation, then rolled forward and lined herself up beside another old woman in a wheelchair. The woman was enormously obese. Under her sweater she wore a bathrobe. Her legs were wrapped in elastic stockings, and there were felt bedroom slippers on her feet.

"Goin' ho'?" asked Catherine courteously, striking up a conversation.

"That's right. My daughter's coming for me."

"Been hosp' long?"

"A whole month," said the woman proudly. "Ruptured appendix. Gallbladder, too." She chuckled gaily. "And anyway, all my insides was, you know, falling out, like I have to keep coming back so the doctor can stuff everything back inside, you know?"

"Oh, yeh," said Catherine. "Goo' i-dee."

Edward Fallfold had bought a bunch of carnations on the street. He carried them up on the elevator to the cardiac rehabilitation floor and inquired at the nurses' station for Catherine Rule.

"She's in Room 28," said Judy Pringle absently, pointing down the hall.

"Oh, I remember now," said Fallfold, who hadn't bothered to visit Catherine again since the day when he had found her apparently feebleminded and senile.

There was no answer to his knock. Walking in, he found the bed empty.

He walked back to Judy and introduced himself, then inquired where Catherine Rule might be.

"Probably in the patient lounge," said Judy. But then she was smitten with a strange recollection. Had she really seen Catherine going *away* from the lounge all by herself?

310

"I'll go look," she said, running around the counter, hurrying down the hall, then racing back. "She's not there," she said to Fallfold in a panic. "Where can she be?"

"How should I know?" said Fallfold testily. "Tell me, how is she doing? I understood her brain was practically dead, but now I gather—"

"Dead?" said Judy. "Catherine's brain?" She laughed. "Oh, no, Catherine Rule's brain is not dead. She's sharp as a tack. Oh, she can't do much talking yet, but she tries hard. She'll be able to communicate before long. I've got a lot of respect for that woman. Just a minute, I'll put out a call on the intercom."

Downstairs in the lobby, sitting in her wheelchair in front of the hospital entrance beside the fat old woman in the sweater and elastic stockings, Catherine heard the announcement—CATHERINE RULE, PLEASE REPORT TO THE NEAREST NURSES' STATION. CALLING CATHERINE RULE. And then before Judy's commanding voice switched off, Catherine heard her begin talking normally to someone nearby. "Mr. Fallfold?" Judy said, and then the loudspeaker made a loud squawk and fell silent.

Mr. Fallfold? Catherine began to tremble. Edward Fallfold was in the hospital. He was looking for her. Her heart began to thump uncomfortably. But then it stopped thumping, as a chunky woman in slacks came through one of the automatic sliding doors, approached Catherine's neighbor, kissed her, and began to trundle her through the door.

"Well, so long," said the fat woman cheerfully, waving at Catherine. "Good luck."

But Catherine had no intention of being left behind. "I comin' too," she murmured softly. Pushing the togglestick of her wheelchair, she followed her new friend outdoors. They made a little procession emerging from Brigham and Women's Hospital, one healthy middle-aged woman and

311

two sick old ladies in wheelchairs. No one paid any attention, even when one of the wheelchairs swerved away from the other and began trolleying around the curving wall of the hospital in the direction of Longwood Avenue.

Catherine's wrinkled hospital bathrobe was tight over the cast on her left arm, her nightgown barely covered her old knees; her fragile feet were clothed in shapeless hospital slippers; her wispy white hair was coming loose from its tiny knot. But Catherine smiled, and her thousand wrinkles flaunted themselves in the warm noonday sunshine of late September.

She was free at last. There were things she wanted to say and do. Crucial things, important things. She must find her way to the Isabella Stewart Gardner Museum and say them and do them, before it was too late.

CHAPTER FORTY-SIX

I N THE TAPESTRY ROOM the arrangements for the
auction were complete. Gerard Fouchelle and his colleagues waited in restless anticipation for the hordes of
bidders who would soon be filling the crowded rows of
chairs.

In the courtyard it was almost time for the wedding. The
guests were beginning to crane their necks, looking for the
bridal procession. And in the Blue Room the bridesmaids
were ready to begin, but the bride was growing uneasy,
wishing she had insisted on taking a look at her bridegroom's wedding finery. What if Titus had chosen something entirely unsuitable? Ducking out of the Blue Room,
Aurora went looking for her husband-to-be.

But Titus was nowhere to be found. Titus had vanished.
The truth was, Titus had merely wandered upstairs to the
Dutch Room to walk slowly among the cardboard boxes
and say goodbye to Titian and Rembrandt and Holbein,
goodbye to Justus Suttermans and Gerard Terborch, goodbye to Botticelli.

But the picture that caught his sorrowful attention most
poignantly, the one that brought the sharpest pang to his
heart in the knowledge that he would never see it again, was
Carlo Crivelli's *St. George and the Dragon.* Holding himself
erect on his rearing horse, St. George swung his long sword
as valiantly as though in one blow he could destroy the
dragon that was Gerard Fouchelle, the ogre that was John
Bodkin, the vampires whose names were Carver and Hillside and Fallfold.

Outside the window, on the balcony of the stairway leading down into the courtyard, Aurora's renaissance quartet strummed and tootled and tweedled in readiness for the most beautiful wedding in the world. But Titus heard them not. He had put the wedding entirely out of his mind.

Standing in front of the painting of *St. George and the Dragon,* he allowed himself to be drawn in. The golden sky bent over him, the white horse plunged at him, the dragon yawned. Willingly Titus sank down into the crabbedness,

the pinched stiffness of the painter's manner, feeling in the tautness of his own nerve endings the cunning skill of the artist. St. George's wry intensity became his own. He bared his teeth like the saint, and felt beneath his feet the stony flatness of the cracked Italian ground.

Walking away from the painting, Titus saw the world for a moment as linear and circumscribed, a golden world with delicate edges. Someone came toward him, and he admired the way her hair fell in slender strands, he noticed the lovely shifting patterns of her skirt as her long legs moved beneath it. The painting had obviously infected him with the linear style of Crivelli's attentive vision. Tomorrow he would choose something painterly to look at, all dabs and blotches, air and light.

Then Titus came back to his senses. There would be no tomorrow. This moment was the end of time.

"Oh, Titus," said Polly Swallow, "you'll be late. You should be changing for your wedding."

Titus looked at her vaguely, then stared down at his shirt, his jacket and pants. Unfortunately he had not bought anything new for the wedding. This morning he had groped in his Kansas Street closet and brought out a tan sport jacket and an old pair of brown pants. Hastily he had pressed the jacket and left a scorch on the seat of the pants. "This is all I've got," he said. "It'll have to do."

"Oh," said Polly. "Well, all right. You look fine, just fine." Together they wandered around the room, looking for the last time at the pictures stacked in Fouchelle's cardboard boxes.

"Well, anyway, I won't miss *her*," said Polly, pointing at Bronzino's *Lady in Black.* "Old sourpuss."

Titus laughed. "Good riddance to bad rubbish."

Somebody was putting his head in the window. It was

3 1 5

the gamba player. "Hey, are you the bridegroom? The bride's asking for you."

"Oh, Titus," said Polly, chagrined, looking at her watch, "it's quarter past twelve."

Grudgingly Titus moved in the direction of the west cloister stairway, walking backward, staring greedily for the last time at the Crivelli, looking back hungrily, too, at Polly Swallow, realizing, too late, opportunities missed, wrong roads taken.

But when Aurora O'Doyle saw his tan jacket and brown trousers, everything came to a halt. Perfection hung in the balance. In the cloisters around the courtyard the wedding guests stood waiting, shifting from foot to foot. On the balcony the musicians played the same airs and fantasias and rondeaux over and over. In the Chinese Loggia the mayor of Boston ran his finger around the edge of the wedding cake. In the Blue Room the bridesmaids grew hungry and hot and the flower girl ate her flowers—while Titus Moon went out into the city of Boston to find something more appropriate to wear.

And in the Dutch Room, in Carlo Crivelli's painting, the gold of the background shimmered with its tireless luster, the sword remained suspended over the shoulder of St. George, the white stallion indefatigably pawed the air, and the dragon yawned, showing his sharp teeth, waiting for the blow to fall.

CHAPTER FORTY-SEVEN

CATHERINE'S ROUTE was clear. On Longwood
Avenue she would turn right, work her way up the
crowded sidewalk to Palace Road, turn left, and
zoom in a straight line down to the museum. It wasn't far,
just two or three blocks. How lucky that the museum and
the hospitals were such close neighbors!

Catherine's only concern was the fear that Edward Fall-fold was looking for her, that he would catch up with her, grasp the handles of the wheelchair and whirl her away, and then kill her more carefully than he had managed to do before. Catherine wasn't afraid of dying—her life had been both long and full—but there were things she wanted to do first, things she needed to say to Titus Moon and the trustees.

The sidewalk on Longwood Avenue was thick with pedestrians. Everyone who worked in one of the hospitals was either going to lunch or coming back. Catherine's wheelchair was caught in a mob collected around a cart selling kosher hot dogs. Then she was entangled in another crush of people waiting to cross the street at a corner where the cars where choked in gridlock, fender to bumper, bumper to fender. Horns squawked angrily, a machine for cutting cement screamed slowly along the sidewalk, a jackhammer battered the pavement, and an ambulance with a squealing siren lunged at the impacted traffic.

In any other part of the city, an old woman in a bathrobe propelling her way along the street in a wheelchair would have been odd and conspicuous. Here on hospital row, among milling throngs of doctors, nurses, patients and relatives of patients, technicians, sick children, weeping babies, hospital administrators, and all the other odds and ends of corporate medical life, she attracted no attention. Slowly she butted her way through the crowd at the corner and began bumping along Longwood Avenue, past Children's Hospital and Harvard Medical School, past the Harvard School of Dental Medicine and the grandiose columns of the Facilities and Maintenance Department.

At Palace Road she found a place where the pavement of the sidewalk had been crushed down into the street. Turning her wheelchair, she waited for the traffic to thin

318

out, then careened down the incline and sped across the road and up a lumpy ramp in front of the Massachusetts College of Pharmacy. On the sidewalk she paused to look back, and her heart leaped in her chest. Edward Fallfold was clearly in view, breasting the clotted melee at the corner. A head taller than the rest, he was staring around, looking for her. Even a block away, she knew when he caught sight of her. At once he shoved his way free of the crowd around him and began galloping along the sidewalk.

Catherine rammed her arm against the control bar of the wheelchair and surged away from the corner, racing down the sidewalk. It was a bumpy ride. The cement had been lifted by the trees growing along Palace Road, and she had to keep veering to the left. Her heart was thumping too fast. Jolting past the parking lot of Boston Latin School, she remembered what the surgeon had said when she came out of her stupor, *Rest and time, that's what you need, Miss Rule, lots of time, lots of peace, lots of rest.* Brick buildings flowed past her—Roxbury Community College, the Massachusetts College of Art. The sidewalk was crazed where heavy trucks had backed over it. Rattling across the shattered concrete, Catherine could hear the pounding feet of Edward Fallfold closing in on her. *Peace,* she said to herself, trying to calm her speeding pulse, *peace and rest. Peace, Catherine, peace, peace, peace.*

By the time Homer Kelly found the right floor of Brigham and Women's Hospital, the place was in upheaval. The phones were ringing. A couple of men in uniform were shouting at a gangly spastic woman who kept laughing and throwing her arms in the air. The woman at the counter was dithering, putting her hands to her head, explaining.

Homer strode into Catherine's room, then galloped back to ask where he could find Miss Rule.

"Good God, I wish I knew," cried Judy Pringle, beside herself with worry. Not only was Judy intensely anxious about Catherine, she was concerned about her job. She was going to have to write an incident report about her patient's escape, and there was no way to gloss over her own responsibility. After all, she had *seen* Catherine leave the ward, an elderly woman in a fragile state of health, and she had done nothing about it. Judy confided in the tall man who had so often visited Catherine. "She left here in a motorized wheelchair about twenty minutes ago. We don't know where she's gone. We're desperate to get her back."

Homer was equally distressed. "Was she alone? All by herself? There wasn't anyone with her?"

"No, no, she was alone. You're the second person who's been here asking for her. Fallfold, the other man's name was. He's looking for her too. But when she left this floor she was all by herself. Oh, Lord, it's all my fault."

Homer didn't stay to commiserate. He took off, lunging through the double doors at the end of the hall just in time to smash into a lunch cart loaded with dirty dishes. Crockery and glassware smashed on the polished floor, slops of milky soup splashed against the wall.

"Whoops," cried Homer. "Sorry, but I've got to go. I'm really sorry." And he raced for the stairs, leaving the dumbfounded orderly gaping after him. The stairway led Homer down, down, down, floor after floor, until at last he confronted a blank wall and a door labeled EMERGENCY EXIT. IF OPENED, THIS DOOR WILL SET OFF AN ALARM. Firmly, joyfully, Homer pushed the door open and ran outdoors, while behind him the hospital squealed with sirens and screamed with a pandemonium of bells.

The sidewalk was jammed with lunchtime pedestrians, the street was choked with traffic. Homer fought his way to Longwood Avenue, then paused at the corner to look over the sea of heads for Catherine Rule. He couldn't see her anywhere, but he saw Fallfold at once. Fallfold was running along the sidewalk, shoving violently through a crowd of women in pink smocks, a whole school of nurse's aides. Pink smocks tumbled left and right, women turned angrily to shout.

Homer himself was caught behind a swarm of wheelchairs, a group of cerebral palsy patients on holiday with their nurse attendants, all gathered around a hot dog cart. He couldn't get through. Wildly he looked for a shortcut. There was only the street, and the cars were bumper to bumper, barely moving.

There was only one thing to do. Wrenching open the rear door of the nearest car, a Rolls-Royce, Homer climbed in, thrust his way past the knees of—good God, an archbishop—and emerged on the other side. "I'm terribly sorry, your Holiness," gasped Homer, sticking his head in the window, "it's an emergency."

The other sidewalk was less crowded. Homer ran in the direction of Palace Road, charging to the left around a cluster of students on their way to a class in the College of Pharmacy, darting dangerously out into the street to pass a corpulent couple with ice cream cones, who took up the entire sidewalk.

At Palace Road he whirled around the corner, then slowed down to get his bearings. The street was empty. There was no sign of Catherine Rule or Edward Fallfold. Not until a ray of sunlight sparkled on Catherine's wheelchair beyond the end of the street did Homer see them crossing the Fenway. Fallfold was ramming the wheelchair across the road, racing it between the two lines of traffic hurtling northeast in the direction of Back Bay and northwest toward the city of Brookline.

Homer was already out of breath, but he ran puffing

down Palace Road and crossed the Fenway in an abandon of caution, yelling Fallfold's name. On the other side of the street there was again no sign of the man and woman he was pursuing. Homer paused, his breast heaving. Then he slid down the gentle slope to the path beside the bulrushes that grew so profusely along the edges of the brook. A little equinoctial breeze was moving across this part of Boston, sending a cooling stream of air over the hot metal rooves of the cars on Park Drive, rustling the leaves of the trees in the park, swaying the feathery fronds of the bulrushes. But it was no little breeze that suddenly started the tall reeds thrashing. Homer stared. Something was moving violently in the jungle.

Fallfold, it was Fallfold! Pawing at the brittle stalks, Homer thrust them aside, his feet deep in mud. In the trampled place in the middle of the jungle he found his quarry.

Fallfold had shoved Catherine's wheelchair up to its axles in muddy water, and now he was dragging her out of it. He was going to dump her in Muddy Brook to drown. Catherine whimpered, but her eyes brightened when she saw Homer, and she grinned at him weakly. "What the hell, Fallfold?" cried Homer.

For an instant Fallfold stared at him. Then, roughly, he dropped Catherine back into the wheelchair and lunged at Homer. Startled, Homer managed to dodge out of the way by pulling one foot out of its muddy shoe. Wheezing, he caught Fallfold and dragged him close, hugging him to his chest. What the hell was he supposed to do now? To his horror he felt himself slipping backward, staggering, going down heavily on his side, with Fallfold on top of him. Fallfold's knee was on his chest, Fallfold had Homer's arms pinned to his sides. Before Homer could take a breath, his head was in the brook.

Savagely Homer rolled and squirmed, but his lungs filled with water, and he felt himself drowning. It occurred to him that if he had been given a choice, he would much rather have drowned in Fairhaven Bay, where the water was certainly a whole lot cleaner, and the setting was certainly more appropriate, symbolically and philosophically, for the death of a respectable transcendentalist.

CHAPTER FORTY-EIGHT

T OM DUCK had not received an invitation to the wedding of Titus Moon and Aurora O'Doyle. His name had been on the bridegroom's list, along with those of the other inhabitants of Kansas Street. But Aurora had discreetly neglected to send them invitations. The poor pathetic souls couldn't possibly appear at her wedding. Anyway, decided Aurora kindly, they would surely feel unhappy there, and terribly out of place.

But no one on Kansas Street had noticed the omission. It never occurred to any of them, nor to Titus himself, that they wouldn't be present, front row center. On the morning of the wedding, while Titus looked doubtfully at the contents of his closet, the others pawed through the box of clothing in the front hall and adorned themselves in ragbag splendor.

Titus had left in a hurry, hours ago, leaving urgent instructions for the rest of them to get to the museum by quarter to twelve. But halfway to the museum on the T, Mrs. Petty remembered she had forgotten her pills, and they had to go back. Then Joe Kelso insisted on having a bowl of soup, so they all had some, and therefore it was half-past twelve when they at last came panting across Evans Way Park, with Tom Duck loping far ahead of the rest.

Tom was happy to be back. Tom loved the museum, he loved the flowers, and in a clumsy way he loved the paintings and sculpture. In some other possible throw of the dice, if Tom Duck had been snatched from his cradle and raised in a different manner altogether, he might have been a person of cultivation and understanding. As it was, he was only Tom Duck, a feebleminded adult, an alcoholic, a punch-drunk exfighter with a broken nose and a ruined mind.

At the museum he was just in time to see a familiar-looking old woman sail past him, her wheelchair propelled across the Fenway in the midst of the rushing traffic by a tall man in a gray suit. Tom gaped at the old lady, who looked up at him as she whizzed by, her mouth a helpless *O*, one frail hand lifted in protest.

"Hey-O, there," mumbled Tom. He watched in confusion as the old lady's wheelchair was catapulted down the little hill on the other side and shoved into the reeds beside the brook. Something was the matter, but Tom didn't know what, and he didn't know what to do. During his long stay in the hospital for the criminally insane, he had learned one

325

lesson very well—to subdue his own physical strength. An enormous barrier had been erected in Tom's mind against the murderous repetitive blows of the prize ring. Tom stared after the disappearing wheelchair, his mind in a jangle. Hey-O, what was up?

And now the big guy named Homer Kelly was racing past him, shouting at the top of his lungs. Jesus Gawd, what in Gawd's name was going on? The old lady had looked so sick and scared. Gawd!

Then Tom made up his mind. "Hey-o, there!" he cried, charging across the street. In an instant he had galloped down the slope and thrown himself into the jungle. Tom Duck made an odd-looking St. George, but he was pursuing the dragon with all his might.

Mrs. Petty, Joe Kelso, and Bobby Dobbins were left on the sidewalk in front of the museum. They looked at each other in surprise. They didn't know what to think. What about the wedding? Their hearts were set on going to the wedding. But they couldn't go without Tom. "We got to wait," said Mrs. Petty stoutly. "We got to wait for Tom."

But he didn't take long. It was only a minute or two before they saw him come out again from the thicket of reeds across the street. He was grinning hugely and yelling, "Hey-o, Jesus Gawd," and pushing in front of him an old woman in a muddy wheelchair.

"Hey, what's he doing now?" said Bobby Dobbins, as Tom parked the wheelchair on the path and made another lunge into the bulrushes.

"Hey, will you look at that," said Joe Kelso. Tom was coming out of the shrubbery again with a tall man on his arm. It was the very same tall man they had seen running across the street only a moment ago, the one who had been shouting so loud. Now the poor man was soaking wet. He had lost one shoe. He was choking and gasping.

"Dear me," said Mrs. Petty, shocked at the condition of the man's tweed jacket and wool trousers, dismayed at the way he was clutching the wheelchair and coughing.

"There goes Tom again," laughed Bobby Dobbins. "No, he's back. Who's he got this time?" Whoever it was, the second man was asleep. He was dangling over Tom's shoulder, his head bobbing against Tom's chest.

"Oh, good," said Mrs. Petty, delighted. "They're coming back. Now we can go to the wedding."

"That's right," said the man in the muddy tweed jacket, piloting Catherine Rule up on the sidewalk. His face was blue and his hair stood erect in pointed spikes, but Homer Kelly was breathing normally once again. "We can all go to the wedding. I hope we're not too late."

The guard at the door wanted to make a fuss, but Charlie Tibby was there, and it was all right. Charlie's melancholy face lit up at the sight of Catherine. Gratefully he accepted the care of the unconscious Edward Fallfold. "He's your man, believe me," said Homer, as the music in the courtyard struck up a festive measure. "Come on, everybody. Look, there goes the bride."

Tom Duck led the way, grandly pushing Catherine before him around the corner into the north cloister, then majestically trailing Aurora O'Doyle as she began her stately progress after her bridesmaids on the arm of the mayor of Boston. Homer Kelly tried to sidle out of the bridal procession, but Mrs. Petty had him firmly by the arm, and wouldn't let go. Oh, well, never mind, thought Homer, running his fingers through his hair. Adjusting his step to the music, he swept after Tom with Mrs. Petty, while Joe Kelso and Bobby Dobbins awkwardly brought up the rear.

The wedding guests were gathered among the flowers. They had been standing in the cloisters surrounding the courtyard for an hour, waiting for the ceremony to begin, and therefore they were glad to see the bridal procession at last. But as the bride approached the Roman throne, their attention shifted to the end of the line. Transfixed by the bedraggled parade, they hardly noticed Aurora O'Doyle.

Titus too saw the unexpected addition to the wedding party. Titus was wearing a powder-blue outfit snatched off a hanger in Kenmore Square. Stepping out from the pillars of the east cloister to take his place in front of the throne, Titus caught sight of Catherine Rule and Tom Duck, Homer Kelly and Mrs. Petty, Bobby Dobbins and Joe Kelso, and his sober face broke into a delighted grin.

The bride was still unaware. Not until she turned around to hand her bouquet to the flower girl did Aurora see them too. Then she dropped the bouquet and stood frozen in horror. The bridesmaids were frozen too, lined up like posies on either side of the throne, gazing at the interlopers in the middle of the wedding procession—an unshaven oafish old man with cattail fluff in his hair, a bag lady in a scarlet tea gown studded with rhinestone sparkles, Homer Kelly in a muddy suit, and a couple of derelicts in the two halves of a single pair of tails, pieced out with overcoats.

But first in line was the dread witch Catherine Rule, in a rumpled bathrobe, her hair in a wild tangle. Catherine smiled. "Hello, Phoebe," she said.

As Aurora started to scream, Catherine's mad yellow eye met the eyes of Titus Moon, and at once he saw the gates of hell and the doors of paradise. Moving in a trance, he walked away from the wedding.

Grasping the handles of Catherine's wheelchair, Titus pushed her around the courtyard to the elevator, and up they went together, while Homer Kelly galloped up the back stairs.

Poor Aurora! She had worked so hard, she had planned so well! The emotional tension that should have been released in lofty ritual and then in the joy and laughter of the wedding reception, found premature release in a paroxysm of tears. She couldn't stop shrieking. Her bridesmaids closed around her, uttering soothing noises, the mayor of Boston slapped her face, Joe Kelso and Bobby Dobbins found the wedding cake, and the wedding broke up in confusion.

CHAPTER FORTY-NINE

I N THE TAPESTRY ROOM the auction was about to begin. But something had alarmed the auctioneer. "What's that noise?" he whispered, putting his hand over the microphone, bending down to Frederique Paquette.

The windows over the courtyard had been closed, but Aurora O'Doyle's hysterical scream was filtering through the glass, unsettling the crowded bidders. In the Tapestry Room and the Raphael Room they were jammed in tight, their chairs too close to one another, their shoulders wedged together. Museum directors from Paris, curators from New York and West Berlin, dealers from Los Angeles and Seoul, London and Taipei, stared at the windows and fidgeted uneasily. In their front-row seats the people from the Getty Museum looked at one another and raised their eyebrows.

Fulton Hillside and Preston Carver were in the front row too, and so were several members of the Harvard Corporation, and all of them craned their necks to see what was going on. John Bodkin stood importantly with Gerard Fouchelle beside the platform and murmured in his ear. Shackleton Bowditch had refused to occupy a seat at the front with the other Harvard Fellows. With Peggy Foley, he was among the standing-room-only crowd at the rear. As Aurora's screams turned to hysterical wails, Shackleton crossed his arms solemnly, and Peggy stood on tiptoe, trying to see out the window.

"Never mind," said Frederique Paquette to the auctioneer, "let's get on with it."

Gerard Fouchelle's premier auctioneer was a brilliant performer with a smooth delivery, a good-humored wit, and a sharp eye for a lifted finger at the back of the room, a nod from a dealer at one of the telephones, a signal from the woman reading mailed-in bids, or a pointing gesture from the girl whose earphones were connected to the bidders in the Raphael Room. He also possessed the extraordinary ability to buoy up the level of excitement and endow each work of art with glamour and importance, while moving the action forward without delay.

"Item number one," he announced easily, his voice reaching to the last row of packed chairs in the Tapestry Room and crackling over the loudspeaker in the gallery next door. "I am open now for bids on item number one,

The Rape of Europa by the Venetian master Titian, perhaps the greatest painting in the western world." Beside him the Titian glowed in pearly pinks and blues, the eye of Zeus flashed fire, and Europa's succulent flesh teetered in glorious perpetual imbalance in the illumination of the spotlights hanging from the rafters. "There is an opening bid on this picture of fifteen million dollars. Do I hear sixteen? Thank you. Seventeen?" The auctioneer glanced down at the Boston Museum's curator of European painting, but the curator was not yet ready to bid. He was waiting for the really serious competition, at which time he intended to come on strong.

The bidding continued swiftly, a million dollars at a time. "Stop," muttered Catherine. "Wait, please stop. Lizzen." But she couldn't make herself heard. Her wheelchair was crowded into the doorway, she was surrounded by museum guards, police officers, and Fouchelle staff members. Homer Kelly loomed up beside her, Titus Moon clutched the handles of her wheelchair. But even Titus couldn't hear Catherine's murmurs of distress. She was helpless. There was only one thing to do.

By this time the bidders had been reduced to two or three, but under the skilful encouragement of the auctioneer the competition had not slowed down. To his horror the Boston Museum's curator of European painting suddenly found himself near his limit. He wanted the Titian very badly, and he tried a bold stroke.

The auctioneer caught his signal. "I believe, sir, that is a jump of five million dollars," he announced smoothly. "Do I hear another bid?"

There was a pause, and then the director of London's National Gallery raised an insane finger. He too had Getty money to spend, and recklessly now he threw it all in one basket.

"Thank you," said the auctioneer, knowing in his bones that he had reached the profoundest depths of the deepest pockets of his richest bidders. Glibly he pronounced aloud the current figure—it was more than had ever been paid for a painting in any auction gallery anywhere in the world, it was enough money to fund an intercontinental missile, a strategic bomber, it was enough to feed a starving nation or carry on a war. "Do I see another bid for this magnificent painting by Titian? Fair warning." For the last time the auctioneer looked around the hall, and then he lifted his hammer.

But Catherine Rule had squeezed her wheelchair through the thick mass of crowded bodies around her. She was raising her left arm, the one encased in a heavy cast. It took the last vestige of her strength, but there was no mistake about what she was doing. She was making a bid, a genuine bid, a winning bid for Titian's *Rape of Europa.*

The auctioneer was stopped cold. He saw Catherine, he saw her raised arm, her plaster cast, her bathrobe, her frowsy head. He paused, and bent down to Frederique. Gerard Fouchelle and John Bodkin hurried to the platform. There was a hasty whispered conference.

"Trustee," murmured Gerard Fouchelle.

"International authority on textiles," hissed Frederique Paquette.

"But perhaps you shouldn't—" warned John Bodkin.

But the momentum was too high, the excitement too great, the sum of money too compelling, and Fouchelle in his turn had been mesmerized by Catherine's yellow eye, which had revealed to him in a single glance the pillars of jasper supporting the stars in their courses.

He winked at the auctioneer, who promptly straightened up, slammed his hammer down, and cried, "Sold! Congratulations, madame."

333

There was an outburst of applause. History had been made this day. There would be headlines in the newspapers of all the capital cities of the world. Once again heads craned, trying to see the bidder. People at the back half-rose in their chairs. There were nudges and pointing fingers. Who was she, the old woman in the wheelchair?

Catherine could feel it, the sudden riveting of attention. She could see the avid faces looking at her. Gently she pushed the control bar of her wheelchair and rolled forward until she came to rest in front of the platform. Plucking the sleeve of John Bodkin, she murmured the news she had been so anxious to impart.

But the auction was forging ahead. The Titian had disappeared. On the tall easel it was replaced by Vermeer's *Concert*. "Item number two," announced the auctioneer, ignoring the whispered conference on the floor in front of him. "For this rare and exquisite painting there is an identical opening bid of fifteen million dollars. Once again I will begin the bidding at sixteen million. Do I hear such a bid? Thank you. Seventeen?"

Gerard Fouchelle had a premonition of disaster. Striding forward, he stooped over Catherine's wheelchair with John Bodkin. Then, as the bidding rose to twenty-seven million, twenty-eight, twenty-nine, he stood up and gave a savage command. Breaking off in midsentence, the auctioneer stepped off the platform to find out what was up.

Homer Kelly leaned against the wall, taking it all in, enjoying himself. He watched as Titus Moon squeezed past him to join the conference. Now Titus was turning away from the huddle around Catherine's wheelchair to hail Shackleton Bowditch and Peggy Foley from the back of the room, and Hillside and Carver from the front row of chairs.

"Continuez," shouted the man from the Louvre, who had been on the edge of his chair, hoping to bag the Ver-

meer. "What zuh hell?" cried an agent for the banana-republic general who wanted a Rembrandt. "Get on with it," demanded a would-be bidder from the Getty, who hoped to pick up one or both of the Botticellis.

But the seven-hundred bidders who were crowded so densely together in the Tapestry Room, and the three hundred wedged into the room next door, were about to be disappointed. While they sat fuming in their chairs, the trustees of the Gardner Museum called the shortest meeting in their history, retracted the vote of June thirtieth, and voted unanimously to cancel the auction.

John Bodkin voted reluctantly, Hillside and Carver heaved deep sighs of regret, but there was no possible challenge to Catherine's trump cards—her colossal gift of money to the museum and her positive identification of the criminal. Edward Fallfold had been responsible for all the trouble, and he would now be locked up. No longer would the museum be subject to foolish and tragic indignities.

Gerard Fouchelle mounted the platform, his face contorted in anguish, grasped the microphone, struggled to suppress the rage in his breast, and dryly announced that the auction was at an end.

The room erupted. Wrathful frustrated bidders stood on their chairs, shaking their fists and yelling at the tops of their lungs. Homer Kelly, pushing through a cluster of angry museum directors, whimpered at Titus Moon, "What did she say? For pity's sake, tell me what Catherine said."

"Gold," roared Titus, grinning at him, wrenching at his ruffled collar, tearing off his baby-blue bow tie. "Her father's oil field in Alaska, a thousand square miles of dry wells. They found gold instead. A mother lode, up in the hills. Nuggets as big as your fist. It's just been sold."

"You mean, it was Catherine's? The whole thing? It all belonged to Catherine?"

"That's right. Her father left it to her, all that worthless territory north of the Arctic Circle, only it just happens to contain the world's richest deposit of pure gold, richer than the Transvaal, richer than the Homestead in South Dakota. Her agents have just sold it, and Catherine's giving half the profits to the museum." Gleefully Titus tore off his powder-blue tailcoat. "Would *you* close down a museum with that kind of endowment?"

Gold, pure gold. Once again Homer was dazzled with the aura of the altarpieces of the Early Italian Room, the beaten goldleaf of halos and gilded skies, the gold brocade of painted robes, the petals of miraculous roses, and now in spectacular abundance this other sort of gold, hidden in secret veins under the ground in the foothills of northern Alaska. Surely it was some patient alchemy of Catherine's that had transformed the base metal of her frozen mountains into something so much more precious than the black gold of her father's fizzled oil wells. "Sorcery," he shouted, leaning down to Titus Moon.

But Titus was thinking about something else. "Have you seen Polly anywhere?" he said, looking vaguely around the room. Abandoning Homer, he pushed through the surge of angry men and women billowing toward the auctioneer's platform. Curators, dealers, and collectors grasped his arm and protested in seven languages.

"No," said Titus, "not now." Shaking himself free, he turned to Catherine, whispered in her ear, and began pushing her wheelchair in the direction of the elevator.

Downstairs they found Polly Swallow in the Spanish Cloister. She was cutting Aurora's wedding cake, handing out slices to the mayor of Boston and to all the wedding guests from Kansas Street. Catherine smiled as Joe Kelso plucked the topmost cherry from a towering molded *parfait*

d'amour, and Bobby Dobbins helped himself to the shrimp on a gleaming *mousseline de poisson.*

The champagne lay ready to hand in its tubs of ice. Titus picked up a bottle with a flourish and went to work on it, grinning at Polly. The cork popped with a loud report and champagne foamed all over the table. Catherine discovered that she wasn't tired at all.

It was a party, a different sort of party from the one Aurora had planned, but better in every way. It soon spilled out into the courtyard. Curators, docents, guards, and trustees appeared from nowhere. The champagne flowed. While angry bidders poured down the stairs, deprived of their Dürer, their Velásquez, their Piero della Francesca, their Rubens, their glorious Vermeer, Titus took Polly by the waist and danced her up and down the red carpeted paths and in and out of the cloisters. The Venetian dolphins spun around her, the dancing maiden on the south wall revolved dizzily, and Tom Duck cried, "Hey-o!" and "Gawd!" Catherine Rule had an anxious moment when one of the bridesmaids cornered Titus—a lovely girl like a Fra Angelico angel or a handmaiden to a Botticelli madonna—oh, there were so many pretty girls in the world! Should she interfere? The boy was such a fool!

No, no, it was all right. Catherine watched as Titus broke away from the bridesmaid. He was making a swoop among the potted orchids, snapping off armfuls of priceless blossoms, thrusting them at Polly Swallow.

Smiling to herself, Catherine looked up at the musicians' balcony. The musicians were gone, but from John Singer Sargent's portrait, Isabella Stewart Gardner looked down on the celebration in hospitable welcome, the cordial hostess, the lady of the house, the giver of the ball.

The festive mood of the party in the courtyard did not filter outdoors to the sidewalk in front of the museum. Here the irate bidders from the Tapestry Room were dispersing, walking angrily away, looking for their cars, whistling for taxis.

John Bodkin was among them, saying goodbye, apologizing profusely. "I'm really so terribly sorry it turned out this way," he said to the director of London's National Gallery. "I mean, we never dreamed anything like this would happen."

The National Gallery man was stiff with ill humor. With-

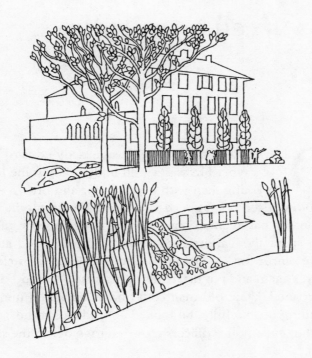

out saying goodbye to Bodkin, he lunged toward a taxi that was drawing up at the curb. But it was not his taxi. It had been hailed by the president of an international brewery cartel with central offices in Heidelberg. The president of the brewery foamed with indignation and there was an undignified scuffle. Pained, Bodkin turned his eyes away.

At once he caught a glimpse of a woman riding past the Gardner Museum on a bicycle. At first he didn't recognize his wife, but then he gave a sudden shout. "Beryl, my God, what are you doing? Stop, stop!"

Beryl Bodkin failed to hear. She was pumping hard, staring eagerly ahead into the traffic. There was a pack on her back, a flush on her cheek, a light in her eye. She was on her way to the baling wire factory in Jamaica Plain, and the welcoming arms of Fenton W. Hepplewhite.

CHAPTER FIFTY

O NE OF the police officers was exactly Edward Fallfold's type. He was a well-built, wholesome-look-
ing young man with a high color and brown eyes.
Fallfold noticed him at once when he woke up on the day-
bed in the basement room where Charlie Tibby's guards
often spent their afternoon breaks. Fallfold stared at the
young officer for a moment without speaking, then closed
his eyes again and put his hands to his head. "Good Lord,"
he groaned, "that old man could have murdered me."

Sitting up carefully, he looked around at Charlie Tibby
and the seven police officers crowded together in the small
room.

Then once again he glanced up into the shiny brown
eyes of Officer Norman Bulger. "Come here," he said,
beckoning feebly. "No, come closer. Sit down beside me."

The young officer raised his eyebrows at Charlie Tibby,
who merely nodded, and then Bulger did as he was told.
Fallfold patted his hand and gazed at him earnestly. "Look,
do you want to know what I did? I'll be delighted to tell you
what I did." Then he glanced around the room in distaste.
"Just send these other people away. They don't need to be
here. I'm not about to fight my way out."

Charlie cleared the room of everyone but himself and
the young officer who had taken Fallfold's fancy, and then
he lectured Fallfold about his right to legal counsel.

Fallfold waved it all aside, and insisted on dictating a
statement to Officer Bulger, looking at him all the while

without blinking, telling him everything, taking great pains with sentence structure, ordering paragraphs, refining phrases, rounding off clauses with elegant ironies and mellifluous cynicisms.

Charlie kept interrupting. "Look, are you quite sure you're okay? You don't want a doctor? You're positive you don't want to call an attorney? Well, okay, then, where were we?"

When Homer Kelly put his head in the door, Charlie was just beginning to read the statement back to Fallfold. Homer came in and sat down to listen, but Fallfold himself seemed to be paying no attention. Instead he began talking in a low voice to Officer Bulger. Homer could hear scraps of the conversation. Fallfold was asking young Bulger about his childhood, his youth, his hopes and dreams for the years to come. At first Bulger kept glancing at Charlie Tibby, but Charlie went right on reading loudly as if nothing else were going on, and before long Homer could see that Officer Bulger was deeply engaged. He was confiding to Fallfold the secrets of his heart.

But when Charlie reached the end and stopped reading, Officer Bulger suddenly remembered in the sudden silence who he was and where and why. With a deep blush, he sprang to his feet.

"Listen, Fallfold," said Homer, "you left something out. It's not all there. What about the music? How did you work that? It was tape players, right? Little ones in the heating system? Or Robbie Crowlie, he had a cassette-player instead of a walkie-talkie?"

Fallfold seemed genuinely puzzled. "Music?" he said. "Titus must have been hearing things. I don't know anything about any music."

So they had to leave it at that. Thereafter, except for the regular concerts in the Tapestry Room, music was rarely heard in the galleries of the Gardner Museum, either in the neighborhood of Vermeer's *Concert* with its music-making trio, or Fra Angelico's *Assumption of the Virgin* with its musical angels, or John Singer Sargent's *El Jaleo* with its guitars and castanets and stamping feet, or even in the Little Salon, where the seventeenth-century spinet and Parisian harp stood silent, year in and year out.

The music of the works of art was of a different kind, inaudible to the human ear, but sweeter perhaps thereby, if Keats was right.

VI

THE TRIUMPH
OF ETERNITY

No more will time be broken into bits,
No summer now, no winter: all will be
As one, time dead, and all the world transformed.
—PETRARCH

CHAPTER FIFTY-ONE

T HE ISABELLA Stewart Gardner Museum continued to survive. A century after the interrupted
auction, while the world outside the museum was

utterly transformed, visitors still strolled through the galleries, and the sunshine still fell into the courtyard in shafts and cascades and floods of light, bathing everything in a soft brilliance, shining on marble shoulders and Venetian balconies, glowing through the translucent petals of Easter lilies. On the walls the colors of the paintings were still luminous and bright, while the bones of the artists who had painted them in countries far away grew yet more brittle in their rotted boxes, deep down under the ground.

In the Long Gallery Uccello's young lady of fashion went right on displaying her patterned velvet sleeve, and Botticelli's madonna continued to gaze at the symbols of the Eucharist. In the Early Italian Room, Love and Chastity, Death and Fame, Time and Eternity still drove their chariots across Pesellino's panels, as they had done for 650 years. In the Titian Room the eye of Zeus never stopped flashing fire as he carried off Europa, and on the other side of the courtyard in the Gothic Room, Mrs. Gardner remained standing in the posture of hostess, her mouth slightly parted as if to say something clever.

During the intervening century the empire of Fatcat had swollen, burst, and at last collapsed. But the woman who had been one of Fatcat's creators, the young girl Homer Kelly had met in her tiny compartment at Fatcat Enterprises, went on to become a wonder in her own right. Her paintings were sought by all the museums in the world, and like Titian himself, she painted to a great age.

When she died at last, everyone else in this story had long since passed away, with the single exception of Catherine Rule. Catherine lived forever. Oh, her body disappeared from sight, that was true, a few years after the events described in this book. But the glance of her wild off eye continued to rove up and down the staircases of the Isabella

Stewart Gardner Museum, and move in and out of the galleries, querying and judging, casting everything into the light of that eternity in which Catherine had always lived.

AFTERWORD

THIS BOOK is a story. Its setting is a physical recreation of the real Isabella Stewart Gardner Museum, but the events are completely imaginary. The characters too are altogether fictional. In actuality the Gardner Museum is wisely run and superbly protected. None of the bad things here described could possibly happen there.

Black-and-white sketches of paintings by masters like Vermeer, Titian, Rembrandt, and Rubens do little more than indicate the subject matter of the originals, which must be seen in their true richness of light and color on the walls of the museum.

The passages from Mrs. Gardner's will are genuine quotations, as are those from her letters and the letters of Bernard Berenson.

ILLUSTRATED WORKS OF ART

352

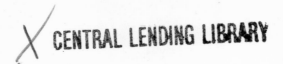
hia

f alarm.